FERAL

VERMIN
BOOK 2

ARDIN PATTERSON

Lost Knot Books

FERAL
ARDIN PATTERSON

Love Knot Books

https://loveknotbooks.ca
An imprint of DAOwen Publications

Feral / Ardin Patterson
Edited by Douglas Owen

This book is written and edited using Canadian English spelling and grammar.

Cover art by MMT Productions

ISBN 978-1-998029-15-0
EISBN 978-1-998029-16-7

10 9 8 7 6 5 4 3 2 1

For my favourite storytellers Nessa and N.J.

1

———

Blood pooled into the bathroom sink, dripping from the vermin's nose. He sniffled hard and turned on the tap. The deep red colour of his blood appeared pink as it circled the drain and dissolved into the cold water. He gazed up at himself in the mirror, dark brown eyes pierced his reflection. *"Iya Misent Leiken Deissu."*

"Are you okay?"

Nicholas turned toward the door, wiping his bloody nose against his sleeve. *"Ha.* Er... yes."

"You shouldn't have bit him," Roland said calmly, leaning against the door.

"He called me a dog," Nicholas grumbled, looking away from him. He held his sleeve under the water, watching the smear of blood fade from the white and blue wool as it ran into the sink.

The young man rubbed his temple, profusely. "Biting him won't help."

Nicholas rolled his eyes. *"Doksot."*

"Pardon?"

"Nothing. Nevermind."

Roland stepped into the bathroom and took the boys face in his hands, lifting his chin up to examine him. "You promised us you would behave. I don't want to have to add another incident to the report."

Nicholas jerked his head back and glared at him. "And you promised Miss Warren that no harm would come to me."

Roland nodded slowly. "Please try to calm down."

"I am calm!"

Roland sighed.

Nicholas slammed his hands down into the counter. "Ugh! *Iigen Bliesso Daknovosa.*"

Roland raised his hands and took a step back. "You really shouldn't talk like that."

"*Stai* Roland! *Iya...*" Nicholas drew in a deep breath and pointed to the door. "Get out."

Roland stood in the doorway and scratched his head. "You should apologize to Peter."

Nicholas bared his teeth, a low growl escaping his lips. His ears twitched as Roland cleared his throat and stumbled out of the room. Once he was alone, he brought his attention back to the sink and began splashing his face.

"How's your hand?" Roland sat across from his friend at the kitchen table. His chin cradled in his hands, head throbbing.

Peter looked up from his notebook and raised his brow. "How's the little mutt's face?"

"He's bleeding."

"So am I."

"Peter, maybe you should take some time off," Roland said, his blue eyes wandering over to the bandage wrapped around Peter's right hand. "How bad is it?"

"Have you ever been bitten by a vermin?"

"No."

Peter shook his head. "I don't recommend it." He slid the

notebook over to Roland. "Guess we're adding this to the report too, eh?"

Roland looked down at Peter's awkwardly scribbled notes. Clearly written with his left. "Don't you think you're exaggerating a bit? You *are* the one who provoked him."

"This time, sure, but what about the incident on Monday?"

Roland scratched his head.

"Or what happened last Thursday," Peter said.

"He's still recovering."

"He's a violent beast. Why do you let him roam about the house so freely?"

Roland averted his gazed. "He starts to annoy me when he's cooped up all day."

"You're terrible at disciplining children."

"Maybe... but at least I've never smacked a child across the face with a coaster," Roland scoffed.

Peter wrinkled his nose and leaned forward. "I'll admit the coaster was in poor taste."

"You think?"

Peter glowered.

"You need a break."

"What I need is for you to have my back."

Roland ran his hand through his curls and nodded slowly.

"You're so busy tiptoeing around Dianna that you've forgotten the boy is a vermin. Nicholas isn't one of your nephews Roland, he's a wild animal and he's getting his strength back. You need to make sure he knows who's in charge around here," Peter said. "Otherwise, we'll have done all this for nothing."

"I just don't think you need to pick fights with him all the time." Roland winced at the sharp pain pulsating at the back of his neck. *These two are seriously stressing me out.*

Peter pouted, crossed his arms, and flinched. "He called me a dot-something. Whatever that means." He looked down at his right hand, gritting his teeth, and attempted to wiggle his fingers. "And I'm pretty sure he insulted my mother."

Roland flipped through the notebook, shaking his head. "I feel sorry for him."

Peter's eyes widened.

"Don't look at me like that."

"He's not some lost puppy you found half dead at the side of the road. He's a vermin you found half dead at the side of the road. There's a big difference."

"And yet you keep calling him a dog."

"Give me a break!" Peter tossed his hands above his head. His cheeks paled as he clutched his hand, cradling it gently.

"Mr. Rissing..."

The two men turned and looked at the vermin peering through the crack in the kitchen door.

"Yes?"

Nicholas crept into the room. His eyes flickered. "Sorry for biting you."

"You'd better be," Peter said sharply.

Roland kicked him.

Peter yelped and cleared his throat. "Is your face all right?"

Nicholas nodded as Peter punched Roland in the arm from across the table and cursed under his breath.

Roland smirked. "Didn't think that through, did you?"

Peter whimpered, his right hand shaking as he bit down on his lip. "No. Not really."

Nicholas tilted his head, watching them. As he did, his long dark bangs slid across his face. He brushed them back, letting them curl beneath his neck. "I didn't know human blood tasted so... *Verjik.*"

Roland and Peter turned to one another, then back to the vermin.

Peter massaged his sore, lightly freckled hand. "What does *Verjik* mean?"

Nicholas shrugged. "It tastes different."

"Different compared too?"

Nicholas bit down on his thumb and knit his brow. "It made me want to vomit."

Peter jolted from his seat, raising his injured hand at the boy. "Then don't bite me!"

"Anyway, there's a rabbit outside. Can I go play with it?"

"Absolutely not," Peter said, about to cross his arms. He caught himself, readjusted and rested his right hand at his side, gesturing instead with his left. "What makes you think you're allowed to go outside?"

"I went out yesterday with Miss Warren."

The two men turned to one another.

Roland sank into his seat. "Of course you did." He leaned his head back and looked at the boy. "Look, we understand your frustration, but because of your behaviour this afternoon, you'll be staying indoors and unfortunately, we'll need to add the incident to today's report."

"That's not fair!"

"Listen here, you little mutt, you're a vermin living in Tavern. You can either behave yourself or–" He slid a finger across his throat.

Roland watched Nicholas' ears twitch.

"Understand?"

"The others are home from school. I'm gonna go upstairs," Nicholas said quietly.

"Get going then," Peter muttered, sitting back down. He glanced at Roland as Nicholas hurried out of the room. "What's with you?"

Roland drummed his fingers along the table, pressing his lips together as the children's voices rang throughout the house.

"Roland?"

He blinked hard, freezing in place.

Peter looked him over. "Off in your head again?"

"Yes, and no."

"Well?"

Roland clasped his hands together and lowered his head. "We should probably get your hand looked at."

"It's not that bad." Peter examined it. "I just don't handle pain very well."

"He broke the skin," Roland said. "Besides, the drive to Dr. Gray's will give us a chance to speak with your cousin" –he pointed up at the ceiling and rolled his eyes–"without worrying about nosy niece's or bored vermin listening in."

ROSE CRISPIN reflexively dodged her younger brothers as they raced past her and into the parlour. The boys left their school bags and wet boots laying at the front door for their nursemaid Lisa to tidy up. Rose gave a huff, peeled her red mittens off and removed her coat before gathering the boy's things and putting them off to the side. *I wish they'd stop leaving everything for her to do. Then again, Uncle Roland does the exact same thing to Tabitha.* She poked the bruises on the back of her hands and grimaced.

Today, school seemed to drag on for what felt like an eternity. The other day her teacher slipped on the ice, so the class was given a substitute. His replacement was the monstress Mrs. Clifford, who for some reason chose to spend the day picking away at Rose for every little thing. Her white blouse was too dressy for school, the embroidery on her burgundy skirt was far too distracting, and her stockings apparently didn't look warm enough. On top of that, Mrs. Clifford insisted that Rose stay in at recess to rewrite her notes because those she said were "Far *too* messy to be legible."

By the end of the day, Rose had buried her head down into her desk, trying desperately to hide behind Philly Tenneson, the tallest boy in her class, who thankfully sat directly in front of her. Unfortunately, Mrs. Clifford was unsatisfied with this and forced Rose to swap places with Eva Evans, who sat in the middle of the first row. When she tried to protest, Mrs. Clifford took the large metre stick from beneath the chalk board and told her to hold out her hands. Now, Rose could barely curl her fingers, and she knew it wasn't because of the cold weather.

All she wanted was to sit down and relax with a nice afternoon snack and a good book.

She dragged herself into the kitchen, and spotted her uncle sitting at the table with Peter Rissing, the two of them watching her brothers hunt through the cupboards for something to munch on.

"There's no food!" Caspian slammed the cupboard door, shooting daggers at Roland, and crossed his arms. "Did you spend the whole day eating or something?"

"No," Roland said defensively. He rocked back on the legs of his chair, peering into the cupboard Julius was rummaging through. "Dianna took Tabby and Lisa to grab some groceries. You'll just have to be satisfied with some cheese and crackers."

Caspian's jaw dropped.

Rose gritted her teeth into a smile, ushering her brothers over to the fridge. "You both like cheese, don't you?"

"We already had that for lunch." Julius pouted, crossing his arms.

"And I'm starving," Caspian said, rubbing his belly.

Rose opened the refrigerator door, yanking on one of the red ribbons in her hair. The boys were right. Not only were the cupboards bare, but the cheese was beginning to mould, and she knew that whatever leftover meal sat at the bottom of the fridge was most definitely rotting away based on the smell. She turned to her uncle, her stomach growling. "Um, Uncle Roland, when was the last time we went for groceries?"

Roland scratched his head and shrugged.

Unbelievable. Rose marched over to the table, eyes burning into him. "You are aware that you don't have to wait around for Tabitha to do everything, right?"

Roland raised his brow, looking up at her. "Money doesn't grow on trees."

"Well then, maybe you should get a job," she said, putting her hands on her hips. "You and your friend here, who seems to forget he has his own house, with his own food and his own bed."

Peter winced, looking away from her.

"We have jobs."

"Doing what exactly?" Rose cocked her head, lips pressed tightly together. "Because it looks to me like the two of you just sit around all day."

Caspian popped up behind his uncle. "Someone woke up on the wrong side of the bed this morning,"

Roland smirked. "Seems like it."

Rose ripped the ribbon from her hair. "Can it, Caspian!"

Caspian stuck out his tongue. "Make me."

"That's enough," Roland said, getting up.

Rose rolled her eyes.

He stepped around her and gestured for Peter to follow him out of the kitchen. "I have to take Mr. Rissing to see Dr. Gray. I'll see if I can stop by the bakery on our way home."

Peter pushed out the chair. "Weren't we going to wait for Dianna?".

Roland shoved his hands into his pockets, his blue eyes leering at the children. "I'd rather not."

Julius latched onto Peter's leg as he got up. "What happened to your hand?"

"Nicholas happened," Peter said, trying to shake the five-year-old boy off him. "Roland, can you deal with this?"

"When you come back from the doctors, will you give me a piggyback?"

"Didn't I give you one yesterday?" Peter said giving his leg a shake, as Roland raced over to pry his nephew off.

Julius giggled.

Roland scooped the five-year-old up into his arms. "Why don't you ask someone else to play with you today?"

Julius looked over at his siblings.

"I have a test to study for," Rose muttered, opening the breadbox. What remained of the loaf was embarrassingly small. Barely a nibble.

Caspian frowned. "Me too."

"Maybe Nicholas and I can build a snowman?" Julius grinned, patting his uncle on the head.

Rose stopped and turned to him. "No," she said abruptly. She looked at the confusion on her youngest brother's face as he stared at her with his big, round eyes. Her face went hot, replaying the tone of her voice in her head. It was harsher than she'd intended it. Even

Caspian and her uncle seemed stunned, watching Rose twist the remaining ribbon in her hair tightly around her index finger. "H-he's probably sleeping."

"You can come with us Julius," Roland said, eyeing her. "And later, I'll build a snowman with you. How does that sound?"

Julius smiled. "Fun!"

"All right then. We'll be going."

Rose waved to them, waiting until they left the kitchen before turning her attention to Caspian.

Caspian backed away from her. "If you hit me, I'll scream."

"I'm not going to hit you." She lowered her voice and forced him to come closer. "Once Uncle Roland leaves, we should search his office for candy."

"Ooh, and under his bed!"

Rose slammed a hand over his lips. "Shh... why are you always so loud?"

Caspian began gesturing wildly, his eyes wide as he murmured into her palm.

She removed her hand, glaring at him. "What?"

Caspian chuckled. "I didn't say anything. You should really get your ears checked."

2

Dianna spun on her heels, spotting Roland and her cousin getting into the Royalton with Julius. She slid on the ice as she raced toward them, leaving Lisa and Tabitha alone with the groceries in the other car. Peter's hand was wrapped in a bandage. "What happened?"

"Oh good, you're back," Roland said, helping Julius into the backseat. "We need to talk."

Dianna pressed her lips together. "About?"

"What do you think?"

She took Peter's hand in hers and began unwrapping the bandage.

"You look very pretty today, Miss Warren," Julius said sweetly.

She gave him a smile. "Why thank you Julius. That's so sweet of you." Her jaw dropped as she returned her attention to Peter's hand. She met his eyes.

"If I were you, I'd act natural. Don't want to upset Tabitha. You know how she gets," Peter said softly.

As if on cue, Tabitha came strutting over to the group, bags of groceries in tow. "Miss Warren, did you not offer your assistance?"

"I-I did." Quickly, Dianna rewrapped Peter's hand. She took the bags from Tabitha, still eyeing her cousin.

"Food! Precious food!" Julius climbed out of the car, got down on his knees and waved his hands above his head in praise.

Alicia dragged a large bag behind Lisa, her mother. Her tiny arms trying desperately to keep it off the ground. "Julius, come see what I got!"

He hurried over to her and peered inside the bag. "Tabby, are you making cookies?"

"I am," Tabitha said, going over to Roland. She pulled him down by the collar of his jacket, whispering something in his ear.

Dianna furrowed her brow, examining the pained expression on his face.

Julius squealed. "Rosie, Caspian! We're having cookies for dinner!"

"No, wait–" Lisa puffed up her cheeks, looking down at her daughter. "And he's gone."

Alicia laughed. "He runs fast, Mommy."

Lisa shook her head. "Yes, yes, he does."

"And Roland, please put on a scarf," Tabitha said firmly. "The last thing we need is you catching another cold."

Dianna smirked, watching the corner of his lip twitch slightly.

He met her gaze briefly, then veered in the other direction. Ever since their argument before Nicholas' meeting with Mayor Hood, Roland had been avoiding her. Most days, he barely said two words to her. *It's probably better this way. Peter's stressed enough as it is. Us fighting will only make things worse.*

"Bring those inside and come meet us in the car," Peter said.

"Are you okay?"

"It looks worse than it feels. Just be quick."

Dianna rushed up onto the porch behind Lisa and Alicia. Her stomach did somersaults as she slid, stumbling backward into the garden. A pair of hands firmly pressed up against the small of her back and propped her up onto the porch. Dianna turned around. "T-thank you, Roland."

He averted his eyes, relieved her of the bags, and went into the house.

She took a moment to steady herself as Tabitha shot her a dirty look. "Should he have let me fall?"

Tabitha merely kissed her teeth and went inside.

Dianna crossed her arms, sat down on the step, and shivered at the cold snow beneath her.

"How did the shopping trip go?" Peter said, making his way toward the step.

Dianna gestured toward the house. "I'm pretty sure that old hag wants me dead."

"If it makes you feel any better, Rose yelled at us."

Dianna stood up and brushed off her skirt. "What did you do this time?"

"Nothing... at least I don't think we did anything." Peter shrugged. "Have you noticed she's been acting a bit strange?"

"You mean since she found out we were all lying to her about Nicholas?"

He nodded.

Dianna linked her arm in his, careful to avoid his injured hand. "Yes, I've noticed."

"It was Roland who didn't want to tell the children," Peter said, moaning as they walked to the car. "You and I were merely–"

"Accessories." Dianna frowned at the snow fluttering down from the sky. "As we always are."

"He bit me, and I hit him with a coaster."

"Roland?"

"Nicholas," Peter whispered.

Dianna pulled away from him. "With a coaster?"

"We were in the parlour."

"Peter!"

"You saw my hand. He... he has no self control."

"Neither do you."

"Okay. Fair, but I don't have built in weaponry." Peter kicked at the snow on the ground. "His strength's coming back and honestly, I don't think we can manage him. Instead of using his words, he gets violent with us. Frankly, I don't know if it's a good idea to have him around the other children."

"He's been avoiding the other children," Dianna said. She shoved her hands into her coat pocket and lowered her head.

Roland emerged from the house, with Julius following close behind. "Ready to go?"

Peter nodded.

Roland scooped up his nephew and spun him around before plopping Julius down into the backseat of the car. Julius squealed and let out a laugh as his uncle playfully pinched his cheek. He held out the keys and turned to Dianna. "Can you drive? I'm not really up to it."

The cousins glanced at one another.

"Sure," she said, taking the keys from him. She climbed into the driver's seat, waiting for Peter to get in the back with Julius, and held her breath as Roland opened the passenger side door. Her green eyes scanned him. "Where's your scarf?"

Roland took a seat and sulked. "Let's just get your cousin to the doctors."

She shook her head and pulled out of the driveway.

OVER THE YEARS, Roland had grown accustomed to the quiet atmosphere of Dr. Gray's office. Despite being just off the main street, there wasn't much commotion during the day. Some nights one might hear a few of drunks cackling outside as they wandered home from the pub, but aside from that the street remained undisturbed.

When Roland was little, Dr. Gray usually came by the Crispin Estate once a week to see him. On rarer occasions, he'd go see Dr. Gray directly at his office with Tabitha or his mother. As a boy, Roland found that the doctor's office had a funny smell to it, like bleach. It wasn't as nauseating as the chemical smells of East Tavern Hospital, but it was strong enough to notice. In addition, there was the awful mint colour of the furniture, which reminded him of the wallpaper in his father's office. The blend of the two made him uneasy, but Dr. Gray, with his kind eyes and hearty laugh, quickly made his jitters fade.

Roland wasn't at all surprised to find Vincent, Dr. Gray's son, sitting at the front desk in the waiting room, flipping through the newest issue of *The Tavern Post*. For as long as he could remember, Vincent had been lingering about the office on his days off; usually tasked with answering calls and scheduling appointments. When they were young, Vincent was one of two children in Tavern allowed at the house to play with Roland. He was also one of the children who didn't mind Adeline Crispin's strict rules about playing quietly, and not getting too excited.

"Roland's a sick boy. Too much excitement isn't good for him," she'd say. However, at that age, almost everything excited Roland and the more fervent he got, the more agitated his mother became.

The article in the paper Vincent was reading caught Roland's attention as Dianna led Peter over to the desk – *Sven Charleston Confesses.*

"Wasn't Sven Charleston the fellow who used to date the Hill sister's?" Roland said as Vincent peered up from the paper.

Peter brushed past him. "That's not important right now!" He plopped himself down into a chair and whimpered, clutching his hand.

Roland cleared his throat and nodded. "Is your father here?"

Vincent nodded, getting up from behind the desk. "He's just finishing with another patient. What happened?"

"A dog," Peter said.

"He was bitten by a wolf," Roland blurted.

The two looked at one another, Peter gesturing wildly as Dianna stepped between them.

Julius shoved his mitten into his mouth, clinging to the bottom Roland's jacket.

"Was it a dog or a wolf?" Vincent took Peter's hand and unwrapped the bandage. His eyes widened. "That doesn't look good."

Peter grimaced. "It doesn't feel good."

As Julius crept out from behind his uncle, trying desperately to sneak a peek at Peter's hand, Roland grabbed him by the hood of his jacket and bent down, whispering in his ear. "I don't think you want to see that."

Julius turned and wrinkled his nose. "Why?"

Roland swallowed hard, studying the crimson moon running between Peter's swollen thumb and the fleshy part of his palm. The two gashes reminded him of the time his older brother Lawrence cut his leg on a rock while playing in the creek. His stomach churned. "It's not very pleasant."

Julius puffed up his cheeks. "Why'd you say it was a wolf when it wasn't?"

Roland caught Vincent glancing over at them as he called for his father. He cleared his throat and tapped Julius on the nose. "I guess it could've been a big dog."

"It wasn't."

"Julius, why don't we go for a walk?" Dianna took him by the hand. "Peter might be a while."

Julius pressed his lips together and nodded.

Roland stood up as Dr. Gray came out of the backroom, with a pregnant woman. He could tell by the look on the older mans face that he wasn't thrilled to see them.

"Roland, you missed your last appointment," Dr. Gray said, shooting him a dirty look. His eyes fell on Peter's hand. He redirected his attention to Roland, then Peter again, his shoulders tense. "Hm. What could've caused that, I wonder?"

Roland's heart skipped in his chest. *Is he angry about the appointment or the vermin?*

"Apparently some sort of large dog bit him," Vincent said, scratching his head.

The pregnant woman's jaw dropped as she tiptoed past Peter. She gave a quick wave to Dr. Gray as she waddled out of the office.

Dr. Gray adjusted his glasses. "A dog. Is that what we're calling it?"

"It might have been a fox," Peter said sheepishly as Dianna ushered Julius out the door. "Do you think I'll need stitches, doc?"

Dr. Gray gestured for Peter to follow him into the backroom, shaking his head. "Vincent, give Roland the usual while I deal with Peter. A dog... you boys must think I'm an idiot."

Vincent nodded, looking over at Roland apologetically and lead him down the hall.

"I think your father's mad at me."

"You missed three appointments," Vincent said. He let out a yawn, stretching his arms out in front of him. "He's also been pretty adamant about me popping in to check on you. Even Tabitha's called a couple times. Personally, I think it has to do with this whole Sven Charleston situation over in Riversburg."

Roland wrinkled his brow as Vincent looked back at him.

"Haven't you been following the news?"

Roland shook his head.

"He confessed to fourteen murders, including the death of his mistress, Felicity Hansen. You know, the actress that played Terri in *The Longest Night*?" Vincent scanned Roland's face and smirked. "You haven't seen it, have you?"

Roland nodded. "I honestly can't remember the last time I went to the theatre."

Vincent shook his head and laughed as he unlocked the medicine cabinet at the end of the hallway.

Roland spied the window beside the cabinet, rubbing the back of his neck. "You'd think after having a vermin break in, your father would move this someplace else."

Vincent shrugged. "Trust me, I've mentioned it. The vermin aren't the only issue either. With this fever going around, people are becoming desperate. My father's been fairly lenient with giving medication to people ever since the incident with that mutt." Vincent smiled at him. "He did, however, agree to keep the majority of the supply locked up elsewhere."

Roland nodded as Vincent rummaged around in the cabinet, taking note of how the botanical patterns of the wallpaper complimented the green pine tree pattern stitched into Vincent's black sweater. "Against the wall here, you look like a forest."

Vincent glanced down at his sweater. "I suppose I do." His voice grew quiet as he looked back at him. "I don't mean to alarm you, but Dianna displayed some questionable behaviour last month. I thought perhaps you should know, seeing as how you two are – what exactly are you, anyway?"

Roland kicked at the floor. "We're just co-workers."

Vincent nodded, then scrunched up his face, looking back inside the cabinet. "Where is this bloody thing?"

Roland peered inside, reached over Vincent's head, and grabbed the small bottle with his name printed on the label.

Vincent shut the cabinet and looked it over. "Oh, I was looking for the tin."

"According to your father, this is supposed to help me sleep."

"You're not sleeping?"

Roland leaned up against the wall. "What was it about Dianna you wanted to tell me?"

Vincent gazed down the hall. "Remember those vermin who stole from my father?"

Roland nodded. *How could I forget?*

"She was there when they were released. Not as a spectator or anything. She was actually *there* with their father. I think she might..." He shook his head. "Did you see how she looked at me when you arrived?"

"No?" Roland pressed his lips together and held his breath.

"She looked at me the way she used to look at you. You know, after you two called off the engagement and–"

"You mean when I was arrested?" Roland said, spying Dianna and Julius out the window playing in the snow.

Vincent followed Roland's gaze and leaned against the window. "I think she might be a vermin lover."

Roland shoved his hands into his pockets, watching his nephew stomp around in the slush. Dianna took a giant leap into the puddle, causing the child to shriek wildly with excitement. He'd forgotten how playful she was. How playful they all had been. "She was in Riversburg for a of couple years. They live alongside vermin over there. You know that."

"Someone from Riversburg should know better." Vincent ran a hand along his collarbone and cleared his throat. "Half or not, those mutts are born evil. I wish those idiots over in Presa would stop breeding them."

"Like you said, those kids just wanted medicine. It's not like they hurt anyone." Roland jumped back as Vincent slammed his fist into the wall.

"You should've seen them. The smug looks on their faces. They think they're better than us," Vincent said sullenly. "They all deserve to burn!"

Roland's eyes widened as they wandered over to the faded scar peeking out from the collar of Vincent's shirt. He lowered his head. "Vincent, I have to–"

Vincent adjusted his sweater, covering it up, and gave him a wry smile. "I'm sorry. I don't know what came over me. What were you about to say?"

"I should give you the money for the medication." Roland dug through his pocket.

"No. It's okay," Vincent said, kicking at the carpet. "No wonder Dianna looked at me like that. She probably thinks I'm a monster."

"You're not a monster."

Vincent shook his head. "I'm not so sure anymore... I read about an old woman who was killed by her vermin in Presa the other day, and I laughed. What kind of person laughs at something like that? All I could think about was how stupid she was. How stupid they all are. Breeding them like dogs and cattle. They're not pets. Would you keep a bear in your house and make it cook and clean for you?"

"No, but there are bears at the circus and the zoo."

"You've never been to the circus *or* the zoo, for that matter," Vincent said nonchalantly.

"No, but you told me there were bears. Besides, my old bedroom is covered in them."

"You're missing the point." Vincent groaned, shaking his head. "These idiots in Presa buy vermin and talk about them the way they do a prized poodle or a corgi, and whenever incidents like this happen, and trust me, they happen a lot, they pretend to be shocked, as if it's the first time a vermin has ever mauled someone to death."

Roland forced a smile as his heart sank into his belly. *If we include today's incident in the report, Kurtis won't hesitate to have Nicholas executed.* He leaned toward the cabinet. *We need to get his temper under control.* He found himself squeezing the bottle in his hand. "Vincent, I was wondering... does your father still have that other medication? The one he used to prescribe to my mother for her nerves?"

Vincent drew in a sharp breath. "Look, I really shouldn't be giving you anything outside of what my fathers prescribed. Mixing too many medications together could kill you."

"You also said drinking would kill me."

"I'm already giving you free medication."

"I offered to pay."

"We both know you can't afford it," Vincent said firmly. He ran a hand through his hair and shut his eyes. "If your mother needs it, you'll have to have her new doctor prescribe it."

"Vincent, please."

"Absolutely not. Roland, for all I know, you might try and use it to–"

"Kill someone?"

Vincent glowered. "I wasn't going to say that."

"You were thinking it."

"My father's been extremely worried about you. Same with Tabitha. I've never seen her so skittish. It reminds me of how your mother was before..." He met Roland's gaze and lowered his head. "Just forget I said anything."

Roland pulled out his wallet.

"Roland."

"Here's the money for the valerian extract," he said, forcefully grabbing Vincent by the hand and dumping out the contents of his wallet into his palm. "Now, if you'll excuse me, I think I'd better check on my nephew. Unless, of course, you don't feel I'm a fit guardian."

"Seeing as how you've been arrested twice..." Vincent uttered, dropping the money onto the floor.

Roland grimaced.

"Like I said, the medications free. My father only prescribed enough for the week. I suggest showing up for your next appointment."

Roland gritted his teeth and hurried down the hall, vision blurring. "You know what? I don't need it," he said, tossing the bottle onto the front desk next to the newspaper. "Tell Peter I went to the bakery!"

Outside, Dianna watched as Julius jumped on a large pile of slush at the edge of the sidewalk. Laughing, she shielded her face as it splattered up into the air.

Julius stood still, eyeing something behind her before raising a mitten covered hand and pointing, causing Dianna to look over her shoulder.

"How's Peter?" She made her way toward Roland as he left the doctor's office.

He slammed the door behind him and rushed past her across the street.

Dianna snagged onto the sleeve of his jacket, tugging him back onto the sidewalk. "Hey, wait! What's with you?"

"Piss off." Roland grumbled, yanking away from her as a car drove by.

She held up her hands and stepped back as his nephew came running toward them.

"Uncle Roland I–"

Dianna noted Roland's lip quiver.

"Stay with Miss Warren."

"Roland, what's wrong? Did something happen to Peter?"

"He's fine. I just... I need to think," Roland said.

She watched him let out a deep sigh as he dragged his fingers through his hair.

He met her gaze. "Why do you always look at me like that?"

Julius wrinkled his nose.

"Like what?"

"Both of you... all of you do," Roland muttered, his voice catching in his throat.

Julius reached for his uncle's hand and clutched it tightly.

"It's cold out here. Why don't we go grab a snack?" Dianna said, taking Julius' other hand. "I don't know about you two, but I'm starving."

Roland turned from her. "A-Are you hungry Julius?"

"Yes, but you probably already knew I was going to say that because my stomach keeps growling." He yanked on his uncle's hand and lowered his voice. "And I really need to go pee."

Dianna smirked, leading them down toward the main street. "Let's go to Jakob's. I'm sure he won't mind letting you use the washroom."

Roland's eyes widened. "Wait, what?"

"It is your grandfather's pub, after all."

3

Roland gazed helplessly at the large red doors of the pub, his legs shaking as Dianna pushed on the handles and lead him and Julius inside. As the doors creaked open, the familiar smells and sounds filled him. For a moment, there was warmth underneath the dim lights, but something slithered within as the doors to the street shut behind him.

The pub was only beginning to fill with people. A group of five teenagers sat at a table by the door, laughing loudly, poking fun at one another. A pair of elderly gentlemen sat at the bar slugging back what appeared to be their third or fourth beer and a woman sat at alone the other end staring into her empty glass, remnants of tears lining the tips of her lashes.

Roland popped up his collar and buried his head down into his jacket. *I should've stayed outside.*

Julius tugged on his hand, large eyes widening as he shimmied back and forth. "Uncle Roland."

Roland blinked hard, adjusting his eyes to the dimness of the room, and nodded as Dianna spun toward him.

"I'll order us some chips while you take Julius to the washroom," she said, giving him a smile.

There was something about her smile that seemed both innocent and malicious, but Roland couldn't quite pin it down. Before he had much time to debate it, he caught a glance of his nephew's face contorting as he squirmed, hopping up and down along the wooden floor. Roland scooped him up and rushed through the tables, toward the small hallway separating the kitchen and the washroom. He opened the washroom door and held his breath.

"It smells really bad in here," Julius said, plugging his nose.

Roland put him down. "Do you need to go or not?"

Julius pouted as Roland pushed on one of the stall doors. "You wait right there and make sure no one comes," Julius said, wagging his mitten at him. He took off his jacket and handed it to his uncle, then slowly closed the door. "I need some privacy, please!"

Roland guarded the door, trying not to inhale the smell of dried piss and alcohol. *Did it smell like this when I was younger?* He looked at his reflection in the mirror and furrowed his brow, combing his hair with his fingers. The curls at the top of his head stuck up every which way and didn't seem to want to lie down, no matter how hard he tried to tame them. *They're worse than Nicholas.*

"All the duckies in the pond say quack, quack, quack and the chickens go cheep, cheep!" Julius sang from within the stall. "But the cow is the loudest of them all. He says moo!"

Roland buried his nose in his sleeve. "Are you actually using the washroom or are you just fooling around?"

"I'm almost done."

Roland lifted his head briefly. "Okay, well, it sounds more like you're singing and not doing very much peeing."

Julius laughed.

Roland groaned, tapping his foot as the washroom door opened. He moved away from the gentleman as he entered, trying hard to hide within his jacket.

The gentleman went about his business, going to the sink to wash his hands.

Roland knocked on the stall door. "Julius, are you finished yet?"

The gentleman peered up at him from the mirror.

"Uh... I need help," Julius said.

The gentleman let out a chuckle, shaking his head. "Don't we all."

Julius propped the door open and looked up at Roland as the gentleman left the washroom. "Can you please help me? I got stuck."

"Stuck? Stuck how?"

"I can't get my boots back on."

"Why would you take your boots off to use the toilet?" Roland sighed, knelt down, and grabbed his nephew's boots from within the stall. "Honestly Julius, what am I going to do with you?"

Julius shrugged. "I don't know."

Roland shot Julius a firm glance and nodded toward the toilet. "Do us all a favour and flush when you're finished."

"Oops I forgot."

"Of course you did."

"Are chips the same as fries?" Julius said, pulling on the handle.

Roland ushered him over to the sink and helped him get his boots on. "Yes."

"But why are they called chips?"

"Because chips are chips and fries are fries."

"But they're potatoes," Julius said, wrinkling his brow as Roland rolled up his sleeves and turned on the tap.

Roland picked him up and held his nephew's hands under the water. "Yes, they are potatoes."

"Did you know you can have potatoes for every meal of the day?" Julius said, messily rubbing his hands together.

"I did know that."

"They sure are *fasinting*."

"Fascinating?"

"That's what I said!"

Roland put Julius down and lead him out of the washroom.

"Where's Miss Warren?"

Roland's stomach churned as he spotted Dianna sitting at what was once their usual table in front of the stage, sipping from a bottle of root beer. *Of course, you'd choose to sit there.* He took Julius by the hand and made his way over to her. "Really, Dianna?"

She grinned cheekily, brushing her strawberry-red hair behind her ear. "I thought Julius might like to hear some music."

"Do you enjoy torturing me?"

She laughed. "I don't know what you mean, Mr. Crispin."

"That toilet was really stinky and really loud," Julius told her, climbing up onto the chair next to her. Roland hung his nephew's jacket on the back of the seat and shook his head.

"Oh no. Maybe I should've taken you to the ladies' room instead. It's much nicer."

Roland sat across from her. "How would you know? Have you ever been in the men's room?"

"Actually, yes, I have," Dianna said, glowering. "That time you got sick and–"

"There you are Dianna. Chips and vinegar."

Roland sank into his seat as the older man placed the basket on the table.

"And who might this little fella be?"

Dianna smiled. "Jakob, this is Julius. Julius, this is Jakob."

"Hi Jakob!" Julius said, waving wildly. He looked down at the basket and furrowed his brow. "May I please have some ketchup?"

Jakob laughed. "Sure thing. Now that your friends have joined you, was there anything else you'd like to order?"

Roland found his legs had reached far underneath the table. His neck was resting uncomfortably on the back of his chair as Jakob turned his attention to him. He smiled sheepishly at the coldness in the man's brown eyes.

"What are you doing here?" He snorted, crossing his arms. He turned to Dianna and shook his head. "I really hope this child doesn't belong to the two of you."

"I don't belong to anyone or anywhere," Julius said, popping a fry into his mouth. "I'm a lone wolf on the prowl."

Jakob raise his brow as Roland sat up straight and gawked at his nephew.

"Excuse me?"

Julius giggled.

"Jakob, do you honestly think I'd have children with this man?" Dianna's green eyes looked Roland up and down as her wine-coloured lips curled into a sly smile.

He stuck his tongue out at her and crossed his arms. "Luckily for you, I loathe children."

Julius' jaw dropped as he jerked his head in his uncle's direction. "What?"

"Well, Roland, I don't know if something happened to your memory over the last few years, but you're still banned from my pub," Jakob said, looming over him.

Roland sighed. "You know you can't actually ban me, right?"

"I have a list of brats like you that don't get service. Using sweet little Dianna won't change my mind. I have no problem giving Officer Umino a call."

Julius got up on his knees and glared at Jakob.

Roland sneered, letting out a short laugh. "Go ahead. Call him."

Dianna shot up out of her seat and stood between him and Jakob as the older man raised his hand.

"You and I both know the boy deserves a smack," Jakob said, grinding his teeth together.

Roland grabbed a fistful of fries and stuffed them into his mouth. "You gonna call Umino or what?" He eyeballed the burly man as he rocked back in his chair.

Dianna moaned. "Would you stop?"

He gazed up at her and swallowed.

"Look, if you'd like us to leave, we'll leave," Dianna said gently.

"I don't have to go anywhere." Roland gestured to the plaque behind the counter. "My names on the bloody wall."

Jakob clenched his fist. "It's not *your* name, you little prick."

"Uncle Roland, you need to eat. You're being cranky," Julius said firmly, holding a fry up to Roland's face. "Come on, say ah."

Sulking, Roland bit the fry and crossed his arms as Jakob swerved around Dianna to look at the five-year-old.

"Is... is that Laurie's boy?"

Roland shot him a dirty look. "No. He's mine. Lawrence is dead."

Jakob took a deep breath as Dianna knelt in front of Roland, green eyes fixed on him.

"Jakob, would you mind keeping an eye on Julius? Roland and I are going to chat outside for a moment," Dianna said.

"I'm not a babysitter," Jakob muttered.

Julius cocked his head.

Roland stood up and sighed, patting Julius on the shoulder. "Can I trust you to sit here and behave until we come back?"

Julius' head bobbed up and down rapidly. "Yes, sir!"

Roland shoved into Jakob, scowling at him as Dianna ushered him out of the pub. *Great going Roland. Now she's pissed.* He leaned his head back and folded his hands over his chest, watching his breath swirl in the cold winter air.

"Why are you like this?" Her voice rose in her throat as she stomped her foot. She slid on the ice and latched onto him.

"You should get a proper pair of boots, Dianna."

"Don't change the subject."

He rolled his eyes. "Look, you and Julius can enjoy your food. I'll just go for a walk like I originally planned."

Dianna attempted to find her balance. Once she felt secure enough, she let go of him and readjusted the black beret on her head. "Is there a reason why you like to take your bad moods out of other people?"

Roland frowned, glancing down at his feet. "I don't try to."

"Well, maybe you should try harder. Baiting Jakob like that in front of Julius was childish, even for you. Honestly, I think that was more reckless than that deal you made with Kurtis Hood."

"I know."

"Then why did you continue to act like a spoiled little–"

"He expects me to act that way. Everyone expects it," Roland said bitterly. He shook his head and groaned. "I have a headache. I think I'll go wait in the car."

"I didn't know Jakob banned you from the pub," Dianna said sheepishly.

He waved her off and shoved his hands into his pockets, kicking

at the snow on the sidewalk as he made his way down the main
street.

4

It wasn't until he reached the Royalton that Roland realized Dianna still had the key. Leaning up against the car, he let out a groan, head swinging back. His blue eyes stared up into the cloudy sky as snowflakes drifted down. He kissed his teeth. *This day just keeps getting better.*

Roland wandered down the main street, shoving his frozen fingers into his pockets for warmth. He could already hear Tabitha lecturing him about not putting on a scarf or hat before he left. Roland sighed to himself, watching as a young woman's legs flew out from under her. One of her black pump's went soaring through the air and into the street. He tried to muffle his laughter as she fumbled about on the sidewalk. When she began to sob, his eyes widened, and he raced over. "Are you all right, Miss?"

She took his hand and let him help her up. "These stupid shoes–" She looked up at him, her brown eyes widened. "Oh…"

He took a step back and cleared his throat, watching the traffic in the street. "You're not hurt, are you?"

"No, I'm fine," she said, rubbing her eyes. "I don't look it, but I am, really."

When the road was clear, Roland hurried into the street and

swept the shoe up into his hand. He hurried back over to her and smiled. "Luckily, it wasn't run over."

She nodded slowly, taking it from him. She slid her shoe back over her stocking covered foot and brushed the snow from her legs. "Thank you, Roland. That was... well to be honest, unexpected."

He furrowed his brow and looked her over.

"Of course, you don't recognize me," she said. "We haven't crossed paths in what, six years?"

Roland examined the small women. "Little Kitty Chambers!"

She made up her face.

Roland cleared his throat. "H-how are you?"

"Well, seeing as how I bombed that interview. I'm lovely. I mean, at least I'm not you."

Roland rubbed the back of his neck. *Probably shouldn't have called her little.* He managed a smile. "Are you looking for a job?"

She nodded. "Where's your better half? Connie said he never called her back after they had dinner a few weeks back."

"Peter? He's... he got attacked by a dog. I just left him with Dr. Gray."

"A dog?"

"It might've been a wolf. I'm not really sure."

Kitty's eyes widened. "You're joking."

"I wish I was."

She fluffed up the thick curls beneath her hat and shook her head. "Seems everyone's been having a string of bad luck lately."

He shrugged.

"You wouldn't happen to know anyone looking for a secretary, would you?"

"No."

Her eyes pooled with tears. "Well, thank you for getting my shoe for me. And for helping me up. That was unexpectedly kind of you."

"It's nice to know you have such high expectations of me." His eyes lit up as he gazed further down the street. "Actually, I might be able to get you a job."

"You?"

He nodded. "If you're still looking for one."

"Is this another one of your practical jokes?" She sniffled back her tears.

He crouched slightly so they were face to face. "Just trust me."

She laughed, rubbing her eyes. "Oh, what the heck! I've got nothing to lose. I've already torn my favourite pair of stockings."

He eyed her left leg. "That you have. Well, come along Miss. I wouldn't want you to fall and crack your head open," he said, taking her by the arm.

"In a weird way, I'm actually glad it was you who saw that embarrassing display and not someone like Miles or Constance," Kitty said, trying to keep her footing as they went down the street. "Sadly, I doubt you'll have any luck convincing someone to hire me. I may be clumsy, but you're well–"

"I'm Roland Crispin."

"Exactly."

He grinned, looking down at the top of her large hat. "Sometimes being Roland Crispin is a good thing."

"Maybe when we were children," Kitty said, turning her head up to look at him.

Nicholas sat perched by the window in the nursery, gazing outside as his ears perked up. The tips of them tingled at the sound of light footsteps making their way down the hallway. *She's probably going up to the library.* He ran his hand through his hair and paused, tilting his head to the side. The footsteps stopped. Nicholas pretended to trace along the window, while taking a moment to glance back, and spotted her round blue eyes peering through the crack in the nursery door. His chest tightened.

Ever since she'd found out who– what he really was, Rose had been distant. He could tell she was frightened. *Biting Mr. Rissing probably didn't help.* She flinched whenever he smiled at her, so he stopped smiling, stopped looking at her, keeping his eyes turned downward. He found that when he met her gaze, Rose's eyes swelled like an animal caught in a trap. Caspian had become weary of him, too. The only Crispin child that seemed interested in him was little Julius so much, in fact, that Nicholas wondered if he were one of the bears painted around the nursery performing tricks.

Nicholas stood up to examine the books on the table that Mr. Crispin had given him. They weren't like the ones Rose read. They were shorter with pictures. He glanced up from the table briefly to look at the door.

Rose pushed the door open gently and stepped into the room, fidgeting with her hair. "What happened?"

Nicholas raised his brow.

She pointed. "T-to your face, I mean. You're all blue and purple."

Nicholas wiggled his nose and winced. "Mr. Rissing hit me with a coaster."

She looked down at her hands and frowned.

He followed her gaze.

Her hands were bright red and lightly bruised. She shook her head. "Seems we were both punished today, huh? Well, I won't keep you."

"I'll see you at dinner."

As Rose walked away, Nicholas noticed a red ribbon lying on the floor and crept over to the door to pick it up, peering down the hall as Rose hurried off to her room. He held it carefully between his fingers and chased after her, sliding up between her and the bedroom door. His pupils narrowed, hair brushing against her cheek as they stood face to face. "You dropped your–"

"I don't have time to play right now. I have to study," she said, backing away from him.

Nicholas' ears twitched. He shoved the ribbon into his pocket.

She eyed him.

He let out a deep breath and lowered his head. "Is Miss Warren home yet?"

"No, she left with my uncle." Rose shooed him away from her

door, watching him shimmy over to the wall. "You really need to stop biting people," she said.

He swallowed hard.

"Acting like that will only get you into trouble."

"Acting like what?"

Rose held the doorknob, pressing her lips together. "Like a vermin."

"Nicholas!"

The two winced at the shrill sound of Tabitha's voice.

"You should go. She doesn't sound very happy," Rose whispered.

"Is she ever happy?" Nicholas groaned, shaking his head. He made his way toward the staircase, listening to the sound of the older woman stomping through the parlour, briefly looking over his shoulder as Rose went into her room. *She says vermin like it's a bad thing. Doesn't she know what human's are like?* Nicholas raced to the edge of the stairs and leapt down onto the main floor; his shoulders tensed as Tabitha came rushing toward him.

"Are you trying to break your neck?"

"No, ma'am."

"Did I not give you a list of things to do before I returned?"

"Yes, ma'am."

"And did you... what did you do to your face?" Tabitha looked him over. "Quick. Answer me. I don't have all day."

Nicholas cracked his knuckles, staring down at the floor. "Mr. Rissing hit me."

Tabitha kissed her teeth and crossed her arms. "What'd you do, run your mouth again?"

Nicholas shook his head.

"You'll want to put ice on that," Tabitha mumbled, taking Nicholas by the wrist, and leading him into the kitchen. "Have a seat. I have to go down to the freezer."

Nicholas watched as she opened the door beside the pantry and faded into the dark. He'd never been to the bottom half of the house, but he knew there was a cellar down there, among other things. Caspian once mentioned the number of cobwebs down there, and for

Nicholas that was enough to deter him. If there were webs, there were bound to be spiders, and if the spiders were anything like the ones back home in Dinara, Nicholas wanted nothing to do with them.

Tabitha emerged, holding the ice between her fingers. She went over to the counter and opened the bottom drawer, reaching in for a hand towel.

Nicholas watched her wrap the ice in it.

"Sit still," Tabitha said, pressing the ice against his skin.

Nicholas recoiled.

Tabitha began inspecting Nicholas' face. "It's bad enough I have to cook and clean and look after the house. If that boy doesn't get a handle on things, I don't know what Evan and I are going to do."

Nicholas cocked his head. "What boy?"

"Sit still."

Nicholas slouched in his seat.

"If Mrs. Crispin saw the state of things here, she'd have a fit," Tabitha said, shaking her head. "It's bad enough having a little brute like you around, but he has that girl living here and that freeloading cousin of hers. People will talk. They're already talking. Oh, the things you could hear with those ears of yours. Makes me glad I'm not a vermin. I couldn't stand hearing more than I already do."

Nicholas closed his eyes, listening to the woman ramble on.

"Dinner's going to be late. I expect you to have the parlour tidied up before Mr. Crispin get's back. Don't worry about cleaning upstairs. You can do it tomorrow."

"*Kheikin Nyla.*"

Tabitha stopped and glared at him. "What was that?"

Nicholas' eyes shot open. "I'm sorry... I meant Mrs. Gibson."

"You know you aren't to be speaking like that."

He winced.

"Take this. I need to finish prepping dinner," she said, handing him the ice.

Nicholas spun around in his chair, watching her go over to the sink. "I can help."

"I don't want your help."

He clutched the ice and looked away from her. "*Beidma.*"

"Excuse me?"

Nicholas sat up straight, pressing his lips into a smile. "Nothing. My face hurts, that's all."

Tabitha raised her brow and waved her hand. "Out! You're distracting me."

"Yes, ma'am." Nicholas pressed the ice to his nose and massaged it gently as he made his way into the parlour. *What am I supposed to be cleaning up in here? Everything is already put away.* He sat down on the couch, propping a pillow behind his head and closed his eyes, holding the ice to his face. *I'll take a nap and clean up later.*

5

———————

"Roland, where are you taking me?"

Roland could sense her concern as he lead Kittyr past the park and West Tavern library. He smiled at her. "Doren shipping." She stopped, pulling away from him.

"What?"

"Isn't that where your father worked?"

He examined the fearful expression on her face. *Typical.* He watched her take a step back, legs shaking.

"Isn't that where he was–"

"Murdered? Yes, it was," Roland said bluntly. He rubbed his frozen fingers together. "Do you want the job or not?"

"I need it but..."

"Miles Jr. works there now. You have no reason to worry."

Kitty dug her heel into the ice.

Roland sighed. "I get it. You don't want to be seen with a murderer. I understand."

Kitty shook her head, steadying her hat with her hands as it flopped about her head. "I-I never called you that."

Roland grinned. "It's fine, Kitty. Really. I'm used to it."

She met his gaze and puffed up her chest. "I'll go. I need the money. At this point, I couldn't care less about what kind of work it is."

Roland raised his brow.

"Wipe that cheeky grin off your face."

"You're far too serious, Kitty," Roland said, shoving his hands into his coat pockets. "Not as serious as Juliet, but serious enough."

"I'm serious? Have you looked in the mirror?"

"Oh no. If I did that, I'd waste away whilst admiring myself."

Kitty laughed. "I see time hasn't made you any less ridiculous."

"Eh, I'm not so bad anymore. I was definitely worse when we were younger," Roland said, starting off again toward the Doren Shipping building.

"Not as bad as Miles and Peter."

"I'll take that as a compliment," Roland said, squeezing his eyes shut as a sharp pain zipped through his skull. *Seriously? Again!* He sighed and glanced at her. "Not to rush you or anything, but if I don't get inside soon, I think my toes will freeze off."

Kitty rushed to his side. "It's days like that that make me wish I lived in Luciole."

"I've never been anywhere else."

"You've been to Riversburg."

Bloody Riversburg. Roland winced. "Th-that's true."

"I went to Luciole and Miao with my folks when I was ten. It was beautiful, but the heat was unbearable!" Kitty told him. "You should try heading out to the islands in the summer. I hear the best time to go is around June. Say, not to be nosy or anything, but why haven't you been anywhere outside of Riversburg? I thought you were moving to Augen for college."

Roland peered down at her, stomach knotting.

Kitty veered her large brown eyes away from him. "I said something stupid, didn't I."

"It's okay."

Kitty nudged him gently with her elbow. "Well, you look like a man who needs a vacation. You should plan a trip over to Luciole with the children. It'd be fun! The children can go swimming and you could lie on the beach and get a tan."

Roland scrunched up his face as they made their way up the steps to the building. "Julius doesn't know how to swim."

"You could teach him," she said, holding the door open for him.

Roland burst out laughing, causing her to jump back.

The woman at the front desk glared at them.

"Don't you remember when I nearly drowned at the lake in the eighth grade?"

Kitty's eyes widened. "Oh gosh! Yes, Miles and Vincent had to drag you out of the water. You were unconscious and everything."

"I'm the last person to teach anyone how to do anything. Heck, I'd rather send the kids out to the islands with Peter. He went there for school. He probably knows his way around... although he had a drowning incident himself back in the day."

"Can I help you?" the woman at the desk said, dragging a pen through her long shiny black hair.

Roland cleared his throat, making his way over to the desk. "Yes actually, I'm here to see Mr. Lévesque."

The woman fiddled with her pen and eyed him. "Do you have an appointment?"

"No, but–"

"Mr. Lévesque is extremely busy right now. I suggest making an appointment and coming back later."

Roland leaned toward her and glanced down at her nameplate. "Mrs. Han, I've never needed to make an appointment to see Charlie before. Sitara always lets me go right on in."

"And that's probably why she doesn't work here anymore," Mrs. Han said, nearly smacking him in the face with her pen.

Roland stumbled back. "H-how about I leave and come back with a coffee and muffin just for you? You look like you're a muffin kind of person."

"Are you trying to bribe me?"

"Yes–" Roland let out of a huff and cocked his head. "Look, lady, I really need to see Charlie."

"And I'm telling you that you need to make an appointment."

Roland glowered and turned toward the door. "My father will be hearing about this."

Kitty's eyes widened. "Wait a minute–"

Mrs. Han jumped from her seat. "Your father?"

A smile crept between his lips as he spun back around, meeting Mrs. Han's eyes.

Kitty tiptoed toward him. "What are you doing?" she whispered.

Mrs. Han chewed on the back of her pen, looking him over. "What's your name?"

He thought for a moment. "Darius."

She furrowed her brow. "And your father is?"

"My father owns this building."

Kitty reared her head. "What the hell are you–"

Roland stepped around her as Mrs. Han twirled her pen around her thumb.

"I wasn't aware the younger Mr. Doren had a brother."

"He doesn't," Kitty said bluntly.

Mrs. Han jabbed the tip of her pen into the front of Roland's jacket, staring him straight in the face. "The Doren's own this building. So, either your father is Sam Doren, or you're lying to me."

Roland leaned toward her, the pen digging into him. "The Doren's name is on the building, but this office and the warehouse belong to my father."

Mrs. Han pulled her pen back and tossed her hair over her shoulder. "I'm bored, but I think I've entertained your little game far too long. Get out of my sight."

"How could you not know who I am?"

"Forgive me for not keeping tabs on every man that tries to bribe me with muffins."

"Other men have offered you muffins?"

She shook her head and groaned. "Go. I've had enough."

Roland rolled his eyes as Kitty tugged on his arm.

"Do I need to call security?"

"No, that'd be quite embarrassing. My father runs the security department," Roland said.

Mrs. Han blinked hard. "And yet you haven't given me his name."

"Is Charlie not in charge of security?"

Her cheeks reddened.

Kitty tugged on his arm again, glaring.

"If I can't go in, then please go fetch him for me. I'm sure he can spare five minutes."

"I-I didn't know Mr. Lévesque had any children."

"There are photos of me in his office."

"What did you say your name was?" Mrs. Han grabbed a piece of paper from her desk.

"Full name?"

"Preferably yes."

"Darius Lawrence Lévesque."

Mrs. Han looked him over, scribbling it down. "That name does sound awfully familiar... Darius Lawrence. Okay, I'll send someone to fetch your father for you. Take a seat over there on the couch."

Roland sank into his seat, watching Mrs. Han hurry off through the doors leading to the rest of the office.

Kitty shoved at him. "Darius Lawrence Lévesque?"

Roland looked up at her. "I may have stolen my father's identity... but it's true, my father does own this building. Well, I suppose my mother does until it passes on to the children."

Kitty sat down next to him, staring straight ahead.

"You've got nothing to worry about."

"How often do you impersonate your father?"

"Seeing as how I hate the man, not often. Plus, it's not like I completely lied about my name. Darius is–"

Kitty groaned, putting her head in her hands. "Oh, shut up."

Roland bit his lip. *If Sitara were here, I wouldn't have had to lie.*

After a few moments, Mrs. Han returned with a thin, dark-haired man in a fitted black suit. She gestured to Roland and Kitty, shaking her head.

The man crossed his arms. "Darius Lawrence?"

Roland scrambled to his feet.

"I should've known." The man kissed his teeth and rolled his eyes.

Roland lowered his head and waved sheepishly. "Hi Charlie."

"He's not your son, is he?" Mrs. Han said, placing the pen down on her desk.

Charlie bit his lip.

"I'll call security."

"Sorry for bothering you at work," Roland said, inching toward them. He gave Charlie a smile and threw his arm around him. "Aren't you happy to see me?"

Charlie pulled away from him. "What are you doing here?"

Mrs. Han hurried toward the doors.

Roland's eyes widened. "Mrs. Han, my father–"

She whipped her head around. "Shut up! I'm done with you. You've wasted both my time and Mr. Lévesque's with this ridiculous game of yours."

"Let me guess, you need another loan," Charlie said, looking Roland over.

Roland gasped playfully. "To think you'd have the audacity to make such an assumption. We both know if I wanted a loan, I'd have gone to your place in East Tavern." He grinned, watching Charlie crack a smile.

Mrs. Han's face reddened.

"Who's your frightened looking friend?" Charlie said, pointing to Kitty.

"She's the reason I'm here."

"Don't tell me you're getting married. I pity anyone who has to put up with your nonsense."

"As do I." Mrs. Han shot Roland a dirty look. "Am I to assume this is your son?"

Charlie's smile faded. "Oh no. He was lying. I don't have any children."

"But you know him."

"Of course he knows me," Roland said matter-of-factly.

"Hush!" Mrs. Han took a deep breath, composed herself, and looked at Charlie. "Who is this lunatic?"

"That's my godson," Charlie said. "His family owns a portion of this building and the warehouses down by the docks. His father was the previous head of security."

"His father?" Mrs. Han eyed him. "Oh... oh no. Darius and Lawrence." Her eyes widened.

"I only lied because I knew if I mentioned I was Darius Crispin's son, that you, being new here and all, might be frightened," Roland said, giving a shrug.

"Y-you're the one who stabbed his father twelve times in the chest."

"He wasn't stabbed, he was shot," Roland said, holding a pretend pistol to his skull. He directed his attention to Charlie, gesturing to Kitty. "Could you do me a favour and give my friend here a job? She's quite smart. She tutored Miles at one point. Couldn't tell you for what subject, but she did. Without her, I think he would have failed the seventh grade. Can you imagine failing two grades?"

"Does your friend have a resumé with her?"

Roland turned to her. "I never asked her. I simply said I could get her a job, and that is what I intend to do. See, you have two options. You can either give her a position now or I'll have to go to my niece and ask her to give Kitty a job on my behalf... seeing as how I have no authority to do so myself."

Charlie nodded slowly, looking Roland over. "Mrs. Han, would you like an assistant?"

"Do I have a choice?"

"Not really."

"Then I suppose I could take on an assistant," she said, going back to her desk.

Kitty's jaw dropped.

Charlie turned his attention to her. "When can you start?"

"T-tomorrow."

"Fantastic. Now, if you'll excuse me, I have to get back to work. Part of our shipment to Presa went missing this morning."

Roland frowned. "Say, Uncle Charlie, I actually do need a loan."

Charlie crossed his arms. "Of course you do. Have Leon bring me the receipts and I'll handle it." He pointed to Kitty. "Once your friend there comes to her senses, let her know that I'd like her here for eight tomorrow."

Roland glanced over at Kitty. She had her head buried in her large black hat. "Kitty?"

She popped her head out. Her face beamed with excitement.

"Did you hear what he said?"

She nodded.

Roland's eyes widened as she threw her arms around his waist and squeezed him tight. He let out a yelp.

"Thank you! Thank you! Thank you!"

He blushed.

"I don't know why Juliet called you the wickedest man alive. You've just done the sweetest thing anyone has ever done for me!"

The sharp pain returned to Roland's head. He stumbled back. The room went dark.

∽

"How old did you say you were?"

"Five."

"Wow. Just wow. I'm losing a game of cards to an advanced toddler. This is great."

Roland sat up quickly, then grabbed his head and groaned. He reared his head as a hand came slamming down onto his shoulder.

"You gave Kitty and Charlie quite the scare."

Roland looked around. "Miles... wait, where am I?"

"My office," Miles Jr. said, placing a card on the table. "You fainted."

"Uncle Roland, do you want to play with us?" Julius looked over at him.

Roland eyed Miles. "Julius, where are Peter and Dianna?"

Julius wrinkled his nose. "Uh, I forget."

"Peter is with my uncle and Vincent. Dianna left to pick him up. I thought you said you would kill yourself if you ever had to be in the same room as her again?"

Roland grumbled, cupping his face in his hands. "When did I say that?"

"I believe it was right after her old man punched you outside the cinema."

Roland peered at Miles Jr. through the spaces between his fingers. He was nursing a drink in his hand while Julius put a card down on the table. *Is that how I looked with Lawrence?* He shook the thought from his head, preferring not to taint the image of his brother any further. Miles Doren Jr. was the boy who tortured him throughout his childhood. Despite being related to Vincent, the two were complete opposites. Miles was loud, rude, rash, and, much of the time, violent.

Julius' eyes widened. "Somebody punched you?"

"A lot of people have punched this idiot," Miles said, eyeing the card Julius placed on the table. "Wait a second. Why did you play diamonds?"

"Because we're matching the red cards to the red cards."

Miles scrunched up his face and took a sip from his glass. "I clearly haven't learned the rules of this game."

"Sometimes I just make a pattern," Julius said.

Miles spun around in his chair, looking Roland over. "You look like sh–shivering. You look like you're shivering. Are you cold?"

"That's why you should have took your gloves and scarf like Tabby said too," Julius said, wagging a finger at his uncle. He picked up a candy bar off the table and bit into it.

Roland pressed his lips together. "Where'd you get that?"

"This nice man gave it to me," Julius said, pointing to Miles.

Nice man. Roland glowered.

"What got you so worked up that you passed out?" Miles said. His brown eyes appeared tired. It caught Roland off guard. "By the way, did your niece like her birthday gift?"

"You gave her a birthday gift?"

"A ribbon for her collection. That and a doll. Didn't know if she still played with dolls. I dropped it off during the party."

Roland furrowed his brow. "You were at the party?"

"For about two minutes. I had some business to take care of in Riversburg, so I stopped by on my way over."

"Is it the doll with the purple dress, the green dress, or the pink dress?" Julius stood up on the chair. "Or the white one? Or–"

Roland moaned. "And this is what happens when you give him sugar."

"I think the doll had on a blue dress. You sister still likes blue, right?"

Julius beamed, leaning toward him. "It's her favourite colour. Do you know my favourite colour?"

"How do you know so much about my brother's children?" Roland cleared his throat, averting his eyes as Miles shot him a dirty look.

"I know just as much about you. The difference is I don't care," Miles said.

Roland gulped.

"And no, I don't think I ever learned your favourite colour. Is it red by any chance?" Miles said as Julius put down another red card.

Julius shook his head, sitting back in the seat. "No."

"Caspian likes black."

"You know that black is actually a shade," Julius said, a hint of pride in his voice.

"Hm. Interesting. I didn't know that."

"Your hair is really black. It looks like the stuff Uncle Roland puts on his shoes."

Miles laughed. "Shoe polish?"

Julius nodded.

Roland massaged his temples.

"Are you okay, Uncle Roland?" Julius peered over at him.

"I'm fine," Roland said.

"Do you need a hug?"

Roland's face grew hot. He shrugged. Truthfully a hug would have been nice but admitting something like that in front of Miles would prompt him to start making jokes about how often Roland cried when they were little, and whenever Miles mentioned such stories he conveniently left out how he was the one who made Roland cry.

Julius climbed down from his chair and went over to the couch. He wrapped his arms around his uncle and smiled. "Do you feel better now?"

"Yes, thank you Julius."

"That man from before he really, really, really hates you."

"What man?"

"The man!" Julius let go and pouted. "With the fries and the cookies."

"Cookies?"

"He means Jakob," Miles said.

"Jakob gave you cookies?" Roland frowned. *Lisa and I are never going to be able to get him to bed on time.*

Julius smiled. "He said you're the rudest boy in the world, but I'm not, because I was good."

"I love how Jakob hates you, more than he hates me." Miles grinned, taking another sip from his glass. "It's just... it's hilarious, honestly. I mean, remember when you and Vincent were the good ones and Peter and I were the bad ones?"

Roland leaned back on the couch. "Yes Miles, I do remember the numerous times you nearly got us all killed."

"But I didn't." Miles gave him a smile. "By the way, my cousin is pissed at you."

"We had an argument," Roland said quietly.

"Yes, I know. He told me."

"When did you talk to him?"

"How do you think Dianna knew you were here?"

"Why wouldn't you call Tabitha?"

"Look. I didn't make the call. Charlie did."

Roland groaned. "And where is Uncle Charlie?"

"Trying to fix this whole Presa shipment mess." Miles shook his head. "Anyway, he said he was giving Dianna your medication."

"Wait what?"

"Does she still not know?" Miles smirked.

Roland glared at him.

Miles held up his hands defensively. "She was already at my uncle's office when we called."

Roland gritted his teeth. "Lawrence told her a long time ago."

"You know, you really put things into perspective for me as a kid. If I didn't know you were going to drop dead any moment, I probably wouldn't have done all those crazy things when we were younger."

Julius' lower lip quivered. "You're going to die?"

Miles put his glass on the table. "Everyone dies."

Julius lowered his head, sulking. "I don't want to die. I want to be an uncle."

"You may want to set higher expectations for yourself," Roland mumbled.

"Why?"

"How old am I?"

"One-hundred?"

Roland and Miles laughed.

"How old do you think Tabitha is?"

"She's smaller than you, so she's only ninety-nine." Julius said, looking at the two of them. "Alicia is smaller than me. That's why she has a little number."

Roland chuckled. "Julius, I'm twenty-four."

Julius wrinkled his brow and eyed him. "How old is Miss Warren?"

"She's twenty-three I think."

Julius turned to Miles. "How old are you?"

"Twenty-five."

"How are you twenty-five if you were in the same class as Uncle Roland?" Julius tilted his head. "Everyone in my class is the same as me."

"He failed the first grade."

Julius' jaw dropped.

The look Miles gave Roland caused his insides to squirm.

"You and Vincent love to casually tell that to everyone, don't you?"

"Yes... I mean no!" Roland slammed a hand over his mouth.

Miles got up out of his chair and sat down next to him and Julius on the couch. He wrapped an arm around Roland's neck and squeezed. "For such a frail boy, you sure like to run your mouth. You've got guts Crispin. You're stupid, but you've got guts."

Julius giggled.

Roland shoved at Miles. "Stop. That hurts."

"Really?" Dianna said, opening the office door. "I've been gone twenty minutes."

"He started it," Miles said, shoving Roland off the couch.

Julius glared at him. "Hey!"

Miles sneered. "We're only playing. See, he's like my little brother."

Roland clenched his fists. *Yeah right.*

"My big brother never, ever, ever pushes me," Julius said, crossing his arms. "He's nice."

"I guess I'm not a very nice big brother then," Miles said, taking a step back. "I'm sorry Roland."

Dianna helped Roland up off the floor. "Stop looking so sour. He barely touched you, Roland."

Roland shook his head. *It's not that. It's his baseless apologies.*

"Besides, it serves you right, running off like that. We were worried about you."

A sly grin slid across Miles' face. "Ooh."

Dianna let out a huff. "Miles, can you not?"

Miles scooped Julius up off the couch and handed the boy to her. "Remember dear, he's broke. Even with his short life expectancy, you won't get anything from him."

Roland rolled his eyes. "You sound like my mother."

"I am your mother."

"Miles, go, go– never mind." Roland stormed out of the office.

"I hope I'll see you all at my mother's luncheon this Sunday!"

"You won't," Roland said under his breath. *I hope you choke on your devilled eggs you–*

"Georgie Bryce will be there!"

Roland stopped, spun around, and cocked his head.

Miles grinned.

"No, he won't."

"He will."

"You're lying."

"I'm not."

Dianna's brow rose. "I actually wouldn't mind going. I've never been to a real Doren party before."

"Me either," Julius said.

"You definitely need to come and teach my grandfather your little card game," Miles said.

"We'll think about it." Roland kicked his feet. "Come on, let's head home."

A mischievous glint hit Miles' eyes. "Are you and Dianna living together?"

Roland craned his neck, glancing between Dianna and Miles, heart hurling across his chest. Shuddering, he jammed his hands into his pockets. There was no escaping it. "Yep."

Miles smirked. "Interesting."

Dianna studied Roland, the medicine Vincent gave her rolling around in her coat pocket. *Should I hand it to him casually or just leave it upstairs on his dresser?* She patted her pocket as the group entered the house, her cousin cradling his freshly treated hand and Roland cradling his exhausted nephew. A smile parted between her lips, peering at Julius flopping about in his uncle's arms. Dianna couldn't help but let out a light chuckle. One of the little boy's mittens dangled by a thread from the sleeve of his jacket while Roland danced about, trying to remove his boots without waking Julius up. *Maybe I should help him?* She inched toward him as her cousin made his way into the parlour, grumbling to himself.

"Got anything to drink?" Peter said.

Roland wobbled about, moving Julius onto his hip. "Ask Tabby."

He looks exhausted. Dianna sat down at the bottom of the step and removed her shoes, still watching Roland struggle. She held out her arms and waved him over. "Give Julius here."

Roland pressed his lips together and carefully lowered the five-year-old into her arms, then knelt down to pry off his boots. He wiped his brow, shaking his head, curls sticking up every which way. It'd been some time since he'd had a haircut.

She smirked. *I wonder if he's decided to grow it out like Nicholas?* Dianna tilted her head, smiling down at little Julius as he snuggled close to her. The afternoon they'd spent at Jakob's pub had been fun, despite the fact that she could barely keep up with half the questions he asked her. It didn't help that Jakob kept bringing over cookies and offering them a soda pop. It had been a while since she'd babysat on her own, and it wasn't until the little boys' words started to morph into an incomprehensible slur of gibberish that she remembered that dreadful time she had when she was thirteen and offered to look after the neighbour's triplets. How a few cookies could make one small child resemble a trio of bouncing ten-year-olds was beyond her.

It was at that point she decided it was time for them to say goodbye to Jakob. She had wanted to discuss Roland with him, but it didn't seem appropriate with Julius there, another time perhaps, but not today.

Julius had told Dianna about a new game he'd invented on the way to the car, where they had to pick a colour and the other person had to imagine every animal in existence as that colour. By the time they reached the Royalton, Dianna realized she never gave Roland the keys and Julius had imagined thirty animals in the colour periwinkle, a colour she herself had always assumed was made up, but according to Julius, Rose had a ribbon in that colour and if Rose had a periwinkle ribbon, then periwinkle had to be real.

They made their way back to Dr. Gray's office where they found Vincent sitting on the outside steps, fidgeting with a bottle of medicine.

He looked up at them. "Where's Roland?"

Dianna furrowed her brow. "He's not here?"

Then the phone rang.

There was a hint of distress and anger in Vincent's voice that she couldn't quite place. After he got off the telephone, he handed her the medicine and told her to go to Doren Shipping. Back when they were in school, Dianna would have never thought of Vincent as the angry or violent type. Out of all of Peter's friends, he was the best behaved. He was polite, rarely raised his voice, and he was smart. Dianna and her best friend Charlotte would often compare the boys in their classes, both usually concluding that Vincent was the nicest of them all and Peter and Miles tied for the worst. After seeing how he had treated Micah and Zana, Vincent was like a complete stranger to her, but when he gave her the medicine, the look on his face was all too familiar.

Roland was in trouble.

Watching him slide off his boots and head into the parlour, Roland *seemed* fine. And if she were to ask, he would claim to be so. Vincent, however, made it clear that Roland was in fact not, and the incident at Doren Shipping only solidified it.

Dianna followed him, Julius still in her arms.

The room was filled with the sound of a heavy sigh.

What's got him so upset?

Roland leaned his head back, gesturing to an angry Peter and a sleeping Nicholas.

Dianna shot daggers at her cousin. "His face is swollen."

"My hand is swollen," Peter said, attempting to shove Nicholas off the couch.

With a huff, Roland took Julius from Dianna and set him down in the armchair by the fireplace. He spun around toward the couch and loomed over Nicholas.

Peter swatted at Nicholas with his good hand. "Get up, you lazy bum."

"Stop that!" Dianna pulled her cousin toward her. "He's clearly exhausted."

"I'm exhausted," Peter said, grabbing Nicholas by the ear.

"Peter!" Roland and Dianna cried in unison, rousing Julius.

Nicholas's eyes shot open. *"Danya Doksot!"*

Julius rubbed his eyes. "What's *Doksot*?"

Peter yanked on Nicholas' hair, forcing the boy to sit up and yelp. "Want to know how many stitches I needed?" He waved his hand in Nicholas' face.

"Peter, stop," Roland muttered, stumbling forward. He drew in a deep breath, swaying back and forth. "Please, just–"

Dianna latched onto him, causing Roland to jerk away. Silence fell over the parlour, all eyes on them. Peter let go of Nicholas, inching away from the couch and toward his cousin. From the corner of her eye, Dianna noted the way he hesitated. She returned her attention back to Roland, whose eyes remained fixed on her. *If looks could kill.*

Tabitha called out to them from the kitchen. "Dinner will be on the table in ten minutes!"

Everyone remained still, even little Julius, who sat in the armchair staring at his uncle quizzically.

Dianna blinked as Roland's expression softened, and he smiled.

"Sorry. You just startled me," he said softly, before heading toward the dining room.

Despite the warmth on his face, the room grew cold.

She wrapped her arms around herself, listening to Tabitha and Roland's laughter echo out from the kitchen. *I'll leave the medicine on his dresser.*

6

———————

Suzanna Wolfe adjusted the green gloves as she looked in the mirror, twisting her body around to examine herself. Her lips were painted with such a shocking red that it made her stomach coil. *Keep it together. You're Lord Wolfe's daughter, you gotta look the part.* She straightened her back, lifting her head high, brushing a loose strand of hair behind her ear, which picked up the laughter from the parlour. The sound of their voices scratched her ears. *It's just your family. I'm sure they won't notice the bruising.* She practiced a smile in the mirror.

"Those pearls suit you," Mrs. Adler said sweetly, glancing over as she carried a drink tray into the other room.

Zana ran a finger along her neck and eyed the necklace her father had left for her.

Human parties were confusing: the clothing, the way they painted their faces, even the music.

She smiled, recalling how she and Nicholas used to sneak out at night and listen to the radio her father bought them, hoping they might catch *The Dolly Song*. Whenever it came on, Nicholas would pop up on his tiptoes to twirl her around his finger, and they'd spin around singing until they went hoarse.

"Lady Suzanna, I believe your father is waiting for you," Mrs. Adler said, coming back into the hall.

Zana swallowed the lump in her throat, gazing at the kitten, heels on her feet, and prayed she wouldn't trip again. She'd spent the past few days practicing in secret, trying to walk gracefully like Ramona Weathers: head held high, hands folded, eyes sparkling beneath a lit chandelier as she lightly stepped across the floor, just like a movie star. Zana nodded to her reflection, drawing in a deep breath, positioning her gently closed lip smile. *That's it. Just like Ramona in Trip to Brine.* She'd only watched the film a dozen times since coming back to Dinara. She could do this.

As she entered the parlour, her father smiled warmly. She returned the smile as a young man took her by the hand and examined her.

He grinned. "Such a charming creature."

Micah glared at him.

Zana's face felt hot as he kissed her hand.

"Kyle Allen," the young man said, still holding her hand.

"Suzanna Wolfe."

"Ah... Lord Wolfe, you never mentioned your daughter had such a rare beauty."

Micah stood up from his seat and took Zana by the hand. "Mr. Allen is our cousin Mordred's stepson." Micah smirked. "Right cousin?"

Mordred grimaced. "And this is my wife, Helena," he said, gesturing to the slender woman standing by the record player.

She shot Zana a look, raising her brow.

Zana blushed. "Pleased to meet you both."

A tall woman stumbled toward her and grinned. "Do you remember me? Your brother thought you might not."

Zana eyed her carefully. "Virginia?"

Her grin grew as she raised a wine glass high above her head. "She remembers!"

"You're a hard person to forget, cousin," Theodore said, gesturing for Zana to come sit next to him on the couch. "That there is my second cousin Kenneth, and with him is his wife Aurora and their daughters Celeste, Marcia and Georgette."

Zana nodded.

"And you may remember Mordred's son from his first marriage, Jordan."

"I... I think so," Zana said softly. She barely remembered anything about her father's house besides the little porcelain doll on her bed.

Theodore pat her hand. "I'm glad you wore the necklace. Do you like it?"

Zana shuffled in her seat. "It's lovely Father... thank you."

"The one in the wheelchair is my great-great uncle Ivan."

"Great... great?"

"We check to see that he's still breathing whenever he takes a nap," Theodore whispered. He pointed to the two young men grabbing drinks from Mrs. Adler. "Emile and Yosef. They're Virginia's wards."

Zana took a moment to scan each and every face. "I don't know if I'll be able to keep track of all of them."

"If you forget, just ask."

She noted the way her older brother eased his way about the room. "Micah seems so at home with everyone."

Theodore laughed. "Well, he was down here to great everyone when they arrived. He's had time to adjust."

"No... he's always been better with people."

Yosef walked over with a drink in hand. "Your portraits don't do you justice."

Zana lowered her eyes and took the wineglass from him. Of course, they didn't. She hadn't had one done since she was nine and any of the photographs her father had of her and Micah seemed ancient.

"Emile was just saying how it's nearly impossible to tell that you're part vermin." Yosef said. "But I suppose there's an air about you... something foreign. Perhaps the fiery look in your eyes."

Zana furrowed her brow. "I'm not sure what you mean."

Yosef sat down beside them. "Is it true vermin eyes glow in the dark, like a cat's?"

Theodore glowered, giving his daughter's hand a squeeze.

Zana laughed. "Like a cat?"

Yosef bit his lip. "I... I'm sorry. That was rude."

"It's all right."

"You were living with your grandmother, correct?"

"Yes."

Yosef gestured to the boy in the far corner. "Emile is too shy to come over. He's a bit scared of you and your brother. I hope that doesn't offend you. We're not used to... your kind."

Zana looked at the other boy. "He looks around the same age as my brother Nicholas."

"He just turned fifteen."

Zana nodded.

"I thought that there were only two of you?"

Zana fiddled with the pearls on her necklace. "Nicholas is... he was like you. Not related by blood. Our grandmother took him in."

"She must've been a very kind-hearted person."

"She was," Zana said, lowering her head.

"I'm Georgette," her cousin said, suddenly looming over them. "Seems you have the Wolfe eyes. A perfect brown. Lucky you."

"How about I let you get acquainted," Theodore said. "I need to check on Uncle Ivan."

Zana's heart skipped watching him get up. *I want to hide.*

Georgette glared at her. "I don't know why everyone is going on about how pretty you are."

"Georgette!" her sister Celeste hissed, marching over with Marcia.

"Well, it's true," Georgette said, crossing her arms. "What's so special about being a vermin?"

Zana folded her hands on her lap.

"I don't even remember Theodore mentioning any children," Georgette said, twisting a curl around her finger.

Marcia pressed up against her sister and eyed Zana cautiously. "Do you have those scary teeth?"

Zana tried her best to picture Ramona Weathers, holding her head high as she shot a dangerous look at anyone who dared oppose her. Unfortunately, Ramona Weathers wasn't a vermin. *Iya Naskit Tes Kot.*

Kyle sat on the other side of her and smiled. "Are you girls jealous?"

"J-jealous of a vermin?" Georgette laughed. "You're joking, right?"

Kyle sneered. "You know Georgette, other ladies are allowed to receive compliments."

Zana pressed her lips together, glancing over at her brother. *Deisso, why are they all flocking to me?* She caught him smiling as the maid Tiani came through with a tray of appetizers. Her eyes widened.

Tiani gave a small curtsy. "Lord Micah."

"Tiani."

Tiani held up her tray. "Devilled egg?"

Micah took one and bit into it. He caught Zana's eye and furrowed his brow. "*Naska?*"

She rolled her eyes, and he went back to chatting with the maid.

After the two of them were released from jail, they barely slept. The noises at night made Zana's chest ache like someone was pressing their foot against her ribs. The few hours of sleep she managed to get was while the two of them curled up together in her room and attempted to read an old book of fairy tales. Neither could remember who the book belonged to, nor make out half the words, but they did remember the little rhyme that went with the picture of the old woman and the large dog. Micah said that one used to make Zana cry as a little girl because the dog died in the end. She didn't remember crying, but it was nice to talk about something other than what happened in Tavern. Anything was better than that.

"I can't believe Theodore had children with a vermin slave," Georgette said, picking at her nail. "It's so gross."

Zana stood, causing Marcia and Celeste to take a step away from their sister.

Georgette smirked. "You may dress like one of us, but you're not *really* one of us."

"Good, I'd hate to think I resembled a *Schlubai.*"

Georgette crossed her arms, pouting. "Y-you can't speak to me like that."

"Then I won't speak to you at all," Zana said, shoving past her and her sisters.

Yosef and Kyle glared at the girls.

Georgette let out of huff. "What?"

Zana kept walking until she reached the open window, taking in the winter night air. The cold felt nice against her skin.

"I apologize for my stepbrother."

She glanced over her shoulder, looking at Jordan. "Who?"

He nodded. "Kyle. He can be a bit forward."

She turned her attention back to the window. "It's fine."

Jordan leaned against the wall. "I hate this family."

Zana raised her brow. "What's there to hate?"

Jordan laughed. "Well, for starters, my gold-digging stepmother... then there's those three idiot sisters. Oh, and Uncle Ivan."

"What's wrong with him?"

"He just won't die."

Zana tried her best not to laugh. "What an awful thing to say."

Jordan shrugged. "I remember you and your brother from a very long time ago."

Zana watched him shuffle his feet.

"I wondered about you when you disappeared," he whispered "Is... is it true you two were imprisoned in Tavern?"

Zana cracked her knuckles. "You heard about that?"

"I go to school in Presa. It was in the paper."

"Oh..."

He smiled at her. "Don't worry, I didn't mention it to anyone."

"Thank you."

"Kyle's still staring at you," Jordan said. "I suggest you don't entertain him. He's very persistent."

"I don't plan on it. He *is* my cousin, after all."

"Stepcousin."

Zana laughed.

"Trust me. All he smells on you is money. He was raised that way by his mother."

"I'm sure they're not all that bad."

"Why do you think I go to school all the way in Presa?"

Zana giggled. "And what about Yosef over there?"

Jordan shrugged. "Virginia spoils those boys a bit too much if you ask me, but... I could say Theodore does the same with you and Micah."

Zana nodded. "So, he's neither good nor bad?"

"He's okay." Jordan smiled. "Still has some maturing to do."

"Jordan, could you come here for a moment?" Mordred gestured for his son to join him and Theodore by the record player.

Jordan nodded. "I should warn you not to sit near Marcia during dinner if you have the option."

"Why?"

"Just trust me. Those girls are evil in its purest form."

Zana furrowed her brow as he walked away.

Tiani made her way over to her and held up her tray. "I have one egg left."

Zana shook her head. "No, thank you."

Tiani spun toward the window and popped it into her mouth. "Good. I'm starving."

"T-Tiani!"

Tiani blushed. "I haven't had anything all evening."

Zana giggled. "I won't tell anyone."

Tiani smiled. "We *Valdinok* have to stick together."

Zana eyed her. "Um... Tiani, my brother does he–"

"*Tiani, Iigen Hasite!*" Mrs. Adler called, gesturing wildly from the hallway.

"Sorry, I have to get back to the kitchen and help Mrs. Adler."

Zana nodded as Tiani raced off. *Maybe I should just ask Micah. Tiani's definitely prettier than Samara, but he really, really liked her...* She rested her chin down on the windowsill and frowned. *I wonder if Samara and her family ever made it to Riversburg?*

"H-hi..."

Zana craned her neck to look at Emile. "Hi."

Emile cleared his throat and lowered his head.

He kind of looks like Nicholas. Small, dark brown hair. She smiled.

Emile's eyes widened. "T-they said you two would look... like, um... well... scary."

"Are you afraid of me?"

"Yes."

"Don't be," Zana said. "Micah's the scary one."

"H-he is?"

She nodded. "Even with those dull teeth of his, he can still pierce a deer's throat with one big chomp."

Emile stared at her blankly.

"Our little brother is about the same age as you."

Emile scanned her face. "T-that was a joke, wasn't it."

"Maybe."

"Oh... haha..." The wine spilled out as he squeezed the stem of the glass.

"Aren't you a bit young to be drinking?"

"Virginia said I could have one, since it's a special occasion."

Zana raised her brow.

"She said you had big brown eyes."

"She did?"

He managed a smile. "She used to tell me stories about you two when I was little... she said that's why we don't keep any vermin slaves at our house."

Zana scratched her head. "All I could remember about her was how she had really long legs and wore very big hats."

He laughed, his glass tipping again.

"Nicholas, *Danya Bloka.* It's gonna get all over the place," Zana said, snatching it out of his hand. She held her breath and cleared her throat. "I mean... Emile."

He blushed. "Thanks Miss Suzanna."

"Sorry. It's just, it'd be bad to get a stain on your white shirt."

"I suppose that's why you're wearing green."

Zana smiled. "Actually, I just like the colour."

Emile nodded. "Your smile isn't... as scary as I thought. It's nice."

She closed her mouth, looking down at her feet. Somehow, she'd managed to keep her balance.

"Did Jordan warn you about sitting near Marcia?"

"He did."

"Good... I told him she had something nasty planned."

Zana frowned. "It's my first time meeting those girls and they already hate me."

"Rumor has it Uncle Ivan is leaving money for you, Micah and Jordan. They said if you two never came back, they would've gotten the money."

"He is?"

"Well, you and Micah are the only ones who carry the Wolfe name."

"B-but we're..."

"He knows what you are." Emile lowered his voice. "Virginia told me that he had an affair with a vermin when he was younger and regrets not doing right by her."

Zana ran a hand through her hair. "I see."

"She doesn't really like your mother... but I'm sure you probably knew that already."

"A lot of people don't." Zana frowned, tugging on her necklace. "Even Micah."

"Virginia told me she always wore a lot of yellow."

Zana nodded, trying to picture it. "Father thought it looked pretty with her hair."

"Dinners on the table," Mrs. Adler announced, entering the room.

Zana drew in a deep breath. *How much longer till I can get away from these Verjik people?* she wondered, catching Georgette glaring at her as they entered the dining room.

"You told them, didn't you?" Marcia shot a dirty look at Jordan as Tiani served the ham.

Jordan raised his brow, cocking his head. "Told who what?"

Emile laughed, knocking over his glass.

Micah snatched as it flew off the table. "I think you've had a bit too much to drink."

Emile shrugged, face bright red.

Micah placed the glass on the table and shook his head.

"Nice catch," Tiani said, putting a slice of ham on his plate. "Make sure you eat your vegetables, Lord Micah."

Micah wrinkled his nose as Mrs. Adler plopped a spoonful of Brussels sprouts onto his plate. *Deisso.* He'd managed to avoid the pickled beets the other night, but it seemed no matter what he did, these people were determined to get him to eat something other than meat.

Tiani and Mrs. Adler winked at Theodore as little Arthur came around with little bowls of potato soup.

Arthur smiled, giving Micah and Zana a bowl. "Here yah go."

"Thank you, Arthur," Zana said sweetly.

Arthur blushed and made his way around the table.

Micah snickered. "I think he likes you."

"*Nei, Danya Bloka.* He's sweet to everyone," Zana mumbled, fiddling with her pearl necklace.

Micah looked her over, taking in the outfit. The last time he'd seen her in a green dress was when they were in Tavern. Her gloves hid the bruises on her arms, and the powder on her face nearly masked the one above her brow. He gave his little sister a smile, nudging her playfully. "*Duvya Kiedunya.*"

"*Duvya Scho Ameilus.*"

He leaned toward her, pinching her cheek. "No really. You're so *Veishii!* Like a garter snake."

Zana recoiled, sticking out her tongue. "Ew... those aren't *Veishii.* They're gross."

"I like snakes," Micah said, wiggling his fingers in her face, his dull fangs peaking out from between his lips.

She shivered, shoving him away. "*Ha,* I know."

Jordan's brow rose. "What's *Veishii?*"

The Wolfe siblings blushed.

"I-it's just a vermin word."

Jordan smirked. "What does it mean?"

"What's this nonsense about vermin words?" Mordred glowered.

"Imagine using such low born language," Aurora said, taking a slender hand and raising up her spoon.

Micah shoved a forkful of Brussels sprouts into his mouth. *Just chew, swallow and keep your mouth shut. Don't embarrass Father,* he told himself. He wanted to gag as he gestured for Tiani to refill his glass.

"Wine or water, sir?"

"Vein, Stabima." He bit down hard on his cheek. *Deisso!*

Tiani poured the red wine into his glass as he watched her tight curls bounce down along her cheeks. Their eyes met.

His heart skipped. *"Dar Danya."*

"You're welcome."

Zana stared at him and wrinkled her brow. "You're still speaking Valdin," she said quietly.

He glanced over at their father.

Theodore waved Tiani over as well. "I'll have some too."

Micah frowned and turned to Zana. "My collar feels so tight."

She laughed.

"Dar Danya, Tiani." Theodore smiled, raising his glass.

"You're welcome, sir."

His relatives stared at him as he pressed the glass to his lips.

"Is something the matter?"

Mordred's mouth hung open. "H-how can you use such foul language, cousin?"

Theodore furrowed his brow. *"Valdin Zungta* isn't foul? Besides, it's important to know the language of the people."

"People?"

"Yes Mordred. People," Theodore said firmly.

"You consider your slaves people?"

"I don't own slaves anymore. I pay both my human and vermin staff. They all have families to feed."

"What a waste." Mordred shook his head. "To just throw away all that money, especially when you have all of your father's old slave houses in the back."

"Those are used as servant quarters now," Theodore said, cutting into his ham.

Micah watched his sister tugging on her necklace again, spooning up a bit of potato soup, trying to mask his shaking hand. He remembered the way his father's family was toward them. His mother prepared him for it. Zana barely had enough exposure before their mother dragged them out of there.

"Theodore, just because your children are impure, doesn't mean that you need to lower your standards." Mordred adjusted his gold cufflinks. "I mean really, cousin. You should look into producing a legitimate heir."

"They are legitimate," Theodore said coldly. "Their mother and I were properly married before they were born. Uncle Ivan approved and witnessed the union."

"Uncle Ivan can't even tell his left from his right! He's a ninety-seven-year-old man!"

"I was seventy-seven then," Uncle Ivan said, pointing his fork at Mordred. "It was the summer of twenty eight. She wore tiny white flowers in her hair... and her dress had little flowers embroidered into it too. She was a lovely bride."

"And look how that turned out," Mordred said sullenly.

Theodore glanced down at his plate. "She didn't feel welcome here..."

Uncle Ivan grinned. "Now that was a wild summer."

Micah winced, looking at the old mans toothless smile.

Uncle Ivan gave him a wink. "If I had teeth like yours, I'd eat a nice big hunk of steak."

Zana tried to muffle her laughter.

"Now I have to cut all the corn off the cob. Takes all the fun out of food. Say, how's that grandmother of yours?"

Theodore and Mordred glared at one another.

"She, um... passed away," Micah said softly.

"And here I am, still kicking." Uncle Ivan groaned. "Funny thing, life is. Poor woman was as radiant as the sun last I saw her."

"You're not kicking anything. We wheel you around everywhere," Georgette grumbled, picking away at her food.

Uncle Ivan raised his brow. "No one was talking to you."

"This is why you're not getting anything," Virginia said.

"I didn't invite you here to insult my family, Mordred," Theodore said firmly.

"We're your family," Mordred said, slamming a hand on the table. "You're *real* family! You haven't seen these two in what, ten years?"

Micah gritted his teeth as his sister sank into her seat. "We still saw our father when we lived with the pack."

Mordred's eyes widened. "Y-you did?"

Theodore nodded.

"W-well, I still think it would be best to have a pure blood human child. I wouldn't be able to rest knowing you left our entire legacy to these two."

Theodore smirked. "Then I'll be sure to leave you restless."

Jordan grinned. "Micah and Zana are entitled to their birthright."

"But they're... look at them!"

Georgette sneered. "Posing in those clothes like we can't smell the brute on them."

"*Iigen Bliesso Daknovosa.*" Zana spat at her.

Georgette sat up straight, mouth hanging open.

"What did you just say to my daughter?" Aurora said, rushing to her side.

The staff giggled, tiptoeing about the room.

Micah smiled his toothiest grin. "As our little brother loves to say, go screw yourself."

"W-why I never!"

"Mother!"

"Shut up Georgette," Celeste said sullenly. "You've been nothing but a pain all evening."

"B-but even you said halflings were gross!"

"Not to their faces."

Micah and Zana turned to one another and clinked their glasses.

"I love our family, don't you?" Micah said with a grin.

Zana nodded. "They're absolutely dreadful."

"Money hungry, *Schlubai,*" Theodore said, giving them a little wink.

"You've put a damn plague upon this family," Mordred said bitterly. "With your lusting and your... your crimes!"

"If love is a crime, then I shall be hanged," Theodore snapped. "Either apologize to my children or get out of my house."

Mordred sank into his seat.

"Father, you're one to talk about lust," Jordan said, shaking his head. "You left my mother for a thirty-seven-year-old actress."

"We don't speak of that woman," Mordred said, stabbing his fork into a slice of ham.

"I'm too old for this nonsense." Uncle Ivan swung his head back and moaned. "I should have the nurse smother me in my sleep. That way I won't have to listen to you spoiled brats whine anymore."

Micah's eyes widened. "Wow..."

"I like him," Zana said softly, turning to her brother. "He talks like Bell."

"Bell was *Verjik,*" Micah whispered. "I still have the scar from when he pelted me with rocks."

"He had his faults... but he was nice to Nicholas."

Micah scratched his head. "True."

Emile hiccupped, resting his head in his hands.

Yosef eyed him. "You alright there, buddy?"

"What a baby," Virginia said, slapping her hand down on the table. "I'm on my eleventh glass and you don't see me keeling over."

"E-eleventh?"

Virginia took a sip and smiled. "I start drinking after breakfast."

Theodore shook his head.

And I was worried about embarrassing him. Micah thought. *These people are the worst...*

"I miss the pack," Zana muttered into his ear.

"*Ha...* I was thinking the same thing."

7

———

The band began playing their third Alana Token song as couples moved toward the dance floor. Dianna Warren leaned up against the wall and smiled, watching them. It was like this at every school formal. She would stand off to the side drinking punch with her older cousin, Phoebe, who was forced to chaperone her and Peter, while her friends mingled and danced in their pretty gowns. Phoebe had been nice enough to lend Dianna one of her own dresses. It was nice having an older cousin who felt like a big sister. Dianna's gaze wandered over to the boys goofing around the snack table, shoving each other playfully and making obscene faces at one another. She smiled.

"You'd better not be thinking about that boy again," Phoebe said, checking her face in her compact. "Not while you're surrounded by all these other charming gentlemen."

Dianna shook her head. "I'm not."

"It's written all over your face," Phoebe said. She snapped her compact shut and pulled Dianna away from the wall.

"Is it?"

Phoebe nodded. "You look like a troubled mistress trying to drown her sorrows."

Dianna cleared her throat.

Phoebe laughed, then pointed across the room. "Is that him?"

Dianna's eyes fell on the dark-haired boy standing next to Peter.

"You have that long-lost look in your eyes." Phoebe pulled at her younger cousin's red hair. "Poor little Dianna. Falling for a pretty rich prick."

Dianna glared at her, turning away from the boys.

"You never mentioned the boy you liked was one of Peter's idiot friends."

Dianna shrugged, pressing the glass to her lips again.

"If you blush anymore, your face will be redder than your hair."

"Phoebe!"

"I'm just saying." Phoebe scanned the boy and grinned. "I won't deny that he's good-looking, but really Dianna? Anyone who hangs out with Peter is probably an idiot."

Dianna glanced over her shoulder and frowned. "Yah, probably..."

"Dianna, is that you?" Charlotte raced over in a crème-coloured floral cocktail dress. "Oh wow. You look so pretty with your hair out!"

Dianna shrugged. She didn't feel pretty.

"If only she'd try and curl it a little," Phoebe said, returning her compact to her purse.

"And... is that lipstick?" Charlotte said, eyeing her. "Wow. My grandfather would have a fit if he saw me wearing red lipstick. Or any lipstick, for that matter."

Dianna blushed. "Phoebe lent it to me."

"Well, if you got so prettied up, why aren't you over there talking to the boys?" Charlotte's brown eyes lit up as she waved over their other friends. "Connie, Juliet come here!"

Dianna lowered her head. She wanted to disappear.

"Doesn't she look nice?" Charlotte said as the other girls wandered over.

Constance nodded quickly, clapping her hands together. "I've never seen you so dressed up before!"

Juliet crossed her arms. "You're not hiding from Peter, are you?"

"If he's picking on you, I'll clobber him," Phoebe said firmly.

"You'd beat up your cousin for being mean to your other cousin?" Constance said, wrinkling her brow.

"I'll beat up anyone who messes with either of them," Phoebe said firmly, adjusting her dress. "Besides, Peter's a brat. I like to keep him in check whenever I visit."

The girls laughed.

"Stop looking at that boy," Phoebe said, glaring at Dianna. "You're only asking for trouble."

"What boy?" Charlotte turned her head toward the snack table.

"No one! I... I need more punch," Dianna said before chugging the rest in her glass. "Look, it's empty!" With that, she raced away from the girls. She drew in a deep breath, clutching the glass to her chest as she hurried to the snack table. *How did Phoebe figure it out? She's only been here a week.*

"Hi."

Dianna thought the glass would shatter between her fingers as she slowly spun around, forcing a smile. "Hello, Crispin."

Roland made up his face, eyeing her.

Well, go ahead. Make fun of me like you always do, she thought, straightening her back.

"You're blocking the food."

"Huh?"

"The food. You're blocking it," he mumbled.

Dianna stepped aside and gulped.

"Damn it."

She glanced over at him. "What?"

"Someone ate all the shortbread," Roland snapped, shoving a cookie into his mouth. He raised his brow. "Oh, it's you Pigtails... you look kinda different."

"Well, it's a formal... so..."

Roland grabbed a handful of cookies and cocked his head. "I guess I can't call you Pigtails if you don't have any."

Dianna rolled her eyes. *Why do I even like you?*

Roland leaned toward her and held up his hand. "You can have one."

"Oh... um thank you?" Dianna muttered, taking a cookie from him.

Roland looked around the room. "Are your parents here?"

"No. My cousin, Phoebe, is my chaperone this evening." She glared at Peter as he started dancing with Josephine Winter. "And I see my other cousin has ditched you."

"I'm used to it." Roland laughed. He looked her over and scratched his head. "I guess I could start calling you Freckles."

"Or you could call me Dianna. That *is* my name, you know," she said, taking a bite of the cookie.

"I know your name."

"Then stop calling me stupid things like Pigtails and Freckles. It's annoying," Dianna said firmly.

"Do I annoy you, Miss Warren?"

She rolled her eyes. "Yes, you do."

Roland popped another cookie into his mouth and looked her over.

"What?"

He shrugged. "We don't really talk unless Peter's around."

Because you make me nervous. Dianna brushed the crumbs off her red and white pinafore dress. *And angry.*

"Um... would you care to dance?"

Her eyes widened. "Are you serious?"

Roland nodded. "Unless there's someone else you'd like to dance with. I could ask them for you."

"I'd never tell you who I wanted to dance with," Dianna said. "You'd probably use it to play a joke on me."

"I don't play jokes like that." Roland held out his hand. "If there's no one else, would you dance with me, Pigtails? I... I mean Miss Warren."

Dianna rolled her eyes, trying to stop her cheeks from burning.

Roland pouted and shoved his hand into his jacket pocket, looking down at the floor.

"My mother said I'm supposed to dance with anyone who asks," Dianna muttered, yanking his hand out from his pocket and pulling him onto the dance floor. *His hand is sweaty.*

Roland pulled his hand away and wiped it on his pants. "Sorry..."

"It's okay."

He held up his hand and placed the other around her waist.

Dianna's stomach churned as she caught a glance of Phoebe staring at her. *He asked! It's just a dance, nothing more.*

Roland stumbled into her and blushed. "I... I think I'm supposed to lead."

"Sorry... I've never danced with a boy before," Dianna said shyly.

Roland smirked. "Me neither."

She laughed. "Are you sure about that?" She raised her brow, watching as he shifted his gaze to the empty piano. "You'd better not be up to anything funny."

"There's no music playing..."

Dianna stopped, quickly pulling away from him. "Y-you're right." She lowered her head. *Why didn't I notice that?*

"Thank you for the dance," he said softly as she wiped her hands on her dress. "It was nice of you."

"Well, thank you for asking."

Roland nodded, still looking at the piano. "How angry do you think Mrs. Clifford will be if I–actually, I don't care."

"Huh?" Dianna's jaw dropped as he made his way up onto the stage and plopped himself down onto the piano stool. "Roland Crispin, you get away from there right now."

"You like that song by Georgie Bryce, right?" Roland placed his hands on the keys.

Dianna bit her lip as he began to play.

He sang, sweetly.

Hug me or kiss me,

Be my one and only.

Stay here with me or I'll be so lonely

I wanna be near you

And have you all to myself

Her heart began racing in her chest. *How did he know this was my favourite song?* She wondered, smiling away as she swayed to the music.

Roland glanced at her.

They say the moonlights
Perfect for kissing.
So darling tell me
What am I missing?

"Winning your heart is all I aim to do." Dianna's voice chimed with a little shy harmony as she, climbed up onto the stage. She leaned up against the piano, getting lost in the music. Somehow, he always managed to pull her in. No matter how much she tried to ignore him, that annoying boy hooked her and reeled her in.

"Mr. Crispin, Miss Warren!" Mrs. Clifford shouted, stomping toward them. "If you wanted to be tonight's entertainment, you should've volunteered."

Roland continued to play, grinning at her.

Dianna blushed, stepping away from the piano.

Mrs. Clifford glared at him, tapping her foot impatiently.

"There was no music," Roland said, batting his lashes at her. "I was just covering for you until you came back."

"Roland," a gruff voice said. "That's enough of that."

Dianna watched as the boy's hands began to shake.

Roland stood up and lowered his head.

The man crossed his arms. "I apologize for my brother's behaviour, Mrs. Clifford."

Mrs. Clifford stuck her nose up. "I expect nothing less from you Crispin boys."

The man pulled Roland and Dianna aside and glared at them. "You beg me to be your chaperone and then you go and pull something like that? I should give you a smack."

Roland smiled sweetly. "I was just trying to liven up the party a little."

"And you." The man started turning to Dianna. He stopped, looked her over, and squinted. "W-who are you?"

"Dianna Warren sir," she said sheepishly, gazing down at her feet. If her parents found out about this, they might never let her go to another dance for the rest of her life. *All thanks to stupid Roland Crispin.*

Roland grinned. "We both know you're not going to tell on me."

"If you're going to do something stupid, at least don't get your friends involved."

Roland laughed. "She's not my friend Laurie. She hates me."

Dianna turned to him and nodded quickly. "R-right. He's really annoying and–"

"I think it's time we go home now, Roland."

"What?"

"Now," the man said, grabbing him by the shoulder.

"But Lawrence I–"

Peter and Charlotte raced over, both giggling.

"Cute duet," Charlotte said.

"Peter, I'll be taking my brother home now," Lawrence said firmly, nudging Roland toward the exit.

Roland shoved his hands into his pockets and pouted.

"Oh, okay." Peter frowned. "You're still coming tomorrow, right?"

Roland glanced up at his older brother.

"Maybe." Lawrence shrugged. "Come on Roland. I can feel Mrs. Clifford's eyes digging into my back."

Roland nodded. "Bye Peter, bye Charlotte."

Charlotte waved. "Bye."

Dianna watched as Roland followed closely behind his brother.

He looked back, grinning slyly. "Goodnight, Freckles."

Her cheeks grew hot as she clenched her fists.

Peter laughed.

Every time I think you're decent... she glared at him.

Roland winked at her. "See you tomorrow."

DIANNA HUMMED TO HERSELF, fiddling around with the medicine bottle Vincent had given her. Roland had retired to bed long before she had a chance to leave it on his dresser, and the thought of just handing it to him made her uneasy. She waltzed around her bedroom in her baby blue ribbed neck pyjamas, staring up at the ceiling as if it would deliver a sign unto her.

"I suppose I could just leave it in the room while he's sleeping," she said, glancing at the bedroom door.

She never intended on staying with the Crispin's this long, but she wanted to keep an eye on Nicholas, and anything was better than being stuck with Peter in his one-bedroom apartment downtown. Her cousin had a habit of bringing women by at all hours of the night without warning, something that she'd hoped he would outgrow after college. The two agreed that if she didn't lecture him about it, then he would continue to convince her parents that she was living with him. She couldn't bear the thought of them knowing where she really was, and she definitely didn't want to go home. At least not yet.

Dianna made her way out into the hallway, wincing at the cold wooden floor as she tiptoed in the dark toward the master bedroom where Roland now slept. She remembered when he used to sleep in what was now Rose's bedroom and how before that he'd slept in the nursery. *I wonder if there's a room he hasn't slept in?* The creaking floorboards made the walk to the end of the hall seem as though it went on forever. Dianna could barely see the handle to the door as she turned it, slowly inching the door open. It groaned loudly, causing her to squeeze the knob tighter. There was a light on in the room. She looked over at the bed and tried not to laugh.

Roland was lying on his back, with little Julius snuggled up next to him, his tiny hand over Roland's face.

She tiptoed over to the dresser, carefully trying not to step or trip over the mess on the floor. Since moving in, she learned that whenever Roland got busy, his room became a disaster.

Tabitha and Lisa complained about the clothes that were constantly being left on the floor.

Once she reached the dresser, Dianna noted the toys and blankets thrown about the room and the picture book resting on Roland's chest. She cocked her head, her pigtails sliding across her shoulders and put the bottle of medicine down on the dresser, picked up the large green sheet laying on the floor and began tucking Julius in. Gently, Dianna began sliding the book off Roland's chest and set it down on the nightstand. As she reached for the blanket, Roland latched onto her hand, eyes fluttering open.

He looked up at her drowsily. "Tabby?"

She glared at him, yanking the blanket up under his chin. "Do I look like Tabitha?"

Roland glanced at Julius, then back at her. He smiled. "Nice hair."

She tugged on one of her pigtail braids. "Go back to sleep."

Julius shot up and looked around frantically, his eyes barely open.

Roland sighed.

"Is it school time?"

Roland looked over at him. "No. Do you want me to bring you to your room?"

Julius rubbed his eyes, laying back down.

"Julius?"

"Miss Warren, will you finish the book?"

Roland groaned. "Julius, it's bedtime."

Julius snuggled up close to him. "Yeah, I know."

"Okay then, close your eyes."

Julius giggled, tickling under Roland's chin.

Roland squirmed, letting out a strained chuckle. "Go to bed."

Dianna shook her head, watching Roland pinch Julius' cheeks and tickle him.

"Go to bed! Go to bed! Go to bed!"

Julius squealed, kicking his legs up in the air, his laughter filling the quiet house.

Roland swatted at his nephew's feet, glancing up at Dianna. "He's never going to go back to sleep now."

Dianna sat on the edge of the bed and held up the picture book. "Lay back down. What page were you on?"

"The one with the old lady and the dog!" Julius said, catching his breath as he crawled under the blanket.

Roland tousled Julius' hair and smiled sleepily, leaning up against the backboard.

Dianna opened up the book and flipped through it until she reached the page. "Oh, the story of Lady Lucy."

Roland yawned. "Wait, did you come in here for a reason?"

Dianna glanced over at the dresser and shook her head. "The light was on, that's all. Now, let's see. Lady Lucy had a doggy..."

8

———————

She dared not speak another word, eyes downcast toward the floor. Had he been able to hear her unsteady heart racing in her chest, he might have seen through her words.

Truthfully, she did love him. Despite it all, regardless of how many times she tried to deny herself, she loved him. Like a silly little fool, loving one with such a devious smile. A boy known to make trouble despite the sweetness of his demeanour, the honey in his voice, the pull of his stare. Roland was in every way beautiful and in every way that beauty frightened her.

He was closer now, arm brushing against her bare skin.

Dianna could smell the cologne on his neck, a gentle scent of sandalwood.

The words fell quietly from his lips, barely a whisper. "The stars sure are pretty."

She nodded, feeling his arm against her shoulder as he leaned back, stretching his neck toward the sky.

It almost appeared as though his lashes were reaching up, trying to touch the sliver of the moon. Then there was that smile again. That smile she couldn't quite place.

"I hope I get to see many moons with you." His eyes were on her now, dark as the night they watched her.

The air grew quiet for a moment, just long enough for her to take in the softness of his voice.

"Me too," she murmured.

Roland laced his fingers in hers. "That would be nice."

How many hands have felt his touch? Dianna tried to suppress the thought, drawing closer to him. Despite the coldness of his fingers, there was a warmth to Roland that made her feel safe. She couldn't care less about the others he'd been with; in that moment, her hand was in his and his smile was for her and her alone.

ROLAND AWOKE to a pitter patter on the window; a sound like pebbles being tossed up against the glass. As he drew in a breath, he could already tell his nephew was laying against his chest. In fact, Julius was laying across him, feet digging into Roland's ribs and head dangling toward the floor.

The pitter patter continued outside as Roland slowly guided his nephew toward the middle of the bed. *What time is it?* He leaned toward the little clock on the nightstand, furrowing his brow as he discovered the other body lying face down in his bed.

One of Dianna's pigtails had unraveled in her sleep and spilled out beneath her cheek.

Julius groaned, rolling in her direction as he stretched both arms above his head.

Roland glanced over at the window. *It must be hailing.* He threw an arm around Julius and cuddled close to him, fixing the five-year-old's hair into place.

Out of the three Crispin children, Julius took after his mother. A mother he'd only known for a brief time. A mother who was hit by a stray bullet while cradling her new baby in her arms.

I wonder if he remembers it? Roland's lashes fluttered as he gazed into his nephew's face. *Do babies retain those kinds of memories or do they forget them once they learn to speak?*

It wasn't a memory he wanted any of the children to carry. It was a month before Rose or Caspian spoke to anyone other than each other and even then, their words were few. Theirs few, his slurred and Julius not speaking at all, just crying through the night.

It was a wonder how soundly he could sleep now with the hail rapping away at the window.

Roland tried not to think about it – the time before – dubbed in his mind the period of blood, bleakness and blackouts. How long was it before he had heard the children laugh again? Was it before or after they mother was forced into psychiatric care? How many nights did he fall asleep drunk wearing Laurie's cardigan? The same one that reminded him of the green decanter he used to sneak sips from as a boy out of boredom. How many hours had strong dejection filled their home? How long did it linger in their hearts and swell and clog their throats?

He shook his head, chasing away the thought. Instead, he pressed his chin into the top of Julius' head and watched the freckles dance along Dianna's brow as her expression contorted in her sleep. Years ago, he would've been nervous having her this close. Now the whole thing seemed silly. Had they been children, he wouldn't have bothered at all. Nothing had happened between them, and for once he'd actually managed to get some sleep.

Knock. Knock.

Roland rubbed the remaining sleep from his eyes as Tabitha propped open the door and peeked inside.

"You gonna sleep the whole day away?" she said, strutting over to the window to pull back the drapes. "I've decided the brute will dust today. Weathers awful. I already called Evan and told him not to bother taking the children to school. Roads are all ice."

"If the weather's so bad, why didn't you stay home?"

She turned toward the bed, hands on her hips. "You couldn't function for five minutes without me. Now, are you going to explain this situation to me, or should I assume the worst?" She gestured to Dianna on the bed.

Julius sat up, eyes closed, head darting back and forth. "Caspian?"

"You fell asleep in my room," Roland said softly.

"Oh..." Julius crawled onto his uncle's lap and shut his eyes again.

Roland gave him a hug, looking back at Tabitha as she tapped her foot impatiently.

She glowered. "Well?"

"Well what?"

"What's this girl doing in here?"

"Sleeping," Roland said matter-of-factly.

Dianna shot up and tumbled onto the floor.

Julius, Roland, and Tabitha stared at her.

Roland wrinkled his brow, trying to muffle a laugh. "You all right?"

She rubbed the back of her neck and nodded.

"I don't want to find her in here again," Tabitha said firmly.

"Oh relax." Dianna rolled her eyes, pulling herself up off the floor. "It's far too early for this type of stupidity."

"Pardon?"

"You heard me," Dianna said, combing through a knot in her hair. "It's no wonder Roland's still single. You think him some fragile-like creature when in reality he's as devious as they come. No woman on earth could corrupt this already flawed man."

Roland cleared his throat, placing Julius back onto the bed, and made his way between the two women.

Tabitha gawked, placing her hands on her hips. "Are you going to let her speak to me like that?"

"I have no control over what she says," Roland said gently. "And I'd rather not start this morning listening to the two of you bicker. I'm not feeling well."

Tabitha yanked him down to her level, placing the back of her hand against his forehead. "I told you to dress properly."

"She did," Julius said, climbing down from the bed.

Roland shook her off.

"Are you trying to catch your death?" Tabitha pulled her hand away, eyeing him.

"No," Roland said.

"Breakfast is on the table. Also grabbed the morning paper for you on my way in. I'm going to assume we won't be expecting Mr. Rissing this afternoon?"

Roland shrugged, glancing over at Dianna as Julius clung to her.

Julius stared up at her with his large, round eyes. "If there's no school today, can we make a fort?"

Dianna laughed and nodded. "If it stops hailing."

Julius ran over and threw his arms around Tabitha. "Good morning, Tabby!"

"Good morning, sweetheart," Tabitha said, her shoulders loosening. She pinched the little boy's cheek, a large smile creeping across her lips.

Roland and Dianna followed Tabitha and Julius out of the room and into the hall, each of them taking turns yawning.

Dianna glanced at him. "How long were we up last night?"

Roland stretched his hand to her pigtail and began unbraiding it, forcing her to stand still at the top of the stairs. "I don't remember."

"What are you doing?"

Roland noted the confused look on her face. "You weren't going to walk around with one pigtail in and the other out, were you?"

She chuckled, gently brushing away his hands. "Obviously not."

He leaned toward her, catching sight of Tabitha spying on them from the bottom of the stairs. "You think Peter will be okay on his own today?"

"Probably."

"What if his hand gets infected or something?"

"It won't."

"But what if it does?"

Dianna shrugged. "Peter's a big boy. He doesn't need his nanny to wake him up and make breakfast for him."

Roland pouted, crossing his arms. "Peter's never had a nanny."

"Exactly. She's not doing you any favours," Dianna muttered. "You'll never grow out of this.," She looked him up and down. "Well, whatever it is, you're going for these days."

Roland cocked his head to the side, watching as she made her way downstairs, long strawberry coloured hair swaying behind her.

9

———————

Her image danced before him, bright and colourful, like the inside of a kaleidoscope. The pub smelled ripe of beer, sweat, heavy perfume, and lit cigars, and the smells swirled together, hovering in the air – a heavy cloud of intoxication.

The band struck up another song, a Georgie Bryce cover played slightly off tempo. The alto, slurring her words into the microphone that she clung to, to keep her balance.

Roland stumbled forward, knocking into Dianna as she called out to him. Her voice was hoarse and sweet, and firm all at the same time. With a gentle hand, she guided him toward the doors, muttering to herself. Roland's ears were ringing. He could feel the music in his chest. Heavy, angry, alive.

"So, this is what it feels like," he said.

Dianna gave him a puzzled look while Roland swayed to the music, eyes unfocused, lost in the song.

Peter had Charlotte on his lap, with her arms wrapped around his neck, kissing her at their usual table near the stage, while Miles Jr. sat with his head down on the table.

Vincent quietly nursed the drink in his hand, that had since gone warm, and Nev and Cato chatted with the other girls, Juliet, Constance and Kitty.

Roland had never been drunk before. He didn't even know how Miles managed to get anyone to serve them. Hadn't it been obvious the group of teens in their bobby socks weren't supposed to be out this late? He tried counting the drinks he'd had on one hand, but his mind was fuzzy. Normally he'd sneak sips out of the green decanter in his father's office, just two or three, so no one noticed anything missing. It smelled and burned his throat, but it helped him fall asleep. Clouded his head just enough that the pain receded when it was time to shut his eyes. Roland had never been this cloudy, but everything seemed warmer, more vibrant, louder. He wanted to tear out of his skin and scream.

"Miles was supposed to take you home an hour ago," Dianna said, yanking Roland by the arm and pulling him from his thoughts.

His eyes fell on the scarf tied around her neck with its swirling patterns. "Miles is drunk."

"So are you," she said, leading him further away from the group. "You look like you're about to fall over."

Roland's body grew cold as a pair of hard blue eyes met his. He took a step back as his father stood up from his seat at the bar, knocking into a woman behind him. Darius only went to the pub on Wednesdays. It was Friday. He was sure, because Friday was when his parents went to have dinner with Lawrence, Wendy, and the babies. Friday was the one night of the week Roland prepared dinner for himself and ate alone with the radio on for company. He knew it was Friday. On Fridays he took the long route home, knowing that his mother wouldn't panic about him getting there two or three minutes late. There was no way he would mix up the date. He couldn't have. He'd been careful. "W-what are you doing here?" he whispered, attempting to shrink himself into the collar of his jacket.

"I was about to ask you the same thing," Darius said sharply, marching over.

Something turned in Roland's stomach, fear perhaps, and rose up his throat onto the wooden floor and his father's shoes. For a brief moment, he understood what it meant to be alive, and now more than ever, he wished to be dead.

THE DRIVE HOME WAS NAUSEATING, and to his displeasure, his father insisted on taking Miles and Vincent back to the Doren's place up at the top of the hill.

Miles was out cold until his grandfather, Miles Sr., yanked him up by his ear from the car and started screaming at him.

Roland chuckled, watching the pained look on Miles' face as he was dragged inside. The chuckle caught in his throat as Darius gripped the steering wheel.

"Nothing about this is funny! What are we going to tell your mother?"

Roland's mind was heavy, still replaying the events of that evening. He couldn't remember what was said to Dianna, but he could've sworn he kissed her. Roland must have. He'd wanted to for weeks.

"Are you even listening to me?" Darius looked back at the boy through his rear-view mirror.

Roland grinned. "Nah," he said, leaning his head against the window. He shut his eyes and slept the rest of the drive home.

10

———

The swelling along Nicholas' upper lip had worsened overnight and created a yellow and purplish hue along his face. The inside of his mouth was raw and made it hard for him to sleep. In the morning, shadows cradled his eyes. He squinted at the light coming into the nursery from the window and forced himself out of bed. There was a mountain of work that needed to be done, and although no one had come to wake him, he knew they still expected him to complete everything by dinner.

Nicholas dressed himself, made the bed, and headed out of the nursery.

Tabitha met him at the top of the stairs and handed him a small decorative piece of paper with writing on it. "I expect you to finish this by the end of the day."

"You know I can't read, right?"

"You can start with dusting and tidying up Master Crispin's room. After you're finished that, I want you to do the dishes, sweep the kitchen floor, and shovel the back step."

Nicholas crumpled the list and shoved it into the front pocket of his grey overalls. "Anything else?"

"Once that's finished, Master Crispin wants to see you in his office."

Nicholas fought the urge to groan, spun on his heel, and made his way back to the master bedroom. Someone had left the door open, and the sheets were laying on the floor. Nicholas scooped them up into a pile and began putting the sheets and covers back onto the bed, being sure to tuck everything under the mattress just as Tabitha had taught him. He stopped for a brief moment to admire the artwork on the wall by the bathroom, a sketch of the gazebo out in the garden, surrounded by flowers and lightly coloured with pencil crayon. There was a small child reading a book on the bench, and a stroller near the pond. Something about the image made him forget the pain in his lips and smile, his fangs peeking out.

The mint green wallpaper complimented the image nicely and warmed the room. When the emerald drapes were opened, the mahogany-coloured furniture created a softness within the space that didn't quite suit Roland Crispin. Aside from the clothes, nothing in the master bedroom seemed to suit the man. As Nicholas observed Roland throughout the day, it seemed that there wasn't a single spot in the house that truly reflected his personality.

The kitchen was Tabitha's, the library, the children's, the guest bedrooms, Lisa's and Dianna's, and the nursery was much too juvenile for the twenty-four-year-old.

Nicholas finished making the bed and cleared off the dresser before going to the linen closet to grab a dust cloth. His stomach growled at the sound of bacon frying in the pan. Soon, the smell made its way upstairs. *That Beidma won't let me eat till I've finished all of this.* He kissed his teeth, the way Tabitha did whenever she was cross – which was often.

Quickly, Nicholas dusted the dresser, being sure to get in between the cracks. Once he finished, he returned the little trinkets and things back. He'd spent time memorizing their placements after the time Tabitha accused him of stealing a gold cufflink from within one of the jewelry boxes. He hadn't even known what a cufflink was, nor did he care. What use was gold to him when he couldn't even leave the property?

After hounding him for an hour and striking him with the end of the broom in front of the children, it turned out Roland had worn the cufflinks while out to lunch with the wife of the mayor. Tabitha never apologized for the incident, but Julius had come and sat with Nicholas in the nursery.

Julius did that sometimes, and although he kept wiping his nose on his sleeve and asking ridiculous questions, Nicholas was thankful for the company.

Nicholas picked up a bottle resting on the floor and rolled it around in his fingers. *Where'd this come from?* He opened it up and sniffed the liquid inside. "Yuck!" He put the lid back on and slammed the bottle down on the dresser, gagging.

"What are you doing?"

He jumped and turned to see Rose watching him from the doorway. *When did her footsteps get so quiet?*

She entered the room, her plaid brown skirt brushing against the dresser as she picked up the bottle and examined the label. "Valerian extract... do you know what this is?"

Nicholas shook his head.

Rose placed the bottle back down and began twisting the ribbon in her hair. There was a little robin embroidered onto her yellow sweater, just beneath the collar. Her ribbon matched its orange belly and her stockings.

"You look nice today," Nicholas said, placing the jewelry box back onto the dresser.

"Thompson invited himself over."

He reached for a photograph of a finely dressed couple. "That's nice."

"Not really."

He glanced over at her, furrowing his brow.

"Don't give me that look," she murmured.

"What look?"

"That one. The one my uncle always gives me. It's like the two of you started sharing a brain or something."

Nicholas placed the photograph on the dresser and crossed his arms. "I just don't get why you don't tell the guy you think he's a *Doksot,* which he is."

She glared at him. "No, he isn't."

"Then what's the problem?"

"He... well, he's just so–"

"Look, I got stuff to finish. Have fun with your friend."

Rose placed her hands on her hips, looking him up and down. "What's got you in such a bad mood?"

"I dunno, maybe it's the bruise on my face, or the fact that I didn't choose to be here, or that half the time you act like I don't even exist and then you come around and pretend to be my friend when you want something." Nicholas pressed his lips together, veering away from her pained expression.

"I'm not pretending to be your friend..."

"*Vint.*"

"I don't know what that means."

"It means get lost. I don't have time to listen to you complain about *Doksot's* like Thompson. I gotta finish cleaning." He could hear the heavy breath she took as she dropped her hands at her side.

"You know, you're being a real jerk."

"I complimented your outfit, didn't I?"

"Obviously, you need time to yourself," Rose said quietly, heading out into the hall.

"It's not like you ever spend more than ten seconds talking to me," Nicholas shot back. He looked down at the photograph, clearing his throat. "What're you looking at, *Bloka?*"

There was the sound of the telephone ringing downstairs, then heavy footsteps, followed by Roland Crispin stumbling into the room, still in his pyjamas. He shoved Nicholas out of the way, nearly stepping on a watch laying on the floor and began pulling a sweater out of the drawer.

"Going some place?"

"The college called."

"Who?"

"The college. It's a school. What did you say to my niece?"

Nicholas gulped. "What'd she say?"

"Nothing, which is highly unusual. She's normally very chatty first thing in the morning... where are my bloody socks?"

Nicholas grabbed a pair from the pile by the bathroom door. "On the floor with the rest of your clothes."

Roland took them and slid them on before pulling off his shirt.

"You're just gonna change here with the door open?"

He stopped and looked at him, then back at the door before yanking the sweater down over his head. "Go downstairs and have breakfast. Let Tabitha know I've taken the car and should be back in" –he looked at the clock– "an hour, given the weather's not terrible."

Nicholas nodded.

"Foods on the table. Lisa's got a plate ready for you in the kitchen. Thompson will be coming by. God knows why, given this weather. Just promise you'll be on your best behaviour."

"What about my lesson?"

"Your lesson?"

"Who's going to do my lesson today?"

Roland cocked his head. "That's right, Peter's not here. Why don't you see if Rose has time. Miss Warren's got to finish going over the report for Mr. Hood, and I'm still feeling a bit under the weather."

Nicholas shoved his hands into his pockets. "Couldn't you just teach me later?"

"I don't have time, I..." Roland looked the boy over and groaned. "Fine. Just fill me in on where Peter left off. Look, I really have to get going."

"Then go," Nicholas mumbled, heading to the door. He scratched his head and looked over his shoulder, ears twitching. "Wait, Mrs. Gibson said you wanted to see me in your office about something."

Roland stopped, looking up at the ceiling. "It can wait... or can it? Yes. It'll have to wait. We'll talk when I get back."

Nicholas nodded and went out into the hall.

A SHEET of ice covered the front steps of the college, forcing Roland to grip onto the front door handle as he struggled inside. He dusted the snow from his jacket, sighing. The drive over had been disastrous and out of all the socks Nicholas handed him, it had to be the one there was a hole in it. *I have so much to do today. They could've scheduled a meeting with me... this had better be important.*

He never wanted to attend the college in Tavern. He was never supposed to attend any college, and never would if his father had still been alive. Roland's classmates had all been much younger than him, many around the same age as Eloise's son Thompson, who was preparing to go off to school at the end of the summer. Darius and Adeline Crispin believed their youngest son could study whatever it was he wanted from the comfort of their home, under their watchful eyes. He never understood why his father acted like he never paid no mind to him as a boy, when it became extremely clear to Roland by the age of thirteen that his father was constantly on him about everything.

"Tuck your shirt in. Comb your hair. Where's your coat? Don't upset your mother."

Thinking back to it as an adult, the last one made his stomach twist into knots. Why hadn't he noticed the caution in his father's voice? The way Lawrence and Darius scolded him for doing stupid things – him always thinking that it was about controlling him, taking away what little freedom he had but in reality the concern was for his mother, who after losing so many children had grown fearful of losing her two boys. The war had already wounded both of his parent's childhoods, uprooting his mother and grandparents from their home in Murienne to Tavern. Like Tabitha and Rose's great-aunt Viola, Adeline's brother was killed in action. Darius rarely spoke of his upbringing, but Roland knew through his god-father Charlie, that the two of them had been a part of the group of young boys sent from different parts of the world to human only zones like Tavern in order to protect their family's large fortunes.

There was a plaque in the trophy cabinet down the hall, with a photograph featuring these boys, nestled together in the courtyard wearing matching uniforms.

Roland hated the image. His father and Charlie with their arms around one another, Miles Doren Sr., behind them like a proud, doting father. It was because of the boys in that photo that Tavern went from being a hole in the wall fishing town, to an established, modern city like Presa.

Whenever others saw the photograph, they liked to comment on how much he resembled his father, which irked him. His mother did that enough. He didn't need nosy strangers reminding him as well.

Roland had wanted to go to school in Augen, where they taught musicians and artists, and brought colour into the dullness of life, but he'd never even taken the train to Riversburg and travelling long distances was absolutely out of the question.

"You need to be near your doctor," his mother would say, and no matter how many times Dr. Gray told them Roland's condition was improving, his parents remained firm.

Roland had to remain in Tavern, and although Tavern was a suffocating place, at least he had Peter and the others until they all graduated from high school and went off to colleges and universities scattering about, leaving him to suffer under the weight of his father's thumb and his mother's anxiety.

Out of his close friends, Charlotte was the only one who remained, and the pair of them suffered together, finding the odd bench to sit on to people watch or sneaking about the library trying to find books with ridiculous titles... a game which grew tiresome after a while.

Once Roland reached the Vermin Studies Department office, he peered into the room where Professor Kidman sat at his desk, drinking coffee. The smell hovered in the air as the older gentleman pushed his glasses up on his nose and cleared his throat. "Got a peculiar call this morning," he said hoarsely, gesturing for Roland to have a seat. "Mayor asked about you. Said he wanted to team you up with one of the students from Presa and is having them transfer here."

"Kurtis said what?"

"The *mayor* says he wants you, the idiot who barely graduated with one of the worst averages in the class, to work alongside Presa's most promising student." Professor Kidman leaned forward in his chair, the dim light flickering in his lenses. "And for the life of me, I can't even begin to fathom why. So please explain it to me, Mr. Crispin. Why is it that you, the one who bombed his presentation to this year's new students, is being given such an opportunity?"

Roland's legs were shaking. No one had mentioned anything about Presa. He steadied his left leg with his hand and cracked a smile. "Must be because his wife asked him to."

"Ah yes, Mrs. Hood is real fond of you." The professor adjusted his glasses again. "It's created quite the stir around here, seeing as how she paid for your enrollment, course fees, books... bail."

Roland swallowed the lump in his throat.

"I hate to ask, but what is your relationship with this woman?"

Roland glared at the man. "Unlike you, Eloise sees the potential of my research and values my contributions to the cause."

"Then what about the kiss?"

Roland tilted his head. "What kiss?"

"After your presentation last month, she kissed you. Several students reported it. It's the main reason why I have absolutely no intention of allowing you or Mr. Rissing to continue to have access to the school's resources for your idiotic vermin project. Using a married woman for her money... you're no better than the scum down by the docks."

"Excuse me?" Roland stood up from his seat. "Eloise is like an older sister to me. You're merely trying to get rid of me because of personal–"

"Yes, I highly dislike you, and I also don't need another reason for this school's reputation to be smeared."

Roland towered over the man, leering down at him. "You'd better hope Eloise doesn't catch wind of this, or Mr. Doren, who might I add, invited me to his home this weekend. I would hate for you to lose your position."

"They won't fire me, boy, not for the likes of you. You're a murderer whose mother paid off the judge and a gigolo using his charms to take advantage of a wealthy woman for his own personal gain."

"Oh, so you find me charming?"

"Get out."

Roland rolled his eyes.

"Have all of your books and resources returned to the college immediately, or you and Peter Rissing will be fined. After that, I don't want to see your face on this campus again."

"You can't do that. I've done nothing wrong."

"Perhaps if you had actually applied yourself more, I would have reconsidered."

"I have applied myself!"

"Raise your voice at me again, and I'll call for security."

Roland slammed his hand down on the desk, causing the coffee to spill over onto the floor. "You're really going to penalize me for having to take care of my mother?"

Professor Kidman got up out of his seat, inching toward the door. "S-security!"

Roland followed, looming over him. "I'd shut my mouth if I were you."

The old man gazed up at him, shaking.

"You seem to have forgotten who I am, and what I am capable of, Mr. Kidman. I pity you for it, I really do because if you ever speak that way about Eloise or myself again, I won't hesitate to destroy everything you hold dear." Roland shoved into him, glancing over his shoulder as he headed out the door. "You'd best start packing up your office. Your name won't be on the door tomorrow morning."

11

———————

Rose ran her finger around the edge of the teacup, watching her reflection in the silver sugar bowl on the table. *I'd be angry too if I was stuck some place I didn't want to be.* She looked over at Nicholas, who sat at the other end of the table, gnawing away on a piece of bacon. Her eyes fell on his fangs.

"You look uglier than usual," Caspian said, grinning at the vermin.

Nicholas gazed up from his plate.

"Shut up and eat," Rose murmured, jabbing her brother with the end of her spoon.

Caspian yelped. "I'm telling Lisa!"

"You're telling Lisa what?" the children's nursemaid said, entering the kitchen. She folded her arms across her chest, looming over the ten-year-old boy.

"Th-that Rose hit me."

Rose's jaw dropped. "I didn't hit you."

Lisa turned to Nicholas, Julius and Alicia. "Well, what did she do then?"

Alicia sank into her seat. "I'm sorry Mommy, I don't want to tattle."

"Me either," Julius said.

Lisa placed her hands on her hips.

Nicholas groaned. "He called me ugly, so she told him to shut up and poked him with that spoon there."

Caspian glared at him. "You traitor!"

Alicia and Julius shook their heads.

"Well, that's what happened."

"Rose, was hurting your brother really necessary?" Lisa said, giving her a disapproving look.

Rose added more sugar to her tea. "Is it really necessary for him to speak that way to Nicholas?"

"He's a vermin. Vermin are ugly. I was only speaking the truth," Caspian said.

"Wow! We think humans are ugly too. Especially the small ones," Nicholas mumbled, a sly grin creeping across his lips.

Julius and Alicia slid their chairs away from him.

"Humans smell bad too."

"Now you're acting no better than a child," Rose said, shaking her head.

"I'm not the one who hits my brother every time he acts like a *Bloka*... I mean... um..."

"Perhaps we should take our meals separately," Lisa said softly.

Nicholas grabbed his plate and stepped away from the table.

"You can eat in the dining room, okay?"

"Okay."

"Why is Nicholas in trouble and not them?" Julius stood on his chair, pouting as Nicholas left the kitchen. "They were the ones being bad!"

Lisa frowned. "Sit properly and eat your breakfast."

Rose gripped tightly onto her spoon, glaring at Caspian. Julius had a point. It didn't seem fair that Nicholas was being punished for her actions.

"I don't get why that dirty animal eats with us anyway," Caspian said.

Rose resisted the urge to smack him and grabbed her plate and cup. "I'll be taking my breakfast in the dining room as well." As she entered the dining room, she spotted Nicholas sitting at the head of the table, staring up at the little chandelier hanging from the ceiling. She plopped herself down in the chair next to him and gave him a smile.

"What are you doing?"

"Having breakfast."

Nicholas lowered his head. "No, I mean, *what* are you doing?"

Rose swung her legs under the table, glancing away from him. "I thought you might get lonely eating by yourself."

"I spend the majority of the day by myself, Miss Crispin."

She tugged on the ribbon in her hair. "I wonder what that valerian was for?"

"Valerian's some kinda plant, right?"

"I'm not sure," Rose said.

"Your name is Rose, and you don't know if valerian is a plant?"

"My mother was the one who liked plants. I barely garden at all. That's Mr. Leon's job."

Nicholas uttered something under his breath and went back to eating.

"It's been a while since we've had a snow day."

"Isn't every day in winter a snow day?"

"No. On snow days, we don't have to go into school because the roads are bad."

"Couldn't you walk?"

"Me, walk to school in my stockings. Are you insane?"

"Wear pants," he said.

"First of all, the girls aren't allowed to wear pants to school."

Nicholas' brow drew together. "Why?"

"I don't make the rules."

"Well, that's a *Bloka*... a... um... it's a bad rule."

Rose giggled. "Secondly, when have you ever seen me in pants?"

"Never."

"Exactly. There's no use in me freezing my legs off walking to school, when Mr. Leon can take us."

"Sounds to me like you're just lazy."

"I am not lazy! I'm really good at jump rope and running, plus last year during the school picnic, Tom and I won first prize in the two-legged race."

"And you do all that in a dress?"

She smiled.

"You're lying."

"Am not," she said, fixing her ribbon. "Ask anyone. They'll vouch for me."

"What's vouch mean?"

"It basically means that they'll tell you I did." She took a sip of her tea and looked him over. "What's *Bloka* mean?"

"You shouldn't say that."

"Why?"

"It's a bad word and you'll get in trouble."

"I just want to know what it means."

Nicholas lowered his voice, looking around the room. "It's like saying something or someone is stupid."

"Hm... interesting. Hey, wait! You called me that the other day!"

He blushed.

Rose shook her head. "How rude. I'm not stupid. Not even the slightest bit."

"Sorry..."

She stuck her tongue out at him. "And I don't smell bad either."

He sank into his seat. "Trust me, you all smell."

She sat there a moment, tapping her chin. "What do I smell like?"

"I don't know. Like a bunch of plants and vanilla and all kinds of stuff. It's too much. It makes my nose itch."

"Oh..."

"I'm sorry."

"No. It's okay," Rose said, going back to her breakfast. *I guess I should stop borrowing Miss Warren's perfume.* She glanced up at him as he squirmed around in his seat. "What smells do you think are nice?"

"I don't know. Bread. I like how bread smells."

She drew in a deep breath. "Yeah, I don't think anyone else would find a person who smelled like bread appealing."

"I miss the food in Dinara."

"What kind of food did you eat?"

"Bread."

"Well, that's helpful." Rose hunched over her plate and sighed.

"Nyla used to make this one thing for Micah's birthday. It had turkey and peas and carrots, and we'd have it on toast. We'd spend forever trying to catch the turkey the day before. Micah and Bell had the same birthday, so we'd split it with his family. One year for Micah's birthday, we got to go to the big house where Uncle Theo lives and had this big dinner with a cake and there was this man who made animals appear from all kinds of places! It was really fun. After we went home, Zana and Micah kept trying to catch animals so that I would think they could make them appear by saying these *Verjik* words into Nyla's pot, but they ended up getting into trouble."

Rose smiled, listening to him talk, his feather earring dangling against his neck as he laughed. "I read in a book that it gets really warm in Dinara."

Nicholas nodded. "Once the snow melts, it's very hot there. Here in Tavern, it seems like it's cold all the time."

"No, the summer is nice. Winters are just really long here. I think it's because we're so close to the water."

"I was born in Ferine, and there it's cold all year... or at least that's what Nyla said. I don't really remember it."

"Ferine is a Vermin only area, right?"

"*Ha.*"

Rose twisted her ribbon around her finger. "And Dinara has humans and vermins?"

"Yep."

"Do the humans and vermins get along?"

Nicholas shrugged. "It depends on the human and the vermin. Some of the older vermin like Nyla were captured by humans and forced to work for them."

"They were slaves?"

"Yep. So, you can see why they wouldn't be very friendly to humans," he said.

"So... basically what my uncle is doing to you right now."

Nicholas stared at her; his pupils narrow.

"If you wanted to leave, I wouldn't blame you."

"I can't leave," he said sullenly. "If I do, they'll kill you."

Rose shook her head. "No... that doesn't... why would they–"

"You're human... you don't know what your kind are capable of. Whatever they've done to me, they will do to you and your family ten times worse if I run away. They will kill you, your brothers, your uncle, Miss Warren, Tabitha, Lisa, Mr. Leon and possibly even your friend Thompson and his family," he said quietly. "It wouldn't be the first-time I've seen humans die for helping a vermin. It happens every day."

"You've seen?"

"Well, Nyla covered my eyes, but yeah. I saw for a second when we had to travel outside of Dinara to get supplies for Zana's coming of age ceremony."

Rose yanked hard on her ribbon, unraveling it in her hair. She began lacing it between her fingers, trying to blur out the memory of her mother's head leaned back in the car as her father threw open the door and ripped Julius from her arms.

"Mama's okay. She's okay. Just take your brothers to Grandmother's. I'll be right behind you."

Rose drew in a deep breath, winding the ribbon around her index finger until it went numb. Her lip quivering.

"The worst thing a human can do is have a child with a vermin. In Dinara, it isn't considered illegal, but usually they drown the half-breeds... Rose?"

"I don't think this is something we should be discussing during breakfast," she whispered.

He nodded. "Yeah. I kinda lost my appetite."

There was a heavy knock on the front door.

"It's Thompson," he said, getting up from his seat.

"I'll get it. Do you mind clearing the table?" She released the tension around her finger.

Nicholas gave her a smile and took her plate.

She brushed off her skirt and stood by the mirror in the parlour for a moment, tying the ribbon back into her hair.

Tabitha raced to the door. "Goodness, are you going to let the poor boy freeze to death?"

Rose shook her head. "I was fixing my hair."

"Girls these days are so vain," Tabitha muttered, unlocking the door. She gave Thompson a warm smile, gesturing for him to come inside. "Good morning, Mr. Hood."

"Good morning."

Rose waited by the piano, while Thompson hung up his hat and coat.

"My mother asked me to bring some treats with me. I also have this," he said, looking at Rose as he held up a small parcel.

She cocked her head.

Thompson made his way into the parlour and sat down on the couch. "Want to see what's inside?"

She took the parcel from him, unwrapping it carefully. A squeal escaped her lips as she threw her arms around him. "Thank you, thank you, thank you!"

He laughed. "It's just books."

She began pulling them out, examining the details of each one. "This one seems a bit scary."

"The film will be playing at the theatre in a couple of weeks. I thought we could go see it."

Rose caught a glimpse of her brothers spying on them from the dining room. "I don't know..."

"We can get popcorn and a bag of candy."

"No, I mean... I don't know if my uncle will let me," she said, cradling the book in her arms.

"Why not?"

"I've never been to a show with a boy before."

"What are you talking about? We've gone to plenty of shows together."

"Not alone."

Thompson cleared his throat, scratching the back of his head. "Well, I guess we could invite some of our classmates or–"

"She'll go," Tabitha said, coming into the parlour. "She's a young lady now. Roland will just have to accept it."

Rose turned to her. "But Uncle Roland–"

"Don't you mind your uncle. I'll discuss it with him later. If Thompson here would like to take you out on a proper date, then I don't see why it's a problem. It's not like he's a stranger."

Rose gulped. "A date?"

"It doesn't have to be one," Thompson said, blushing.

Tabitha shook her head. "Back in my day, if you fancied someone, you asked them on a date. Simple as that. Lisa and I will be doing a bit of baking. If the boys are bothering you, send them to me and I'll find work for them to do."

Rose fiddled with her ribbon.

"Oh, and let me know when your uncle gets back from the college."

"Why's he at the college?"

"My father met someone in Presa who he thinks would be able to help your uncle and Mr. Rissing with... well... the creature," Thompson said.

"Nicholas."

"Yes. Him."

"But I thought it was supposed to be a secret?"

"From what my father said, he thinks we could actually get to a point where Tavern is just like Presa."

"In what way?"

"Well, you know, they keep vermin as pets and such."

"How ridiculous," Tabitha said, going into the kitchen.

"Nicholas is basically like your family pet." Thompson smiled.

Rose pressed her lips together.

"What's the matter?"

"Nicholas isn't a pet. He's..." She stopped twirling the ribbon around her finger. *Why would anyone want Tavern to be like Presa? Mama hated it there.* Rose folded her hands in her lap as Thompson leaned in close.

"Aren't you going to look at the other books?"

She shuffled slightly. "Do you think what my uncle is doing is wrong?"

Thompson scrunched up his face, shoulders tensing up. "Where's this going?"

"Well, it's just I... this whole thing gives me knots in my stomach. I just have a really bad feeling. Like... maybe Tavern shouldn't be like Presa. Maybe we should just stay as we are."

"Phew... for a moment there, I thought we were going to get into another argument," he said, giving a light chuckle. "This whole vermin thing makes me really uncomfortable. I mean, Nicholas doesn't look like any of the vermin from the books I got from the library, but there's just something about him that makes me uneasy. It's like my body instantly goes into fight or flight. I keep thinking about the stories my father told me about vermin charging through the streets, slaughtering everyone in sight... I don't think I could sleep with a creature like that in my house."

Rose cocked her head. "There are books about vermin in the school library?"

"No, the public one downtown. It's a small section. There were only three books."

She leaned closer, pulling her legs up onto the couch.

"Don't look at me like that," he said, his voice cracking slightly. "My father thought it might be beneficial if I read up on the creatures, but honestly, there was nothing helpful in those books at all. It's no wonder your uncle wanted to study a live specimen."

"What do you mean?"

"Well, for starters, your vermin doesn't have tusks. One book had this illustration of this tall looking creature with thick hair all over its body, antlers like a deer and these" -Thompson waved his hands in front of his face- "disturbingly long bushy tails. Imagine a furry walrus, but with a deer's head and a bear's body... but the bear had a squirrel's tail. It was so bizarre. I've had nightmares about it."

Rose giggled, watching him. "Tusks and a busy tail?"

He nodded, his shiny black hair flopping about his head. "That wasn't even the weirdest depiction. In another book it said that vermin use their teeth to kill their prey, and their elephant sized ears allow them to hear something as small as an ant crawling across the floor. Oh, and they have faces like cats."

Rose laughed, shaking her head. "I wonder what sort of things were in my uncle's textbooks."

"Being that we live in Tavern, I'd say the details were very much the same."

"How could someone think a vermin looked like that? I mean, really, bushy tails and antlers?" Something tugged on Rose's ribbon, forcing her to glimpse behind the couch.

Nicholas let go, flashing a toothy grin at the pair as Thompson turned around.

Rose's eyes widened. "How'd you get back there?"

"I crawled," Nicholas said, still playing with the ribbon. "What's an elephant look like?"

Thompson pulled Rose toward him, glowering. "A giant grey creature with big ears."

Her face went hot.

Thompson tapped a finger impatiently on the edge of the couch. "Was there a reason why you decided to interrupt us?"

Nicholas wrinkled his nose, ears twitching. "Uh... um... well, you were talking about vermin books."

Rose watched Thompson's expression soften as she shifted away from him.

"Yes, and?"

Nicholas shrugged. "I've just never seen an elephant."

Thompson took Rose by the hand, still keeping his eyes on Nicholas. "I don't suppose you've got a tail hiding somewhere, do you vermin?"

"No, but I know what vermin do."

Thompson tilted his head as Rose slid her hand away and knelt up on the couch to face Nicholas.

"Some of us have tails and antlers."

"Are you pulling my leg or something?"

"I'm not even touching you," Nicholas said.

"That's... never mind. Rose, do you want to go skating?"

Rose looked at Thompson, then back at Nicholas. "Do vermin really have tails?"

Nicholas nodded. "Certain packs do. The *Mivos* attach fox and wolf tails to their coats. Vermin packs who wear lots of furs usually come from Ferine."

"Where you were born."

"*Ha...* I think my father must've worn antlers. I remember someone putting them on my head when I was really small."

Thompson chuckled. "What kind of lunatic wears antlers?"

"Tom, don't be rude," Rose said, shooting him a dirty look.

"Lunatic? Hm... oh that's the word human's use for people who are *Verjik*." Nicholas slid out from behind the couch and sat on the floor. "Why do humans go skating?"

"It's fun."

"But it's not safe to go on the ice."

"Not always. You have to make sure it's thick enough," Thompson said. "Rose, you said he was born in Ferine, right?"

She nodded.

"That place is supposed to be a frozen wasteland. You've never been skating?"

Nicholas shook his head.

"My parents would kill me if they knew I was choosing to make conversation with a dog but... I have to ask, the vermin girl that was in the newspaper, Lord Wolfe's daughter" –Thompson lowered his voice as Lisa walked through the parlour– "is that typically what vermin girls look like?"

Nicholas blinked hard. "What do you mean?"

"Well, you look like you," Thompson said. "Humans. We all look human... but we have different features and such. Like Lisa's hair, it's so fair it almost looks white. Mine is black. Do vermin have different fang sizes or heights or anything like that?"

Rose sat up straight, examining Nicholas carefully. She knew Zana and Micah were his siblings, but Nicholas had been adopted by their grandmother. The only thing she could remember off the top of her head was that all three of them had brown eyes. The Wolfe siblings both had thick blonde hair and olive skin. Nicholas' complexion was similar, but his hair was a much darker shade of brown versus hers or her uncles. She glanced at Thompson and shook her head. *That was a stupid question.* She opened her mouth but shut it immediately as Nicholas lifted his upper lip with his finger.

Thompson trembled.

"Half-breeds don't usually have fangs this noticeable," Nicholas said, before running his tongue over his upper teeth. "Mine are fully grown in but one of the women in my pack. She had the strongest fangs out of everyone. She led every hunt. Her daughters were a little older than I was. They could move so quickly and quietly you'd never know they were coming. My brother liked the one daughter, Samara. She was an amazing hunter. I caught them kissing in the cave once." He smiled gently, then laughed, tugging on the sleeve of his shirt.

"So, all vermin don't look like you," Thompson said.

"Of course they don't!" Rose's cheeks went red as the boys stared at her. "Well, I mean...humans don't all look alike."

"That's true... I guess it was a stupid question."

"You should hear some of the questions Mr. Rissing asks me," Nicholas said.

Thompson stood up off the couch. "You're a lot chattier than I expected."

"I don't get out much."

"No... I suppose you don't."

Rose got up and adjusted her skirt. "Before I forget, Thompson, Nicholas doesn't believe that we won the three-legged race while I was in a skirt."

Thompson laughed. "We did. Speaking of which, this'll be my last year competing."

"Did you decide on what college you're going to attend?"

Nicholas furrowed his brow.

Thompson frowned. "My mother wants me to go to the school your father attended in Presa. I think that's why my parents went there in the first place."

"Why do humans do so much school?"

"Who knows," Thompson said. "I'd rather just attend the college here in Tavern while I wait for you to graduate."

A knot twisted in Rose's stomach.

Nicholas laid down on the floor, staring at her. "Nyla always says not to wait on other people. Folks have to do things at their own pace."

Thompson glared at him. "Who the heck is Nyla?"

"His grandmother," Rose said softly, taking Thompson by the hand. "Nicholas, you should probably get set up for your lesson. If Tabitha's looking for us, we'll just be in the library."

"Okay," Nicholas said.

Rose led Thompson out of the parlour toward the stairs. "Why were you being so invasive?"

"What do you mean?"

"Asking him all those questions. He spends all day having people poke and prod at him like that. Why can't you just be his friend?"

Thompson squeezed her hand gently. "I know it may not seem like it, but that was me trying to be nice. It's not easy for me. I... I don't trust those things."

"He's not a thing."

"I don't want to fight with you."

"We're not fighting. I just..." Rose glimpsed the strained look on his face and sighed. "Thank you for trying."

12

Roland knew he should've went home immediately after his conversation with Professor Kidman, but inside he was fuming. He somehow found himself at Doren Shipping again, a place he usually avoided.

The face Mrs. Han made when he came through the door was enough to cause him to take a step back.

"Is Mr. Doren in?"

"What do you want with him?" She put down her pen.

"I..." Roland stared at her; his legs were shaking.

"Well?"

"Would you ask if he'd see me?"

Mrs. Han brushed a strand of her silky black hair behind her ear. "Young man, there are three Mr. Doren's present today. This is Doren shipping after all. You'll need to be a lot more specific."

He nodded, clearing his throat. "Right um... could I please speak to Miles Sr. if he isn't too busy?"

Mrs. Han frowned. "You *are* the same gentleman who came in here claiming to be Mr. Levesque's son, right?"

"I am..."

"Roland, right?"

"Yes."

"Why don't you take a seat. I'll grab you a cup of coffee," she said softly.

Roland sat down, trying to ease himself as she left her desk and went through the large wooden doors. *Professor Kidman's a jerk, but he's not bad at his job.* He shook his head. *No. I can't go back on my word. I'm already here.*

Mrs. Han returned with a plain white mug and handed it to him. "I only did a milk and sugar. I hope it's okay."

"That's fine," he said, even though it wasn't. Roland hated coffee. He only started drinking it because it seemed like the adult thing to do. The smell was soothing and holding the warm cup helped reorient him whenever he dreamt about his father. He took a sip and forced it down before directing his attention to Mrs. Han.

"Mr. Levesque informed me of your situation," she said softly. "I'm sorry. I can't imagine what you've been through."

Roland's knuckles turned white as he held the cup.

"Mr. Doren will be ready for you in a few minutes. There was an issue with another one of our shipments. Seems the vermin are getting bolder."

"Vermin?"

She clasped her hands together. "Usually, they hit the trains or the warehouses, but this time, they attacked one of our ships. We've been trying to find out if there are any survivors."

"This sort of thing happen often?"

"Didn't it when your father was here?"

He took another sip. "I guess so... he was in charge of security. I can remember a few meetings that took place at home. Didn't realize it was vermin robbing the trains."

"Since I've been here, it's been almost non-stop. Luckily we haven't lost any of our Tavern staff, but at the branch in Riversburg there have been three deaths."

"Oh, wow..."

"Your father died in this building, right?"

Roland eyed her.

"It must not be easy for you to come here. I'm sorry."

"What did Charlie tell you?"

"You're Roland Crispin. I've heard your name all over Tavern, especially on the west end. You've been looking after your brother's children since he and your father were killed."

So, he left out the murderer part. Roland pressed his lips together and nodded slowly.

"He also said that the incident the other day isn't uncommon."

"Incident?"

"When you fainted. He said you're not well."

"I'm fine."

She gave him a smile that wrenched his gut. "I was wrong to be so harsh with you the other day. The staff here speak very fondly of you."

They do? Roland rubbed the back of his neck as Miles Doren Sr. opened the door and waved him over.

"What can I do for you today, Roland?" He motioned for Roland to follow him into the rest of the building.

Roland drew in a deep breath. "Well, Professor Kidman has decided that I can no longer use the colleges resources and that I'm not welcome on the property."

The older man pointed to the mug in Roland's hands. "And what did you do to warrant such action?"

"Nothing."

"Well, you must've done something, boy," he said, going into his office. "I've never known Kidman to ban students. Did you speak with the dean?"

"No. I came here. I told him I'd speak to you about it." Roland stood sheepishly by the door while the man fiddled around with the papers on his desk. "Apparently other students have been questioning my relationship with Eloise and because I was selected to work with a student from the Vermin Studies program in Presa, Professor Kidman believed their claims."

"Eloise has a fondness for you."

"He also called me a murderer." Roland lowered his voice. "And a, um... gigolo."

"So, you've come to tattle on him?"

Roland blushed. "W-well... look, I don't care what people say about me–"

"Yes, you do."

"Okay... I might a little, but Eloise doesn't deserve to have her reputation dragged through the mud."

"Your father never wanted you to go to the college in the first place," Mr. Doren said, curtly. "And yet you defied his wishes after his passing."

Roland lowered his head. "I'm sorry..."

"No, you're not. You hated him." Mr. Doren put the papers back down on his desk and gestured for Roland to have a seat. Quickly he scanned the hall, then shut the door. "I don't know how you turned out to be such a disappointment. You had so much potential."

"I just–"

"Out of all of my grandchildren, I never thought you'd be the one to fall this far... you weren't drawn to trouble like Miles, and Vincent... Vincent has always surprised me with his ability to lead. He'd be a shoo-in for mayor. You, on the other hand, are a lazy drunk."

Roland sat up straight, furrowing his brow. "I quit drinking."

Mr. Doren crossed his arms. "I raised your father from the time he was nine years old."

Roland clung to the mug in his hands, letting the warmth fill his palms. *Not this story again.*

"Why else do you think you and your brother called me Papa Doren?"

"Because everyone else did?"

"Can I ask you something?"

"Sure."

"Why did you hate your father so much?"

A lump swelled in Roland's throat.

"Look, you're right. Eloise doesn't deserve to have people speaking that way about her, but it is because she chooses to dote on you that people believe the girl is having an affair," Mr. Doren said.

"Papa Doren–"

"Every action we make has a consequence. For instance, you getting arrested for breaking into my office."

"I really am sorry about that... I was–"

"Drunk. Yes, I'm aware." He slowly lowered himself down onto the couch next to Roland. "When I lost my little girl, I asked you to sing me a song. Do you remember that?"

Roland frowned. "Yeah."

"You were... you were so much like your father." Mr. Doren's tone softened. "I know you hate hearing that, but you were. People used to say you were, darling. Now they call you a murderer and a gigolo, because of your actions. You gave people like Kidman, a reason to distrust you, a reason to speak ill of you... and because you never fully understood your place in this community you managed to single-handedly smear the Crispin name after everything your family sacrificed to send your father here during the war."

"I'm sorry..."

"If you really were sorry, you'd turn yourself in to the police and confess."

Roland's heart dropped. "Papa Doren... do you and Uncle Charlie hate me?"

The old man wrung his hands together, stopping to glance up at the ceiling. The wrinkles around his eyes smiled before his lips did. "No boy. No. I could never hate you."

Roland waited quietly, keeping his eyes on Mr. Doren.

"It isn't your fault, little one," he said, placing a hand on Roland's shoulder. "You had a hiccup, is all. A minor lapse in judgement. I could never hate you for that."

Roland relaxed.

"I'll be sure to have this whole Kidman thing sorted out. I assume you pulled a Darius. Made some big threat?"

"I might have."

"Of course you did. I'd expect nothing less. I'll sort it all out."

"Thank you..."

Mr. Doren began to get up, steadying himself with the corner of his desk as he did. "Now, might I ask you for a favour?"

"Sure. Anything."

"We're having a party at the house. I'd like you to come and bring the children with you."

"Miles already invited us, actually."

"Did he?"

Roland nodded.

"Good. Good. I'm glad. I was really disappointed about not receiving an invitation to Rose's party."

"I didn't think you'd want to come."

"Nonsense. I'm old, I'm not dead. I plan on dancing until–"

Roland laughed. "Until you're dead as a doornail."

Mr. Doren straightened out his back. "I'd like you to sing a song for us on Sunday. Would you do that?"

Roland jumped from his seat, spilling coffee onto his jacket.

"Don't look so startled. You used to play for us all the time."

"When I was a child! I couldn't, possibly."

"Just one song. Please."

Roland started to shake his head, then stopped and placed the mug onto the desk. "Did you have something in mind?"

"How about that old Alana Token song? The one you always sing for your mother."

"Who told you that?"

"Adeline."

"When?"

"When I went to visit her a few weeks back," he said. "I know it's far, but the facilities in Presa are–"

"I wouldn't be able to see her if she was in Presa."

"I know..."

"All her friends are here," Roland said, rubbing his hands together.

"I know Roland. I know… she said the same thing when you were taken to the hospital in East Tavern. She didn't like it one bit."

"I'd rather she came home," Roland said, swallowing the lump in his throat. "I don't think I'm cut out for this parenting thing. I can barely take care of myself, and like you said… the people around me continue to suffer because of my actions. If she were there she could–what are you doing?" The old man pulled out his chequebook.

"Giving you some money."

"Why?"

"Well, for starters, you've soiled your jacket."

"It'll come out."

"And I'd like you to go pick out something for your mother for me. All you ever do is bring that woman sweets. Why not get her some perfume or a nice hat?"

"I don't know anything about perfume and hats."

"Please Roland, it'd make an old man really happy. Your father always gave her something nice to pull her out of her melancholy. She gets awfully blue this time of year, poor Adeline."

Roland sighed. "So, you want me to sing at the party and get a gift for Mama. Anything else?"

"Yes actually. That lovely young lady who you had us hire. What was her name?"

"Kitty Chambers?"

"That's it! I think Miles is sweet on her. Would you find out if she's currently seeing anyone?"

"She'd never go out with Miles."

"Why not?"

"Papa Doren, not to be rude or anything… but Miles didn't make a very good impression on the girls at school."

"Hm. Well, he's matured since then."

"Not really," Roland muttered.

"Pardon?"

"Oh nothing. I was just saying I'm feeling a bit sleepy."

"Well, I'd best let you go then. One of these days I'd like to get the children in here, so that they can learn a few things about the family business. They have shares in the company, after all."

"Right."

Mr. Doren opened the door to his office and smacked Roland on the back, causing the young man to stumble forward. "Charlie and I will be covering your expenses until you can get back on your feet. Don't sigh and pout about it. I don't want you working yourself to death."

Roland pressed his lips together, holding back a sigh, instead giving a little grunt and a nod.

"Go on now. I've got to check in with Sam and Charlie about one of the ships."

"Thanks Papa Doren."

"Thank you for coming to me."

For some reason he could barely remember what she liked. White roses? The scent of freshly made coffee? Red cardinals?

Several things came to mind, but Roland wasn't sure if these were things that would bring his mother joy. For much of his early childhood, he'd watched her paint, host parties or lie in bed with the curtains pulled shut, staring off at the ceiling. Her smiles came and went, but winter always made her blue, Lawrence had told him.

Papa made her smile. Roland stopped for a moment, digging his shoe into the icy sidewalk. *But he's not here anymore...*

He often wondered if his gloomy disposition stemmed from watching her all those years. She didn't hold him at a distance like his father did, but over time, she became more hesitant. As a child, Roland could remember going into his parent's bedroom, climbing up onto the bed and chatting with her – sometimes brushing her hair while asking questions about when she was a little girl, other times he would recite what Lawrence had read to him the night before. Falling asleep in his parent's room was a comfort at first, but it wasn't long until the room turned on him like the rest of the house. Not long after his mother was moved into the asylum, Roland realized that the only ghost at the Crispin Estate was him; him and the memories that haunted his dreams.

A faint tune pulled him from his thoughts toward a small trinket shop in the middle of the street. Roland peered into the window, hot breath fogging the glass. The bell above the door rang out as a young couple left the shop, arms linked and grinning. In the few seconds the wind held the door open, the little plucking sounds from a music box drew Roland inside. As he slipped through the door, all eyes fell on him.

A trio of women huddled together, gawked at him from beneath their fur coats, while two shopgirls chatted amongst themselves before the taller of the two stepped out from behind the counter and made her way over.

"Can I help you?" She fiddled with her red beaded necklace. She looked around the same age as his niece. Maybe a few years older.

He tilted his head. "That song. I was curious about it."

"Song?" She spun around, her skirt floating beneath her. "Oh! Do you mean this?" She rushed over to the table with the music boxes.

"It's him, Greta. I'd know those murderous eyes anywhere," a woman said with a hiss from the other end of the shop.

"Shh…"

Roland looked at the trio of women and sighed. *How typical.*

The shopgirl brought the music box over, holding it out to him.

Roland examined the weight of it in his hands. The music box was designed to look like a carousel, horses and all. The tune sang out into the shop as the horses went up, down and around. *I know this song.* His stomach churned.

"Aren't you Rose's uncle?"

His eyes remained on the music box. "Yes, I am."

"Sofia Muller," she said, doing a little curtsy.

The music came to a halt. "Do you know what song this is?"

She leaned in close, lowering her voice. "The owner buys a lot of these from Augen and Presa."

"And?"

"Well," she said, looking over at the trio of women ogling them. "It's probably made by a mutt. Cheap to buy but hard to sell. Most folks around here don't want to spend money on something made by a v–"

"I'll take it."

Sofia took a step back. "Pardon?"

"The foul are always drawn to the foul," the woman in the brown fur coat said, haughtily.

"Oh, bugger off!" Roland grumbled, waltzing toward the counter.

"Excuse me?" the woman said, stomping her feet as she made her way to him. "What did you just say to me? How dare you speak to me like that!"

Roland glimpsed at her from behind his shoulder as Sofia raced over to the other shopgirl standing behind the counter.

"You've always been a disrespectful little wretch. It's no surprise you'd enjoy that filth."

A new word crawled up his throat and tickled his tongue. *Keep it together.* He handed the music box to Sofia. "How much?"

"Twenty-six dollars."

He nodded, pulling out his wallet, while the angry woman tapped her foot impatiently behind him.

"Are you even allowed to serve people like *him*?"

The smaller shopgirl turned to Sofia. "Uh... well um–"

Before she could continue, a sound flew from Roland's lips. "*Doksot.*"

Everyone went quiet, except Sofia, who was wrapping the music box. "We don't get paid enough for this."

"No, you don't," Roland said, handing her forty dollars from his wallet.

The girl's jaws dropped.

Roland grabbed the neatly wrapped package with the music box inside and turned to the trio of older women, giving them a smile. "Say hi to my father when you see him, won't you?" he said, winking at them as he pushed open the door and exited the shop.

Walking toward the car, his body seemed light. *Why did I say that? I don't even know what that word means! I've been spending too much time around that boy...* He looked at the package, humming the song back to himself. *Maybe I heard Nicholas singing this in the nursery?* He stopped at the car and groaned. "I need to be more responsible with my money."

13

———————

Roland twiddled his thumbs, sitting in Adeline's room as she unboxed the package he'd brought. That afternoon, she seemed more distant than usual, barely saying a few words at a time.

"It's from Darius, and Mr. Doren," he said as she pulled out the music box.

She pressed her lips together. "It's pretty."

"You play it by twisting the top," he said, demonstrating for her.

As the horses began to go around the miniature carousel, Adeline pushed it away.

"You don't like it?"

She sat there for a moment, watching the horses bob up and down. "You usually bring sweets."

"Uh... well, Mr. Crispin wanted to get something to brighten the room a bit and I–"

"Nothing could brighten this place." Adeline pulled the pillow onto her lap, squeezing it tightly. "And that song– your father..." Her eyes filled with tears.

My father? Roland placed the music box on the nightstand by her bed.

She glared at him. "Take that thing home with you."

"Have you painted anything lately?"

"Not really," she said, brushing back the greying pieces of her hair. Adeline reached out a hand, placing her palm to his cheek. It was small and cold. "You stupid boy," she whispered, lifting his chin. "All we ever did was love you."

Roland averted his eyes. "What are you talking about?"

"Look at me." She yanked him by the arm. "I said look at me!"

He pulled away, his hands shaking.

Adeline chuckled, rolling her watery eyes. "What did you do to them after you locked me in here?"

"I'll go get your nurse. All right?"

Adeline latched onto him again, nails digging into his wrist.

"Mama, please, you're hurting me," he said softly.

"You're such a stupid boy," she said, glaring at him. "I should've given you something stronger."

"L-let's listen to the music box. Doesn't this horse kind of remind you of Dusty?" he said, trying to pry her off of him.

She let go and stood, pacing back and forth. "Something's not right."

Roland examined the red scratch marks along his wrist, attempting to rub them out by smoothing them over with his thumb.

"W-wasn't it your birthday yesterday?"

"Pardon?"

"Oh dear, I should've had Freya bring us some tea," she said.

He sighed. *Here we go again.*

She looked around the room, then back at him. "You shouldn't be out of bed."

"Mama–" He gulped.

She stopped and stared at him. "What on earth is all over your coat?"

"Nothing. It's nothing. I just spilled some coffee earlier."

"Of course you did. I'll have Tabitha wash it," she muttered, waving her hand. She tapped a finger to her chin, then pointed it at him. "Wait a minute, don't you hate coffee? Great, now I've got that song stuck in my head!"

He was startled by how alert she was. "Do you know what it's called?"

She nodded. "Your father used to sing it to you."

Roland drew in a deep breath. *She's probably mixing me up with Laurie again.*

"You must remember. You're always humming it when you're trying to get Julius back to sleep," she said. "Why are you staring at me like I've got four heads?"

He wrinkled his brow. "Why did you think it was my birthday?"

Adeline's expression changed. She stood quietly for a moment, then smiled. "The boys, did they send any letters?" She wound up the music box. "Darius, do you remember how you used to sing this to them?"

"I–"

"You're such an awful singer." She laughed. "But I like it. Your voice is so warm when you sing. I know it's not easy looking after Roland while Tabby's away. I know that. I picked a rotten time to get into one of my moods, huh?" She sat down on the bed, fiddling with the music box. "I suppose I shouldn't have spoken to her like that. It's not her fault Roland got so sick; where did you and Charlie learn this song again? Was it at school?"

Roland lowered his head. *Is she getting better or worse?*

"Darius, doesn't this horse remind you of Dusty?"

Roland struggled to remember whatever memory his mother was recalling. He got a brief image of being snuggled up in bed. Lawrence, already fast asleep across from him, while their father sat on the edge of the bed feeling his forehead. Had Darius been singing them to sleep? Lawrence would've known, being seven years older. Laurie always remembered everything Roland couldn't.

His father used to say, "Your mother thinks you look like a porcelain doll."

He remembered that, and he'd asked his father something before falling asleep to Laurie's loud snoring.

"Could you sing the song to me?"

Roland shook his head. "I don't know the words."

"Of course, you do."

"I-It's been a while. I don't remember."

His mother frowned. "That's too bad. Why don't you ask Charlie and sing it next time you come? Bring the boys with you. Roland sings it to Pippi while you're at work. It's quite cute. He gets awfully shy whenever the staff catches him."

Roland gave her a smile.

"I never should've let you take them to see her," she said sullenly. She wrang her hands together. "I shouldn't have yelled at Tabitha. Roland's only gotten sicker since she left. It's not her fault. It's mine. I'm a horrible mother, I know that..."

"You're not a horrible mother," he said, kneeling down in front of her. "You just have bad days sometimes, that's all. Lawrence loves you so much, and Roland has fun keeping you company while you work. We all love you."

"Tavern mothers aren't supposed to have bad days," she said quietly. "They're supposed to be strong, protective, and nurturing."

"Oh, trust me, you're very protective," Roland said nonchalantly. "Overly protective even."

"That's not protection... that's fear. I'm afraid. I'm always afraid."

He took her hand. "Of what?"

"We lost so much. The twins, baby Darian. I... I don't want to lose another child. I can't, but we never should've trust that woman."

What woman? Roland raised his brow. "I understand."

"Please beg Tabitha to come back. She can bring her boys to work with her if she has to. Offer her more money. Roland might die without her. She's a better mother than I'll ever be. I don't care if he calls her Mama. It was a stupid thing to fuss over. Please tell her I'm sorry... please Darius, I'm begging you. I can't lose my baby."

"It's already taken care of Addi," Roland said, using the name his father called her. "Tabitha's with the boys right now. She got Roland to eat this morning, and he was feeling well enough to get up out of bed and play a game of cards with her."

Adeline wrapped her arms around him, sobbing.

Roland rubbed her back gently. "It's all right. Everyone at home is safe. You just focus on getting better."

She shoved him back, staring at him as tears ran down her face. "W-who are you?"

"I'm–"

"No. It's not possible." She was shaking. "Where's my husband? Who are you?"

He sighed, running a hand through his hair.

She leaned forward, eyes fixated on him. "Roland..."

He met her gaze, causing her to shiver.

She jumped up and bolted for the door.

"Mama, wait," he said, climbing to his feet.

"Help! Please, someone help me!" she screamed.

Roland stood by the bed, shoving his hands into his pockets. He drew in a deep breath.

I am crawling,
My knees bleeding,
Looking high and low.

He sang softly. That was the song his father used to sing. The one he would sing to Pippi, while the maids hovered by the door.

Adeline's nurse, Freya, came running into the room and held her.

"I need to see my babies," Adeline said between sobs into Freya's shoulder. "I need to save them from him!"

"Take a deep breath. Just breathe, okay?" Freya said, looking over at Roland. "The weathers getting worse. You should head home for the day."

He made his way to the door.

"Please, I need to see Rose!" Adeline pulled away from Freya and leapt at him, slapping him hard across the face.

Roland winced, his right eye stinging.

"I know what sort of beast you are," she said as Freya grabbed onto her again. "Stupid, foolish, boy... you stupid boy..." Adeline sank into Freya's arms, staring at him. "Let me see them. Stop lying to me."

Roland's lip quivered as he cleared his throat. "I told you to never lay hands on me again."

She glared at him. "I hate you."

"So, does everyone else," he mumbled, heading out the door. "I'll be sure to bring you some candy next time I visit."

"Don't bother," a man said, coming through the corridor. "Freya, help Adeline to bed," he said, shoving Roland out into the hall. "And you, Mr. Crispin, I think it would be best if you didn't visit for a while. From what your mothers said during her time here, your presence is deeply disturbing."

"What did she say?"

The man folded his arms across his chest.

Roland backed away from him and turned to leave. "I'll send someone else."

"I think that would be best."

14

Micah woke in a cold sweat, taking harsh, shallow breaths; his brown eyes darted about, scanning the vast darkness surrounding him. *It's okay. We're okay.* Sitting up, he smoothed back his long blonde hair. His ears perked up as he listened to the noises within the house. He wasn't used to sleeping alone in such a large bed. For years, it had been him, Zana and Nicholas all crammed together in a tiny bedroom while their grandmother Nyla slept on a lumpy, fur covered mattress by the fire. Micah traced the faint scar running along his neck. It was easy enough to hide beneath his hair, but there was no hiding from his nightmares of that place.

Tavern had scarred him. If he had just listened to Bell, and kept going with the rest of their pack, everything would have been fine. They might've been able to get Nicholas to Riversburg and gotten him help. Maybe they might have even been able to save Nyla if he'd pushed back a little more and made her stay with the group.

Being back in Dinara, back in this house, with its crystal chandeliers, white pillars and marble floors, was excruciating. He shouldn't be here. He couldn't be. Nicholas was in Tavern, enslaved by humans wishing to experiment on him, while Micah and Zana were kept within the safety of their father's home, sheltered from the rest of the world.

He cracked his knuckles, still trying to ease his pounding heart. *And I've been fooling around with that girl.*

Tiani had been a welcome distraction. She was funny, and pretty, and sometimes smelled like lemon and ginger. Having her around made him feel something other than fear. All the vermin in the house seemed to ease him. It was the humans, that tiptoed around him that made the hair on his neck stand on end. There was a little boy named Arthur who ran errands for his father, and whenever Theodore praised the child. Micah's chest hurt. *I'm not jealous. I'm not.* He could remember before his mother had taken them from the house, how all the staff called him and his little sister *Valvenok* – half-vermin. At the time, they were rarely ever addressed by their names. *Valvenok* had been their identity. Even during the brief time that he was in school, the word mutt was hurled at him by the other students. *That's why Mother left us... and why Father never came for us.*

It wasn't until the first time Micah dug his teeth into a rabbit's neck that the other children in the pack began to warm up to him. He was a hunter, and therefore he was a *Valdinok.* A real vermin like the rest of them. *Bell would hate it if he knew what those Doksot's did to our home. Marking it with their Verjik Lilik Morin.* Micah had asked Tiani to scout the small clearing in the woods where his pack once resided. The red, gold, and blue carvings that hung from birch trees had been taken down. The entire place had been redecorated with purple ear shaped markings – long and curved, painted above the windows and doors of every cottage. The vermin that resided there now braided purple thread into their hair, embroidered it into the sleeves of their jackets and used purple paint to colour their skin. They had offered to merge with his pack, but Nyla and the other elders refused.

"The *Lilik Morin* are just as bad as the *Mivos.* Vermin in Dinara have already been slaves to the humans. Why would we want to be slaves again to our own kind?" Nyla had said.

The vermin in Dinara were free. Tolerated to some extent. Their existence was mostly peaceful, as long as they didn't interfere with human affairs. Micah had only heard stories about the *Mivos* from Ferine, but he knew that vermin like him – *Valvenok* – were killed at birth there, and that when the *Mivos* arrived, Nicholas was brought to live in Dinara.

Nicholas... Micah's heart ached. It hurt more than the night his mother left without a word to anyone. He could hear that man, Vincent Gray's words, in his head while he slept. *Sordt Starod Elde Feiv.*

That place, Tavern, was evil.

15

———————

Dianna waited off to the side while the Crispin children ran to the door to greet their uncle. Roland was covered in snow, head to toe. He took off his jacket and shook it in the children's faces, causing them to squeal and jump back as little chunks of snow flew up at them. His cheeks were rosy, lips a little blue.

"You missed supper," Dianna said.

Julius clung to his uncle's arm, giggling.

Roland grunted and looked down at the boy. "Why are you three so wound up? Didn't you go outside today?"

"We had cookies!" Julius shouted. "And hot chocolate, and I made you something."

"*We* made you something." Caspian pouted, crossing his arms.

Roland directed his attention to Rose. "Did Thompson head home already?"

She shook her head. "Didn't you see him outside with Mr. Leon and Nicholas shoveling the snow?"

Dianna titled her head as Roland eased Julius off of him and removed his boots.

"No."

Something's wrong.

"Come see what I made," Julius said.

Caspian shot daggers at him. "We, as in all three of us."

Roland pat Julius' head. "Give me a minute. Okay?"

There it was: the deep sigh, the downcast eyes, the sunken shoulders.

Roland rubbed the back of his neck, before stepping around the children and making his way into the parlour. "Where's Tabby?" The boys followed closely behind him.

Dianna stopped Rose. "Does your uncle seem a bit..."

"Grumpy?" Rose evened out her skirt. "He hasn't eaten yet."

Right. He's probably starving. Dianna forced a smile.

"The college said what?"

Dianna and Rose raised a brow at one another, then ran into the kitchen to find Tabitha, slamming the clean pot onto the counter.

"I already talked to Mr. Doren about it," Roland said, sitting at the kitchen table.

"The nerve of those people!"

"It's fine Tabitha."

"It's not fine. Nothing about that is fine, Roland!"

Dianna eased toward the table. "What happened?"

"Peter and I... uh... the college doesn't want us using their resources anymore," he mumbled, while Caspian brought him a plate of food. "Thanks Cas'."

She inched closer. "What does that mean?"

"It doesn't matter. I don't really feel like talking about it. I just want to eat and go to bed."

"Can you read me a story again?" Julius stared at him with big round eyes, like a dog begging at the table for scraps.

Roland hung his head over his plate. "Why don't we pretend *you're* the grownup and you can read me a story instead?"

Julius pouted.

"Oh right... Rose, you grandmother asked for you," he said, rubbing his forehead.

Rose's face contorted. "She did?"

"Tabitha, would you take her? I don't think I should go for a while."

"I didn't know you were going to see your mother today?" Tabitha said. She eyed him, coming over to the table. "Lisa, why don't you take the boys upstairs and get them ready for bed. Rose, would you be a dear and get Alicia cleaned up?"

Rose nodded, taking Alicia by the hand while Lisa ushered the boys out of the room.

Tabitha glanced out into the dining room, then back at Roland. "Why were you so late getting home?"

He shovelled a mouthful of potatoes into his cheeks, keeping his head down.

Dianna drew near and sat down beside him.

"I can smell it on you," Tabitha whispered, wringing her hands together. She shut her eyes, kissing her teeth. "I thought Jakob banned you."

"He did."

Dianna frowned. There was a faint smell of alcohol on him.

"It won't happen again," he said.

"I'm going home for the night. I'll leave this one to you, Miss Warren," Tabitha said, untying her apron.

Once she was gone, Dianna gave Roland a light poke in the shoulder, causing him to glance away from his meal momentarily. "Did you go to the Tavern hotel?"

"No. I... I'm sorry Dianna."

"Why are you apologizing?"

He shrugged, pushing his plate away.

"Are you okay?"

"I don't know."

She nodded slowly. "Well, Tabitha made cookies. They might still be warm. Do you want some?"

He turned to her.

"Roland?"

"I was with Charlotte."

~

DIANNA WATCHED Roland break off a strand of licorice and pass it to Charlotte as they went to their usual spot behind the library. A nice shady spot, away from the prying eyes of adults. Her stomach did somersaults, noting the way Charlotte leaned into him, laughing as she wagged her half in his face.

"You should get Roland to help you with your homework," Charlotte said, turning to Dianna, who was attempting to braid together what she hoped would be matching bracelets for the two of them.

"What for?"

"Well, for starters, I'm a genius," Roland said, fishing around in his paper bag. He pulled out a pack of candy cigarettes and held it out to her. "Plus, Charlotte said you were struggling."

Dianna's face grew hot, but she eased herself and grabbed one of the chalky white candy sticks from the box. Their hands brushed briefly, causing him to jerk away. A tingle ran through her fingers.

Roland cleared his throat, plopping the box down onto the grass.

"You're so lucky your parents give you money for sweets. Grandpa would never," Charlotte said, reaching for the pack.

"Actually, my brother gives me the money."

"He was at the formal, right?" Dianna tucked her half-made bracelet into the front pocket of her dress.

He nodded, leaning up against the wall. "Are you gonna show me your homework or not?"

Dianna hesitated, then pulled the loose papers from her bag. She handed it to him and sat quietly while he went through them.

Roland gave a low whistle, popping a candy cigarette into his mouth. "Ah yes, the dreaded importance of trade assignment. I hate to say this, Pigtails, but what you've got here is... well, it's not great."

"I know that already," Dianna said, crossing her arms. "And stop calling me that."

He glanced up at her and smiled.

Her heart leapt in her chest.

"Okay *Freckles.*"

Charlotte smacked him on the shoulder. "Stop that. You're good at this stuff. Just help her."

Roland gestured for Dianna to come closer, taking a pencil from his book bag. "The entire point of this assignment is to get us to understand how Tavern works. The majority of the people living here work for Doren Shipping. Here in your paper, all you've written is that trading allows us to get nice things from our neighbours... which is true, but it's much more than that. For example, my brother Laurie works for Doren Shipping, and his job is to help broker deals with all of the cities surrounding Tavern. Since we've got direct access to the water, we're able to make deals with islands like Luciole and Miao, while also using the trains to transport product to places like Augen."

Dianna squinted, trying to see what he was writing.

"Now, my father and uncle, who also work for Doren Shipping, make sure that each shipment arrives on schedule. That means keeping close tabs on the merchandise they procure from Presa, Augen, Riversburg and wherever else. What most folks don't know is that next to Dinara, Tavern is the second biggest exporter on this side of the country, despite having only a quarter of the population and–"

"Could you slow down a minute? I can't keep up," Dianna said, blinking hard.

Roland twirled the pencil around in his hand, then tapped it on the paper. "If you want a good grade, just focus on how trade has transformed this small fishing town into a fully functional human-only city."

"Can you talk like a normal person?"

"Dianna, he's trying to be helpful," Charlotte said, taking another piece of licorice from the bag.

Roland sighed, scribbling on the paper. "Honestly, I find the whole thing boring, but it's important to understand it if you wanna go to college."

"College? I'm in seventh grade!" Dianna's eyes widened. "College is millions of years from now."

"My poor, sweet child," Roland said, wagging a finger at her. "It's not as far away as you think."

Charlotte nodded. "He's right."

Dianna frowned, turning to her friend. "You'll both be in college before me."

"Only for a year, and Juliet will still be here," Charlotte said, reassuring her. "Besides, I don't even know what I wanna do."

"There are only so many things you *can* do in Tavern," Roland said, grabbing another candy. "Work for Doren Shipping or go into Vermin studies. Neither of which sound even the least bit exciting."

"Vermin studies is neat," Dianna said, picking at the grass. "My uncle teaches it at the school in Riversburg."

"I just don't understand why we need to learn about a bunch of extinct mongrels."

"They're not extinct, they're all over the place," Dianna said firmly. "And they're not mongrels."

Roland and Charlotte eyed her.

"The teachers here are idiots. Vermins and humans are basically the same," Dianna said firmly.

"How would you know?" Roland asked, leaning toward her.

Dianna held her breath, glancing at Charlotte. "W well, I've seen them in Riversburg. They're very nice, and this vermin boy named Patrick taught me how to say a couple words in his language."

Roland grinned, crossing his arms. "*Right,* and can Peter verify this tall tale of yours?"

"He wasn't there..." Dianna muttered. She sat up straight, glaring at him. "But it's true! Just ask Phoebe next time she comes to visit."

"Sure thing, Warren." Roland handed her the papers and nodded before turning to Charlotte. "I'd better get going. I have–"

"Piano lessons. Yes, we know," she said, snatching the bag of candy.

Roland climbed up onto his feet, stretching his arms above his head, before pointing at Dianna. "Small population. Big profit. Okay Pigtails?"

Dianna gritted her teeth.

Roland stumbled forward, catching himself.

A devious smile crept between her lips. "Maybe I'll start calling you Sir Trips-A-Lot."

He knelt down, putting his face right up close to hers. "I'm surprised you didn't think to make fun of my bushy eyebrows."

"Would you two get a room?" Charlotte said.

Roland swung his head around, cheeks bright red.

"I'm only teasing. Go to your piano lesson before someone sends your poor nanny out looking for you."

"She's not my nanny!"

Charlotte smirked. "She is. Miles *and* Vincent confirmed it."

Roland stuck his tongue out at her, picked up his book bag and hurried off, leaving the girls alone.

"He forgot his candy," Dianna said, pointing to the bag in Charlotte's hand.

"Speaking of candy. He's sweet on you, you know that, right?"

Dianna shook her head frantically. "That's impossible!"

"He doesn't even like candy cigarettes. He bought them because that's what you picked out last time we got together."

Dianna looked at the box sitting next to her in the grass. "But I like peppermint patties. I only got these last time because they ran out."

Charlotte laughed, twirling a short curl around her finger. "I know that. Here, look." She dumped out the rest of the bag.

Dianna gawked at the four packs of candy cigarettes, spilling out onto the grass, along with a small box of peppermint patties. She spun around, watching Roland run off up the hill, her cheeks burning. "If that boy likes me, he must've been born with one too many screws loose."

"CHARLOTTE'S BACK IN TAVERN?" Dianna said, watching Roland eat. She waited patiently for him to swallow what was in his mouth before nudging him with her elbow.

His eyes drifted up from his plate and met hers. "I keep forgetting you weren't at the wedding."

"Right... she's married."

He nodded, resting his fork on the edge of his plate. "We hadn't talked since she left for Augen."

Dianna puffed out her cheeks, cupping her chin in her hands.

"What's wrong?"

She leaned toward him. "Do you mind if I ask why Tabitha was so cross with you?"

He sighed. "Only if you tell me why you and Charlotte stopped speaking."

Dianna shrugged. "She didn't like how I ended things with you."

Roland cleared his throat, catching her off guard. He poked away at his potatoes again. "That's unfortunate."

"If I learned anything from our relationship, it's that it's best to avoid sharing friends with one's sweetheart."

"And how many sweethearts have you had?"

She smirked, looking him over. "Wouldn't you like to know."

He gave a light chuckle, nodding slowly.

"So, what happened? The two of you went for drinks?"

"Something like that."

What's that supposed to mean? Dianna brushed some hair behind her ears. "And that upset Tabitha because?"

"I don't drink anymore."

She thought for a moment, then smiled. "Well, it's probably for the best. You were never good at handling yourself."

"You were gone for the worst of it," he breathed, moving the potatoes to the edge of his plate.

"Roland?"

He turned to her.

"Is something the matter?"

"It's nothing. Guess I'm not as hungry as I thought. I'll just head upstairs and see if I can find something short to read to Julius."

"I can read to him. It's no problem."

Roland got up from the table, clearing his plate. "My brother read to me every night, no matter how bad his day was... the least I can do is try, and give that to Julius."

How often does he think about his brother? Dianna pushed the chairs in around the table. "Sometimes you seem so... different."

He scratched his head.

"Mature. I guess. What I mean is you're more mature."

"Oh... well, I didn't really have a choice in the matter. You should pay Charlotte a visit. I think she could really use a friend right now."

Dianna eyed him.

"Don't stay up too late, okay?"

"I should be the one saying that to you," she said, folding her hands together.

He gave her a smile. "We don't get much sleep in this house."

She wrinkled her brow.

"Goodnight, Freckles."

Her cheeks burned, watching him exit the kitchen.

He glanced over his shoulder. "I mean Dianna."

A chill rushed through her. *Dianna?* She turned from him, nodding. *Something happened with Charlotte. Something must've happened.*

Two large brown eyes watched eagerly as the young man dug at the frozen earth, hands trembling as dirt buried itself beneath his fingernails. Nicholas listened to a heavy sigh as the man sat cross legged, stretching his arm above his head.

"*Nul. Daknov Musa Elde Iigen Vui Naskit Matya.*"

Nicholas crawled toward him.

The man pulled him up into his arms, nuzzling their cheeks together. "Aren't you cold?"

Nicholas shook his head, feather earring dangling back and forth.

The man's breath swirled about as he gazed toward the camp, brushing the toddler's curious fingers away from his ears. "Quit that, I'm trying to think."

Nicholas wrinkled his nose before burying it into the man's chest. "*Iya Lieken Yurna.*"

"I don't see how that's relevant." He held the boy up, twisting him side to side. "What's the matter? Are you hungry?"

"*Ha.*"

The man wrapped him up in a blanket, securing the little boy to his chest. "We can't drink the water; the animals are sick... Ferine is falling apart."

Nicholas gazed up at him.

"I have no idea where your mother buried the money, and I'm a terrible hunter. Promise me you'll be better at it than me," he said gently. "Okay, *Yunenik*?"

Nicholas rested his head against the man's chest, listening to his breathing. The cold air bit away at the tips of his ears as he whimpered.

"I know, little one. Just a bit longer, then we can find *Musa* and go."

NICHOLAS RUBBED the drool from his cheek, raising his head from the pillow. The blankets had become entangled around him, as if he were a blue robin's egg, warm and safe in its nest. Normally, Zana would end up hogging all the blankets, leaving him and Micah shivering on winter mornings like this, but now he had more sheets than he knew what to do with.

He let out a yawn, patting around the bed. For the past while, he'd been secretly curling up at night with the stuffed bear he'd found in the nursery closet, the one Roland called Pippi. Nicholas preferred to call it Bear, although Pippi wasn't a horrible name. Bear just seemed more practical. He'd learned at an early age not to name the animals, since most of them ended up on his plate, and so Pippi was now called Bear.

Bear was worn, and although he claimed to be too old for toys, having something to hold was the only way Nicholas managed to fall asleep. At first, he would cling to books Rose had lent him or a pillow, but Bear proved to be a more comfortable solution, and to top it off, Bear couldn't scold him for speaking *Valdin Zungta*.

Reaching around with his other hand, Nicholas latched onto something firm and meaty. His pupils narrowed as he sat up. "*Deisso...*" He let go of the small human's arm and inched away from him, lifting up the sheets. *Why is this thing here?* He groaned, yanking Julius up onto the pillow before crawling out of bed.

He spotted Bear on the floor by the nightstand and quickly shoved him under the bed, praying Lisa wouldn't check under there while cleaning. The last thing he needed was for one of the adults to find it and mistakenly give it to Julius or Alicia.

Julius wasn't heavy, or at least not as heavy as his older brother, but the five-year-old seemed harder to move when he was asleep.

Nicholas wanted nothing more than to shove the kid onto the floor and go back to bed, but his conscience wouldn't let him. If he did, Julius would cry, and he would get far worse than a slap of the wrist for an offence like that. Everyone was protective of Julius. *Even Rose would wring my neck.* He threw the little boy over his shoulder and made his way down the hall. *Why does he keep sleeping in my bed? There's a whole other bed right there! Bloka, Verjik Hiloven Kokinok!* He propped open the door to the master bedroom and peered inside. "Mr. Crispin?"

Roland was sitting up in bed, massaging his forehead. He glared at them, then gestured for Nicholas to put Julius down next to him. Roland pulled Julius up onto his lap and pet his head gently, running his fingers through the little boy's hair. "Caspian must've kicked him out again."

Nicholas shrugged.

"He doesn't sleep well."

"Looks like he sleeps just fine to me," Nicholas mumbled, crossing his arms.

Roland peered up at him. "Cas' doesn't... Julius, on the other hand, can and will sleep anywhere if given the opportunity."

"Yeah, well, it seems like he's forgotten I was sick not that long ago."

Roland nodded. "Your recovery was fast. I've been thinking I might donate the leftover medication to Dr. Gray. I heard there's a family in town who–"

"I don't like doctors."

Roland gave him a smile.

Nicholas tiptoed backward, away from the bed.

"You've only ever met one doctor, and Dr. Gray is a good person. Despite what you might think of him."

"Vincent Gray isn't." Nicholas noted the way Roland pressed his lips together, taking his hand away from his nephew's head.

"Vincent's..."

"He hurt my family."

"I know, but they broke the law."

"He hurt *me*."

"I..." Roland sighed, nodding. "I'm sorry."

"Will there be any lessons tomorrow before you all go off to your party?"

"How confident are you feeling about your spelling?"

Nicholas picked away at the skin around his thumb, lowering his voice. "I don't wanna learn how to write words like that. I wanna learn stuff like... like how to spell Dinara and words like dainty or pastry."

"Pastry? Look, the words you're learning right now are small, but they're useful. Off the top of your head. Can you spell something for me?"

Nicholas held his breath. "S... uh... O..." He hung his head, tugging on the sleeve of his shirt. "C.A.T. Cat."

Roland smiled. "See, you're making progress. Peter's a good teacher."

"I'd rather you taught me instead."

Roland got up out of bed. "Trust me. Peter's way better at that sort of thing."

"Every time I do something wrong, he..." Nicholas shook his head, hair flopping side to side. He knew better than to try and explain his displeasure. The humans weren't obligated to teach him anything. Peter reminded him often that being able to roam the Crispin Estate was privilege enough. Vermin living in Presa were treated far worse. The fact Nicholas was allowed to dine with the family was bizarre. Anywhere else it would've been considered scandalous. He cleared his throat, meeting Roland's gaze. "I'll keep practicing."

"Are you up to going for a walk?"

Nicholas' ears perked up. "Outside?"

Roland nodded, squinting slightly as he craned his neck. "Get dressed. I'll go see if Miss Warren's awake."

Isn't he worried about me running off? Nicholas hurried out into the hall, back to the nursery.

He'd mapped out a handful of escape routes in the sketchbook he'd gotten when he'd first come to the Crispin Estate. Peter and Roland often flipped through it, supposedly for research purposes so Nicholas made sure that the maps were properly hidden. Each of the trees he drew was a map, and their branches would stretch out into different pathways in and around the house. Currently, he only knew of one path outside, which led to a smaller guest house out in the woods. He'd only been there for a short period, and barely remembered how he got to and from there, but now and then he would catch Mr. Leon shoveling outside, and it seemed he went a long way away from the main house.

If I could get out there again, maybe I could find a route to Riversburg? He knew it was possible. Rose had mentioned a trail somewhere on the property that went all the way up there. Apparently, her uncle had used it once in his youth to run off.

What will happen to them if I leave? That was the question that haunted him.

Nicholas contemplated it as he changed into a striped knit sweater and overalls, pulling his argyle socks up over his feet. If he left Tavern, would the Crispin's be killed? His stomach turned at the thought of what might happen to little Julius. If he had been afraid of Nicholas, he wouldn't constantly follow him around the house like a duckling. Julius even snuck snacks up to the nursery whenever Nicholas was made to stay there. Once he'd brought up an entire sandwich and two fistfuls of salted crackers. Of course, everything was smooshed during transportation, but it was the thought behind it that truly mattered. Julius was just a little kid. Annoying, yes, but not annoying enough to die. *Peter, on the other hand...* Nicholas smirked, his ears tingling at the sound of footsteps outside the nursery door.

"Are you dressed?"

The smirk faded at the sound of Dianna's voice. *She'd be sad if anything bad happened to her cousin.* Nicholas pouted and opened the door. Peter would have to live, for Dianna's sake.

Dianna placed her hands on his cheeks, turning his head from side to side. "You're looking a bit thin."

"*Stai!*" Nicholas shoved her back, rubbing his face. "I'm fine."

"Roland thought you might like to get out for some exercise. He's already downstairs."

Nicholas nodded.

"Are you sure you're feeling okay?"

He raised his brow, looking her over.

"Sorry. I'm just a bit worried, is all. It's cold out, and I want to be sure you're well enough. I have no idea what Roland's planning. He's been acting strangely."

"What do you mean?"

"I don't know. He said he wants to take you up to the stream."

Nicholas cocked his head, earring flopping to one side. "What stream?"

"Come, he'll show you."

Nicholas followed her downstairs to where Roland waited, already in his coat and boots. To his surprise, the man was also wearing gloves and a scarf. Normally, someone had to yell at him to do so. Nicholas also noted how Dianna was wearing a pair of black slacks instead of a dress or skirt. *The stream must be far if she's dressed like that.* He finished getting dressed, being sure to put a hat on to cover his ears, and followed them into the kitchen, toward the backdoor.

Roland led them up the snow-covered path, and then took a turn heading up into the trees, Dianna right on his heels, chatting away with him.

Nicholas found himself taking sharp breaths once they started going uphill, deeper into the frozen wood. The air smelled of pine, while the snow crunched beneath their feet. The smell of the humans seemed stronger now that they were outside, the mixture of scents tickling his nostrils with an array of florals and spices all mingled together. Nicholas sneezed loudly, scaring the nearby birds. He groaned, watching a red cardinal fly off overhead.

Dianna and Roland looked back at him.

"You're moving a little slow. Are you cold?"

Nicholas eyed him.

"Maybe we should take a break?" Dianna placed a hand on Roland's arm.

"I'm fine," Nicholas growled back, his teeth chattering together. The smell of pine filled his nostrils again. His stomach knotted in the place where his bruises had finally yellowed. *Vincent Gray.* He looked back over his shoulder, then turned to Roland and Dianna. His ears twitched. "Did you hear that?"

Roland motioned for him to come close. "It's probably just a rabbit. We've got a lot of those here."

Nicholas hurried up the hill after them, still wheezing. He grabbed onto a maple tree for balance, glaring at Roland as he brushed pine needles from his jacket. *Vincent Gray smelled like pine.* There was the ache again.

"We're almost there," Roland said.

Nicholas trembled. "What are those?"

Roland and Dianna turned, looking at the carved, snow-covered stone figures nestled beneath a large tree.

Nicholas had noticed similar stones spread about as his pack crossed over onto Tavern's boarder.

"That's a headstone." Roland glanced back at him, then continued up behind another group of trees.

Nicholas gulped down some air, dragging his feet through the snow. *What's wrong with me?* Dinara didn't get as much snow, but he was born in Ferine. He was kissed by the frost at birth. All vermin born there were more than capable of dealing with the cold, but he was struggling. He'd never struggled to keep up. His heart sank. *Did they do something to me, to make me weak so that I can't run away?* He eyed Dianna as she turned back and held out her hand.

Nicholas took it, allowing her to pull him into the clearing where

Roland was waiting. There was a small frozen stream, and more little stone figures. Nicholas went over to one, running a gloved hand along it. "Do humans make these?"

Roland nodded.

"What are they for?"

"To mark graves."

Nicholas backed away.

"It's all right." Dianna laughed, putting a hand on his shoulder.

"The one you saw down there was my mother's cat," Roland said. "And these three are my siblings."

Nicholas cocked his head. "You turned them into these rocks?"

"No?" Roland and Dianna exchanged a look, then turned back to him. "They're buried under the ground."

Nicholas lifted a foot.

"They died," Roland said nonchalantly.

"Obviously," Nicholas muttered. "But why are there these rocks?"

Dianna placed a hand on his shoulder. "The headstones are what we humans use to mark where our loved ones are buried."

Nicholas ran his thumb along the back of his earlobe, feeling where the earring was hooked in. "So, you bury the bodies and leave these stones with them when they die?"

Dianna nodded. "Something like that. Most of the time, we bury people in graveyards. Not at home but..."

Nicholas turned to her. "But why are the rocks shaped like babies with butterfly wings?"

Roland smiled, loosening his scarf. "Well, these two little babies side by side are supposed to be my sisters. And this one here is my brother. They died long before I was born. Oddly enough, I used to talk to these statues. I thought they were fancy garden gnomes."

"Gnomes?"

"Don't you have garden gnomes?"

Nicholas wrinkled his nose. "Our garden got a lot of bugs and dandelions."

Roland shoved his hands into his pockets, a wide grin spreading on his face. "Dandelions huh?" He chuckled. "So, I was thinking we could build a snow fort up here, and when everyone's awake, surprise them. I don't have much experience with it... but I figured you two might." His gaze began to wander over to Dianna as she crouched down in the snow, bunching up a ball of it in her hands.

Nicholas got low to the ground too, removing his glove to tracing a large paw print in the snow. *A fox maybe? No...*

"Don't even think about it," Roland snapped, shooting her a menacing look as Dianna got to her feet, a perfectly round snowball in hand.

Nicholas' ears perked up again, pupils narrowed.

Dianna giggled. "But packing snow is perfect for–"

Nicholas sprang up, leapt behind her and tackled the animal to the ground, holding onto it as tightly as he could. The wolf yelped, snarling at him.

Roland grabbed Dianna by the hand, pulling her beside him.

"W-what do we do?" She trembled; eyes swollen with fear. "Roland, what do we do?"

Nicholas could hear both of their hearts racing as he struggled to wrestle with the wolf. *Why can't I hold it?* His stomach fluttered again as the wolf pawed at his neck. Nicholas opened his mouth, fangs jutting out and dug them into the wolfs back, doing his best to avoid the neck. *Sorry...*

Dianna clasped her hands over her mouth as the wolf swatted at him again. "Nicholas!"

Nicholas removed his fans, roughly pinning the wolf down onto its belly, hissing in its ear, silencing it. Blood spilled from his mouth as he drew in a deep breath. "*Bloka...* you scratched me."

The wolf gazed up at him, large eyes glazed over as it whimpered.

Nicholas patted it gently where he'd bitten, trying to sooth it. "*Duvya Brolki* wolf. *Duvya Brolki.*"

"N-Nicholas are you okay?" Dianna said, creeping toward him.

Nicholas looked over his shoulder. "Are you?"

"I'm fine, but your... your lip is bleeding."

Roland removed his scarf, his face pale. "Is it dead?"

"Are you crazy? I couldn't kill this little guy, he's just a baby!" Nicholas scratched the wolf behind its ears.

"That's a big baby," Dianna said, turning to Roland.

Nicholas got up off the wolf, guiding it gently into the wood. "Sorry for biting you," he said, patting its neck. "It won't happen again, so long as you don't try to hurt my friends. Go on. Get outta here."

The wolf looked back at him, then hurried off, tail between its legs.

Nicholas rubbed the scratch along his neck, turning back to Roland and Dianna.

"Your face..." Roland uttered, backing away from him.

Nicholas and Dianna watched as the man went and leaned over, taking in several deep breaths.

"I'm gonna be sick."

Nicholas rubbed his neck again. "It's just a little scratch," Nicholas said, licking his fangs.

"That's not..." Roland began to gag, shaking his head. "What is wrong with you? What is wrong with you?"

Dianna gave Nicholas a small grin, patting him on the shoulder. "You're going to have a hard time explaining those stains to Tabitha," Dianna said, looking him over. "Anyway, we've still got some time. Why don't we follow the stream and see if we can find that tree Miles broke his arm falling out of?"

Roland stared at them.

"He's a vermin. They bite things. It's normal," Dianna said, tossing her hair over her shoulder. "The least you could say is thank you."

"There is nothing normal about this... I-is that what you did to Peter?"

"No..." Nicholas said sheepishly. He wanted to add what he'd done to Peter had been minor compared to what he was forced to do to that poor wolf. Normally he would've just wrestled it to the ground, but his body felt weak. *That's proof... they must be poisoning me.* The only time he ever dug his teeth into an animal was when he knew he couldn't frighten it away. He licked the blood from his fangs and spat it into the snow.

Dianna looked him over. "Are you hurt anywhere?"

Nicholas frowned. "No, but there's fur in my mouth."

She turned to Roland, who was pacing back-and-forth muttering to himself.

"Maybe I should brush my teeth," Nicholas told her. *I can't just go around saying I think the humans are poisoning me, especially since she promised they weren't. Still, there's no other explanation for it. I've been able to take wolves that size since I was ten. That should've been easy.*

"Roland, I think we should head back. Nicholas is covered in blood," Dianna said, turning Nicholas from side to side. "Roland?"

Nicholas' ears perked up as the man flew face forward into the snow.

"Roland!"

Nicholas pulled away from her, moving toward him. He rolled Roland over, tracing the man's forehead with the back of his hand. "He feels warm. I'll carry him back to the house. You should call…" He swallowed hard, heart racing in his chest. "You should call Dr. Gray."

Going down the hill should've been the easy part, but with a grown man on his back, Nicholas' legs wanted to give way. *Why is he so heavy?* Nicholas let out a harsh grunt, trudging through the trees after Dianna, the smell of pine filling his nose again. He'd carried Micah on his back plenty of times, just for the fun of it, but there was absolutely nothing fun about this. Roland was heavy, his clothes were wet, and he smelled awful. *Why do humans drench themselves in those Bloka oils?* The tips of Nicholas' ears tingled as he pushed on. *Sounds like our friend the wolf is back.* "Miss Warren, do the Crispin's have a gun?"

Dianna turned to him. "I don't know."

Nicholas sank waist deep into the snow, Roland sliding down his back. He gripped onto the man tightly, shivering.

Dianna ran over. "Did he seem sick to you?"

"I'm fine. I got it."

She backed away, nodding as Nicholas forced his way out onto the main path at the bottom of the hill. "I don't understand. He hasn't shown any symptoms of the fever."

"Can we talk later?" Nicholas growled, arms shaking beneath the man's weight. "That wolf is right behind us."

Dianna nodded, hurrying toward the house.

Nicholas wanted nothing more than to dump Roland on the ground and leave him there. His arms and legs were numb, and his neck hurt. *Micah and Zana carried me all the way to Tavern. I can carry this Bloka a little longer.* One foot at a time, Nicholas pushed on, knees buckling every so often. He couldn't stop. His siblings didn't abandon him like the rest of his pack. Roland didn't leave him to die that day he and Rose found him out in the snow. He made a promise that he'd keep the Crispin's safe. He had to honour his promise. That's what Nyla would do.

Once they reached the back door, Dianna peeled Roland off of Nicholas' back and laid him out on the kitchen floor.

Nicholas sank to his knees, wiping the sweat and blood from his face, while Dianna picked up the phone. "W-what... what should I–"

"Hello. Dr. Gray, it's Dianna. I'm at the Crispin's. Roland collapsed. I-I'm not sure. There was this wolf and... yes... thank you. Okay."

Nicholas leaned over Roland, eyeing him. His skin crawled.

"What's going on?" Rose said, entering the kitchen. She stopped, staring at Nicholas, face growing pale.

"Dr. Gray and Vincent are on their way. Rose, take Nicholas upstairs and hide him," Dianna said, hanging up the phone.

Rose backed away. "W-what..."

Dianna helped Nicholas up off the floor, looking over at Rose. "Is Lisa up?"

Rose shrieked, causing both her brothers to race into the room.

"Why are we screaming?" Julius cried before bumping into his brother.

Caspian latched onto his sister, knees shaking.

Julius looked at them, then at his uncle, and then at Nicholas and Dianna.

"Take them into the other room," Nicholas said softly.

Julius nodded, grabbing Caspian's other hand, eyes on Nicholas' teeth.

Nicholas noted the way Rose and Caspian squeezed each other's fingers. The unreadable expressions on their faces. In that moment, Julius seemed much older than both his siblings, barely flinching at all as he led them to the couch in the parlour and had them sit down. Nicholas waited in the doorway, watching Julius grab one of the Afghans and place it on his brother and sister, before snuggling up beside Rose and kissing her cheek.

"It's okay Rosie."

Nicholas forced his way up the stairs, Lisa racing by him toward the parlour, calling out to the children. *Tabitha and Mr. Leon must be late getting here because of all the snow.* He gripped onto the railing, arms aching. *Did I give him the fever? Are all of them sick now?* He lugged himself into the nursery, little Alicia peering at him from Rose's bedroom, holding one of the porcelain dolls. It wasn't until he sat down on the bed that he realized he still had his boots on, the ones that were a size too big for him. He undid the laces and pried them off his feet, along with both socks.

Alicia came into the room, rocking back and forth on the balls of her feet. "What's all over your face?"

Nicholas ran a hand along his mouth and looked at his fingers. *Blood?* He looked at her, lowering his head. "Strawberry jam. I ate a bunch in the woods. You should go downstairs, okay? I think Julius might need your help."

"You're not supposed to eat berries you find in the woods. My mommy said that could make you sick."

I feel sick. Nicholas looked up at her through his bangs. "You should take the extra blankets on that bed and give them to Miss Warren. Mr. Crispin's really cold."

Alicia nodded and went over to the other bed across from him, scooping the blankets up in her little arms the best she could. "You need a bath, mister. You smell."

Nicholas stared at his hands. *Is this what they saw?* He placed his head in his hands, trembling. *Maybe vermin are monsters?*

17

———————

Blood. Fangs. Blood. Fangs. Blood. Fangs.

Nicholas.

It was Nicholas. Wasn't it? Rose's eyes fell on her youngest brother, who was patting her hand gently. She glanced at Caspian on the other side of her. Her fingers were numb. He was squeezing them just as he did that day. She closed her eyes.

There was a heavy knock on the door.

"Please, please be the doctor," Lisa said.

Rose held her breath, running through the events in her head. She heard Dianna in the kitchen, went inside and saw her uncle laying on the floor. Blood covered Nicholas' face. *Did he attack him?* She shook her head frantically.

A hand came down on her shoulder.

"Rose..."

The voice was warm, gentle, familiar.

She opened her eyes. "Mr. Gray, my uncle. He–" The words were clogged in her throat, eyes still on Vincent.

He turned his attention to Julius. "Have you had anything to eat yet?"

Julius shook his head.

He nodded slowly, green eyes scanning the room until they fell in a puddle on the floor. "Would you like to go out and get something to eat? The diner should be open."

Rose squeezed her eyes shut, then opened them again.

"I'm not leaving Uncle Roland," Caspian said firmly.

Vincent smiled at him. "My father will take care of him. We'll come right back as soon as we're done."

"I'm not going."

Vincent gave Rose a sympathetic look. "I don't think it'd be wise for me to try and cook while my father's working. I wouldn't want to get in the way."

"I don't care. I'm not going," Caspian said again, glaring at the man. He was squeezing Rose's fingers tighter now. His hand shaking.

Dianna came into the parlour, wringing her hands together.

"What happened?"

"We were walking up by the stream and this wolf came out of nowhere–"

Julius stomped his feet. "It wasn't a wolf!"

Vincent turned to him.

Dianna pressed her lips together. "Let's talk in the office."

"It wasn't! It wasn't a wolf!" Julius jumped up off the couch.

Rose was glued to the seat, watching her younger brother ball his fists, round cheeks reddening.

Vincent placed a hand on Dianna's back, leading her toward the parlour doors. "When you arrived this morning, did Roland seem off?"

"Um... well actually–"

"Stop lying!" Julius shouted, grabbing onto Dianna's arm.

Caspian let go of Rose's hand, jumped up off the couch and latched onto their younger brother, yanking him away from the adults. "Shut up Julius!"

"B-but–"

Alicia pushed Caspian away from Julius and glared at her. "Everybody just stop yelling and saying mean things!"

Caspian raised a hand at her, then backed away, shaking his fist. "I outta pound the both of you into meat pies."

"I'm not scared of you," Alicia said, crossing her arms.

Caspian turned to Dianna and Vincent. "Sorry."

Rose eased her way up off the couch and took Caspian by the hand. "Let's... let's go up to the library."

Caspian hung his head.

She held her hand out to the younger children. "Julius, Alicia, are you coming?"

Julius nodded. "Yes... but Miss Warren–"

"Miss Warren needs to talk to Mr. Gray privately. We'll wait upstairs for them to come get us," Caspian said firmly.

Julius lowered his head, taking Alicia by the hand.

What if Vincent sees Nicholas? Rose's chest tightened, watching the adults go into the office while she led the smaller children upstairs. *Nicholas...* She tiptoed past the nursery, heart thumping loudly, as if everything else had emptied out of her. She was hollow, like the inside of a drum, beating and beating endlessly. *Would Miss Warren lie to keep Nicholas safe? Would I?*

AN HOUR HAD PASSED while the children hid up in the library, waiting for someone to come get them.

Alicia and Julius seemed oddly calm, despite being the youngest ones there. Caspian was pacing and muttering quietly to himself, a habit he'd picked up from their uncle, and Rose pretended to read, but doing so was impossible when images of blood and bodies muddled her mind.. Her thoughts seemed unending.

Caspian kicked the wall a few times, then spun on his heels and went back to stomping back and forth, wildly gesturing with his hands. "It's not that you were wrong Julius. It's just, if you told Mr. Gray the truth, then Uncle Roland would get in a lot of trouble. Yes, lying is bad but sometimes you *have* to do it. I lie all the time."

Alicia glared at him, shaking her head. "My mommy says lying is naughty."

"Well, your mommy is an idiot, because right now, lying is the only option," Caspian said, jabbing her belly with his finger.

Alicia gasped, placing her hands on her hips. "That's not nice!"

"Stop fighting," Rose murmured, lacing her black ribbon between her fingers. She couldn't remember when she'd pulled it out of her hair, but she'd gone from using it as a makeshift bookmark to fidgeting, as if wrapping it around her index finger would somehow help her unravel the thoughts in her head.

Caspian turned around. "I'm not fighting. I'm reasoning. *Reasoning,* Rose."

"Saying it twice won't make you sound more convincing," she said.

"Well, thanks to you, we're in a crisis," Caspian said.

"What did I do?"

"Nothing. You did absolutely nothing, and now we all look suspicious."

Rose pulled the ribbon through her fingers, staring at him.

"Julius is only five. He doesn't know any better. You're the oldest. You're supposed to make sure he doesn't screw up."

"That's not fair."

"Life's not fair, or have you suddenly forgotten?" Caspian said, sullenly.

"Why do you get a free pass? I'm barely three years older than you!"

"Because Papa told you to take care of us!" Caspian's voice rose in his throat. "And you're too busy with your stupid parties, and boys and your dumb hair!"

Rose slammed the book down onto the floor, getting up onto her feet. "Excuse me?"

Julius crouched down behind the couch.

Caspian puffed up his chest. "None of this would've happened if you didn't decide to play hero and rescue some stray mutt."

Rose rolled up the sleeves of her sweater. "Don't ever bring up Papa like that."

"Why? Because you know it's true?"

"You're the one always getting into trouble at school and making problems! Uncle Roland probably hates you. Honestly, I think everyone does. That's why you don't have any friends!"

Caspian's lip quivered as he drew in a deep breath. "Friends? You think those kids at school are your friends? They'd never talk to you if it weren't for Thompson."

She glared at him.

"I don't want friends who always talk bad about me when I'm not around."

"Well, I didn't want you for a brother, but here we are!" Rose cried.

Caspian brushed past her toward the stairs.

"Fine, run away. See if I care."

"Oh, go eat a rat!" He slammed the door.

Alicia turned to Julius, shaking her head. "Well, that was dramatic."

Julius frowned. "Rosie... are you and Caspian fighting because of me?"

Rose sank down onto the couch. "Please, just... be quiet."

18

———————

Vincent stood by the small bookshelf in the office, a room that at one time was forbidden to children when they came to the Crispin Estate. He watched as Dianna tidied up the papers on the desk, placing them in one of the drawers, her long red hair draped over her shoulder. It'd been several minutes since they entered the room, and he had so much to ask.

"Sorry about the mess. We didn't clean up last night."

"We?"

"Peter's been at home most of the week, so things have kind of piled up. Plus, I'm sure you know that Roland's not the most organized person on the planet." She gazed up at him, coming out from behind the desk. "Do you think he's going to be okay?"

Vincent examined her small frame. "How'd you get him back to the house?"

"Pardon?"

"You said the two of you were up at the stream."

"We were."

"Is that where he collapsed?"

She nodded, then shook her head, then nodded again.

"Dianna, are you all right?"

"I'm fine... just a bit startled. He seemed fine. He wanted to make a snow fort for the children. Then that wolf showed up."

Vincent scratched his chin. "Wolves again, huh?"

She nodded. "It jumped out at me and then he..."

Vincent watched as she clasped her hands together, taking in a deep breath. *Julius seemed convinced that it wasn't a wolf, but she doesn't seem to be lying.*

Dianna pressed her hands to her cheeks, slapping them hard. "I've never seen a wolf up close like that. Not even on the farm. After it left, Roland just collapsed."

He nodded. "I don't think he's been taking his medication. Did he show any signs of the fever at all? Rose had it a while back, its possible he got it from her."

"No. That's why I'm so confused. He seemed perfectly fine, except..."

"Except what?"

"He mentioned he was with Charlotte. I didn't ask."

"Charlotte, huh?" Vincent crossed his arms, nodding. "I wasn't aware she was back."

"Something happened at the college. Roland saw his mother and then when he came home, Tabitha was awfully cross with him. He was really late. He's never late for supper."

"You were here for supper?"

Dianna blushed.

"Are you..." He cleared his throat. "Are you and Roland living together?"

"Technically yes, but not in the way you think," Dianna said quickly. She took off her beret, running her hands through her hair. "I've just moved in temporarily. It's a long story."

There was a loud bang upstairs.

Vincent gazed up at the ceiling, furrowing his brow.

"It's the children."

"They seemed frightened."

"They were," Dianna said. "Rose especially."

"You're positive what attacked you in the woods was a wolf?"

Vincent said, looking her over.

She nodded.

"How did you get away?"

"There was... a man. Boy. He was hunting."

"No ones allowed to hunt on the Crispin land."

"I know, but I never would've gotten Roland down the hill without him."

Vincent eyed her. "Where is he now?"

"I..." Dianna gave a light shrug, laughing. "Honestly, I don't know. One minute he was there, the next he wasn't. It was almost like... like a divine moment or something. I didn't even get a chance to say thank you."

"Could you describe him for me?"

Dianna cocked her head. "You're not going to charge him for being on the property, are you?"

Vincent shook his head. "No, but I'd like to ask him if he's seen a lot of wolves up there. Seems there's a lot around the property. If I were Roland, I wouldn't be letting the kids out of the house. At least not without a gun present."

"I don't think he owns one."

"He does." Vincent noted the puzzled look on her face. "His father did anyway. I'm sure they're just tucked away someplace safe, so the kids can't get at them. Maybe ask Mr. Leon."

Dianna nodded.

"So, about the boy who helped you. What did he look like?"

"Well, he was wearing a red and black checkered hat and coat. Uh... brown hair. I'd say he was around your height... no, maybe a bit shorter. I'm sorry, that's all I can remember."

Vincent smiled at her. "I'm going to go check in with my father. How good are you with the kids?"

"If they don't want to talk to me, I'll send Lisa."

"All right." With that, Vincent went out to the parlour. His father and Lisa had Roland resting on the couch, wrapped up in a bunch of sheets. He leaned over his father's shoulder, watching him. "Do you need me to run back to the office and grab anything?"

His father shook his head. "I'm going to stay the night and keep an eye on him. Fainting like that twice in one week is highly unusual... I'm almost thinking he should go to the hospital."

"The hospital's all the way in East Tavern."

"I know."

"And the kids are already freaked out," Vincent said softly.

"I'm aware of that, Vincent."

He took a step back at the harshness of his father's tone. "You seem uneasy."

"It's nothing."

"No. You're acting strange. Everyone is. What's going on?" Vincent turned his head as Caspian entered the parlour.

Lisa hurried over to him, wrapping her arms around the boy.

Caspian eyed Vincent, squirming away from his nanny. "Could we go to the diner?"

Vincent gave him a smile, then turned to his father.

"Go on," his father said. "I can handle things here."

Vincent nodded, leading Caspian to the door. "Aren't you going to get your brother and sister?"

"Nope." Caspian put on his coat.

Vincent brought the boy out to the car and waved at Tabitha and Mr. Leon as they pulled up the driveway.

Tabitha hurried out to greet him. "What a pleasant surprise! Where are you two off to?"

"I wish this were a social visit," Vincent said, gently placing a hand on Caspian's shoulder. "But there's been an accident. Roland collapsed. My father is with him now. I'm taking Caspian to the diner to get some breakfast."

"Collapsed? Why? What happened?"

Mr. Leon ran over, gliding on a patch of ice.

"Dianna said there was a wolf. I don't know. Hopefully, once everyone's calmed down a little, it'll be easier to understand what happened," Vincent told them.

Tabitha rushed toward the house as Mr. Leon stopped to tip his hat.

"You'll be good for Mr. Gray, right?" he said, looking at Caspian.

Caspian grunted, opening the car door.

The drive was quiet until they reached town. Caspian wasn't usually as chatty as his brother and sister, but he wasn't shy. It wasn't until Vincent reached for the radio that Caspian opened his mouth.

"Is my uncle gonna die?"

Vincent gripped the wheel. It was a question he and his cousin Miles often asked about Roland as children. Roland hadn't collapsed like that since his trial. Back then it was caused by stress, and a lack of sleep. Prior to that, Vincent could only recall a handful of times, all random, two of which sent Roland to the hospital. He remembered how upsetting it was, listening to the adults argue about possible causes and treatments. He decided then he didn't want to be a doctor like his father. Vincent observed the way the ten-year-old squeezed his hands together in his lap. "I don't know. I'm not a doctor. I hope not."

"But your dad's a doctor."

Vincent gave a quick nod. "Sometimes doctors don't know either. Your uncle's been sick for a long time. So, we really don't know."

"If he dies, we'll be orphans."

Vincent took a deep breath.

"What would you do if you knew someone was doing something that might be bad?" Caspian asked.

Vincent pulled over in front of the diner.

"Like, what if the person was someone you cared about, and you didn't want them to get in trouble, but you also thought that maybe what they were doing might get them hurt?"

"Is your uncle doing something bad?"

Caspian squirmed around in his seat.

"It's okay. You can tell me."

The boy peered up at him. "Well... well, Uncle Roland, he..." Caspian curled his fingers into two tight fists. "He did something that made Tabby really upset, and I found a bottle in his room."

"A bottle?"

Caspian nodded. "Like from when I was little."

Damn it Roland. Vincent pat Caspian on the head. "Thank you for being honest with me. I'll let my father know when we get back, and we'll try and help your uncle. Okay?"

Caspian nodded, tears spilling down his cheeks.

"It's okay. I understand. I really do. Sometimes grownups need help too, but they don't know how to ask. Your uncle is very lucky to have you, and he loves you all so much. If I have to, I'll knock some sense into him like last time. I bet Peter will too."

Caspian sniffled, rubbing his eyes. "Can I get pancakes?"

Vincent smiled. *Just like his uncle.* "Of course. Anything you want."

19

There was a pulsing sensation as heat rushed through Roland's skull. The dizziness hit as he lifted his head slightly to gage his surroundings. Immediately, his head went back down, his chest rising and falling rapidly. *Laurie. Where's Laurie?* Slowly, he turned his head, vision blurry, black and white spots dancing before him, and then came the red. Deep blood red. His chest tightened. "Laurie. I need Laurie..."

A gentle hand smoothed back the short curls sticking to his forehead. "Shh..."

He gulped down some air, glancing up at the strawberry-coloured locks flowing down in two long braids. *Red.*

Dianna laid a hand down on his chest, humming gently.

Roland's eyes fluttered. "Pigtails."

She smiled at him. "You had us all worried."

"Where's Laurie?"

She pressed her lips together again.

More red. Deep red. Blood red. Roland eased himself up again, head spinning, as he looked around. His hands shook violently. "Wait... why am I in the parlour? Where's Laurie?"

Dr. Gray came over, holding a thermometer. "Open."

Roland did as he asked, taking the thermometer in his mouth while Dr. Gray looked down at his watch.

"Is he awake?" Tabitha said. She was standing next to the piano with Mr. Leon, holding a cup of tea.

"He's asking for Lawrence again," Dianna said softly, getting to her feet.

Roland squeezed his eyes shut. *Red. Red. Red.*

Dr. Gray removed the thermometer and held it up, adjusting his glasses. "He doesn't have a fever, but he is delirious. Did he bump his head when he fell?"

Roland eyed him. "I fell?"

"You collapsed out by the stream. Do you remember?"

Teeth. Blood. Roland gripped his stomach, leaning forward.

Dianna rubbed his back. "I don't think he hit anything. He fell forward, though. He seemed fine earlier."

"Fine. He's been far from fine for weeks," Tabitha said, harshly.

Mr. Leon placed a hand on her shoulder, then turned to Dianna. "His behaviour's been odd."

"Not that this girl would notice."

Roland took a deep breath. The image of fangs danced in his mind. "Where's the boy?"

"The boy?" Dr. Gray looked over his shoulder. "I've already spoken with him. He's fine."

"I need to see Laurie. I... I saw a vermin. I saw a vermin in the woods. I have to tell Laurie."

"He's... Lawrence went out," Tabitha said, coming closer. "Do you want something to eat? I made soup."

Vincent stepped out from the parlour doors. "A vermin in the woods?"

Roland turned to him, nodding slowly.

"He's confused," Dr. Gray said softly. "He was going on about licorice earlier."

Vincent crossed his arms. "Caspian told me a few things... could I speak with you and Tabitha for a moment?"

Dr. Gray glanced over at Tabitha, the both of them nodding, then following Vincent out into the hall.

"Caspian?" Roland looked into the hall. "Wait... where are the children?"

"Just relax," Mr. Leon said. "You need to calm down. You had a little too much excitement today."

Dianna nodded slowly, inching toward the parlour doors.

"Leave them be," Mr. Leon said firmly. "Whatever happens, happens. It's for the best."

"No... none of you were there," Dianna said sharply.

"How do I know that you aren't covering for him?"

Roland held his stomach again, lowering his head. "Dianna, where's Charlotte?"

"Charlotte?"

He looked around the room, vision blurring again. "Charlotte. I... we saw a vermin in–"

CHARLOTTE SAT across from him on Lawrence's old bed in the nursery, hands folded neatly in her lap. Her brown eyes fixed on him, unwavering. The mix of curiosity and confusion on her face made Roland uneasy.

No one had looked at him like that. Most wouldn't even look at him. He'd forgotten what it was like to be noticed.

"It's my first time in a boy's room," she said. "I didn't expect it to be so... delicate."

"What's that supposed to mean?"

"It just doesn't seem like you, that's all."

Roland scratched his head.

Charlotte tapped her index fingers together, rhythmically. "I'm sorry about what happened."

"It's fine."

She cocked her head. "Is it?"

Roland started nodding while something bubbled in his throat. He tried swallowing it, but then the tears poured out.

Charlotte's shoulders sank. She got up and sat down beside him, putting an arm around him.

Why was he crying now? He hadn't even cried at the funeral.

Charlotte held him tight. "Vincent sent Peter a letter. We thought it might be nice if you had your best friend come for a visit. I'll come by as much as I can. If you need me, I'm just a phone call away, all right?"

"Have you heard from Dianna?"

Charlotte squeezed his shoulders.

"Why won't she write back? Did something happen?" He started to sob.

Charlotte reached into her cardigan pocket, pulling out a small black box.

Roland eyed it. His heart sank.

"She gave it to me when I went to see her in Riversburg... I should've told you. I just..."

Roland held the box in the palm of his hand. "It's fine. I don't care," he said quietly.

Charlotte rubbed his back. "That's not true."

He turned to her. "You should go... it's getting late."

"I'll wait until your mother gets home."

"It'll be dark then."

She smiled. "That's all right. I like the dark anyway."

Nicholas remained in the nursery bathroom until noon, staring at himself in the mirror. The long, thin scratch along his neck. His fangs. His cheeks were hollow and tired eyes. His hair was longer. The longer he stared at himself, the more he loathed his ears, his teeth, the way his pupils narrowed like a cat. He could hear all the conversations in the house, and that man. Vincent Gray.

How could someone like that honey their words when they spoke. He remembered their first encounter, how Vincent seemed gentle, but then still left him there to die.

He could've at least had the decency to kill me.

Nicholas curled up on the bathroom floor, looking at his hands, curling and uncurling his fingers. *Is Mr. Crispin okay?* He pressed his back up against the wall, the floral wallpaper scratching his bare skin. The feather earring dangled up against his neck, hidden beneath his long, dark hair. He pressed his thumb into the sharp end of the hook that held it in place, pushing up into the metal and forcing it out of his earlobe. As he held the earring in his hand, his ear tingled. He'd never been without the earring. It was always there, a reminder of a family he didn't know. Of people he'd probably never see again. He went over to the counter and placed the earring down by the sink, looking at himself in the mirror once again. He brushed his hair behind his left ear. It felt naked.

Am I a monster?

He gripped the counter. *Why else would she have screamed like that?* He shook his head, brown hair covering his face. *The humans will always be afraid of me. Why wouldn't they be? I nearly tore Mr. Rissing's hand open, and I took down a wolf. Of course, they'd poison me. Even when I'm at my weakest, I could still hurt someone.*

There was a knock on the nursery door, followed by unfamiliar footsteps.

Nicholas remained still, slowing and quieting his breathes.

"I know you don't like me much, but would it be all right if I took a quick look at you?"

It was Dr. Gray.

Nicholas crept toward the door.

"I promise. All I've got here is a little peroxide and some bandages."

Nicholas opened the door hesitantly, peering out at the doctor. "W-what's peroxide?"

"It's just so your cut doesn't get infected."

Nicholas backed away from the door, letting the doctor enter.

Dr. Gray shut the door behind him and began pouring an odd smelling liquid onto a cotton ball. "It'll sting a little."

Nicholas nodded.

"You're smaller than I remember," Dr. Gray said calmly as he turned to face him. He looked the boy over. "What are you, twelve?"

"Fourteen."

"Fourteen huh?" He inched closer with the cotton ball between his fingers as Nicholas stepped back. Dr. Gray took a deep, shaky breath. "Seems we're both a bit nervous."

"I won't hurt you," Nicholas said gently. "Mr. Crispin says you're a good person."

Dr. Gray edged toward him. "I don't have many good experiences with vermin... but from what I understand, Roland never would've gotten back to the house if you hadn't been there."

Nicholas remained still, shoulders tense.

"I'm sure your experiences with humans aren't great either." Dr. Gray pressed the cotton ball against Nicholas' neck.

It sizzled, burning against his skin. Nicholas winced. *Lisa used this on me before.*

"My wife used to teach Roland piano lessons, back when he was a little boy," Dr. Gray said, dabbing the cotton ball lightly under Nicholas' chin. "She taught him these old vermin songs she learned while she was a student in Augen. You look like the boy who – a vermin killed her. Tried to kill Vincent."

"I'm sorry."

"It was our fault. We were naïve." Dr. Gray backed away slowly. "If you hurt Roland or anyone in this house again, like you did to Peter, I'll take my shotgun and blow a hole through your skull. Understood?"

Nicholas pinched his wrist, digging his nails in tightly. "Yes, sir. I'm sorry... it won't happen again."

Dr. Gray threw the cotton ball into the wastebasket. "Vincent and I will be staying the night. I suggest you find someplace else to sleep. We'll most likely be using the nursery."

With that, the doctor left, leaving Nicholas alone again.

He snatched the feather earring from off the counter, going out into the nursery to grab a clean pair of clothes. *I guess I'll have to sleep up in the library.* He looked upstairs, stomach turning. *But only if they want me there.*

20

———————

Zana puffed up her cheeks, adjusting her turtle earring in the mirror as her brother waltzed down the hall with Tiani. She caught a glimpse of his hand around the girl's waist, pulling her in close before stealing a kiss. *Bloka Yunenik.*

Micah had been popular with a handful of girls in their pack, and even during his brief time at school, seemed to attract the attention of the odd human girl. Many often commenting on his deep tan and dark brown eyes. The one girl in their pack that he seemed smitten by was Samara. She was a year older than he was, and he would find flowers near the cave and bring them to her. Whenever he did, Samara would put them in her hair and give him a peck on the cheek. Zana always assumed they'd be mates, but Tiani seemed to push Samara far from Micah's mind.

Lately Micah slept in his own room, rather than coming to look at picture books with her. Zana didn't even want to imagine why. The idea of it was enough to turn her stomach. Yes, Micah was of age, but she didn't need the constant reminder. *At some point, Nicholas will be too...* She shook the thought from her head and picked up her comb. *Ew. Nope.* It was hard to picture either of her brother's giving shy, longing glances at their mates. They couldn't even grow facial hair yet.

Zana ran the comb through her hair, parting it as she listened to Micah and Tiani giggling in the hall. *He knows better.* She tried to shrug it off, but her ears twitched as the two started whispering. Her cheeks grew hot. "Micah!"

Her brother came into the room, shoving his hands into his pockets. "What's the matter?"

She spun around on her stool. "I can hear *everything* you're saying to her. At least go somewhere more private."

He blushed, nodding.

Zana took a look at his face. "What's going on?"

He shrugged. "I've been trying to find a way to get Nicholas back." *Despite all the distractions.* Zana raised her brow. "Any ideas?"

"Only one."

Zana sat up straight, eyeing him. She hadn't expected that.

Micah glanced out into the hall, lowering his voice. "The *Lilik Morin.*"

"What about them?"

"Tiani's set up a meeting with them tonight to see what they'd be willing to take in exchange for invading Tavern."

"*Yarya Danya Verjik*?" Zana let out a growl, getting to her feet. "If you ask them to shed blood, they'll ask you to do so in return. On top of that, going to war with Tavern means going to war with *all* humans. Think about Father."

"What about him? He enslaved our mother and forced her to marry him. Doesn't that bother you?"

"He loved her," she said meekly.

"Well, clearly she didn't feel the same way, otherwise she'd be here right now," Micah said firmly. "It's us or them. There's no in between Zana. You and Nicholas will always come first, no matter what. You're my family."

"Micah, we're in between..."

"Says who? What does being a *Valvenok* even offer us, huh? Had we not been Lord Wolfe's children, we'd be dead. Most mutts outside of Riversburg are drowned at birth. You know that."

"Why are you acting like this?"

"Because I want my brother back!" Micah turned from her, shoulders shrinking. "If it means I need to make a deal with the *Lilik Morin* then so be it."

"Fine… then I'm coming with you."

Micah eyed her.

She crossed her arms. "And instead of offering blood, offer them land. We may be mutts in their eyes, but we're also wolves. Where we're weak in terms of physical strength, we make up for in influence. Nyla taught me that."

There was a glint in her brother's eye. He smiled, holding out his hand. "I'll have Tiani finalize the meeting."

Zana shook it firmly. "Let's bring Nicholas home."

MICAH AND TIANI woke Zana after midnight, and together the three of them snuck out through the servant's entrance at the side of the house.

Zana noticed the way Tiani's eyes glimmered under the moonlight, a blue halo around her iris, the colour of hot flames. Nicholas' eyes were the same colour under the shade of night. Nyla said that vermin were born from the flame, while the humans came from the earth and so the humans were forced to make their own light to protect themselves from what lingered in the dark.

Micah took Zana by the hand, keeping her close, just as he did the first time they'd left their home as children with their mother. His eyes were black as the sky. It was difficult for him to navigate in the dark, which was why he had always hunted in the early mornings as the sun came up.

Zana struggled in the dark as well, but not as much as her older brother. She could rely on her ears, which were just as good at

Nicholas' or her grandmother's. As long as Micah held onto her, she could keep him safe.

Tiani looked back at them, flashing a toothy grin as she pointed at the small glowing lights dancing in the distance. "Looks like they've sent someone to meet us."

Micah's grip on his sister's hand tightened.

"*Hallet!*" a voice called in the dark. "*Vare Elde Tes?*"

"*Tiani, Ata* Lord Wolfe's *Yunenik Ata Maedkasho!*" Tiani held out her arm in front of Micah and Zana, looking around.

A figure moved toward them, a single pair of footsteps. Zana noted the lightness of each step until the vermin was in view, eyes burning into the blackness of night. He tilted his head, the purple thread braided intricately through his long black hair, slid past his shoulders. The vermin inched closer, stretching out his purple painted fingertips. "*Hiloven?*"

"*Nei. Valvenok.*"

The vermin nodded. "*Latu Serni Kesa?*"

Zana turned to her brother, then looked at Tiani.

"*Chonig.*"

A little? We speak Valdin fluently. Why is she lying? Zana met her brother's eyes, her heart racing as the vermin approached them.

"*Maedkasho,* girl... what is your name?"

"Suzanna."

The vermin smiled. "Suzanna. *Kimlich.* You were the vermin girl in Tavern."

She nodded slowly.

The vermin took her free hand and kissed it.

Zana's face grew hot as the vermin's eyes met hers. She studied the deep purple powder lining his bottom lashes. His face was small, and boyish like Nicholas'. *What's he doing out here by himself? Nicholas never wandered this far out alone at night.*

Micah squinted at the vermin. "What's your name?"

"Keirsi. Come, *Vedsoter* is waiting for you."

They followed Keirsi through the trees, to the glade near the caves where they used to play with Nicholas and the other children.

Part of the land was in the bog, but up by the caves, the earth was drier. Keirsi looked back at them, being sure to point out loose rocks or logs laying on the path, long black cape flowing behind him, as the winter wind blew through the trees.

Zana could hear the crackling of the fire as they approached, followed by a chorus of whispers. *They're talking about us.*

Once they reached the meeting point, Keirsi took a seat on the ground in front of an older vermin with long pointed ears, the tips decorated in purple paint. The other vermin watched carefully as Tiani curtsied, gesturing to Micah and Zana.

"I hear you want to make a deal with me," the older vermin said, scratching his long red beard.

Micah nodded. "We would like to ask the *Lilik Morin* to help us get our little brother out of Tavern."

"Tavern?" the old vermin said, baring his fangs. "Why would I send members of my pack to die for one child?"

"We're willing to give you something in return."

The group of vermin, young and old, looked to one another, mumbling in *Valdin*.

"What could *Hiloven* give us that we don't already have?"

Zana caught Keirsi rolling his eyes, waving a ring covered hand at the older vermin.

"*Vedsoter,* this land was theirs before ours. They're half-breeds, not humans. I'm sure they've thought of something that might be of interest."

"*Ha...* yes, the Wolfe children. I gave your pack the opportunity to join us, and your leaders refused." The older vermin stood and approached them. "Therefore, before we can make any deals with Wolfe's, we'll require blood."

Micah turned to his sister, then Tiani. "Blood?"

"Will you take land?" Zana met the older vermin's eyes.

"And whose land are you offering us?"

"Land that once belonged to our mother. It's outside of the bog and would be a great spot for building."

The older vermin nodded slowly. "We have no need for land at this time, nor do we wish to fight the humans. You'd have better luck approaching the *Mivos*. Blood, blood is what's important."

Micah and Zana looked at one another.

"By blood, I assume you mean for one of them to join your pack?" Tiani said, running a hand through her thick curls. "Or a token?"

Zana's ears twitched. She watched Keirsi, getting up onto his feet as the older vermin nodded.

The older vermin examined them. "Why have you not gone to your own pack with this?"

"We were separated. We don't know where they are," Micah said softly. "And the *Mivos* are too far. Ferine's on the other side of the country."

The older vermin shook his head. "Wolfe's with no pack. *Verjik. Nei.* I won't spare any of my blood for one of yours. Our numbers are low as it is with this fever going around."

"I'll go," Keirsi said, creeping around the older vermin and placing a hand on his back. "*Inrohai* Papa?"

"*Nei!* For all we know, the humans could be using these two as spies."

Zana removed her cloak, rolling up the sleeves of her dress to show the fading scars and bruises on her body. "*Elde Hiloven, Schlaryend Matya Kalo, Matya Halya Ata Arkan.*" She growled out her words, exposing her fangs. "*Serni Hoten Matya Brani. Serni Yarya Feiv!*"

The vermin stared at her, listening to the fire crackle away as she drew in a deep breath, trying to compose herself.

Keirsi knelt at her feet and turned to the older vermin. "What if we spoke with one of the packs in Lupinus?"

"For one child?" The older vermin threw up his hands. The purple tips of his fingers turned upward toward the night sky. "The last time a group of vermin went into Tavern they were captured and burned alive. Or did you forget what happened to your mother?"

Keirsi wrung his hands together slowly, the flicker of the flames dancing in his eyes. "More reason for me to go."

The older vermin shook his head, stomping away from the group toward the woods. "*Bloka!*"

Keirsi stood face to face with Zana, taking her hand, examining the bruises along her arm. "Do you know where they're keeping your brother?"

She nodded. "He's being kept by a man named Roland Crispin."

Keirsi pulled back as the older vermin spun toward them.

"Crispin?"

"*Ha...*"

The vermin began murmuring amongst themselves again, exchanging looks.

"We'll need to discuss this further," the older vermin said gently. "Tiani, take them home. Keirsi, come."

Tiani nodded, picking Zana's cloak up off the ground and ushering her and Micah away from the pack.

"That didn't go as planned," Micah mumbled as Tiani handed the cloak over to Zana. "Perhaps we would have a better chance talking to the *Mivos?*"

Zana shook her head, putting her cloak back on before reaching for her brother's hand.

"Tiani, do you have any ideas?"

She linked her arm in Micah's. "I'll go back later and speak with them."

"Can you get us in touch with a member of the *Mivos* pack... or possibly the *Glamend Varot* Tusin?" He let go of his sister's hand.

Zana eyed him. "Tusin's no where near Tavern. If you're going to try reaching out to other vermin for help, you should try somewhere like Riversburg or Murienne."

Micah glared at her. "They don't have the numbers."

"But–"

"If it comes down to it, we'd be better off using a unified group, not a bunch of small, scattered packs like ours."

Zana shook her head, walking ahead of him. "We don't need to invade Tavern. We just need one or two vermin to go to the Crispin house and get our brother, *Danya Bloka!*"

Tiani reached out to her. "Lady Suzanna, please wait!"

"*Stai!*"

"Zana!"

Zana raced through the dark, blind, her ears picking up the light footsteps behind her. *Not Micah's.* Her older brothers were heavier, clunkier. These steps were like Nicholas', quiet and quick. Quicker than hers. She spun on her heels, her dress and cloak swirling around like maple seeds floating to the ground. She jerked her hand back as Keirsi latched onto her and pulled her close. Her heart racing.

"Doher Latu Danya Rebit?"

She met his gaze, the glow from his eyes on her face under the moonlight. "I... I live at Lord Wolfe's manor."

"On the hill."

She nodded.

He took her hand, opening up her palm. "I'll come find you tomorrow. Please tell your brother not to try and make a deal with the *Mivos*. They want war and don't care if you're half-vermin. If they smell any *Hiloven* on you, they'll kill you." He placed something soft in her hand.

She looked at it, holding it up under the moonlight. "A doll?"

Keirsi smiled, stepping away from her as she examined the tiny purple rag doll with yellow hair. *"Zat Danya. Vui Ayen Daknov Chonig Schistra.* She'll keep you safe."

Zana eyed the boy. "Thank you."

Keirsi nodded, turning toward the trees. *"Nelich Norch,* Suzanna."

She waved. *My little sister, huh?* She brushed the doll's yarn hair. *Okay. Until I get my brother back.*

21

Nicholas made a makeshift fort out of the pillows and blankets in the library, beneath the table that sat between two of the larger bookshelves. At night, the library was dark, and it creaked and groaned along with the rest of the house. He'd never noticed it before, but there was a large window in the room, and from it the moon peered into the house. He couldn't remember the last time he just stared up at the night sky, admiring the stars, trying to recall their names.

When they were little, Micah had told him and Zana that every star had a name and a story, just like every flower in the forest. They didn't know the names of each star, so they made up their own.

Bolkiss Brani, Chonig Brani, Chonig Schistra.

Micah, Nicholas and Zana, all lined up in a row. He always managed to find the three stars side by side.

Looking at them, Nicholas' chest tightened. He crawled into his fort, bringing a picture book with him, and began flipping through it, reading aloud to himself the best he could.

"See the..." He traced the words with his index finger. "B-Big red apple tree. My cat–" Nicholas held his breath, ears perking up at the sound of footsteps on the stairs. He hoped his fort was hidden well enough that no one would notice. The Crispin children were always making forts up in the library. It wouldn't be too strange seeing one in there. His heart raced.

The door opened.

Nicholas could see the dim light from the lantern waving about the room.

"Hello?"

He peeled back one of the blankets, spying out at Rose as she laid a silver tray down on the floor. His stomach grumbled.

Rose shut the door and put the lantern on the coffee table before going back to grab the tray. "I brought you something to eat."

Nicholas crawled out from his hiding place, causing her to stumble back.

She glared at him. "You startled me."

"Sorry..."

She inspected his fort. "May I join you?"

He nodded, going back inside and moving the pillows around to make room for her.

Rose pushed the tray inside, then crept in. "Lovely place you've got here. Very nice use of blankets." She grinned, a small giggle escaped her lips.

Nicholas glanced away from her.

She removed the lid from the tray, revealing the array of things she brought. "I made you a ham sandwich, an brought some chocolate chip cookies and since you didn't have breakfast... or well... anything to eat. I brought what was left of the chicken and potatoes, too."

"Thank you." He could feel her eyes on him as he reached for the sandwich.

"I'm sorry I screamed at you before."

He watched her fiddle with the white ribbon on her pink baby doll nightgown.

"I... all I saw was the blood. I'm sorry."

"It's okay."

She shook her head. "I should've came to see you hours ago. I must've hurt your feelings. I just... I did an awful thing and assumed you hurt my uncle when instead you saved him."

"I just carried him down a hill."

"And fought a wolf," she said. "Miss Warren told me. I feel really bad, so I wanted to pinky promise that I'd never, ever assume something that awful about you again." She held out her pinky.

He furrowed his brow.

She gave a huff, taking the sandwich out of his hand, and rearranged his fingers to match hers. "When you pinky swear, you lock your pinky with someone else's, and make a promise." She wrapped her pinky around his. "So, I pinky promise to never judge you like I did today, and to always be your friend."

"Do you really want to be my friend?"

She nodded, plopping the sandwich back into his hand. "You're the only kid I know who isn't too scared to come over and play... well, other than Thompson."

"That's because I have to be here."

Her cheeks flushed. "Y-you're teasing me, aren't you?"

Nicholas smiled, taking a bite of the sandwich.

"Apparently Caspian told Mr. Gray that my uncle's a drunk, even though he's not. Well... he was, but not anymore."

Nicholas swallowed what was in his mouth, then turned to her. "Why'd he do that?"

"Because he was going to blab about you, but instead said my uncle had bottles and things in his room."

"He does."

Rose eyed him.

"Your uncle does have bottles of spirits in his room," he said before taking another big bite out of the sandwich. He watched Rose's downcast eyes.

"Oh..."

He nudged her gently with his elbow and held up a cookie.

She took it, twisting it around between her fingers. "When my parents were alive, my uncle was a bit of a degenerate... that's my aunt Viola's word for him, anyway. Mama said he was always getting into trouble, but it was little things like singing too loudly while walking home from the pub or being obnoxious. Uncle Roland used to be really silly, and he'd tell me these crazy stories and used to make these weird-looking cookies, which made Tabby really angry." She smiled, looking at Nicholas. "I didn't know anything was wrong with him... Uncle Roland's always been good at keeping secrets from me."

Nicholas handed her another cookie, despite her barely having touched the first.

"Caspian's right... I'm a horrible big sister." Her eyes filled with tears. She wiped them away with the back of her hand, sniffling. "I should've been the one to find that out. Not him. He's just a kid."

"You're both kids."

"But I'm the oldest."

"So what?" Nicholas lifted the blanket up and pointed to the window. "See those three stars there? They're two brothers and their sister. They're all in a line because they look after each other, even if one is bigger than the others."

"I thought those were a belt?" she said, taking a bite of one of the cookies.

Nicholas scratched his head. "Yeah, I'm not sure what you humans call things, but I could've sworn those were called stars."

A big grin spread across her face. "No, not the stars. Never mind. I like your story better, anyway."

Nicholas smiled at her.

"Thanks for always listening to me. I know I talk too much sometimes," she said. "If you want, you could tell me things too. Even if you want to say them in vermin."

"I don't really know what to talk about."

"Anything you want." She tucked her legs under her, popping the rest of the cookie into her mouth.

Nicholas sat for a moment, chewing the last bit of his ham sandwich. "How do you say this word?" He slid the picture book in front of her.

Rose looked down, tilting her head. "Sally?"

"Sally. Hm."

"It's the name of the girl, and the cat's name is Fluffy."

"What kind of name is that?"

"Sally or Fluffy?"

"Fluffy," he said, shaking his head. "I've been calling it Flantony."

"Flantony? What did you call the girl?"

"Slayden."

Rose laughed. "You're ridiculous."

"I can't read."

"You had me fooled."

"Can you tell me what happens? All I know is Slayden's cat is stuck in the apple tree," Nicholas said, grabbing a piece of chicken.

"Her name is *Sally*. Hey, don't you want a cookie?"

"*Iya Lieken Yurna.*"

"What does that mean?"

"I like beef..."

Rose stared at him. "That's a chicken."

"Yeah... I know. I was pretending it was beef, though."

She wrinkled her brow and gestured to the tray. "Have a cookie, dear. You're sounding a bit mad."

He picked one up and popped it into his mouth.

"Your table manners are worse than my uncles."

"He's the one who's been teaching me."

Rose laughed, clapping her hands together. "Wow! Yeah, that makes perfect sense."

Nicholas' ears twitched. He held his finger to his lip.

Rose slammed her hands over her mouth. "Stay in here. I'll pretend I was up here alone." She crawled out of the fort and went over to the bookshelf by the coffee table, grabbing a handful of brightly coloured books with illustrations on the covers. She sat on the couch, kicking her legs up as she giggled, flipping through them.

Nicholas hid himself away, listening to the doorknob rattle. He recognized the familiar sigh immediately.

"What are you doing up at this hour? You'll wake the whole house."

"I was reading comic books," Rose said.

"Comic books?"

Nicholas' heart sank. *How many types of books are there?*

"I haven't read a comic book since... it must've been the last year of high school," Roland said.

Nicholas listened to Roland's footsteps. *He doesn't sound sick.*

"What are you doing up? Shouldn't you be resting?".

Roland shuffled his feet. "I heard noises upstairs and... I don't know I thought I heard Laurie."

"You were asking for Papa all morning, that's why."

"Was I?"

"You also said there was a vermin in the woods."

Roland cleared his throat. "I-I did?"

"And Caspian told everyone you're a drunk."

"Wait... what?"

"He found the bottles in your room, Roland," Rose snapped.

Nicholas peered out through a little crack between the blankets.

Roland sighed, rubbing the back of his neck. "I don't drink anymore."

Rose glared at him.

"Those bottles are for medicine, that's all."

"Medicine?"

He nodded.

"Is that what that valerian stuff was?"

Roland sat down beside her. "To tell you the truth, I haven't really been taking my medication..."

Rose crossed her arms. "No wonder you passed out."

"It... it doesn't prevent that from happening. Most of the medication Dr. Gray gives me is for my headaches, and those... well, they've been worse, that's all. I wasn't intoxicated when I went for a walk this morning. I just fainted."

Nicholas watched Rose study him carefully.

"I don't think we should go to the luncheon tomorrow," she said. She groaned. "You forgot, didn't you? The Doren's party."

"Right... sorry. I still don't feel quite like myself."

"Exactly. You should go back to bed and rest."

Roland nodded slowly. "Try not to stay up too late, okay? And keep it down, would you? People are trying to sleep."

Rose opened up the comic book, smiling at him. "Okay."

"Goodnight," he said, heading for the door.

"Night. Love you!"

Once he was gone, Rose snatched the comics and hurried back to the fort.

"That was a close one."

Nicholas nodded.

"Did you eat that entire chicken while he was here?"

He blushed. "*Ha...*"

"My goodness," she whispered. "I should have you enter in the Tavern pie-eating contest. You'd win first place for sure."

22

Dr. Gray took Roland's temperature early in the morning, then gave him a glass of water and a handful of pills. "Here."

Roland popped them into his mouth and swallowed.

"Did you not think it might be wise to ask what they were for?"

"I trust you."

Dr. Gray shook his head. "Tabitha, how do you deal with the boy?"

Tabitha sat up in the chair, her face tired. "As long as he's eating, I know he's healthy."

Dr. Gray gave her a smile, which faded quickly as he shot Roland a menacing glare. "You should go to the hospital and see a neurologist."

Roland frowned. "Didn't we already try that twice?"

"And make an appointment with the phycologist as well."

Roland sighed, taking a sip of water.

"Looking at the state of things here, it's very plain to me that you're not taking care of yourself. On top of that, you're drinking habits–"

"I don't drink anymore. I swear."

Tabitha gave a huff. "Really? What's this bottle of spirits doing here, then?"

"I gave a little to Nicholas while he was sick. It helps me sleep."

"You've got medication to help you sleep!" Dr. Gray slammed his hand down onto the nightstand, curling his fingers into a fist. He inhaled sharply, then pushed up his glasses. "How many times must we go over this? If the medication I prescribe isn't helping, we will try something else."

Roland rubbed the back of his neck. "Truthfully, I haven't given the valerian much of a chance."

"I've noticed."

Roland glanced over at Tabitha. *She looks more devastated than disappointed.*

"The fact that Caspian was aware of this is what I find most upsetting. It was your actions that sent your mother to the asylum. You promised that if the children were under your care, you would clean yourself up."

"Mama's not there because of me," Roland whispered, bowing his head.

Tabitha rose from her seat, gripping the skirt of her dress. "You pushed her down the bloody stairs, Roland!"

Dr. Gray went to her, placing a hand on hers.

"I've been protecting you, keeping your secrets, lying for you... for... for as long as you've been alive!" she cried. "And I am tired of it. I have children of my own. My boys grew up without their mother because of you. Because my husband and I didn't have the luxury to deny a job offer from the Crispin's. And all you've ever been is reckless! You don't give a hoot about how much other people have sacrificed for *you*. Look at Peter, for goodness' sake!"

Roland eyed her.

Dr. Gray nodded slowly as Tabitha's eyes welled with tears.

"He transferred schools because Vincent and Charlotte asked him to come back after your brother died. He was thriving in Luciole! He'd probably be teaching at the high school had he not been tied up in your nonsense... and don't even get me started on poor Vincent, how you nearly sabotaged his chances of making officer."

"I didn't make them–"

"You didn't have to. You pull people in and you infect them. How you even managed to lure that girl back into your life is beyond me! She was better off in Riversburg. You were never the victim in that situation. You tortured that poor thing endlessly."

"She abandoned me."

"Good!" Tabitha threw her arms above her head. "Perhaps you should think long and hard about why."

Roland held his breath, hands shaking as he tried to steady the glass. "I... Tabby I didn't–"

"Miss Warren may have broken your heart, but she did you a favour by leaving. I wish I'd seen it before, but you clouded my judgement. You're not a child anymore. Evan and I can't keep treating you like a child."

"I just wanted to–"

"And what on earth were you doing with Charlotte, robbing the bank?"

"No, we were... she..." Roland placed his head in his hands.

"What then? What could you have possibly wanted to meet up with that girl for?" Tabitha wrang her hands together. "Or is that another secret I have to keep on your behalf to spare poor Peter any heartache?"

Dr. Gray removed his glasses, cleaning them with the bottom of his sweater. "Perhaps I can set up an appointment with Dr. Kohli?"

"I don't need to see Dr. Kohli. There's nothing wrong with me."

"Nothing wrong with you?"

Roland gazed up at Tabitha.

"You're just as bad as your mother... constant denial. Your father and brother were murdered! Your mother had a complete breakdown, and... and you're keeping that *thing* in the nursery."

"It's either Dr. Kohli, or I speak with one of the neurologists at the hospital," Dr. Gray said softly. "I'll get Charlie involved if I have to."

Roland shook his head. "Don't. I'm fine. It was all the blood... it made me dizzy. I'm fine."

"And before that, when you collapsed at Doren Shipping?"

"I wasn't well... but yesterday it... I–"

Tabitha crossed her arms. "Let me tell you what I think happened. The night before last, you decided that since you'd had a rough time that it'd be fine if you went off and had a couple of drinks. Then you recklessly drove yourself home, which personally I don't think you should be driving at all, given your state. And please, don't try to lie to me. I know you were drinking. I could smell it on you, and there were stains all over your jacket."

Roland glared at her. "The stains on my jacket were from coffee, and yes, I did have a bad day, but I didn't drink anything. I'm not an idiot."

"Stop lying to me."

"Ask Charlotte then. Go on!"

There was a knock on the door.

"Um... Uncle Roland?" Julius entered the room, sheepishly.

"Not now!" Tabitha massaged her temples. "Whatever it is, go to Lisa."

Julius opened the door, peering inside.

"Julius, please," Roland said gently.

"There's someone here to see you."

Roland climbed out of bed. "Who?"

Julius looked around the room, stepping back into the hallway. "Um... Detective... Detective uh–"

The adults groaned in unison. "Detective Carson."

Julius nodded.

Dr. Gray tilted his head. "Are you sure he's not here for Vincent?"

Julius nodded again. "He wants to see Uncle Roland."

"Go on then, get it over with," Tabitha muttered. "Martin, would you please make a list of what it is Roland needs to be taking and when. I'll be sure everyone in the house knows. Obviously, he's incapable of managing this himself."

Dr. Gray nodded. "I'll get you Dr. Kohli's number as well."

"Thank you."

Roland glared at them, heading toward the door.

"You're not going to make yourself presentable?" Tabitha grabbed him by the back of his blue pyjama shirt.

Roland shot her a dirty look. "Don't touch me."

She pulled her hand back.

"Where's the detective?" He guided Julius out toward the stairs.

"Having hot chocolate with Mr. Gray in the parlour. Alicia and I made it for them by ourselves. Want one?"

"That would be lovely, thank you."

Julius tugged on Roland's sleeve. "Why was Tabby so upset with you?"

Roland winced. "A lot of reasons."

"I never, ever heard her yell for so long," Julius said, bewilderment in his eyes.

"I have," Roland said quietly as they went downstairs.

Vincent waved him over as he entered the parlour.

Detective Carson glared at him. "Were you with a young woman named Charlotte the other night? Lennox Keating's wife."

Roland nodded.

"Could you tell me where and when?"

"I think I ran into her around five o'clock on Friday." He scratched his head. *Charlotte Keating. Was that her name now?* "I saw her on my drive back from the asylum and gave her a lift into town."

"And then?"

"Did... did something happen to her?" Roland turned to Vincent.

"Answer the question, please," Detective Carson said firmly.

"We went to the hotel," Roland said.

Vincent's jaw dropped as he fumbled with the mug in his hands.

"And how long were you there?"

"We sat and talked in the lounge. We never checked in. I bought her a few drinks at the bar, and I think I left at around seven-thirty."

"If I were to question the staff of your whereabouts, would they corroborate your story?" The detective pulled out his notebook, scribbled inside it.

Roland nodded.

"I'm also going to assume this is the Taylor's hotel, correct?" he said through a tight-lipped smile.

"Yes, the one here in West Tavern."

"The one owned by Eloise Taylor-Hood?"

Roland nodded again.

"Wonderful. As per usual, the staff will confirm your presence. It wouldn't be the first time they lied for you," Detective Carson said sullenly.

"I *was* there."

The detective raised a brow. "I just find it so convenient that every time I come to question you, you're suddenly sick with some sort of make-believe illness."

Vincent leaned forward. "Not to overstep, but my father has copies of Roland's medical records. I'm sure if you were to ask, he'd give them to you."

"I've already seen the records." Detective Carson took a swig of his hot chocolate, glancing at Julius, then placed the mug down on the table. "Luckily for you, your story matches up perfectly with our witnesses."

"What's happened? Is Charlotte all right?" Roland grabbed hold of Julius to steady himself. *I never should've left her alone.*

"Did her behaviour come across as odd to you in any way?"

Roland thought back to Friday evening, how he'd seen Charlotte walking aimlessly in the middle of the street without a coat. He'd nearly run her over with the car. If she'd not been in that bright red sweater, he may never have spotted her out in the blizzard. He'd pulled over and gotten out of the car, grabbing her.

"Roland?" She'd stared at him a long while as he led her toward the vehicle. She seemed lost, like his mother often did. There was nothing usual about her behaviour at all.

He gave her his jacket in the car and asked where she was heading, noticing how the red polish on her fingernails was chipped. Her hair was a windblown mess. Mascara smudged under her dark lashes. She was trembling and staring at him with those big brown eyes unblinking, as if she'd seen a ghost.

"Sorry for nearly running you over. I honestly didn't see you." As he drove, Roland contemplated taking her home, but with Nicholas around, he decided it would be best to offer to take her some place else.

"You should've called to tell me you were visiting," he said. "Are you staying with Constance or Juliet?"

"My husband."

"Right, you got married." He tapped the steering wheel, squinting to see through the heavy snow. "What are you doing all the way out here without a coat? Did your car breakdown?"

Charlotte reached for his arm, fingers trembling. "I-I... Roland about Augen."

"You're shaking like a leaf. Are you okay?"

She didn't answer.

An uneasy feeling had swelled in Roland's gut. *She seems scared.* "Charlotte, is everything okay?" He watched her, waiting for a response as they entered the downtown area.

"Let's go to the library," she said, pointing toward the snow-covered steps.

"It's already closed."

"Do you still have that room at the hotel?" Her voice was steady now.

Roland scanned her. "I haven't been there in a long time, but we can go to the lounge if you'd like."

And they did. Charlotte nursed one drink after the other, staring into her glass until it had emptied. Roland offered to get her a coffee, but she refused.

"I need something stronger."

It wasn't uncommon for Charlotte to have a few drinks. He'd seen her drunk maybe once or twice. She didn't seem drunk. She didn't seem real. Perhaps after not seeing her for all those years, he'd forgotten what she was really like? Maybe his memories had morphed into a fictionalized version of her? Then again, anyone who knew her would've found her behaviour out of the ordinary. Charlotte was always well put together, and it wasn't like her to be so quiet. So distant.

Detective Carson waved his pen around as Roland hunched over.

"When I picked her up, she seemed scared," Roland said finally, coming back to the present. "Even when I left her at the hotel, she didn't seem... it was like she'd..."

"Could you describe to me how she appeared? Something she said?"

"She didn't really say much. She mentioned her husband briefly, and Augen. The last time I saw her was when she boarded the train to Augen and that was years ago. I don't know what else to tell you other than that she just didn't seem like herself."

The detective got up off the couch, tucking his notebook into the inside of his jacket. "Thank you for your time, Mr. Crispin."

Roland grabbed him, his voice rising in his throat. "What happened to her?"

Detective Carson gently removed his hand, meeting his gaze. "I'm not obligated to say anything at this time."

Roland's heart raced, chest squeezing. He blinked hard.

"Thank you for the hot chocolate," the detective said, directing his attention to Julius.

"You're welcome," Julius whispered, clinging to his uncle's leg. He gazed up at Roland, then looked at Vincent.

Vincent stood up, following the detective to the door.

Roland pulled at the collar of his shirt, swallowing the tightness in his throat. *I shouldn't have left her alone.* He hurried toward the stairs, Julius chasing after him.

"What was that about?" Tabitha peered downfrom the top of the stairs. Dianna poked her head over the railing, unbraiding her hair.

23

———————

I t seemed like a poor day for a party, and to Rose, it seemed like
the dreariest Sunday of her entire life.

She never truly understood her family's relationship to the
Doren's outside of the fact that they worked together. She found them
overly flashy, as if they were constantly trying to remind the citizens
of Tavern of their superior eminence. A live band for a luncheon was
a bit much and to top it off the excessively large dining room was
decorated in an array of reds and golds, fancy tiered trays lined the
table, everything perfectly polished and pressed, each dish exquisite,
laid out in a way that exuded an almost unattainable excellence. To
top it off, the older Mrs. Doren wouldn't stop bragging about getting
the best and latest from Presa, flitting about the room in her new
ruffled lavender ballgown.

What's the big deal with Presa, anyway? Rose crossed her arms,
slouching. Her mother's stuck up snob of an aunt lived there, so it
couldn't possibly be as remarkable as others made it out to be. She
wanted so badly to roll her eyes at the woman, but knew it was best to
put on a pretty smile. She couldn't risk embarrassing her uncle, who
seemed completely out of sorts, and had wandered off with Miss

Warren as soon as they arrived, leaving her and her brothers unsupervised. *He should've stayed home.*

Julius managed to get the attention of Miles Doren Sr., chatting away as he always did. It paid to be the youngest. Julius had always been better behaved than Caspian, who looked as bored as his sister felt.

Rose thought about scolding him for sulking, but the two hadn't spoken since the other morning. She knew her brother well enough to know when to back off.

Rose caught a glimpse of Peter Rissing waltzing into the room, wearing a fine black suit and bowtie, shoes sparkling with fresh polish. Her eyes widened. *He actually looks like a gentleman.* She went up to him, examining him carefully. *He's much better at putting himself together than Uncle Roland.*

"Well, hello young lady. I haven't seen you in a few days," he said, smiling at her. "How've things been while I was away?"

She tugged lightly on her ribbon, rocking back and forth, studying the bandage wrapped around the fleshy part of his palm and thumb. "How's your hand?"

"It doesn't hurt as much anymore."

"That's a relief."

"What's with Caspian?"

"Things have been really, really bad..." Rose whispered. "Worse than the time you babysat us, and Julius peed all over you and then you almost set the house on fire. You know, before Lisa came to live with us."

Peter knelt to her height, blushing. "You and Caspian swore to never speak of that again."

"Exactly. But that's how bad it is... it's worse than that. Worse even then when you and Uncle Roland mistook that skunk for a cat and–"

"I understand. Where is your uncle, anyway?"

"Probably looking for some place to hide or wherever the food is. I lost track of him and Miss Warren a while ago."

Peter looked around. "There's food everywhere. It's a luncheon."

"Must be hiding then." Rose clapped her hands together as a group of girls approached, led by Sofia Muller, in her green tulle gown. She latched onto Peter. "Don't leave me alone with these people."

He stood up straight, eyeing the five girls.

Sofia looked Rose up and down. "What a pretty dress. Don't you think it's pretty?" she said, turning to the other girls, who nodded quickly, smiling.

Delores scowled. "I tried to get my parents to buy me a new dress for the party, but they made me wear my old one from the Frost Festival."

"Well, not all of us have wealthy uncles," Sofia said, smiling. The tone of her voice was so sickeningly sweet, Rose wanted to vomit. Sofia batted her lashes like she often did at school around Thompson. "Why, your uncle gave Kiyomi and I these gorgeous bracelets."

Rose looked at Sofia's wrist, then at Kiyomi's, knitting her brow as she studied the matching turquoise bracelets. *Those are pretty... wait a second–* She placed her hands on her hips. "*My* uncle gave you those?"

The girls nodded, grinning from ear to ear.

"We wanted to thank him," Kiyomi said, blushing as she looked down at her yellow heels.

"Kiyomi thinks he's handsome," Delores said, shrugging. "Not sure what's so handsome about a murderer, but hey, whatever floats your boat."

Rose's skin boiled.

Peter took her by the hand and smiled. "Young Miss, I believe Mr. Doren would like a word with you."

Rose smiled. "Oh, right. I'll see you girls later."

"Bye Rose," the girls said, smiling and waving.

As Peter led her away from the group, Rose let out an exasperated gasp.

"I absolutely hate those–"

"Have you ever tried giving one of them a good ol' punch in the nose? Always worked for me," Peter said, lowering his voice.

"Trust me, I'd love nothing more. Sofia and Kiyomi aren't even in my class. They're in Thompson's."

"You should make up some story about them, so they're never invited to one of Mrs. Doren's parties again. Their mothers will be furious. These parties are big for girls at their age. It allows them to meet respectable husbands."

"That'd be mean. I don't want to get them in trouble."

"Wow, you're way nicer than I am. I got four kids banned when I was even younger than you."

Rose glared at him. "How could you?"

He stuck out his tongue. "I was only joking. Relax. I'm not that cruel."

She squinted, looked him up and down.

"What?"

"I almost thought you'd act more grown up, wearing something like that, but you're exactly the same. I'm a little disappointed."

Peter laughed, waving Miles Jr. over.

"Hello Peter, Rose." Miles rolled his eyes, stirring the olive around in his martini. "Peter, how much could I pay you to kill me?"

Rose's jaw hung open. She closed it promptly, checking to see if anyone had overheard.

Peter raised his brow. "What's wrong?"

Miles groaned. "My grandfather's trying to set me up with Nanette."

Peter cleared his throat.

Rose looked around. "Who?"

"The pretty girl, over there next to my mother in the pink gown."

"What's wrong with her?" Rose examined the woman's elegant posture and glowing smile.

"She's impossibly boring," Miles said.

Peter nodded. "But a good kisser."

The two men exchanged a look, then looked down at Rose, who was scowling at them.

"That was highly inappropriate," she said, hands on her hips.

Peter pat her on the head. "Where's your uncle?"

"I saw Rolly boy with your pretty cousin." Miles snickered. "It looked to me like he was making a complete idiot of himself."

Peter's nostrils flared.

"What?"

"You're not Miss Warren's type," Rose said, fixing the white gloves on her hands.

Miles leaned forward. "Oh, yeah, says who?"

"If she finds my uncle irritating, she'd absolutely despise you."

"Wanna bet?"

"No," Peter said, stepping between them. "Miles, children can't gamble. Don't be irresponsible."

"I'll give you fifty-dollars if she refuses a dance with me," Miles said.

Rose scoffed, waving him off with her hand. "Please, do I look like a child? I want at least seventy-five."

"Sixty and I'll sneak you and your brother's extra pudding."

She thought a moment, pretending to stroke an imaginary beard. The men laughed.

"Okay. You have a deal. And if she does dance with you, then I'll direct that Nanette girl to a more suitable gentleman."

Miles laughed, slapping Peter on the back. "This is why she's my favourite Crispin."

Peter chuckled, shoving his hands into his pant pockets. "I'd wish you luck, but it'd be cruel to get your hopes up."

Miles handed Peter his drink, strutting to the other end of the room.

Peter shook his head, putting the glass on the table.

"Tell me, what are my chances of winning?" Rose got up on her tippytoes, neck stretching to see past the guests crowded around the table chatting.

"This could go one of three ways. Dianna says yes, and you lose. Dianna says no, and you win, or my personal favourite, Miles and Roland duke it out, which neither of you factored in as a possibility, but me knowing better, being that I'm older and wiser, and not an idiot or a thirteen-year-old knows from my many trips around the sun, that this in fact, will be the result, as it always is when it comes to Miles and Roland vying for dominance."

"What?"

"Just watch," Peter said.

Rose shaded her eyes with her hand, as if looking out over a great distance. Her eyes fell on Dianna in her slim, green tube dress with the Bardot neckline. Then she spied her uncle in his dark pinstriped suit, leaning up against the wall, staring up at the ceiling while his godfather chatted away.

Miles came up behind Dianna, placing a gentle hand on her shoulder.

To Rose, it looked as though his hand was hovering, barely touching her at all. Butterflies fluttered around her stomach while she watched Dianna give him her attention. *She's smiling.* Rose surveyed her uncle, eyes growing wide as he stepped away from the wall, arms folded across his chest.

"And now, the idiots will fight and get a scolding from Mrs. Doren," Peter said, nonchalantly. "Happens every time."

Rose scrunched up her nose as Caspian came over.

"What are you doing?"

"Trying to drain Miles's wallet," she said, spinning him around in the direction of their uncle. "Or at least see something interesting."

They watched Miles take a step toward Roland, who was combing a hand through his hair.

Dianna took Miles by the hand, nodding.

Rose groaned. "I wish I could read lips."

"Or had vermin ears," Caspian whispered, looking up at her.

She nodded. "You're right. That'd be highly useful in these types of situations."

Peter's jaw dropped. "Is... is he just letting him take her away?"

The children nodded slowly as Dianna and Miles walked hand in hand, joining the others on the dance floor.

"This is completely unacceptable. I refuse to believe it." Peter said, throwing his hands above his head.

The Crispin children shrugged.

Rose looked over at her uncle, who was looking longingly at Miles and Dianna. A lump grew in her throat. "I'll be right back."

Peter and Caspian nodded.

She pushed through a group of older girls, squeezing between them. "Excuse me. Sorry!" He stepped out in front of her uncle as he turned toward the exit.

He frowned. "Oh, there you are."

"Do you want to dance with me?"

He raised his brow. "Wouldn't you rather dance with Thompson?"

"I haven't seen him yet."

Roland gave her a smile and held out his hand. "I'll help you look for him."

She crossed her arms and pouted.

"What did I say?"

She turned up her nose.

"Flower... w-what did... never mind. Fine, I'll dance with you."

She smiled, grabbing both his hands and dragging him to the dance floor next to Miles and Dianna.

Roland put a hand on her shoulder and held up her other hand, keeping his eyes off the pair beside them.

"I meant to ask. These girls from school said you bought them bracelets... which seemed a bit odd."

Roland cocked his head, twirling her around his finger. "Why would I buy bracelets for a bunch of girls at your school?"

"Exactly. I knew Sofia was lying," Rose said, shaking her head.

"Sofia? Oh..."

Rose glared at him.

"There were these two little girls who came and thanked me for giving them money the other day."

"You *gave* them money?"

He blushed. "It's not a very interesting story."

She groaned.

"Did I do something wrong?"

"They always talk bad about you at school, and now they're acting like you're *so* special because you had to go and give them free stuff like an idiot."

"Roland is special. Isn't that right, Rolly?" Miles said, leaning toward them.

Dianna froze in place, eyes wide. "G-G-Georgie… Georgie." She pointed at the band.

Roland swallowed so loud that Rose could hear the gulp go down his throat. She turned around to look at the man holding the microphone as the music picked up. She glanced back at her uncle, watching the smile spread across his face.

She tugged on his hand. "Who's that?"

"Georgie Bryce."

"That's Georgie Bryce?" Rose gave a loud whistle, then slammed her hands over her mouth. *How embarrassing!*

Roland laughed, throwing an arm around her. "We have this album at home."

She eyed him. *We do? This sounds nothing like what Uncle Roland played on the piano.* She jumped at the loudness of the man's voice, booming out into the crowd as the adults began racing to the dance floor. She noticed her uncle holding out his hand to her. She took it, letting him spin her out as he sang along.

Roland pulled her back beneath his arm.

Rose's heart raced. Her eyes widened as he picked her up by the waist and spun her around. She giggled. "Put me down, you're gonna break your back."

"I will not!" he scoffed, grabbing her hands and twirling her around.

Georgie Bryce's voice came ringing out into the room as the trumpets roared.

Poor little me didn't
Know what to do
Went peddling round

To my bicycle blues.

Rose spotted her little brothers attempting to bop. Julius mostly just jumping from left to right, occasionally throwing his hands up in the air and spinning around. Caspian, on the other hand, rocked his head back and forth to the music, while Peter stood there laughing.

Rose imagined herself a spinning top, the white skirt of her dress swirling around beneath her, a wide smile on her face as the music filled her from the tips of her toes all the way to the top of her head. Her curls bounced around, the black ribbons she tied at each end waving about like flags blowing in the wind. Her laughter echoed throughout every inch of her.

Her uncle chuckled as the song came to an end and pulled her in for a hug. "I told you I wouldn't break my back."

The guests applauded loudly.

Perhaps a live band wasn't as flashy as she'd initially thought. It was fun.

Georgie Bryce held up the microphone, his grin revealing the little dimples in his cheeks. "I'd like to thank Mr. Doren for inviting me. It's always nice coming back home and singing for you all." He gestured to the older Mr. Doren, Miles Sr. then handed him the mic.

"I'd like to let the band take a short break. I'm sure they're hungry." Georgie Bryce walked off the stage with the rest of the band, waving. "In the meantime, I'd like to invite Roland Crispin up here. He's going to treat us to an Alana Token song."

Rose held her breath, watching her uncle's face pale. "You are?"

"I... I guess."

Oh, no... She watched her little brothers rush toward the stage with Peter, then turned to Dianna and Miles. She could already hear the girls from school giggling as her uncle climbed up on stage. She shut her eyes, squeezing her hands together. *Please. Please. Please don't do anything embarrassing.*

Miles Sr. laughed. "I should add he hasn't played in a while."

She listened to the stool squeak as her uncle cleared his throat.

She opened one eye, heart thumping against her ribs as he placed his hands on the keys.

A coolness washed over her uncle as he opened his mouth.

> Tell the postman
> My letters taking too long
> Before I know it
> My baby'll be gone...

She opened her other eye, hands falling to her side. *Grandmother used to like this song.* Roland's voice was warm, bright. He didn't talk like that. He sang, sweetly.

> He's probably left
> For Ferine,
> Where he will
> Never be seen
> Again.

It was the first time in forever that she'd heard the little lilt in his voice. She glanced at her brothers.

Julius' mouth hung open wide as he listened.

"I think I'm in love."

Rose turned her head and, shooting Sofia a dirty look, watched her and the other girls swoon. She brought her attention back to her uncle as his voice sailed through the room.

"Such a waste." Dianna fiddling with the white pearls around her neck.

Rose furrowed her brow. *What's that supposed to mean?* She spun back toward her uncle as the song came to an end.

The guests were quiet.

Roland stood up, stumbling away from the piano as he cleared his throat. He opened his mouth, then shut it, pressing his lips together tightly as Mrs. Doren came running up onto the stage.

She squished his cheeks between her hands, smooching his face. "Thank goodness you sound nothing like your brother!"

Roland's eyes widened. "Uh... okay?"

"Again!" Julius shouted, clapping loudly.

"Would you?" Mrs. Doren said. "Please. Until Mr. Bryce is finished eating."

Roland backed away slowly, knocking into the piano. "I'm... I'm not–"

"Woo! Rolly boy!" Miles shouted.

Dianna smacked him on the back of the head.

"What, I'm trying to offer encouragement?" Miles pouted.

"I'm afraid I don't know many songs by heart," Roland said sheepishly, bowing his head.

Rose watched him shuffle his feet, shoving his hands into his pockets. *One's enough. He's not feeling well.* Rose started toward the stage as Mrs. Doren forced Roland back onto the stool. *He needs rescuing.* Her eyes widened as her uncle reached for the guitar. She followed his gaze. His blue eyes fell on Dianna.

"I know one more song," he said softly, breath being picked up by the microphone. He adjusted the capo, moving it down to the second fret. The air changed as he opened his mouth.

> Some boys are silly
> Some boys are charming
> Some boys are too much to bear.

Rose's heart sank in her chest, listening to the tone of his voice. The sweetness and warmth was gone.

> Some boys are gentle
> Some boys are sweet.
> Some boys just don't care.

Roland glared at Dianna with each word as if he were saying

them to her. His strumming grew heavier, the guitar louder as Dianna gripped her necklace.

> But wicked boys
> Wicked boys are so
> Cruel.

Dianna climbed up on stage, opening her mouth, forcing Roland to take the harmony above.

> Kiss you once,
> And then they leave you.

Mrs. Doren backed away from them.

"What just happened?" Rose turning to Miles.

"The song's a duet," he said, crossing his arms.

Rose's jaw dropped, listening to their voices blend together. Although Dianna's voice was weaker, it complimented Roland's.

The guests jumped as Roland slammed the guitar down on the stage. His left hand shaking. He cleared his throat as Dianna spun toward him. "E-excuse me..." He hurried off the stage, staggering toward the exit.

Dianna lifted her dress, chasing after him.

Mrs. Doren took the microphone. "Uh... well... that was um..."

Rose gritted her teeth, listening to the chatter around the room. *It can't end like this.* She marched up to the stage, sat at the piano, and began to play the song her uncle had taught her when she was little.

ROLAND STOOD IN THE HALLWAY, knees buckling as he gripped his left hand tightly in the other. The tips of his fingers burned. He hadn't played guitar since Julius was a baby. He'd forgotten how much pressure was needed to push down on each string. The tips of his fingers were bright red and raw, just as they had been when Lawrence gifted him the used old acoustic the summer before Roland entered school. He gasped for air, pressing his back up against the wall.

Dianna ran past him, then spun around, nearly tripping on her dress. She looked him up and down as she approached. "Are you all right?"

He managed a smile.

Dianna glanced out into the dining room, "Who's playing the–"

"Flower?" He peered into the room, out at the stage, where his niece sat at the grand piano playing, a very poorly timed version of the song from the music box Roland had given his mother.

Dianna held out her arm, allowing him to use her weight to steady himself. "She's..."

"Awful." He chuckled, a slight grin on his face.

"I wouldn't say that. Then again, I can't play any instruments."

"Why'd you come sing with me?"

"It's a duet. Remember, Charlotte and I used to sing it."

"And throw grass at Peter and I." He nodded. "I didn't forget."

"I thought you hated that song," she said softly.

His face grew hot. "I learned it for Charlotte after you went to Riversburg."

"You look a little pale. Do you need to sit down?"

"I'm fine." He winced as his niece played the wrong note. "I can't remember the rest of the words to this one."

Dianna shrugged. "Oh? I've never even heard it before."

Roland stood up straight, adjusting his cufflinks. "I think I've had enough fun for one day. Would you ask Georgie Bryce for an autograph? I'm going to head out."

"How are the rest of us going to get home if you take the car?" She followed him to the coatroom.

He pulled out his jacket. "I'm just going for a walk."

"No, you are not. You weren't even supposed to be dancing!"

He lowered his head. "I have a hard time saying no to my niece."

"She would've understood, given yesterday's events."

"It's fine. I wanted to."

"Did you now?" Dianna placed her hands on her hips. "Because when Nanette asked, you had no problem declining."

"I didn't want to dance with her," he muttered. He cleared his throat, running a hand through his hair as she stared at him.

"You should stay," Dianna said as he headed for the door.

He looked over his shoulder. "Why did you want to dance with me, Pigtails?"

She averted her eyes.

"That's what I thought."

24

———————

Zana's ears perked up as she wandered through the vast courtyard, amongst the lavish stone sculptures, herself cold and still as she stopped and listened. It had been her fourth time outside that day. More than once she mistook a bird, or one of the staff, for the vermin boy who'd promised to meet her.

There was a low whistle, followed by three quick, high-pitched ones.

Zana pushed hair back behind her ears, listening to the gentle footsteps approach. She turned her head as Keirsi positioned himself atop one of the sculptures and smiled, fangs glistening in the afternoon sun.

"*Hallet Maedkasho.*"

"*Hallet.*" She examined the purple markings under and around his eyes. They ran down along his cheeks like tears.

He propped his chin in his hands, head cocked, long black hair pulling to the left of his body. "*Nelich Rolossmok.*"

"It's not a castle," she said, feeling his eyes on her, adjusting her scarf.

"Do you know why the Crispin's took your brother?"

"For research, or at least that's what we were told."

"*Deisso.*"

"What?"

He wiggled his ears, scrunching up his face. "A long time ago, before The Burning, a Crispin came to Esque."

"Burning?"

He nodded. "You know *Hiloven*. We're made of fire, so they think burning us will help cleanse the earth of our blood."

Zana rubbed her shoulder, nodding slowly, as the winter wind picked up. It wasn't as cold as the winds in Tavern, but it pricked at her skin just the same. Her mind wandered to when she asked Vincent Gray why he hated vermin so much. The coldness of his expression had nearly numbed her. Nothing was colder than that look.

Keirsi gnawed on his knuckle, staring off.

Zana watched him carefully. "Were the Crispin's a part of the burning?"

"*Nei.* They were looking for a woman."

"How long ago was this?"

"Uh... *Tabet Trasat Jare's?*"

"Thirty years ago... do you know anything else about it?"

He nodded, fixing his gaze on her. "The woman was *Mivos.* She promised them something... or at least that's the rumour. After they left, the other *Hiloven* came and burned everything in sight."

The Crispin's definitely never mentioned a vermin woman, and that man, Roland, didn't look much older than Micah. Maybe they don't know anything. Maybe it was some other Crispin family or a distance relative or something. Zana's foot tapped rapidly with each new thought. She bit down on her tongue, wincing slightly. *Did we really abandon our little brother with a group of murderous Hiloven?*

"What is this creature? Some sort of bird-horse?"

Zana drew in a deep breath, looking up at him. "It's called a Pegasus."

"*Kiedunya,*" he whispered, patting its neck.

"Would you like to come inside?"

Keirsi tilted his head from side to side. "*Ha.*"

She waited for him to jump down off the Pegasus statue and lead him through the courtyard into the house.

Micah glanced in her direction briefly, then shot his head back around as Keirsi came through the large double doors. "Zana, *Danya Bloka!*"

Zana held up her hand, stopping her older brother as he ran toward them.

Micah bowed his head, shoving his hands into his pockets. "You're uh... the guy from the other night, huh?"

Keirsi grinned. "Keirsi."

Micah waved, then scratched the back of his head. "What brings you here?"

"I invited him," Zana said.

"Does Father know?"

She shook her head.

"Cousin Mordred's here again. Having a vermin around, looking like that, might set him off."

Zana smiled wryly. "What's wrong with how he looks?"

Micah raised his brow.

Keirsi stared up at the ceiling, squinting at the chandelier. "*Verjik Ata Blesein.*"

"*Ha.* It doesn't look bad when it's lit," Micah said, gesturing for them to follow him through the hall. "The leader of your pack. Is he your father?"

"*Vedsoter? Ha...* well, kind of. It's–"

"Complicated?"

Keirsi nodded, stopping to look at a painting on the wall.

Zana turned to her brother, watching him fidget with his earring. "Why's Mordred here?"

"I tried listening in, but you and Nicholas are much better at that than I am."

There was a pang in her chest. "Keirsi said not to make a deal with the *Mivos.*"

Micah held his breath.

Keirsi turned to them. "How difficult was it to get across the Tavern border?"

"Don't," Zana said firmly.

He cocked his head, staring at the siblings.

"We appreciate that you want to help, but the humans there aren't like the ones here in Dinara... and you're a full-blooded vermin like our brother. You won't survive."

Keirsi's ears twitched.

Micah jerked his head. "What is it?"

"Why are the *Hiloven* talking about *Musa Elde Mivos*?"

Zana eyed him. "Who?"

"The leader of their pack."

Zana glanced at her brother, then gestured for Keirsi to come close. "I'm not sure, but Micah's right. You don't want to have a run in with Mordred. Let's go to the sitting room. We'll be able to hear them better."

Keirsi grinned.

In the sitting room, the three sat in a circle on the floor, eyes shut, listening to the voices coming from the room next door. Zana winced at the nasal voice of Cousin Mordred. From this room, she knew it'd be easier for Micah to hear as well.

"These mongrels will stop at nothing," Mordred said. "Threatening to expand... they're coming for our family's land. *Our* land Theo! We're already struggling to handle those purple freaks. If we don't get this under control, Dinara will be lost. We'll have to leave."

"Purple freaks?" Keirsi whispered. "*Lilik Morin* aren't freaks... what's does freaks mean, anyway?"

Zana opened one eye. "Probably something like *Verjik.*"

"*Rubreilich...*"

"Mordred, your fear of vermin is making you act irrationally," Theodore said.

"Your love for them makes you irrational! Do you have any idea what you've done to this family? You've poisoned our bloodline. There is *no* greater sin. Even those vermin scum would never do that.

In the past, we would've disowned you and stripped you of your titles."

Zana dug her nails into her knees, holding her breath.

"You're talking about arresting innocent people."

"Vermin are not people. People don't steal and eat infants or burn holes into crops just by touching them."

"Neither do vermin. Those holes five years ago were caused by caterpillars and other insects."

"Insects brought by the *Mivos* from Ferine!"

"Seriously, Mordred, read a book. These delusions of yours are ridiculous. Everyone knows there aren't any caterpillars in Ferine. They'd be more likely to bring over seals or puffins or some other animal that clearly doesn't give a damn about what's growing in your garden," Theodore said.

"For your information, I've done plenty of reading. Did you know that your two little half-breeds were arrested? You've got criminals under your room!"

Zana listened to her father groan.

"Look at me. Mordred, just look at me for a moment. There is no wild conspiracy. The vermin are not plotting to kill us or destroy our food supply or take over Dinara. I'm well aware of the fact that my children were arrested in Tavern. They're not criminals, they're just two kids who happened to end up in a city with ludicrous laws which allow humans to commit heinous crimes against vermin."

"How can you be so blind?"

"I'm not."

"Breena never loved you. The whole thing was a charade. She made you believe she cared about you. Those slaves of yours probably coached her, Theodore. You showed her too much affection. She was meant to be your pet, nothing more."

"No one coached her... she probably didn't think she had a choice," Theodore said quietly.

"She got her claws in you, while you were vulnerable and when the time was right, ran off with our family jewels, abandoned your children and left you for some other man."

"You speak as if you know her mind," Theodore said.

Mordred chuckled. "That woman is conniving. Your children being arrested was probably all part of some scheme. Cut them loose."

"Do you hear yourself right now?"

"She's leading the *Mivos.*"

"She's also my wife."

Zana's eyes shot open, hands falling to the floor. *Nei.*

"Looks like we can ask them for help after all," Micah said, looking at her.

Keirsi shook his head. "I wouldn't go anywhere near them if I were you."

"She owes us," Micah said bitterly. "If you won't come with me to talk to them, I'll go by myself."

Zana sat quietly, tuning out the conversation coming from behind the wall. *I don't even know if I want to see her.* Her eyes met her brother's. She could tell there was no stopping him. He was willing to burn for her. Willing to risk hanging to get Nicholas medicine. With a shaky breath, she nodded. "Okay. Let's do it."

25

———————

Roland squeezed the tips of his fingers, watching the blood rush to them as the cool air nipped away at his skin. He wasn't used to being around that many people, and it was clear from the moment he arrived at the Doren's luncheon that his presence was unwelcome by the majority of the guests. A breath of fresh air was what he needed, that, and something to snack on.

The streets were just as slippery as they had been earlier in the week, but a fresh layer of snow had created a soft blanket along the sidewalk, and it crunched beneath his brown oxfords. As a flurry of snowflakes fell from the sky, Roland stuck out his tongue reflexively. He caught a few and smiled. On days like this, his parents would've ordered him to stay indoors bundled up beneath a heavy layer of quilts in the nursery. Being outside, hands and face exposed to the winter air, was nice.

He squinted slightly, spotting a figure up ahead, crouched down on the sidewalk, tracing their fingers in the snow. He panned over the snow-covered red sweater as the woman's brown eyes lifted, catching his gazed. "Charlotte?"

She gave a weary grin, shivering as Roland fumbled toward her, sliding down the sidewalk, feet kicking about wildly.

He latched onto her, nearly toppling the two of them onto the ground. "What are you doing?" He steadied himself, kneeling beside her.

"I'm not sure."

He leaned forward, noting the shadows under her eyes. She was wearing the same clothes she'd had on the other day.

"I should go…"

"Where are you headed? I'll walk with you."

She shifted away from him.

"Look… Vincent and Detective Carson came by and…" He shook his head, removed his coat, and wrapped it around her, as he'd done before on the way home from the asylum. "Come with me. The Doren's live just up the street. We can talk there."

She drew in a sharp breath. "What did you tell them?"

He sighed, the heat from his lips swirling around them. "I thought something awful had happened to you. I… I thought… I thought it was going to be like Laurie all over again. Could we go somewhere and talk?" He forced a smile. There was no way he was leaving her alone. He held out a hand, letting her put hers in it. It was smaller than he remembered. He adjusted his grip, trying to hold her gently. "Lead the way."

They walked in silence down the street. The Doren's place lit up with its bright, shimmering lights fading in the distance. They drew nearer to the docks, catching sight of ships leaving the harbour, pushing through the icy water. This end of town was nicknamed by Tavern's residents as The Deadman's Dock. At thirteen, Roland had been dared by his classmates to sneak into one of the nearby warehouses, only to be discovered by a friend of his brother, who gave him a well-deserved lecture, before taking him home. He'd never found out what was in the warehouse, nor had he ever ventured near that part of town again. Sully was scary when he got angry, and Roland never wanted to see him like that again. *I wonder how he's doing? I haven't seen him since the funeral.* Walking by the large brick building with its high windows made his insides squirm. *What was I thinking?*

Charlotte squeezed his hand. Her pace quickened. She pulled him firmly toward the docks, where the air grew colder. "The folks around here wouldn't hesitate to take the shirt off your back."

"You already did," he said, gesturing to his jacket.

There was a hardness in her stare.

"Sorry... bad joke." He shoved his hands into his pockets, watching her slip off her flats and tiptoed along the edge of the frozen wooden dock. It creaked beneath her weight. *She must be freezing.*

"Do you remember when we all used to play at the lake in the summer?" Charlotte stopped, still propped up on the balls of her feet. She cocked her head, rubbing her hands together. "Miles pushed you off the diving rock. You couldn't swim."

"Is everything all right?" Roland stretched out his arm as she slid, latching onto the sleeve of the jacket. "It's freezing. Why don't we go inside? I bet the library will be open?"

Charlotte's brown eyes darted about as he drew her toward him, guiding her away from the edge. "Why didn't you come with me?"

Roland grabbed her flats and laid them at her feet. "Pardon?"

Charlotte removed the coat and held it out to him.

"It's freezing."

She wrapped her arms around herself, scrunching the ends of her sweater between her fingers as they dug into her ribs. Tears pooled along her lashes, re-wetting the smudges of dried mascara beneath them. "You... you can't tell anyone."

"I won't," he whispered, taking her in his arms. He smoothed back her short curls, resting his chin on her head as she cried. "How about we go somewhere warm, okay?"

"Please don't say anything to Vincent and Peter."

"What?"

"Roland please. Please don't say anything. I'm begging you." Charlotte shook.

Roland rubbed the back of his neck. "Where were you and your husband staying? Do you want me to walk you there?"

"I can't go back there," she said, her voice rising in her throat.

Roland fished around in his coat pocket for his wallet. "Well, I'm sure there's a place around here to get something to eat. Why don't we do that?"

"I... I can't."

Roland cleared his throat. *Maybe I should get Dianna?* He jumped as she started to cough. "Charlotte, put the coat on. You'll get sick."

"Why didn't you go to Augen with me?"

Roland winced, hands returning to his pockets. "You know why. Look, let's go to the Doren's. My car is there. I can drive you to Dr. Gray's and get you looked at."

"No."

"Charlotte, you're in the same clothes I saw you in days ago," Roland said gently. "And from the looks of things you clearly need–"

"I don't need anything. Just go," she said, pounding her palms into his chest.

Roland lost his footing.

"I didn't mean to!" Charlotte cried, trying to hold on to him. "I'm sorry Roland. Really, I am. You were supposed to go with me! You said you'd meet me there, but you didn't come."

Roland trembled, trying to pull himself away from the edge without dragging her off with him. "My mother–"

Charlotte drew in a deep breath, yanking him as hard as she could. Her fingers slipped. "Roland!"

26

The air was hot, fire consuming everything in its path, crackling and popping, until night looked like day. He gazed over his shoulder, blue eyes fixed on her.

"You have to stop them!" she said, pupils narrowing.

"Let it burn," he muttered, lighting a cigar, unbothered by the shrieking coming from the village at the bottom of the hill.

DIANNA TAPPED HER FOOT IMPATIENTLY, arms folded as she stood near the doorway of the Doren's mansion. She could feel Miles' gaze on her, but had no desire to humour him any further. *He puts on airs in front of his family and acts like a child the moment his mother isn't within earshot.* She groaned. Roland had been gone for over an hour, and the majority of the guests had already left. Had he remained at the party, like she insisted, she would have been able to hide with him and eat at the bottom of the stairs. Roland was good at sneaking away from large groups of people, especially at parties. *At least I got to meet Georgie Bryce.*

Georgie Bryce, with his curly black hair, muscular shoulders, and deep brown eyes.

No one should be allowed to be that gifted and beautiful. She scrunched up her face slightly, heart skipping as her thoughts drifted to Roland's gentle voice filling the room. Somehow she'd managed to forget it, the way he used to call after her in the schoolyard, or how he'd hum quietly on their walks. How easily he'd go from shy to wildly outspoken and bold, and how his entire being lit up whenever he sat down to play a song. *A lot changed.* She frowned, as her cousin approached for the fourth time, to inquire about his missing friend. *As if I've seen or heard anything new in the last six minutes.*

Peter nudged her with his elbow. "Do you–"

She flicked her wrist up, holding up her index finger against his lip as she drew in a sharp breath.

"I didn't even–"

She turned her head, staring him down.

He grumbled and pouted, mirroring her by crossing his arms.

She returned her attention to the door. *Where on earth is he?* Dianna glanced at the children, sitting and chatting with Miles Jr. and a few other guests, one of which she recognized as the rich older gentleman from Micah and Zana's trial. *The monster who wanted to buy Nicholas' sister. I'd love to punch that old fart in the nose.* She shook the thought from her head and took another deep breath. *Why am I in such a bad mood today?*

"I'm gonna look for him," Peter said gruffly, going toward the coatroom. "For all we know, he could've passed out somewhere. Why'd you let him leave, anyway?"

"I'm not Roland's keeper."

Peter threw on his jacket and scoffed.

"What?"

He raised his brow.

Her hands dropped to her side. "What?"

"Funny he says the same about you," Peter said. "You're usually a lot more persistent with him. He listens to you."

"He does not. Roland's as good a listener as that rug," she said, pointing to the one by the door.

"He actually cares about what you think."

"He couldn't care a lick about me."

"That's not true," Peter muttered.

Dianna's heart leapt.

He smirked, as though he could see right through her, and put on his jacket.

She placed her hands on her hips, head shaking from left to right. "Fine, go look for him. I'll ask Miles if he can lend you a hand."

Peter winced.

"Or not?"

"Those two managed to survive an event without one having the other in a headlock. I don't want to jinx it."

"Good point."

The door flew open, cold air filling the entryway.

Dianna shivered.

"Where's your jacket?" Her stomach twisted in knots as she raced over, looking Roland up and down. "Why are you soaking wet?"

"Peter, can you drive the kids back?" Roland's legs trembling. He cleared his throat and went to the coatroom. "Dianna, do you mind driving the car for me?" Roland pulled out her coat and hat and handed them to her, meeting her eyes briefly.

She felt the chill of his hand on her skin. "Your lips are blue."

"I'm all right. I just slipped and fell in the water." He looked over at Miles as he brought the children over. "Caspian, help your brother with his coat, please."

Caspian scrunched up his face, taking Julius' jacket from his uncle. "A bit early for a swim, don't you think?"

Roland smirked. "Peter's going to take you home. If you get there before us, could you ask Tabby to make some tomato soup?"

Rose nodded, buttoning up her long red coat.

Caspian looked over at the door. "Who's that?"

Dianna examined the figure standing just outside the door in Roland's jacket.

"A friend," Roland said softly. "Come on, hurry up and get dressed. The weather's getting pretty nasty, and I'm freezing."

"Thanks for inviting us to your party, Mr. Doren," Julius said, shaking Miles' hand as his older brother forced the five-year-old's hat onto his head.

Miles smiled at them. "You're very welcome."

Dianna caught a glimpse of Roland shivering. She grabbed him and wrapped her scarf around his neck, forcing him down to her eye level. "What happened?"

"I fell," he said, trying to pull away.

"What were you doing out by the water when you know you can't swim?"

He shook his head, this time prying her fingers from the scarf. He held them gently in his and sighed. "Would you do me a favour when we get back?"

She raised her brow.

He removed the scarf and put it over her shoulders. "Please try and understand that I'm asking you for a good reason and not because I want to hurt anyone."

Her shoulders drooped. "What are you talking about?"

Peter raised a hand. "All right kids, who wants to ride up in the front?"

Caspian and Rose looked at one another, then raced to the door.

"No running in the house!" Roland shouted, the Doren's heads veering toward the children. He glared at Peter. "Seriously?"

Peter blushed. "What?"

Rose whipped open the door, sticking her tongue out at her brother. "I win!"

Dianna's gaze fell upon the woman standing outside. "What's she doing here?"

27

"You're a real prick, Roland." Charlotte snatched the apple from his hand.

"So I've heard." He laughed, shivering slightly at the cool autumn breeze as the two teens sat on a bench across the street from Doren Shipping.

Charlotte raised the apple up above her head, examining it carefully. "Did you have to take such a big bite? I only have the one apple."

"You said I could have some."

She shot him a dirty look. "I was expecting you to nibble."

Roland leaned back, stretching out his legs. "I was hungry."

"When are you not?" Charlotte said, slapping him on the belly. "You'd better be careful. My grandpa says your food'll catch up to you."

"Me specifically or…"

"All of us," she smirked. "Bloody damn teenagers."

"You ever think about being dead?"

Charlotte furrowed her brow. "It isn't top on my list of daily thoughts. Why?"

Roland took the apple and made up his face. "I think about it a lot. How it'll just sort of happen one day, folks will be all sad and say how tragic it is because I'm *so* young. My parents will give me my special place by the creek, next to the others. I bet my eyes will go white," he said, rolling his eyes back into his head. "And my tongue'll stick out and–"

"Stop that!" Charlotte groaned, smacking him on the shoulder. "Your eyes'll get stuck like that."

Roland blinked, putting his tongue back in his mouth.

"You're always so morbid," Charlotte said, arms crossed. "It worries me."

"Why?"

"Because you talk about death like it's a joke?"

Roland chuckled.

"It's not funny."

Roland wrapped an arm around her. "When I'm a ghost, I'll be sure to visit you."

"Oh, my–"

"Late at night when you're fast asleep," he said, voice breathy in her ear.

Charlotte jumped up off the bench, glowering.

Roland took another bite of the apple. "What? I've seen you asleep before."

"You're an idiot," Charlotte mumbled, kicking at the sidewalk.

"I know," he said quietly. "I'm just bored."

Charlotte lowered her head and sat back down. "Your stupid antics got me fired. No one's going to want to give a job now. I could barely afford that apple."

Roland eyed her. "Charlotte, you stole this apple."

She pouted. "What time does the pub open?"

"Late."

"Ugh!"

Roland sank further in his seat, listening to the red apple crunch beneath his teeth. He'd been bored many times in his life, but there was something unbearable about being bored after summer ended.

"You two got nothing better to do with yourselves?"

Roland sat up straight at the sight of his father exiting Doren Shipping. He scrambled to tuck in his shirt. "Where're you headed Papa?"

"Does your mother know you're out?" Darius said.

"She was sleeping when I left."

"And how do you think she'll react when she wakes to find you missing?" Darius grumbled, gaze falling on the apple in Roland's hand. "There's a worm in that."

Roland gagged, tossing it over his shoulder.

Charlotte sulked. "Hey! I never even got a bite."

"It was poisoned!" Roland beat his chest, choking.

Charlotte frowned. "You owe me an apple. I'm not going back to the Warren's to get another."

Darius shook his head. "You're not to go anywhere near that girl's house."

Roland rolled his eyes. "She's not even there. She's in Riversburg. Or did you forget how you made her parents send her away so that they could keep their farm?"

Darius pressed his lips together.

"You didn't even let me say goodbye," Roland said bitterly.

"I don't have time to discuss this with you," Darius said. "I have to catch the next train."

"Oh, so you can leave town at random without informing Mama, but I can't go to Augen and study music for a year?"

"There's a college here in Tavern. You don't need to go to Augen," Darius said firmly, shoving his hands into his pockets.

"Yeah, well, I ain't going there either, am I?"

"You *aren't* going there," Darius said.

"You won't let me leave Tavern. I can't go to college. You made Dianna go away, and last night you fired Tabby!"

Charlotte spun her head in his direction, eyes wide.

Darius gritted his teeth and drew in a deep breath. "And whose fault is that?"

Roland swallowed hard.

"Perhaps if you'd have been home instead of off drinking at

Jakob's, your nanny wouldn't have been let go," Darius said bitterly. "If anyone is to blame for that, it's you."

"You just didn't like that she stood up to you." Roland frowned, averting his gaze. "Come on Charlotte, the libraries probably opened up by now."

Charlotte bowed her head and followed him up the street.

Roland's chest hurt.

"Why didn't you tell me about Tabitha?"

"What for?"

"We're friends. We're supposed to tell each other things like that," she said, grabbing him by the hand as they reached the library steps. "Hey, look at me for a second."

Roland rolled his eyes.

Charlotte pulled him around the corner, behind the building, and placed her hands on her hips. "What's going on with you?"

Roland shoved his hands into his pockets. "Isn't this where you and Peter used to fool around?"

"Shut up."

He pressed his lips together, nodding.

Charlotte drew in a deep breath and sat down in the grass, patting the earth next to her. "Sit."

Roland untucked his shirt and rolled up his sleeves, and kicked at the wall.

"Did Tabitha get fired because you were with me at the pub yesterday?"

"No."

"Then what happened?" Charlotte said, fixing her ponytail.

"My mother was upset because she didn't know where I was all day. You know how she gets? Well, I guess I was being too mouthy and my father decided to smack me," he said sullenly, giving a little shrug. "Tabby told him off. Said if he laid another finger on me, she'd let him have it. Papa didn't like that. He told her not to interfere. It was his choice how he disciplined his kids. She started listing off everything, and I mean everything my parents did to me that she thought was unfair. Everyone, all the other staff, came into the parlour. Her and my father were screaming at each other. Then, out of nowhere, he tells her we won't be needing her services anymore and drags me up to the nursery."

"She lives close by, right? You can always go visit her," she said gently. "Maybe... maybe you could ask to stay with her?"

"I can't..."

"Then come stay with me," she said as he lowered himself onto the ground.

"Do you know why Dianna hasn't written me back?"

"I haven't heard from her," Charlotte said softly.

Roland frowned. "I wanted to try and meet her at the hotel we ran off to in Riversburg. I thought maybe I could find a job there and save up some money for us to move to Augen."

"Move to Augen?"

"She wants to live by the water when we're married, and I read there's a nice lake there. I bet if I worked in Riversburg for a little while, we could find a small house and fix it up."

Charlotte let out a surprised squeak, her eyes wide. "When you're married?"

"We're old enough to get married," he said meekly. "Besides, we've been engaged for almost an entire year."

"Yes, but are you sure you're ready?" Charlotte cocked her head. "Like *you* specifically because last night you spent your last dollar on beer and, well... um... you kind of need money to start a family, Roland."

"My family has plenty of money." Roland shrugged. "I know what's worth what. I can just take a few items, pawn them off, and use that to hold us over until I get a job."

Charlotte shook her head. "You need to stop stealing from your parents. It's not right."

"You stole an apple."

"Look, it's not stealing if my best friend's parents wave to me while I'm taking it."

"Look. I don't care. I just want to be with her. I'd do anything for her," Roland said. "I'd even kill for her if I had to."

Charlotte threw her hands above her head. "Not sure if anyone's told you this, but killing folks is illegal and not at all romantic!"

"I said if I had to," he said. "Like if she was being attacked by a bear or something."

"A person's more likely to get attacked by a vermin than a bear."

"True. Regardless, bear, vermin, human. I'd slaughter them."

Charlotte picked at her nails. "Could I come with you to Augen?"

"Absolutely."

"Why do your parents treat you like that?"

Roland sighed. "Papa says I'm a nuisance."

28

———————

"She's a nuisance," Mrs. Doren said, shaking her head.

Rose leaned forward on her tippytoes to get a better look at the woman through the doorway. *I wish I had Nicholas' hearing.* She stretched her neck as far as she could, trying to filter out the other adults. Her eyes widened, catching sight of her uncle's hand latching onto the woman's, under the glow of the afternoon sun. Her cheeks flushed pink.

"Mother, please." Miles stepped around the Crispin children, glancing at Peter. "Her husband just died."

"Move along," Peter mumbled, guiding Rose away from the door. "Quit being a pest."

"I wasn't being a pest. I was–"

"Being nosy."

Rose frowned. "Mrs. Doren doesn't seem to like that lady much," she said, hoping to pry something out of him.

"Figures."

Caspian cocked his head. "Who's that lady with Uncle Roland?"

"We all went to school together," Peter mumbled, taking the car keys out of his coat pocket. "Now, how about you nosy, little booger eaters mind your own business."

Rose put her hands on her hips. "Well, that was both childish and uncalled for."

"Yeah, Peter," Miles said, throwing an arm around him.

"Sorry... look, my hand still hurts and I'm feeling kind of grouchy. Let's just go home."

Miles grinned. "Grouchy because of Charlotte?"

Rose giggled. "Ooh! Is she one of your sweethearts?"

Caspian threw his hands above his head. "He was about to let it go. Why'd you keep bugging him?"

Rose rolled her eyes, brushing her hair up into a ponytail. "I was curious."

"Well, curiosity killed the fox," he said, sitting down on her bed.

"Cat."

"Whatever. Curiosity killed it either way. Sometimes you just gotta know when to not ask people things."

She frowned. *Says you.*

"I think Uncle Roland might've been a two-timing, no good, cheat," he said, holding out a hand to Julius so he could get up onto the bed.

Rose shook her head, tying a blue ribbon in her hair. "That's impossible."

"Oh yeah? Well then, how do you explain how strange the grownups are being?"

"They're always like that," Rose said. "And Uncle Roland's far too preoccupied to string along a bunch of women."

"Says who?"

She rolled her eyes. "I think we'd know if he had women coming by the house, don't you?"

Caspian shrugged. "He doesn't tell us anything."

"But he tells Peter *everything.*"

Caspian eyed her.

"So, I just thought if I kept asking, eventually he'd spill the beans."

Julius whimpered, putting his head in his hands. "He called us booger eaters… and now Mr. Doren is mad at us too."

Caspian looked at him. "You should hear what he calls Nicholas."

Julius perked up. "What'd he say?"

"He called him a dirty–"

"Caspian." Rose tightened the ribbon, turning toward her brothers. "Don't repeat those kinds of things to Julius."

Julius groaned, kicking his legs. "But I wanna know."

"Anyway, that lady can't be Uncle Roland's sweetheart. Didn't you see poor Peter's face? He looked absolutely distraught."

Julius cocked his head. "What's that mean?"

"Who cares Rose? Why are you so obsessed with this kind of stuff?" Caspian grumbled, laying back on the bed.

"I'm not."

"You are. You're always obsessed with stuff that's none of our business."

"What's *du-straw* mean?" Julius asked again, looking back and forth between the older two.

Rose glared at Caspian. "Look, we can't expect the grownups to keep Uncle Roland out of trouble anymore. Grandmother's not around, and Tabby and Mr. Leon are getting old. Uncle Roland's gotten too good at hiding things from them, so it's up to us to keep tabs on him."

"Us? You're thirteen, I'm ten, and Julius doesn't even know what distraught means!"

Julius crossed his arms. "I'd know if one of you would just tell me already!"

"Last time our uncle was acting all sneaky, and people weren't telling us things, we ended up with a vermin in our house," Rose whispered, fussing with a loose thread on her checkered navy-blue skirt.

Caspian sat up again. "And the time before that, he got arrested."

"Exactly."

Julius gasped. "Uncle Roland got arrested?"

Caspian slammed a hand over his mouth. "Not so loud, you ding-dong!"

"Everyone in Tavern knows. It happened back when you were still a baby," Rose said.

Julius nodded.

Caspian let go of him and shrugged. "Well, from what I've heard, lots of grown-ups have been talking about Uncle Roland running around with some married woman. Apparently, it's incorrigible behaviour."

Rose's jaw dropped. "What? Where'd you hear that?"

"Some of the teachers at school."

Julius glowered. "Stop saying stuff I don't know."

"Just go play with Alicia or something," Caspian said.

Rose's face grew hot. "He would never!"

Julius cocked his head. "Yes, I would. I love Alicia. She's my best friend."

"I think she means Uncle Roland would never run around with a married woman."

"What's so bad about running? It's fun. I like it," Julius said proudly.

Caspian made up his face, trying not to laugh. "We mean kissing."

Julius' eyes bulged, his face reddening. "Oh..."

Rose looped the thread tightly around her finger until it was purple and yanked it from her skirt. "First, he's a murderer, now he's Sofia and Kiyomi's favourite person, and a home wrecker?"

"Relax Rosie, people always say a bunch of really bad stuff about our family," Caspian muttered.

"Yeah," Julius said gently.

"Did someone say something mean to you?" She sat down between them. "Because if they did, I'll give them a piece of my mind."

"Some girls at the party were talking bad about you, so we put caviar in their coats when they were leaving," Caspian said, while Julius snickered.

Her eyes widened.

"You know, the gross fish eggs that make Uncle Roland throw up every time he eats them?"

"Caspian," she tried to muffle her laughter. "That's so evil!"

"And you know what else?"

She looked at Julius.

"I kicked Sofia," he said proudly.

"They had it coming," Caspian said, crossing his arms.

Julius grinned. "They all do."

Rose and Caspian stared at him.

He eyed them. "What?"

"N-nothing. Thanks for sticking up for me, but no more pranks, okay?" Rose said, hugging him.

Caspian moaned, putting his head in his hands. "I can't wait till I'm old enough to get out of this stupid town."

She frowned. "And go where?"

"I dunno. Presa."

Presa again? Rose mustered a smile, deciding to humour him. "What's so great about Presa?"

"Mama and Papa met there." He sat quietly, picking away at a scab on his arm. "I hate this house. There's too many people here. I liked things before."

"Before Nicholas?"

He shook his head. "Before like when we were little kids."

"We still are kids."

"Not really..." he said bitterly. "Julius is, but not you and me."

She held his hand.

"If it were up to me, I'd be a grown up already and move away and never come back... but you two can visit me."

"I don't want you to move away," Julius said quietly.

"We can't leave Tavern. We're supposed to work for the Doren's like Papa and Grandfather," Rose said, lowering her head.

The boys frowned.

"Didn't that lady look really sick?" Caspian said, changing the subject.

Julius nodded. "And that policeman was asking about her this morning."

Rose and Caspian shot their heads in his direction.

"Wait, what?" they said in unison.

29

———————

Dianna squirmed as Roland rummaged around in his sock drawer. "What are you looking for? Are you okay?"

"I'm fine. I'm just cold."

Dianna's stomach knotted while he continued to pull things out. *Why won't he look at me?*

Roland held up a sweater from off the floor and tossed it over to Charlotte, who was sitting on the bed. "Here. Put this on."

Dianna had never seen Charlotte in such disarray, and Roland's frantic behaviour made her uneasy. Charlotte had always been the type to fix every curl in place, make sure that not a wrinkle appeared in any of her skirts, and put extra attention on looking her best for every occasion. It was something that she had in common with their friend Constance, and why everything about today seemed so bizarre. "Roland, your clothes are soaked. Why don't you change?"

Charlotte glanced over at them, nibbling away at a chocolate chip cookie. She folded her hands onto her lap. "Sorry again..."

"It's okay, Charlotte, I just want to make sure you're okay," Roland said, pulling something from the dresser.

The last time Dianna saw Charlotte, the two had gotten into an argument over him. Charlotte had been furious with her. Her chest ached. Dianna caught a look in Roland's eye that turned her stomach. It was a look she hadn't seen since the night he took things too far at the lake. That was a few weeks before she went to Riversburg, and the incident that led up to his father's death. "Roland?"

He turned to her, that glimmer still in his eye. "Take this to the pawnshop."

Dianna took the small black box from his hand.

Charlotte curled up on the bed, tucking her legs into her chest. She buried her head in her knees.

"Hopefully you can get a good price for it," Roland said gently.

Dianna opened the box. Her insides squirmed. "What is this?"

"Your ring."

Dianna eyed him. "Why do you still have this?"

He cleared his throat, rubbing the back of his neck.

"Don't look at me like that."

"Like what?"

"Like I just scolded you."

"You *are* scolding me," he said, raising his brow.

"Roland, I can't sell this ring," Dianna said, eyeing him carefully.

He shrugged and began unbuttoning his dress shirt. "Why'd you dance with Miles?"

"Don't change the subject."

He looked at her. "You didn't seem to care this much when you gave it to Charlotte."

She pressed her lips together, spying the Crispin children popping their heads into the master bedroom. "What's that supposed to mean?"

"You could've at least waited until we buried my father," he said coldly. "Instead, you left me in this town to rot."

"You know I didn't want to leave," she said harshly. "And I can't sell something that doesn't belong to me."

Roland leaned his head back and sighed. "Well, I can't exactly take it myself."

"Well, maybe if you didn't steal all of that stuff from your parents, you wouldn't need me to go there on your behalf." She shook her head. "As for that comment about leaving you here to rot, I will gladly discuss our relationship with you, but not in front of Charlotte and the children."

Roland's eyes widened as they fell on the children, spying through the door.

Dianna crossed her arms.

Roland cleared his throat, gazing down at his feet. "Dianna please just–"

"Have you ever once considered how I might've felt knowing you stole this ring? Or thought about how cruel it is to ask me to sell it?"

Roland winced.

"I'm going for a drive," Dianna said bitterly, clenching her fists. She tossed the ring box onto the dresser and stormed past the children out into the hall toward the stairs.

"Dianna, wait, just let me explain," Roland said, chasing after her.

Dianna threw on her coat and grabbed the keys before heading into the office. "Why?"

"I wouldn't have asked you if I had another option," he whispered.

"You never should've given me that ring in the first place," she said, opening the door.

He threw himself into it and glared at her. "I gave it to you because I love you."

"Move."

He held the doorknob firmly, gazing into her face. "I'd never do anything to hurt you, but I need the money to–"

"I said, move!"

"Roland!"

The two of them turned to look at Tabitha.

Roland stepped aside, lowering his head.

"I've had it up to here with you!"

"T-Tabby I–"

"Go to your room!"

"But–"

Dianna watched his face pale as Tabitha pointed up the stairs.

"If you act like a child, Leon and I will treat you like a child. Go to your room and don't come down until I call you for dinner."

Dianna recoiled as Tabitha smacked Roland on the hand. "Tell Peter I went to Jakob's."

He met her gaze. "Don't go."

"Good. That's the smartest decision you've made since moving back here. Go to the one place in Tavern. This idiot can't get all wrapped up in whatever mess you've created," Tabitha said, dragging Roland back upstairs.

DIANNA POURED MORE vinegar on her fries, watching Jakob pet the little black and white kitten he held in his large palm.

"You were with that idiot today," he said. "I can see it on your face."

She nodded.

"Why do you bother with him, eh?"

"We work together," she mumbled.

"Doesn't mean you need to spend every minute of the day together. I ran into your mother recently. She knows you're not staying with your cousin."

Dianna froze.

"I saw him going into the hotel with Lottie."

"Peter?"

Jakob put the kitten down on the counter and leaned in close. "You know I'm not talking about Peter, and I know that you know, that I know who you're staying with. Why, is the real question."

"Did you tell my parents?"

"I didn't see a point in adding more strain to that relationship."

She frowned. "Thanks Jakob."

"You were free of that boy for five years. Why come back? Did something happen in Riversburg?"

"My cousin Phoebe got engaged."

"Well, that's nice."

"It is... isn't it?"

Jakob eyed her as the kitten rubbed up against his hand. He picked it back up and scratched beneath its chin. "Did something happen between you and Phoebe?"

Dianna shook her head. "I figured she didn't want her little cousin living with her and her new husband once they were married. Peter offered to let me stay with him."

"And you somehow ended up living with your ex-fiancé?"

Dianna glanced over her shoulder as a group of gentlemen entered the pub. "It's not all bad. We work together anyway. I just... I never intended on staying. It was supposed to be temporary. I was just helping out."

"And now he's been spotted around town with another woman, and you're upset."

"I'm not upset about that," she said, eating a few fries. "It's been five years. I've seen other people, just as I'm sure he has. It's just that I don't know if I can trust him."

"Well, it's hard to trust someone after they've been accused of several murders."

"Two."

Jakob shook his head. "Three. Everyone always forgets about poor Wendy. The children lost both their parents. I still can't understand how he managed to gain custody of them... then again, it's possible Wendy's aunt was never informed that Adeline Crispin was no longer with the family."

"The thing is... I don't think Roland isn't capable of hurting anyone."

"Except for your classmate Etienne at the lake," Jakob said. "Or did you forget about that?"

Dianna shivered, wringing her hands together.

"The kid almost lost his eye."

"That was different."

"Why are you still defending him? Even Vincent can admit what happened to Etienne was messed up."

"Etienne and Miles took things too far. Roland wasn't himself... they knew that."

"And that gave Roland the right to try and attack him?"

Dianna sat quietly, twirling a fry between her fingers. "No."

"You know, after his father died, he and Charlotte were spending a lot of time together. Put on airs, like they were real sweet kids, but those two were... if it weren't for Vincent, things would've ended badly. Rumour has it Charlotte's in the family way."

Dianna's heart sank. *Was that why he wanted me to sell the ring?* She stood up and grabbed her jacket.

"If you need somewhere to stay, Hester and Prudence are renting rooms from Mrs. Keswick. I'm sure she'd be happy to take another old student of hers as a tenant."

"Do you know if Dr. Gray's around?"

"Vincent picked up lunch for his father a couple hours ago. Listen, if you ever need to talk to someone, I'm here. Okay?"

She nodded. "Thanks Jakob. I appreciate it."

30

———————

Vincent was rocking back in a chair, gazing up at the ceiling, when Dianna Warren came bursting into the doctor's office.

"I need to talk to you," she said as the chair tipped over with him in it.

He crawled out from behind the desk. Blood rushed to his cheeks as the patients sitting in the chairs along the wall stifled their laughter. Mr. Timmins, unfortunately, couldn't hold back and cackled away, his glasses bobbing down his nose.

Dianna held out her hand. "Are you okay?"

He took it hesitantly while she pulled him up. "I'm fine. Did something happen to Roland?"

She let go of his hand, eyeing him carefully.

"I doubt you'd come see here about anything else."

"Is your father with a patient right now?"

"Yeah, it's been a busy day," he said, gesturing to the four patients sitting behind her. "Is something wrong? Do you need me to come by the house?"

"Can we talk somewhere a little more private?"

Vincent eyed her as she wrang her hands together. "Of course. Follow me. We can talk upstairs."

She nodded, following after him.

He glanced her over. "You look nice. Going somewhere special?"

"I was at your grandmother's luncheon. I just haven't had a chance to change."

He winced. "Oh, that's nice. Well, you look really pretty." He caught a glimpse of her smiling and turned his attention forward. "I hope my grandmother didn't say anything weird. I think she's trying to find a suitable girl for Miles, now that he's finally getting a handle on things over at Doren Shipping."

"Your cousin actually behaved himself. He was the one who invited me. Oh, and Georgie Bryce was there."

"Really?" Vincent looked back at her again as they walked past the upstairs window, toward his father's file room. "Guess I should've accepted the invitation after all."

"Why didn't you?"

"Like I said, it's been busy... besides, I'm a Gray, not a Doren. I've never really fit in with that lot. So, what's going on with Roland? My father's still waiting to hear back from Dr. Kohli, but we're hoping she can see him sometime next week."

"Roland didn't mention anything about another doctor?"

Vincent cleared his throat, opening the door to the file room. *Whoops.*

She nodded. "The reason I came was because of something Jakob said about Roland and Charlotte."

Charlotte? Vincent held the doorknob firmly. "Have you seen her?"

Dianna pressed her lips together.

"Detective Carson and I still have some questions to ask her," he said, forcing a smile. He didn't need to tell her the police suspected Charlotte had coaxed Roland into helping her get rid of her husband.

"She and I haven't really spoken," Dianna said softly.

Vincent's mind was already racing as he entered the room. *If Detective Carson's right, that would mean that Roland spent time going back and forth between Tavern and Augen. How couldn't he have been in two places at once unless someone was covering for him? Besides, the train station would have some sort of record of him boarding the train.* He rubbed his chin. "What was it Jakob said?"

Dianna followed him into the room and waited for Vincent to shut the door behind them. "He said he saw Roland and Charlotte go into the hotel together."

Like he told the detective and I. He let out a sigh of relief, relaxing his shoulders. He still wasn't sure why Detective Carson was making him tag along, but the whole idea of Charlotte killing anyone made him uneasy.

"You knew?"

He looked at her and nodded.

"Jakob seems to believe something happened between them."

Vincent fiddled with the loose button on his sleeve.

"He brought up what happened in high school, with Etienne." Dianna's voice grew soft. "And he said that he'd heard Charlotte was pregnant. Roland... she was at the Doren's with him."

Vincent drummed a hand along a stack of papers and kissed his teeth. *There's something she's not telling me.*

"Vincent."

He balled his hand into a fist and knocked on the desk. "Etienne forgave him for the whole eye thing. He tells people he got the scar fighting with a vermin, while delivering shipments to Presa."

"Vincent... did Charlotte come see your father at all about being pregnant?"

He ran a hand through his black hair, craning his neck. "No, but Connie mentioned something about it."

"And the father?"

"Are you trying to ask me if it's Roland's?"

"That's what Jakob led me to believe."

Vincent chuckled as she wrung her hands together. "I wouldn't know." He grabbed them gently, eyeing her. "Besides, even if the two of them did get together, you called off the engagement. It's all in the past now."

"She was Peter's girlfriend... *my* best friend!" Dianna pulled away from him. "Would you do something like that to your best friend?"

Vincent hung his head, shoving his hands into his pockets, thinking for a moment. He met her eyes. "You still love him, don't you?"

"This isn't about me."

"You could've went straight to him and asked, but instead you came here. You were trying to spare someone the heartache, and given that look on your face, I'd say it was yourself."

Dianna turned from him.

"Do you know where Charlotte is now?"

"No, but I'm worried. If she's pregnant–"

"Pregnant, according to Constance," Vincent said.

Dianna raised her brow. "So, you're saying it's probably just a rumour?"

"I'm saying that there's no point trying to open up old wounds."

She was staring at him intently now, green eyes locked on.

"Fine. We'll go bug Connie on her day off and see if she knows anything. Is that what you want?"

Her face softened. "Really?"

"Yes really. I know you. Once you get an idea in your head, you can't let it go. I'll run and tell my father I'm stepping out for a bit. I was bored anyway."

DIANNA WASN'T sure why she'd let Jakob get into her head, but seeing Vincent only added to the unease she felt in the pit of her stomach. There had to be some explanation for Roland wanting her to sell that ring. He'd kept it all those years. *Did he say he loved me? Or that he loves me?* She fiddled with her bracelet.

Vincent rang Connie's doorbell, and within seconds, the pair could hear her running through the house.

"Coming!" she sang sweetly.

The door swung open, and there she was, Constance looking as polished as ever.

"Dianna, Vincent, what a surprise!" She looked around. "Peter's not with you, is he?"

"No," Dianna said.

"Good." Constance pulled them inside and shut the door. "I hate that dirty, rotten scoundrel," she muttered, gesturing for them to follow her into the kitchen. The radio was playing in the background. Compared to Roland's place, the little house was filled with reds and blues, paintings of flowers and foxes decorated the walls, and the entire place smelled like cinnamon. It was very Connie. "So, what brings you two here?"

Dianna winced at the cheery grin plastered across Connie's ruby coloured lips.

"We wanted to ask about Charlotte. Have you seen her lately?" Vincent said, as Connie turned her attention to the oven.

"I'm actually in the middle of baking some things to bring over to her hotel. Poor dear, did you hear about her husband? What an awful mess. She's been through so much these last few years. I thought some pies would cheer her right up... well, maybe not right away, but I know I'd want someone to bake me a pie if I was going through it."

"Are they expecting?"

Vincent shot Dianna a dirty look. "Straight to the punch, are we?"

She waited for Connie to pull the pie from the oven.

"Sugar. Charlotte loves sugar pie. I got the eggs from your folks. You've got one of the prettiest farms in all of Tavern. Remember how we all used to help your folks feed the chickens as girls?"

"Connie..."

"I know, I know I heard you," she said, turning down the radio. She took off her red oven mitts and sat down at the table.

Vincent sat across from her and leaned forward. "A while back you told me–"

"She told me was pregnant."

"And?"

"And then I don't know," Connie said, looking at what appeared to be freshly painted nails. "Suddenly she was back in Tavern, and Lennox was dead in their hotel room."

"What happened?"

Dianna took a seat. "Is it Lennox's baby?"

Constance sat up straight, eyeing them, eyes wide as saucers.

"She knows something," Dianna said, turning to Vincent. "Her right eye is twitching."

Vincent cocked his head. "How did you notice that?"

Connie exhaled deeply, throwing her head onto the table. "Do you know how long I had to keep that a secret? Almost four months. Four! It's not Peter's if that's what you're worried about. The two of them haven't spoken since they broke up after high school. Plus, she just got back to Tavern a couple of days ago."

Vincent gave a slight nod. "We know that... but do you know who the father is?"

Dianna looked at the top of Connie's head, watching the long lump of black hair snake along the table as their friend groaned loudly.

"I told her she was marrying him too fast, but she wouldn't listen to me. I thought if I told you" –she gestured to Vincent, lifting her head slightly– "that you'd put a stop to it."

"Me?"

"But *no,* you did absolutely nothing, and Juliet didn't see an issue with it. Figured it'd be harder for Charlotte to raise a baby on her own. Of course, it'd be hard, but at least she'd have her friends. I would've helped her. I offered to help her, but she didn't want to burden me. Instead, she burdens me with this secret and has me worrying about her every night as I fall asleep. I have dark circles because of her. Circles. Under my eyes. Like Roland!" She took a deep breath, sitting up straight, brushing the hair from her face. "Pie anyone?"

"I thought you were bringing those to Charlotte?"

"I've made six. I doubt she needs six pies."

"Six!" Dianna clasped her hands together, trying to restrain herself. "Why uh... why'd you make six pies, Constance?"

"Because her husband died!" Connie said, tears flooding her eyes. "I haven't even stopped by the hotel to console her. I've just been baking pies. I'm a terrible person."

"Oh... no that's not true," Vincent said quickly.

Connie glared at him. "Shut up! Why'd you worry Dianna with the whole baby thing, anyway? Making her think Peter's that irresponsible. He's a jerk, but he's not heartless. If he had a child out there, he'd do right by it."

Vincent blushed. "Like I said, we didn't think it was Peter's."

"Well, who else could the father be?" She threw her hands above her head. "You?"

Dianna watched Vincent squirm around in his seat. She took Connie by the hand. "Vincent wasn't the one who told me. It was Jakob."

Constance's jaw dropped. "J-Jakob?"

Dianna nodded.

"Why would he tell you something like that?"

"He was trying to protect me."

"Oh dear... oh... Dianna, are you pregnant?"

Dianna blushed. "No."

"Well, that doesn't make a lick of sense."

"He thinks Roland's the father," Vincent mumbled, staring up at the ceiling.

"R-Roland Crispin?" Connie burst out laughing. "That's... no. There is no way those two. Nope."

Dianna and Vincent stared at each other while Constance continued to laugh. They watched the tears stream down her face, streaking bits of her makeup. Although it irked her, Connie's laughter was a bit of a relief.

Connie shook her head. "I'm sorry. Wow, I haven't laughed like that in forever."

Dianna squeezed her hands together. "So, she never told you who the father was?"

"Even if she had, it wouldn't have mattered. Lennox told his family in Augen that they were going on holiday. They came to check out the children's home in East Tavern. See, he was supposed to find somewhere for her to stay until she gave birth and then they'd put the baby up for adoption and go back to Augen. Outside of myself, no one knew, so it seemed simple. I figured they'd pull it off... but I know she didn't want to give up her baby. That was his idea. He said it'd be too hard for him, raising a stranger's child."

Dianna's stomach knotted. *Does Roland know about this? Is that why he took her to the house?*

31

Roland rubbed the back of his neck, glowering at Tabitha as she paced the upstairs hallway. "Go home Tabby."

"I don't want to hear a peep from you!" she said, not turning her attention to him. "Besides, I'm waiting for Evan to finish up outside. He's my ride this evening."

Resting his chin in his hands, he stared at the front door from the stairs, praying for Dianna to emerge. He'd tried reciting what he'd say, but every explanation he had was worse than the next. Even sitting there, with Tabitha furious at him, the children ogling from Rose's bedroom, and poor Lisa exposing herself once again to the fever by checking in on their guest, Roland couldn't contain himself. *How did she know the ring was stolen?* A grim smile crept between his lips. *Mama probably had something to do with that.*

"You stupid, reckless boy." Tabitha marched toward him, finger wagging away. "Do you ever think about the rest of us? What you're putting us through? If Adeline were here, she'd–"

He turned to her, raising his brow. "But she's not, is she?"

"Shut that mouth before I shut it for you."

"Then stop talking to me."

Tabitha groaned, grinding her heel into the carpet. "Twenty-four years I've spent raising you, when I've got my own two boys back at home. Twenty-four years of cleaning up after your messes, and here you are making yet another. I'm going grey because of you. My whole head! Mr. Leon's going bald in the middle!"

"He's going bald because he never takes his cap off."

"And Lisa and the children barely sleep, with you always bickering with Dianna or Peter or that... that... bloody thing." She puffed up her chest. "I can't even yell at you properly because we've got a guest, and who knows what you've told her."

"I told her nothing," he said calmly. "What was I supposed to do, let Charlotte freeze to death?"

"You could've taken her to the police station."

Roland stretched his arms up above his head.

"But you and that disastrous little brain of yours had to scheme up some awful trick. You couldn't just do the right thing."

"I haven't done anything wrong."

"R-really? Because last time I checked, you put a target on this family's back and jeopardized every effort your mother made to keep you out of trouble. She should've just let them lock you away. Maybe a few years behind bars would've straightened you out."

"Like I said, you're free to leave. I'm not stopping you."

"And if I go, who'll make sure nothing happens to these children?"

Roland glared at her. "The children are fine."

Tabitha motioned to them. "Do they look fine to you?"

Rose stepped out from the doorway, taking Tabitha by the hand.

Roland looked her up and down, then turned away. "It's been over thirty minutes. That's how long you've been hounding me, Tabitha."

"Pardon?"

Rose gave him a kick in the side. "Stop acting like a brat."

He grimaced.

She yanked him down, squeezing his jaw between her fingers as she jerked him toward her. "Instead of sitting here, waiting for Miss Warren, why don't you just have someone else sell that ring?"

He eyed her.

"I'm sure no one would think twice about Peter or Lisa doing it."

Roland pushed her hand away, nodding slowly. *Why didn't I think of this earlier?* Roland stood up, brushing past his niece and opened the door to the library stairwell.

Tabitha gripped his wrist. "Dianna won't forgive you for doing this."

"What do you care? You don't even like her," Roland said, heading upstairs.

"But you do."

Roland opened the door to the library. "I have a job for you."

The vermin nodded. "I know."

NICHOLAS STUDIED HIS REFLECTION CAREFULLY, taking notice of anything that one might consider inhuman. The teeth were always the first giveaway, that and the ears. Other differences were more subtle, easier to mask. He wrapped the scarf around his nose and mouth, then put the hat on his head. As long as he got back before dark, no one would notice anything out of the ordinary about his eyes.

"I still think we should wait for Miss Warren," Nicholas said, looking over at Roland. An ache formed in his chest. *Why's he doing this? If I go in there and someone realizes what I am, it's over for the both of us.*

"Nicholas," Roland said sternly, causing him to jerk his head back. "All you have to do is go in, ask them how much they can give you, and come straight back to the car with the money."

"But I heard you before, what you said to Miss Warren."

Roland sighed. "I know."

Nicholas watched the man shuffle in his seat. "Is this ring really that special?"

Roland nodded.

Nicholas held his breath as he opened the car door. "I'll be in and out, just like you said."

As he opened the door to the shop Nicholas' eyed widened. *Deisso. Deisso. Deisso!* He pulled the black ring box from his pocket and walked up to the counter, as instructed. Hands trembling as he set it down.

The man eyed him.

"How much?"

"Who's is it?"

"My mothers. We need to buy medicine," Nicholas said, reciting what he'd been told to say by Roland. He looked back at the car.

The man opened the box, nodding slowly and inspected the ring. "This is a beautiful piece. Lovely design, very unique. All right, I'll give you two-hundred bucks. How's that sound?"

Nicholas glanced toward the window, looking at the Chevy Deluxe, and nodded. "Uh sure."

32

"Hey, can I talk to you?" Roland said, face redder than the apples in her family's orchard. He hung his head, shuffling his feet.

Dianna bolted from her seat on the picnic blanket, brushing the crumbs from her dress. "About?"

Roland rubbed the back of his neck. "D-do you have any plans tomorrow?"

Constance and Juliet giggled, while Dianna looked him over.

"Look, I... I kind of was... I'm trying to–" Roland sighed, shaking his head.

Charlotte stood, took each of them by the hand and lead them away from the others. "Sorry about those two. Now, what was it you wanted to ask Dianna?"

Roland rummaged around in his pocket and pulled out a ticket. "Do you want to go?"

Dianna scowled. "Go where?"

"With me..." Roland gulped, pulled another ticket from his pocket and handed both to the girls. "Actually, um, I have a piano lesson. So here. You two can keep these."

"These are tickets to the Georgie Bryce show tomorrow," Charlotte said, wide eyed.

Roland bowed his head and darted off toward the group of boys on the other side of the lake.

Dianna knitted her brow, turning to Charlotte. "There's something very wrong with that boy."

"Well, that didn't go as planned," Charlotte said, twirling one of her curls around her finger.

"What?"

"He was supposed to ask you to go with him!" Charlotte threw her hands above her head. "He's been trying to ask to you for months!"

Dianna blushed. "No, that's impossible. He thinks I'm annoying. Peter said so."

Charlotte crossed her arms. "Peter lied."

Dianna gasped. "Is that why Roland spilled paint on himself last week while we were making posters for class elections?"

"Yes."

"And why he keeps buying candy and leaving it behind the library?"

Charlotte laughed. "Yes Dianna!"

Dianna eyed her. "Is that why you made me walk home with him the other day?"

Charlotte groaned, stomping off in the direction Roland went.

"Why didn't you tell me he liked me?" Dianna said following after her. "I mean, I told you I liked him..."

"Because both of you made me promise not to tell the other," Charlotte muttered.

"If he likes me, then why does he keep calling me Pigtails and Freckles?"

"Because Dianna, Roland's an idiot," Charlotte said, grabbing Dianna by the arm. "He thinks the only way people will pay attention to him is if he causes trouble... but he's a really sweet, and he really likes you."

"Why would he even like me?"

Charlotte turned to her, hands on her hips. "Why do you like him?"

"I don't know... he just does these things and–"

"Hello ladies," Miles said, strutting toward them. "Are you planning on going for a swim?"

"We didn't pack out bathing suits," Charlotte said, brushing past him.

"That doesn't mean you still can't go swimming."

"Piss off Miles," Roland said, tossing a rock at the older boy.

"We might play a game of tag if you girls want to join," Miles said, hurling the rock back at him.

"That sounds fun," Charlotte said, giving him a smile. "Can Connie and Juliet play too?"

"The more the merrier."

Dianna stood next to Roland under the tree and held the ticket out to him. "I thought you had a piano lesson."

He scratched his head. "I do."

Charlotte's smile grew wider. "Dianna, you're on Roland's team."

"Pardon?"

"For tag," Charlotte said as their schoolmates gathered around.

Roland shoved his hands into his pockets.

"I don't dislike you," Dianna said softly.

Roland's eyes widened.

"Do you dislike me?"

"Of course not," he said, turning to her. "Actually, I... well I um..."

She smiled at him. "Same."

Roland ushered Nicholas into the house, only to have Mr. Leon, Tabitha and Lisa corner them at the door.

"What were you thinking?" Tabitha said, screaming in their faces.

"Only one person saw him. He was dressed like this the entire time," Roland said, removing his coat.

Nicholas took the hat off, smoothing back his hair.

Tabitha crossed her arms. "What did that girl give you to sell this time?"

Nicholas tiptoed around her. "A ring."

Roland held his breath. "Go to the nursery."

"Yes, sir."

Tabitha shut and locked the front door, while Lisa and Mr. Leon guided Roland toward the dining room. Mr. Leon sat smoothing back his grey hair.

As Tabitha entered, she gestured for Roland to take a seat and stood behind his chair, resting her hands upon his shoulders.

Roland squirmed, feeling her fingers dig into him. "What's going on?"

Mr. Leon leaned forward, looking the young man up and down. "That's what I'd like to know."

"You're not sleeping," Tabitha said firmly.

Roland sank into his seat.

"Lisa's heard you up at all hours of the night."

"I didn't sleep before."

"Stop with the excuses, Roland," Leon grumbled. His expression softened. "Tabitha, would you allow us a few moments?"

Roland glanced back as her hands left his shoulders. "This isn't about my sleeping habits, is it?"

"It is not," Leon said, as Tabitha and Lisa shut the doors to the parlour.

Roland flinched at the slight click the doors made as they came together. He couldn't remember the last time they'd been closed. Mr. Leon cleared his throat, catching his attention.

He clasped his hands together on the table. "I've worked for your family a long time. This house and your parents represent something to this city... or they did. Look, I'm going to be brutally honest with you, because Tabitha, though she means well, struggles to see you for what you are."

Roland glowered, sitting up straight. "And what am I exactly?"

"An adult."

Roland, chin resting in his hand, tapped the table with the other, eyes rolling. "Obviously."

"Everyone in this house is aware you're not taking proper care of yourself. Nicholas included, and I don't think you realize how dangerous that is. You're putting all your attention into this project, which truthfully, it's nice seeing you so passionate about something again. I know your parents would've–"

"Let's leave my parents out of this one, please," Roland said, groaning as he brushed the hair from his brow.

"Well, that's just the thing. Despite how you feel about them, you are a Crispin. Your reputation has been damaged, possibly beyond repair. Being a Crispin in this city used to be... how can I explain this to you? Kids your age seem to forget–"

"Kids my age?"

"Stop interrupting me! And quit fidgeting," he said, swatting at Roland's hand.

Roland folded them onto his lap, nodding.

"Folks like myself and Tabitha, we grew up here. Our families were fishermen or farmers. When those rich families started sending their children here during the war, this city came to life."

"And then they opened up trade, blah blah blah. I know all this. It's the only thing I was allowed to study before I attended a *real* school."

"What did I say about interrupting?"

Roland swallowed hard. "Sorry... go on."

"You're a spitting image of your father. I know you hate hearing that, but by the time he was your age, Darius was a crucial pillar in this community. Crispin's, Taylor's, Doren's... these families helped establish Tavern into what it is today. Your name means something. It's not just a word you can throw about to scare folks. Do you see what I'm getting at?"

"Not really."

Mr. Leon shook his head. "You can't be yelling at old women in shops or picking fights with Jakob."

"They started it," Roland muttered.

"Stop. Please. Just listen." Leon frowned. "You really need to work on cleaning up your act. I know you don't care, but this isn't about you. Attending that party at the Doren's today was a great first step! Allow people to see you in a positive light. Interact with folks around town. Stop glaring at strangers and threatening your professors."

"I didn't threaten him."

"We both know you did. You're the same kid who threatened to have me fired when you were six because I scolded you for mucking around in the garden."

Roland scowled. "Professor Kidman was out of line."

"Roland, you're an adult. Stop pointing fingers at other people."

Roland slouched.

"And stop pouting! You're responsible for *three* children. Your brother's children. Sure, your work is important, but it's also important to take care of yourself, so that you can be the best guardian possible. Laurie and Wendy wanted them to stay here in Tavern for a reason. We both know how Viola is."

Roland shuddered. "Yeah..."

"Try to mend past relationships. Leave the house more. Let people see you for who you are, not who they expect you to be."

Roland leaned his head back, sighing heavily. "But that's too much effort."

"The effort isn't for you, it's for the children. Rose and Caspian are only a few years away from graduating. If they were to apply to college right now, I doubt they'd be accepted."

Roland sat up straight, eyeing him.

"I hear the things folks say to and about them when I pick them up from school. You're known as far as Florus from what I gather."

"Th-that's not–"

"And if word were to get out about your project, there will be no saving them. Do the work now and give those three a fighting chance. What'll they do when you're not here anymore?"

Roland shifted in his seat.

"You brought Charlotte here, knowing she's wanted by the police. You never should have done that. You absolutely cannot make mistakes like that. You need to think things through before taking action. We've talked about this... multiple times."

"She needed help."

"I'm aware of that, but Tabitha doesn't believe that's the reason she's here. So, tell me... is the child yours?"

Roland blinked hard. "Pardon?"

Mr. Leon blushed, clearing his throat. "Is the child yours? I-is that why you're so concerned about her?.

"I don't know what you're talking about?" Roland chuckled, shaking his head. "Evan, what sort of relationship do you think Charlotte and I have?"

"Listen, I don't usually get involved in those types of personal matters, but for the sake of everyone involved, I need you to be honest with me. If you do that, I can try and warm Tabitha up to the idea."

"The idea of what, exactly?"

Mr. Leon gave a wry smile. "Perhaps we need to have *that* talk. Did anyone ever–"

"I'm twenty-four. I think we've passed that point. Besides, Peter and Miles told me enough. What does any of that have to do with my reputation?"

"That doesn't make me feel any less uneasy..." Mr. Leon said, shaking his head. "Roland, Lisa thinks Charlotte is with child."

Roland laughed, then scratched his head. "Wait..."

"So?"

Roland lowered his voice. "Is that why you sent Tabitha out of the room?"

Mr. Leon shot up out of his seat. "How could you put that poor girl through all that?"

"I'm confused... what did I do exactly?"

Mr. Leon frowned, easing himself back into the chair. "Sorry. I promised myself I'd remain calm. The ring you had Nicholas sell. Was it Charlottes?"

"No, it was my mothers."

"Roland..."

"I have a few other things I could sell, like Papa's pocket watch and the decanter. I never use them. With the money, I could see if Eloise will help me hide her. Maybe get her sent to Dinara. She'd be safe there," Roland said softly.

"You are not responsible for her."

Roland met the older mans gaze. "And she wasn't responsible for me, back then. Without her, I would've died. You know that. Let me help her, please."

"You're an idiot."

"Tabitha's told me at least a million times. I know it was stupid to send Nicholas in there, but Dianna wouldn't let me explain. It was the only thing I had of value... and if Charlotte is pregnant like you say, I don't want Detective Carson getting his hands on her."

"Give me the pocket watch. I'll take it in tomorrow and see what I can get for it."

Roland nodded. "Thank you."

ROLAND PUSHED the door open slightly, peering in through the sliver of a crack at Charlotte resting on his bed. He'd lent her one of his mother's nightgowns, which hung loosely on her. It was definitely old fashioned, and seeing Charlotte in it made him chuckle slightly, but he decided, given the current situation, that he should keep the teasing to a minimum.

Charlotte was staring at the ceiling, eyes panning over the dimly lit room.

Roland gave a little knock, then went inside, carrying a tray of food that Tabitha had put together. "Dianna went out," he said, wincing.

Charlotte sat up, watching him put the tray on the bed beside her. "I know. I heard your two arguing."

Roland blushed. "Yeah... I was hoping you didn't. A-are you hungry?"

"Did she just get back? Are you two married?"

Roland cleared his throat, fingers drumming against his knee as he sat down. "We work together, that's all."

"But she lives with you."

"She... yes. Yes, she's been living with me."

Charlotte smiled, taking a cookie. "Well, now that we've all grown up a bit, perhaps you two can fix things?"

"I don't know how to fix anything, Charlotte. You know me. I'm a disaster."

Charlotte frowned.

"How did you meet your husband?" he said gently.

"He worked as a tradesman. Was always coming by the pub I worked at. Guess he had a thing for barmaids... I never should've married him."

Roland eyed her as she picked away at the chocolate chip cookie.

"Lennox wasn't a bad man. I just... it's just... I'm pregnant."

Roland smiled, relieved to hear it from her own lips. "Wow, that's–" He studied her expression, then sighed. "Charlotte, you look like you could use a hug."

She nodded.

Roland pushed the tray aside and wrapped an arm around her. "Is that what you were trying to tell me before?"

"The baby isn't his." Tears flooded her eyes. "I came back so I could find you or Connie to see if you'd help. Lennox knew. He knew, and he wanted me to tell the police. To tell Vincent."

"Tell them what? Your relationship with your husband isn't anyone's business," Roland said firmly.

"Roland, the baby's father isn't... he's not like us."

"What do you mean?"

She was shaking.

"Charlotte, did you love him?"

"I thought I did, but then he disappeared. Lennox... I think he had him disappear, and now I've lost everything. I don't know what to do."

"It's going to be okay. I'll help you, and I'll get in touch with Constance if you like. We'll all work together. Okay?"

"Roland, the father's a vermin."

Roland drew in a deep breath, holding her tighter. "That's... that's okay. We'll be okay."

Charlotte rubbed her eyes.

"Yeah. It'll be fine. I studied vermin in school. I've actually learned a lot," Roland said, trying to convince himself as his mind raced. "And I've had plenty of experience with babies. I'm basically an expert now."

Charlotte laughed. "You're taking this well."

"Truthfully, I'm a little surprised but well, um... I uh..." He shut his mouth. *If I tell her about Nicholas and the police find her here, there's no telling what she'll say in order to protect herself. If I were in her shoes, I'd throw him to the wolves.* He cleared his throat. "The police are looking for you. Did Lennox tell them anything about the baby?"

"No. He... he got sick."

"I hate to ask, but you need to be completely transparent with me. Did you kill him?"

Charlotte shook her head. "I left the hotel to get him some medicine, and when I came back he... he wouldn't wake up."

Roland nodded.

"There were bite marks along his throat. I... I think he angered someone back in Augen and they followed us here."

"By someone, do you mean..."

"Yes."

33

The Wolfe siblings stood hand in hand just outside of the beach the *Mivos* currently occupied. Micah didn't want to let go of his sister's hand. If anything happened to her, he'd be alone, and even Tiani's sweet voice wouldn't be able to pull him from that.

He straightened his back, taking in the smell of sea salt.

Zana rocked back and forth on the balls of her feet. "What if she doesn't recognize us?"

Micah pointed to his earring with his free hand. "Vermin always recognize their children."

Zana nodded slowly, turning her attention back to the beach.

Micah's stomach turned with the waves. When they'd gone to the *Lilik Morin* for help, Keirsi had come to meet them long before they got this close. The fact that none of the *Mivos* had approached them made the hair stand on his arms. He caught his sister's ears twitching. "What is it?"

She stepped in front of him, letting go of his hand.

"What do you hear?"

"Speak Valdin. They think we're human."

Micah sniffed his shirt, catching a whiff of their father's cologne, and growled. "*Deisso.*"

"Micah, *Stai.*"

"Don't tell me to shut up."

"Micah!"

He pressed his lips together, irritated. *I should've let that kid come with us... I don't think I could take a Mivos in a fight, and Zana's...* He looked over his younger sister. *If she's busy trying to protect me, she'll get herself hurt again.*

"Tsk. Tsk. Tsk. You *Hiloven* never learn, eh?"

Micah's jaw dropped as the hulking vermin approached.

"*Unya Valdinok. Misent* Breena Misk," Zana said.

"*Naska Latu Danya Voshen Iin Zat?*" Hereyes panned over the pair.

"*Iin Unash Musa.*"

The vermin towered over them, baring her teeth. "*Rodlich Valvenok.*"

Micah fought the urge to roll his eyes, instead forcing a smile.

The vermin gave a quick grunt, crossing her arms. "*Na?*"

"*Iya* Micah, *Ata Iin Elde Matya Schistra* Suzanna," he said. "*Ata Danya?*"

She smirked, leaning in close. "*Telchsci.*"

"Is that your actual name, or just what they call you?" he asked, pupils narrowing as she put a hand on his shoulder.

Zana stepped between them. "We just want to see Breena."

"*Ha. Inrohai.* This way."

The two followed the vermin *Telehsei* toward the beach, where a group of vermin stood waiting in front of a run-down house. The wind chimes hanging by the door sang out as they waltzed inside. *Telehsei* kneeled before the group of vermin sitting around what looked to be a fur blanket, lined with an assortment of food laid out on pieces of driftwood.

Micah caught sight of her instantly. The tawny-blonde bangs dangled in her face, nearly the colour of white sand.

Breena's eyes looked through him as sharp fangs peaked out from behind a smile no one could read.

The vermin sitting on the floor leered.

This was a bad idea. Micah rubbed his frozen fingers together.

"So, you've finally found me," Breena said, taking a piece of meat and popping it into her mouth, sucking the juices from her thumb. "Your kind aren't normally welcome, but I assured the others you wouldn't be staying."

Micah's ears twitched. He glanced at Zana.

Breena cracked her knuckles, leaning back in her seat as she looked them over. "Come now, *Yunenik*, what is it you want?"

Micah blinked hard. He'd forgotten the brittle sound of her voice. Micah's ears perked up at the tightness of her words. *She doesn't want us here.*

"We need help getting our brother out of Tavern," Zana said softly, not meeting the woman's eyes.

"Brother?" Breena scratched her head, glancing around the room. She wrinkled her nose. "You wreak of your father. Have you been to see him?"

"We've seen much more of him than you." Micah barked out his words, causing the others in the room to stir. "While we were in jail, you were with these *Feiv Valdinok*, not giving us a second thought."

"*Yunenik, Danya Misent Verjik.*"

"Our brother, the child you brought from Ferine, is in Tavern," Micah said, as she got to her feet. "Do you not remember dumping him on Nyla like you did us?"

Breena smacked him across the face, sending Micah stumbling back into his sister. Her pupils narrowed.

Micah pressed a hand to his cheek, eyes burning.

Zana pulled him back, standing face to face with their mother. "Our brother is from Ferine. I thought the *Mivos* always looked after their own."

"Go back to Nyla and have her retrieve him."

"Nyla's dead," Zana said.

Breena turned up her nose, circling around her daughter.

Micah steadied himself. "We know you're planning on taking Dinara."

Breena shot her head in his direction, nostrils flaring. "Don't speak of things you can't possibly understand."

"All we want is our little brother back," Zana said, reaching for their mother's hand. "No one else will help us... please, *Musa,* we need you."

Her face softened. Breena turned to the rest of the group. "*Telehsei?*"

The woman groaned, then shrugged. "Nyla vowed to watch over the child. If he's in Tavern, we need to get him. It's what she would've wanted."

Breena rubbed her temples. "But Tolya..."

"Regardless of what he's done, the boy is important to us."

"This throws off our entire plan," Breena said, grumbling as her ears twitched.

"We were going to hit Tavern eventually," she said, glancing at Micah and Zana. She wrinkled her nose and shuddered. "Where's he being kept?"

"He was taken by the Crispin's."

Breena grabbed her daughter by the shoulders, squeezing tightly. "W-what did you say?"

"The Crispin's. Roland Crispin."

Breena let her go, shaking her head.

Micah raised his brow. "That's how the *Lilik Morin* reacted when we went to them."

Breena nodded. "Go home. We'll need to discuss this matter privately... *Telehsei*, bring Tolya to me."

Micah glowered.

"Where are you staying?"

"With Father," Zana said.

"I'll come see you later, after we've made our decision. Tell Theo."

Micah stormed from the house, followed by his sister, cheek still stinging. He turned to Zana. "You okay?"

"*Ha... Danya?*"

He bit his lip. "I'm starting to think we left Nicholas with some really bad people."

34

———————

Dianna arrived back at the house with Vincent and two of Connie's sugar pies. "If Roland's face is stuffed with food, he can't ramble on and dodge my questions," she said, snickering as she unlocked the door.

Vincent leaned forward, glancing down at her hands. "You have a key?"

She blushed. "W-well, yeah."

Vincent shook his head as she opened the door and followed her inside. "Hello?"

Tabitha rushed to greet them. "Vincent, what a lovely surprise!" Her entire face lit up until she turned to Dianna. "Miss Warren, I didn't expect to see you back so soon. Where'd you get the pies?"

"Constance," Vincent said. "Do the children want any?"

"Most likely." She gave him a smile, wringing her hands together as she looked at Dianna. "Roland's in your room."

Vincent raised his brow.

Dianna groaned. She could only imagine what was going on in Vincent's head. "I see. Tabitha, do you mind bringing this to the kitchen?"

Tabitha shook her head, taking the pie.

Dianna went upstairs, catching sight of Nicholas hovering outside her door. "You shouldn't be out here," she whispered, glancing toward the stairs.

He nodded, brushing hair over his feather earring. "Mr. Crispin's in there."

"Tabitha told me."

He lowered his head. "*Kem Havochen Verjik.*"

Dianna knocked on the door, taking a deep breath. "*Narem?*"

He shrugged. "I don't know. Stuff. Stuff about you."

Dianna propped the door open just enough to pop her head in. She spotted him there on the floor, playing with the white bed skirt.

"Hi," he muttered.

She entered the room, taking off her heels. "Tabitha said you were up here."

"Nicholas, shut the door and go to the nursery," Roland said quietly.

Nicholas nodded, doing as instructed.

Dianna could see the strain on Roland's face. She knelt down beside him. "Are you upset about our argument?"

He shook his head. "That's not why I'm here."

"Okay… well then, what is it?"

He cleared his throat. "Charlotte's wanted by the police."

"I know."

He glanced at her briefly, then back at the bed skirt. "I had Nicholas go to town and sell the ring, so you don't need to worry about it anymore."

"Why would you put him in danger like that?"

"I needed the money."

She pressed her head into the edge of the mattress. "Roland."

"If I can get some money together, will you help Charlotte leave Tavern?"

"What? I-I don't–"

"Maybe you could take her to stay with your cousin Phoebe in Riversburg? Just until we find something more permanent."

"Roland, Vincent is downstairs. He's looking for her. A lot of people are looking for her."

"Well then, why the heck would you bring him here?"

Her voice caught in her throat. "Why would you sell my ring?"

He balled his fists. "Five years ago, you wanted nothing to do with it."

Dianna threw her head into her hands. "Because you stole it and became a murder suspect!"

"Charlotte needs us," he said sullenly. "And if we can't help her, then I at least want to know her kid is safe."

She smoothed out her dress. "So, it is true. She's pregnant."

He sighed deeply. "Why did you have Charlotte break up with me on your behalf?"

Dianna pressed her lips together as his eyes finally met hers. "Where's this coming from?"

"We never finished our discussion. I want you to be honest with me."

"Vincent's downstairs. T-there's pie and–"

"I don't give a damn about pie!"

She took his hand and squeezed it gently. "I don't think we should talk about it right now."

"When?"

Her voice shook. "Why do we even have to?"

He ripped his hand away, climbing to his feet.

She tucked her knees into her chest. "Did anything ever happen between you and her?"

Roland's fingers drummed along his thigh as he stared at her. He inhaled sharply, then smiled. "It was so easy to hate you while you were away."

"You didn't answer my question."

"We should go eat that pie. I don't want Vincent to get suspicious."

35

———

Roland sat across from Vincent at the kitchen table, carving out a slice of sugar pie. He resisted the urge to excuse himself to check on Charlotte. It was bad enough having a vermin in the house, but now he was harbouring a murder suspect. A murder suspect who was carrying a vermin's baby.

Dianna hadn't said a word since leaving her room. She was still in her gown, jabbing away at a piece of crust on her plate, not making eye contact with either of the men she sat between.

Vincent looked around. "Where's Peter?"

Roland forced down another piece of pie. "He's working on a paper. It's due at the end of next week."

Vincent gave a slow nod. "I heard Charlotte was at the Doren's. Did my cousin invite her?"

Dianna peered up from her plate. "She came with Roland."

Roland went to shoot her a dirty look, but instead gave a smile. "She wasn't invited. I just saw her out on the street without a jacket on and didn't want her to freeze."

"Any idea of where she went after?" Vincent said.

Roland ate another piece of pie, chewing slowly.

Julius came running into the kitchen, climbed up onto the empty chair and shook his uncle's arm wildly.

Roland turned to him. "Yes?"

"Have you seen Harry?"

Roland frowned. "I have not."

Julius pouted, scratching his head. "I can't find him anywhere."

"I'll come help you look," Roland said gently. He stood up, scooping Julius into his arms.

Vincent eyed him. "Roland, did Charlotte say anything about where she was going?"

"Charlotte?" Julius wrinkled his nose.

"The lady from the party," Roland said. He turned to Vincent, shaking his head.

"Do you mean the lady with the red sweater like Harry's?" Julius said, looking over at Vincent.

Roland shot his head around as Dianna choked loudly.

"Are you all right?" Vincent said, turning to her.

Dianna pounded her fist against her chest, eyes watering.

"We'll be right back. Harry's a very important bear in this house," Roland said, inching toward the kitchen door. Roland could feel Dianna's eyes burning into him as she scarfed down a glass of water. Roland let out a deep sigh. "Hopefully, this shouldn't take too long."

"How did you two get mixed up in this? You haven't spoken to Charlotte in years," Vincent said, rubbing the back of his neck. He raised his brow, eyes darting back and forth between Roland and Dianna.

Roland shrugged, wincing at the look Dianna gave him as she cleared her throat.

Vincent sat up straight. "Oh! Did you hear about the *Mivos*?"

"The what?" Roland scrunched up his face.

Vincent shook his head. "I don't know much about them or any of those feral mutts, but they've apparently reached Dinara. I have no idea how they managed to get that far. If cities like Riversburg weren't so lenient with their laws, this never would've happened."

"The *Mivos* are from Ferine, aren't they?" Dianna said, wringing her hands together.

"Why are we talking about vermin?" Julius said quietly.

"Oh sorry. We're just having a grown-up discussion," Vincent said gently, giving Julius a little smile. "Would you like me to help you and your uncle find your teddy bear?"

"We're not supposed to talk about vermin," Julius said firmly as the phone began to ring.

Roland shushed him, heart racing. "Julius, don't be rude."

"It's okay," Vincent said. "I understand. They can be scary."

"I'm not scared of them. They're nice," Julius muttered. He pat his uncle on the shoulder. "Can you help me look now?"

Vincent's jaw hung open as Dianna rose from her seat.

"I think I'll change into something a little more comfortable," she said, clearing the dishes from the table.

Vincent turned to her, then back to Roland. "Julius, vermin are very dangerous. Especially ones from Ferine. That's where the last of their army went after the war."

Julius clung to Roland's neck. "No! He's just a little bit grumpy sometimes."

Roland held his breath as Lisa came dashing into the room and grabbed the telephone.

Vincent stood and inched toward them. "He? Julius, who are you talking about?"

36

The Wolfe family sat quietly in the tearoom, staring at the stranger they once called wife and mother. Every memory of Zana's early childhood had been tainted the moment their mother struck Micah. Something broke inside Zana, and for the first time in her life, she wanted to take all the rage building inside her and put it to use – but she didn't. If she couldn't fend off a group of humans in Tavern, there was no way she'd be able to take down a full-blooded vermin.

Breena gazed around the room, not letting her eyes fall on Theodore even once, despite the obvious way he watched her. "We have yet to make a decision about going to Tavern," she said, eyes finally resting on the teacart.

Zana glowered.

"It's not because we fear the humans that live there, but because of who is currently in possession of your brother. You see, I struck a deal with the head of the Crispin family before marrying your father. I cannot go back on that deal even if they have Tolya's child."

Zana watched her carefully. "You made a deal with the Crispin's?"

Breena pushed back her uneven bangs, revealing a light bruise along her brow.

"Was this about thirty years ago?"

Breena's pupils narrowed. "A little less, but yes."

Zana stood. "During the burning of Esque?"

"What are you going on about, Suzanna?" Theodore turned to his daughter as she began pacing back and forth.

"What sort of deal did you make with them, Mother?"

"He and his wife lost a child. I guaranteed the next one would survive," Breena said nonchalantly, folding her hands onto her lap.

"How?"

Breena sucked in her breath. "Well clearly it worked, because now they have Nicholas... I haven't seen them since what happened in Esque. Do you know what they named the child?"

"Roland, I believe," Theodore said, as Micah reached for his sister's hand.

Breena's grin caused Zana's stomach to knot. "Nicholas will be safe with them. The family provided aid to the vermin of Esque at my request and worked alongside my crew for many years to free vermin being shipped to Presa. You have nothing to fear."

"Except Tavern! Where they locked us in cells and beat us!"

"If anything happens to Nicholas, the Crispin's will be killed."

"W-we don't want you to kill them," Zana said softly. "We just want our brother back."

"I never said the *Mivos* would do it. Humans who harbour a vermin are to be hung by the neck until dead. It's their law. Surely the Crispin's are aware of this."

Zana shuddered.

"The gentleman you made a deal with is no longer alive, Breena," Theodore said, finally drawing her attention. "I don't believe Roland Crispin has any knowledge of your agreement."

"The mother does."

Theodore shook his head. "I didn't see Mrs. Crispin at the house. To my knowledge that young man is the only adult Crispin present."

Zana watched her mother squirm.

"I see... That must've been what Tolya was hiding from me."

"You know I don't wish to hear that name in my house…" Her father folded his hands on his lap.

"You still believe I chose him over you?" Breena sneered, shaking her head. "All these years, and you still know nothing."

"Who's Tolya?" Micah said, glancing up at Zana as she pulled away from him.

"He stayed with us when you were a baby," Breena said. "He's Nicholas' father."

Zana turned to her. "You've been with his father this entire time? *Danya Doksot!*"

"Don't speak to your mother that way," Theodore said firmly, gesturing for Zana to take a seat.

"Someone needed to look after him," Breena mumbled. "He was getting involved with the *Mivos*."

"And look where you are now."

"I control the *Mivos*. I'm not slaughtering half-breeds and killing helpless humans in their sleep."

"No, you're just robbing trains and threatening Mordred," Theodore said.

"Mordred. Mordred. Screw that whiny little *Doksot!*"

"Okay, let's all just stop for a second," Micah said coolly. "What's important right now is Nicholas, not Cousin Mordred."

The others nodded, averting their gaze.

"You made some deal with the Crispin's, right? Could you possibly strike a new deal in exchange for Nicholas?" he asked.

Breena leaned forward and shrugged. "Like your father said, we're not sure this younger Crispin knows anything about our deal, and even if he did, it's not like he currently needs my assistance."

"Well, if he doesn't know, then the *Mivos* should just go to Tavern and get our brother."

"I don't think you understand what it is we do, *Yunenik*," Breena said gently.

Zana eyed her brother as he winced. She dug her nails into her palms, holding tight onto the fury within. *How can she still call him that after what she did to him earlier?*

Theodore exhaled deeply, patting Micah on the shoulder. "Your mother steals from all those ships and trains heading into Tavern."

Micah's jaw dropped. "You're a thief?"

Breena shrugged. "If you want to call it that."

"*Musa...*"

"Theo, *Bovyabik*, would it be possible for you to get in touch with the Crispin's and invite them here? Ask for the wife specifically. She may have simply been absent during your last visit."

Theodore frowned.

Zana's throat tightened, watching her father's demeanour darken. *She called him that as if it meant nothing.* Zana wanted to scream, her face growing hot.

"Whatever you wish, Breena."

"All will be well. Your father can handle things from here. I best get back."

"Or you could stay..." Micah whispered.

Breena furrowed her brow. "What for? There's no reason for us to play catch up. You've both grown taller, your father's still... well, himself... and Nyla's dead. I have all the information I need. I do wish you hadn't let your brother get taken. You're lucky he isn't dead."

"Nicholas wasn't the one getting beaten and starved," Micah said sharply, his pupils narrowing. "But you don't seem to give a damn about what happened to us."

"The two of you have the ability to use your father's name whenever it suits you. Nicholas doesn't have such luxury. He's not a half-breed. In fact, if the humans knew anything of his breeding, they might think twice about keeping him alive."

"I'll see if I can find the telephone number Miss Warren left me," Theodore said, getting to his feet. "She's the only person I trust in that city. She may be willing to help us."

Zana nodded, watching her father wander out of the tearoom. She barred her teeth, glaring at her mother. "Why did you make us live with Nyla?"

Breena blinked hard.

"Father cares about us. He doesn't think like the other humans.

He forced them to let Micah go to school... and if you hadn't taken us, Micah would be in college right now. Vermin can go to college in places like Riversburg! And we could've taught Nicholas to read and write, and the other kids, too. If you let us stay, maybe our cousins wouldn't be so hostile towards us. Maybe people would treat vermin better. You broke his heart; you know that don't you? Nyla's too... she couldn't even talk about you because it hurt so much. Why would you just leave us... We're your family."

Breena drew in a deep breath. "I couldn't bring you with me to Ferine."

"Then why weren't we sent back to live with Father?" Micah took his sister's hand again.

Zana was thankful for it, squeezing as tight as she could. They'd always have each other, no matter what. He'd never abandon her.

"Because these humans would've torn you to shreds!" Breena said, pointing to their father. "You're delusional if you think growing up here would've changed how they treat us. I spent my entire childhood in this house listening to them whisper. I could hear every *Bloka* thing that came out of their mouths. Everyone knew that I couldn't be the wife Theo wanted, but your father was just as foolish and naïve as you are. I thought I was untouchable because of my connection to this family, but I will always be a *Valdinok*, as will you. No amount of schooling or fancy clothes, or *Verjik Hiloven* customs will change the way others perceive you!"

Zana brushed the hair behind her ears as they twitched. "That still doesn't explain why we haven't seen you in ten years."

"It sounds like your father's gotten a hold of the Crispin's," Breena said, crossing her legs. "I'll stay until we know what's going on. You're right, I can't leave Nicholas in Tavern. If Nyla's gone, the child is my responsibility."

Zana sat beside her brother. "And we're not?"

"I didn't say that... it's just that the *Mivos* only came to Dinara to retrieve him. He'll be of age soon and expected to mate with one of the eldest *Maedkasho's* of their pack. I've taken the liberty of selecting suitable candidates. Nyla knew this."

Zana's eyes widened. "A mate? He's too young for a mate! Micah doesn't even have one!"

Breena turned to her son, pupils narrowed. "Nyla was too protective. Her pack only had a handful of potential mates. She knew you were to participate during *Jare Guntin*."

Micah crackled his knuckles, shrugging. "There were more important things going on during my spring, and Suzanna is only behind by a year."

"Also, Micah's *Iinayadin* left Dinara. He probably would've chosen her for his mate. She's the most skilled hunter from our pack," Zana said, desperately trying to ease their mother. The truth was that Samara's family had been skeptical of her being with a half-breed. She was incredibly talented, and although Micah worked hard to prove himself amongst the other vermin his age, he still fell short in terms of strength.

"The *Lilik Morin* kicked us out and took everything," Micah said.

Breena frowned. "Those *Doksot's* are out of control..."

Micah snarled. "How is your new pack any different?"

"The vermin in Dinara got too comfortable, thinking the humans would eventually allow for things to be equal between us. There can be no peace between us when there are children still being bred for the purpose of slavery. To this day, there are still more vermin in captivity than there are free. The *Mivos* only wish to change that."

Zana furrowed her brow.

"Your father purchased me the way he did that pretty dress you have on. Despite being a child, he selected me, and thought it was some good, generous deed, because it meant I could remain with my mother. Many of the vermin that work in this house have been here so long they've forgotten they were bought. They worked for free! I was Theo's companion. I had no identity outside of him, and then in the end I took his name as my own... because of that I can't determine if I really ever... loved him," Breena said quietly, in that brittle voice that had once been familiar to them. "I don't think our kind are meant to love. It's a very human concept. We choose a suitable mate because we want to strengthen our packs. I failed mine by being with

Theodore. You two are weaker because of your father... and I'm sorry for that. After I left Dinara, I realized why both humans and vermins believe *Valvenok* were cursed. Finding mates will never be easy for you... unless, of course, someone takes into consideration that you will inherit your father's wealth and influence, which is not something we vermin value. In our terms, you're undesirable. Nicholas, on the other hand, is exceptional... and needs to seek out a proper mate. The candidates I've selected may be taken if he's still in Tavern by *Jare Guntin*."

Zana heard her father breathing just outside the door. No one had ever called them undesirable. "Is that the only reason you want to get him back? To make up for your mutt children?"

Theodore swung open the door, looking right at her. "I-I spoke with a woman over the phone, who informed me that Mrs. Crispin is currently receiving treatment at a local asylum. Her husbands passed, along with the eldest son. So, the man I met, Roland Crispin, is currently head of the household... and he wasn't available either. She said she would have him contact me. But based on that call, I don't believe anyone in the household is aware of this deal you made."

Breena shook her head. "That's unfortunate."

"That aside, why not take Micah to *Jare Guntin*, instead? Surely you'd want one of your own children to find a proper vermin mate, to help strengthen the pack."

Breena glowered. "Don't act like you know anything about our customs."

"Don't call our children undesirable."

"Micah already–" Zana pressed her lips together tightly as her brother cleared his throat.

Theodore eyed them. "Micah's what?"

Micah shifted in his seat, cheeks flushing pink. "*Iya Lieken* Tiani."

Their parents exchanged a look that made Zana's heart flutter.

"She's a vermin who works for me," Theodore said softly.

Breena left out a huff, turning from him.

"Does she like you as well?"

"I think so," Micah mumbled.

"Like father, like son. I'd advise you to put a stop to this, Theo. It won't end well for either of them."

Theodore glanced back at her. "I've known her since she was a child. She's a lovely young lady."

"You know what, Theo, you're right. I should bring our mutt children to *Jare Guntin*. Perhaps being around *real* vermin will open their eyes, since it seems you and my mother have done everything in your power to blind them to the realities of this world," she snapped, heading for the door.

"Breena, *Stabima*..."

"Festivities will begin in the next month. I'll send *Telehsei* to assist with preparations," Breena scoffed. "And once you're able to get a hold of Mr. Crispin, I'd like to speak with him."

37

Dianna looked from Roland to Vincent as Lisa spoke quietly on the phone.

"Yes, of course. I'll be sure to have Master Crispin call you right back," Lisa said, then hung up the phone.

Vincent titled his head, running a hand along his collarbone. "Julius, can you tell me about this vermin?"

"I'm not supposed to," Julius said softly, burying his face into his uncle's shirt.

Roland cleared his throat. "Lisa, who was that on the phone?"

Lisa pressed her lips together, brushing back her pale blonde hair. "Lord Wolfe."

Vincent turned his attention to Roland. "Why would Lord Wolfe want to speak with you?".

"Are you sure it wasn't for me?" Dianna said, causing Vincent to jerk his head around. "I've been meaning to check in with him."

Lisa bowed her head. "He... he asked for Mrs. Crispin but she's absent, so he was wondering if he could speak with you instead, sir."

Roland blinked hard. "My mother?"

"Yes sir. He said it was urgent."

"I wasn't aware he knew my mother."

"I wasn't aware he knew you," Vincent said firmly, cracking his knuckles. He leaned in close, examining Roland, then Julius. "Could you describe the vermin for me, Julius? Was it a girl around the same age as your sister?"

Julius shook his head.

"Julius has never seen a vermin," Roland said quickly. "He's just been spending a lot of time with Peter and I while we've been working."

"Roland, Lord Wolfe's children are vermin. The vermin that robbed my father. The vermin that Dianna helped get out of Tavern, without even a slap on the wrist!" Vincent motioned to her.

Dianna's stomach twisted into knots as she wrung her hands together. She went over to Roland and held out her arms. "I told Theodore we were married," she said, avoiding Vincent's gaze, praying he'd buy the lie. She took Julius and held him. "I didn't think he'd speak with me unless I came from a prominent family."

"Speak to you about what?" Roland raised his brow.

"About coming to Tavern to get his children," Dianna said, lowering her head. "It must've been me he was asking for, not your mother. I... I should've said something. I'm sorry."

Vincent tapped his foot, looking them over. "He's probably calling to see if Tavern is willing to help Dinara with their vermin infestation. He should've thought of that before pushing to change all those laws."

"Vermin deserve rights," Dianna said firmly.

"They're dangerous."

"So are we!" She threw her hands above her head. "Humans lie and cheat and steal and kill, just like they do."

"They're monsters. A human wouldn't attack a defenseless child!"

Julius covered his ears.

"You can't just use the actions of one vermin to judge an entire group. That's like saying that because Roland's a murderer, all Crispin's are murderers!" Dianna let out a huff, glaring at him.

"But Roland isn't a murder!"

"You don't know that!"

Vincent stared at her blankly.

She turned to Roland, face hot. "W-what I meant was–"

"Lisa, I'd like to speak with Lord Wolfe. Could you call him back, please?" Roland said, averting his gaze. He turned to Dianna and Vincent. "I think the two of you should leave. Tell Connie thanks for the pie."

Dianna hung her head. "I didn't mean it like that."

Vincent stormed toward the kitchen door, then spun on his heels. "Julius, what was the vermins name? The grumpy one."

Julius hid behind his uncle.

"I said go," Roland muttered sullenly. "I don't have the energy to deal with either of you right now."

Vincent glared at him and pushed open the kitchen door.

Dianna frowned. "I'll be upstairs... okay?"

"No."

She eyed him as Lisa handed Roland the phone.

"I don't want you staying here. Just go home," Roland said hoarsely. He pressed the phone to his ear.

38

Roland wrapped the black cord around his finger, as Dianna stepped out of the kitchen. He could feel her eyes on him still as the door closed behind her. He let out a gentle sigh the moment Theodore's voice came through the speaker.

"Is this Roland?"

He glanced down at Julius, who was clinging tightly to his pant leg. "Yes. You wanted to speak with me?"

"Actually, I was hoping we could speak with your mother. Is she around?"

"No..." He gripped the cord, pulling the phone away from his ear. *So, it was my mother he wanted to speak to... but why?*

"Hello?"

"I'm still here," Roland said.

"Are you the only adult Crispin currently living at the estate?"

"I am. My mother's been hospitalized."

"I see. I'm sorry to hear that. Well, Breena would like to speak with you. Are you alone?"

Roland frowned. "My nephew and the nanny are here in the room with me. Should I ask them to leave?"

Lisa raised her brow.

"Yes. That would be best."

Roland gestured for Lisa to come closer. "Help Julius find Harry, and make sure Vincent and Dianna have both left."

"Yes sir," she said, taking the five-year-old by the hand. "Come along, little one. Perhaps Alicia's seen Harry around?" Quickly, Lisa led Julius from the kitchen.

"I'm alone now."

"Good. Breena's here," Theodore said.

"Hello Roland," the woman said gently. "I hear you have my boy."

The goosebumps raised on Roland's arm. *Nicholas?*

"Did your father ever mention me?"

"No?"

"He and I had an arrangement. You see, I'm the reason you're here."

His heart dropped. "P-Pardon?"

"I tried to save your brother, but your parents came to me too late. It's always easier to start while the child's still growing. How's your health? Your father did reach out once... something about intense migraines?" she said softly. "I can help with that, if you'd like."

Roland furrowed his brow. "I'm sorry. I don't know what you're talking about."

"I am crawling, my knees bleeding, searching high and low." Her words slithered into the phone.

Roland's eyes widened.

"It's a song from Ferine. Did you know that?"

His stomach turned.

"If you refuse to return the boy to me, I may have to break my promise to your father, and since he's no longer here, I really don't have to honour our agreement," she said, chuckling lightly.

"I don't know anything about an agreement, nor do I know anything about you."

"Go ask your mother and call us back in the morning." There was a click, followed by silence on the other end.

Roland hung up the telephone, hair standing up on the back of his neck. He turned slowly toward the kitchen door, heart dropping in his chest. *Was that Nicholas' grandmother? No, she sounded young.* He raced from the kitchen, heading upstairs and opened the door to Dianna's room. "Do you–" Roland looked around. *I told her to leave.* Roland shuddered, hurrying downstairs. He unlocked the front door. "Dianna?"

"She left with Mr. Gray," Lisa said, poking her head out from over the railing.

"I-I have to go visit my mother," Roland said quickly. "When Dianna gets back–"

Lisa frowned, pointing to the coat rack. "She took a bag with her and left the key. It's in your jacket."

"Wait... what?"

She shook her head. "I'm sorry. I wasn't much help back there." She came down the stairs. "Mr. Rissing is still upstairs. Would you like me to get him?"

Roland shuffled his feet, looking around. "No. I... I won't be long. Keep an eye on things for me while I'm gone."

"Is something the matter?"

"I'm not sure," Roland said, giving a weary smile as he put on his boots. "Did Dianna say where she was going?"

"Home, like you told her."

Roland nodded, threw on his coat, and sighed. "I see."

39

———————

Roland climbed into bed, pulling the sheets up halfway while Lawrence called out to him from the bathroom.

"Did you pick something?"

"Yep!" Roland called back, grabbing the novel from the nightstand. He traced his finger over the raised lettering on the cover and smiled, the bumps tickling his skin. He'd observed how his older brother selected books: the spine, the feel, the cover, the summary on the back, the first few pages. Roland always knew Laurie would love a book if he read more than the first few chapters, and Laurie always found the most marvellous books.

He waited patiently for his brother to finish brushing his teeth, and then once Lawrence was ready, scooched over to make room on the bed.

Laurie took the book from him and grinned. "Nice choice." He nodded, rubbing his chin the way their father often did. "I haven't read this since I was about your age."

Roland leaned into him. "Do you think Papa's ever seen a pirate?"

"No... but they usually don't attack trains. They rob ships."

"I wish I could ride the train all around the entire world, and then sail somewhere that had no rules or bedtime and you only could ever eat cake," Roland said.

Lawrence chuckled. "When I move to Presa, you'll have to take the train to visit me."

"Why are you going so far away? Why can't you just stay here for school?" Roland pouted. Laurie had told him many times that someday he'd be too big for the nursery, and that eventually he'd have a house of his own, with another family, but Roland secretly wanted things to stay as they were forever.

Lawrence opened the book, careful not to put too much pressure on the hardcover spine. "Well... they have a writing community there." His gaze went far off, like he was some place Roland couldn't be.

It made his stomach flutter.

"I secretly enrolled in one of the universities writing programs. They liked my writing portfolio... and accepted me," Lawrence said quietly. He pulled Roland close. "You can't tell anyone. Not a soul. Not even Tabby."

Roland cocked his head, heart racing.

"Promise?"

He smiled big, nodding. "I promise. Cross my heart, eat a fly, swear on Tabby's apple pie."

His older brother tousled his hair.

Roland beamed. It wasn't every day that Laurie trusted him with a secret. He'd keep it forever. He'd never tell a soul, not even a ladybug or the wind. This was a special secret between him and his brother.

"I THOUGHT we advised you not to visit for a while," the man at the desk said, as Roland bowed his head.

"I know, but it's urgent. I really need to see her."

"Visiting hours ended five minutes ago," the man said.

"Please." Roland's throat tightened. "I... I have to ask her a question about my medication so I can have Dr. Gray order it for me.

She got it from another doctor and... and I've started blacking out again."

The man eyed him. "I'm sure Dr. Gray can–"

"He doesn't know who the doctor was."

The man leaned back in his chair as Freya approached.

"Mr. Crispin, what are you doing here?"

"He wants to see his mother," the man grumbled. "But as I just told him, visiting hours ended five minutes ago."

Freya clapped her hands together. "I think Mrs. Crispin could use a quick visit. She's been asking for you by name."

Roland furrowed his brow. "S-she has?"

Freya nodded. "How does ten minutes sound? Can we spare him ten minutes, Mr. Pike?"

The man shrugged, kicking his feet up on the desk. "I'm willing to look the other way, if you're willing to compensate us for the time."

Roland sighed. "Do you have a pen?"

Mr. Pike handed one to him and a piece of paper.

"Call this number and ask for Charlie Levesque. He'll cover the expenses. Just tell him Roland needed extra time with his mother. He'll understand."

Mr. Pike grinned. "Enjoy your visit Mr. Crispin."

Once they reached Adeline's room, a lump grew in Roland's throat. During his last visit, his mother had slapped him. He wasn't sure how she'd react to seeing him again.

Roland entered the room, giving her an awkward grin. "Sorry I didn't bring and candy this time."

Adeline stared at him, then turned to Freya.

"I was wondering if I could ask you about one of Darius' friends? Her name is Breena," Roland said, glancing back at Freya as his mother came close.

Adeline looked him over. "Who told you about Breena?"

"She did."

Adeline gave a slow nod, then turned to Freya. "I'd like to speak with him in private."

Freya pressed her lips together. "Are you sure?"

"I'll call for you if I need you," Adeline said gently.

Freya left the room, closing the door only partway.

Adeline gestured for Roland to follow her toward the window. "Don't go anywhere near that woman."

"She said you had an agreement with her," Roland whispered, looking over his mother carefully.

Adeline glowered, pressing a hand against the window. "She's the reason you're drawn to such evil. From the day you entered this world, I knew. I tried to keep you safe... to lock you away. I think that's why you spared me."

Roland held his breath. "I'm not evil. I'm–"

"Sometimes my mind plays tricks on me. You, you play tricks on me. You look so much like him that sometimes it's easier to pretend you are. To pretend you didn't take him from me... but your eyes. Your eyes are like that woman's. That's how I know."

Roland placed a hand on her shoulder. "Mama, who is Breena? What's this deal she's talking about?"

Adeline shoved him off, taking a step back. "When Darian was sick, we took him to Esque. It's just outside of Dinara. Your father had heard of a girl there. She said Darian was already giving up, but that if we wanted, she would protect our next child," Adeline said quietly. "Your father wanted a large family. He said we should try again, just one more time... but when you were born, you had no heartbeat. We thought you were dead. We thought she killed you. She did kill you. It's the only thing that makes any sense."

Roland had heard the story before. How he had been delivered at home, and how his mother had been very sick during the delivery. How he didn't cry when he entered the world, but instead remained still and silent. Dr. Gray had put him down in the basinet by the bed and chose to tend to Adeline at Darius' request. There was no saving the child, but he could save the mother.

It was Laurie who noticed the tiny hand move. He insisted that he had to see the baby, even if it was to say goodbye. He whispered in Roland's ear, and that was when Roland started to wail. The pink coming to his face.

"What did this woman do? How could she... how did she know about the migraines?" Roland asked.

"Her blood runs through you," Adeline said, keeping her voice low. "A vermins blood. She'd done the same with Darian. He was with us another year but... but he–"

Roland steadied himself against the wall. "I-is that why you tried to kill me?"

"I wasn't trying to kill you. I was trying to keep you safe!" She began wringing her hands together, her voice wavering. "You were going to run away again. You would've hurt someone else, like you did that classmate of yours. I couldn't let it happen again."

Roland shook his head. "I-I don't understand. By blood, what... what did she do?"

Adeline stepped back as Freya came into the room.

She glanced at Roland. "Is everything all right, Mrs. Crispin?"

Adeline wandered over to her bed. "Go home Roland. I don't want you getting caught in the rain."

40

———————

Rose woke the next morning, with Julius' foot digging into her face, and Caspian curled in a tight ball, nuzzling her shoulder. She laid there a long time, staring up at the ceiling. The day before had been absolute chaos. Currently, there was a stranger in the house. Miss Warren vanished, and Vincent had been questioning Julius about Nicholas. *Did Uncle Roland come back last night?* She tickled the bottom of Julius' foot, causing him to sit up, eyes closed, head darting wildly.

He smacked his lips. "I dreamed an evil bunny was trying to eat me."

"Oh, no. Were you scared?" Rose said, patting Caspian on the head.

Julius shook his head as Caspian groaned.

He squinted slightly to look at his sister. "What?"

"We've got school," she said.

"I'm not going," Caspian said, pulling the blue sheets over his head.

Rose crawled around Julius and got up off the bed, stretching as she went over to her closet. "If we don't go, people will think something's wrong."

"The bunny was orange, and it smelled like oranges. I'm never eating oranges again," Julius said, finally opening his eyes. "Why are you in our room, Rosie?"

"This is her room," Caspian said, gesturing to the piles of books on the floor.

Julius stared at him. "No wonder I dreamed of evil bunnies."

"Are you implying that I'm evil?" Rose said, placing her hand on her hips.

Julius shook his head, pointing to the painting of brown rabbits in a carrot patch. "I don't trust carrots."

Caspian and Rose exchanged a look, brows raised, then turned to their younger brother.

"Why not?" Caspian said, getting out of bed.

"They're orange."

"Come on, let's go get ready for school," Caspian said between yawns. He turned to Rose as she pulled a long red dress from her closest. "Wait a minute... why didn't Lisa wake us up?"

Rose pulled one of the ribbons from her braid. "Hm. That is odd, isn't it."

"Maybe we should go check on her?"

Rose nodded, following the boys out into the hall. Her heart nearly jumped from her chest as she spotted their uncle sleeping beneath the grandfather clock in the hallway.

"What's he doing?" Caspian whispered.

Rose shook her head, tiptoeing toward him. "Uncle Roland, are you okay?" Rose tapped him gently. *He smells awful!* She turned to her brothers. "I think we should get Lisa."

Julius ran and knocked on the door to Lisa's room, while Rose shook their uncle again.

The Crispin children stood in the hall; jaws dropped as their uncle stirred, revealing the large purple bruise around his eye.

"What happened?" Caspian said as Lisa opened the door.

"Should we call Dr. Gray?" Rose knelt down, examining their uncle's face.

"Why do you smell like that?" Caspian said, pinching his nose.

Julius pulled Lisa toward the grandfather clock. "You smell like that place with the cookies!"

"Shh!" Rose and Caspian said, glaring at their younger brother as Roland massaged his head.

Roland squinted his right eye. "I, uh... I need to make a phone call."

Lisa crouched down next to Rose, taking his head in her hands and tilting it side to side. "You're drunk."

The Crispin's jumped back as the door to the nursery popped open.

Rose covered her eyes. "Nicholas, where are your clothes?"

"Relax. I have pants on," he said, hoarsely. "Mr. Crispin, you can come sleep in here. I changed the sheets for you."

Anger washed over Caspian's face. "You knew he was like that, and just left him here?"

"Last night this *Bloka* went all *Verjik* and started making a mess of the kitchen. When I tried to stop him, he tried to hit me, so I made him sleep out here on the floor."

Rose uncovered her eyes.

"You got your clothes dirty, Uncle Roland," Julius said. "Tabby's going to be so upset!"

"Look at what he did to my arms," Nicholas said, turning them around to show the deep red scratches.

"How big of a mess did he make?" Rose watched as Lisa helped Roland to his feet. "Maybe we can tidy it up before Tabitha gets here?"

Roland sniffled. "D-do you remember when grandmother...Do you..." He stumbled forward, nearly knocking into his niece.

"Easy now," Lisa said softly. She shook her head. "It's already bad enough the children have to see you like this."

Rose glared at Nicholas. "Would you please put a shirt on?"

He marched into the nursery.

"There's no way we'll be able to hide this from Tabitha," Caspian said as Rose took Julius' hand. "We can't just leave him."

"Maybe we should tell Mr. Leon instead?" Julius said, looking between the two of them.

"Don't worry about the mess downstairs, I already took care of that," Nicholas said, pulling a grey shirt over his head.

Rose studied him briefly and gulped, looked at the ceiling. "What time did he get home?"

"Early this morning."

Rose frowned. "Do you know what happened to his face?"

"No, but the police dropped him off."

"Great, that means everyone's going to be talking about it at school," Caspian said, stomping toward his room as little Alicia peered out into the hall.

"Tabby's going to give Uncle Roland a spanking," Julius said firmly, following his brother.

"No one's getting a spanking," Rose said, shaking her head as Lisa shut the door to the nursery.

Lisa folded her hands together. "Nicholas, did you say the police dropped him off?"

"*Ha.*"

"Would you keep an eye on him for me? I'll call the station and see if they can tell me where he was last night. Rose, go get ready for school, okay?"

Rose frowned, going back to her room. *I thought Uncle Roland didn't drink anymore?*

SUNLIGHT POURED in through the curtains as Roland rubbed the sleep from his eyes. His nose caught the soothing scent of coffee, and for a moment as he sat up, listening to the radio playing, he saw a glimpse of his father staring back at him. Roland blinked hard, shaking his head before opening his eyes again. Tilting his chin up, Roland angled his face, examining Peter as he waltzed into the room and flopped down onto the bed across from him.

"Lisa called," Peter said, handing him a mug. "We told Tabitha you we're up all night working and needed some sleep."

Roland shrugged. Tabitha was the last thing on his mind. *Why does my face hurt?*

"So, you paid your mother a visit last night?"

"Yeah."

"And then you ended up drinking your fill and going to my cousins," Peter grumbled, before glugging down half of the coffee in his mug. He exhaled, looking up at the ceiling.

Roland followed his gaze. There wasn't anything there.

"My uncle nearly killed you," Peter muttered.

"Huh?"

Peter stared at him for an instant.

Roland cleared his throat. "Sorry... I'm not really–"

Peter smirked. "It's fine."

"I feel like my head's about to explode."

"Yeah, my uncle gave you a really good hit, according to Dianna."

"I had a bit to drink last night," Roland said, blowing on his coffee. He took a sip and wrinkled his nose. "It's not sweet enough."

Peter chuckled. "It's coffee. Not liquid sugar. And you had more than a bit."

Roland sulked. "My mother... after Laurie died she tried to..."

Peter eyed him.

"What?"

"You do realize you went to my cousin's house in the middle of the night and embarrassed yourself, right?"

Roland's ears went hot. He nodded, nearly choking on the fresh stream of coffee going down his throat. *It's way too bitter.*

"I thought you didn't drink anymore. At least that's what you told me a while back?" Peter said, looking a bit hurt.

Roland rubbed the back of his neck. "I don't. Please don't say anything to Tabitha. My head's killing me."

Peter leaned back. "She's going to find out, regardless. My aunt called the police."

"Promise you won't tell her? She'll worry and so will the children." Roland stood up and eased himself toward the window. "My mother said something yesterday, and I don't know what it means."

"Yeah?"

Roland glanced back at Peter, watching him trace the rim of the mug with his finger. "What's wrong?"

"I'm usually the one asking you that," Peter said softly.

Roland took another sip of coffee. It was still bitter, but at least it didn't make his insides recoil in disgust. He turned to face Peter again, looking him over carefully. "What's the matter?"

"What happened between you and Charlotte after I left for college?"

Roland held his cup firmly. "Why?"

"Dianna seems to believe something happened," he said softly.

"It was nothing."

"Then tell me."

Roland took a quick gulp of coffee. "We stole from Doren Shipping."

"I know that. Obviously..." Peter grit his teeth. His expression softened. "Whatever it is, I won't be angry. I just want to understand what's happening here."

"She was with me, the night my father died... we were at Doren Shipping."

Peter eyed him.

"We were in his office."

"Okay... and?"

Roland sat down beside him. "We... we found the body."

Peter drew in a deep breath and held it, eyes wide.

"My mother thinks I was born evil... and I think that maybe she's right," Roland said softly. "What I did to Etienne and what I did to her. I could've killed both of them."

Peter exhaled. "You're not evil." He poked Roland playfully in the side, causing him to swat back.

Roland chuckled slightly, finishing his coffee. His hands were shaking. "Do you know what it means to have vermin blood?"

"Doesn't it just mean someone's part vermin?"

"I'm gonna be sick..."

Peter raised his brow. "Why? What's wrong?"

Roland turned his head. "Was Dianna there, at her parents?"

"Yes," Peter said.

"Did I say anything to her about my mother?"

"You'll have to ask her that, although I'm not sure she wants to see you right now."

Roland gripped the mug by the handle. "How does someone know if they're part vermin?"

"I don't know?"

His stomach ached. *Maybe I should call that woman back?* He drew in a deep breath, getting up off the bed. "Did Dianna tell you about last night?"

"You're going to pull the handle off," Peter said, gesturing to Roland's fingers curling tighter around it.

Roland let go, looking at the redness of his hands.

"Look, I don't like getting in the middle of you two."

"I did a lot of stupid things yesterday."

"At the party the other day, I could've sworn you were about to murder Miles with the look you gave him, but you didn't. I see how you look at her, okay? It's hard not to... but you're an idiot, Roland."

"You sound like Tabitha," Roland muttered, looking down at his feet.

"One minute you hate my cousin, the next you're in love with her."

"I never said I hated her."

"You did. Multiple times, both before and after she broke it off with you."

Roland frowned.

"It's not like you didn't see other people while she was away," Peter said.

"I didn't see anyone else." Roland's voice was so soft, it was just above a whisper. His entire face burned.

"Pardon?"

"Your cousin's the only girl I've ever been with," Roland murmured, shoving his hands into his pockets.

Peter stifled a laugh.

"What?"

"Wait, so all this time you never even tried to meet anyone else?"

"What sane woman would want to be with me? Everyone thinks I'm a murderer."

Peter cocked his head. "You've never kissed another woman?"

Roland gave a huff and glowered. "Of course, I have."

"Like who? Tabitha and your mother don't count."

Roland sighed, easing himself away from the bed. "I don't kiss and tell." The truth was, he couldn't. Not now, not with everything going on.

Peter burst out laughing. "You know what? I'm going to make it my mission that you get a kiss from a woman by the end of the week."

"That's stupid."

"No, you're stupid," Peter said with a laugh. "Come on, let's get you cleaned up."

41

———

Rose sensed the eyes on her and her brothers as they waited for the bell to ring. The chatter filled the schoolyard. Their uncle's name coming from students, teachers and parents.

Rose noted how Julius hesitated to leave her side. She gestured to his classmates, who were building an oddly shaped snowman by the front steps. "Don't you want to play with your friends?"

Julius hung his head, fiddling with his mittens.

Rose glanced at Caspian as he knelt down in front of their little brother. He hadn't said a word since they left, but the scowl on his face softened as he gave Julius a big, wide smile.

"Want me to help you with your laces?"

Julius nodded.

Caspian pulled Julius' boot forward and tied a knot. He peered up into Julius' face and pinched the five-year-old's cheek. "What's the sour look for, eh?"

"I want to go home," Julius said, voice catching in his throat. He sniffled slightly, rubbing his eyes.

Caspian turned to Rose. "It'll be a long walk back. Besides, I don't think you want to be home right now. Uncle Roland is... well..."

"He's not feeling well," Rose said quickly. She didn't like lying to

Julius, but it was easier than trying to explain. Caspian had been the same age as Julius when their uncle would stagger about the house. Usually, Roland would sit in the parlour, glowering at their grandfather's chair. Sometimes he would leave and wouldn't come back for days. It made the knots in her stomach tighten. Caspian would ask if she thought he was coming back, and she never knew the answer. Julius was too young to remember, and she was thankful for it.

"Are you three all right?" said Miss Pearson, Julius' teacher. She put a hand on Rose's shoulder, pouting. "I heard about the police and your uncle. I can only imagine how frightened you all must be."

Caspian wrinkled his brow. "Frightened of what?"

"Your uncle," she said, plainly.

Caspian stood; arms crossed. "Why would we be frightened of him?"

Rose gave a smile as Miss Pearson eyed them. "We're not sure what you mean about the police. Our uncle's been a bit under the weather recently, that's all."

Mrs. Clifford marched toward them. "The man's a drunk."

Rose flinched, reaching for Caspian's hand.

"I don't know why they let him go. They should've locked him up."

Miss Pearson frowned. "Mrs. Clifford, I went to school with Roland and–"

"And I was his teacher," Mrs. Clifford said sullenly. "The boy was a monster, as was his brother and as are you three. I've yet to meet a single decent Crispin."

Caspian gritted his teeth. "What does an old hag like you know about monsters?"

Rose shot her head in his direction, eyes wide.

"E-excuse me?"

Miss Pearson folded her hands together. "Caspian, dear, that wasn't a very polite thing to say."

Mrs. Clifford grabbed him by his jacket, yanking him away from Rose.

The other students and teachers were watching.

"What? You gonna call my mother?" Caspian said, glaring at the teacher. "Go on. I'm waiting."

Rose's heart dropped. "Caspian please–"

Whack!

The students gasped.

Caspian winced, cheek red.

"Apologize." Mrs. Clifford stomped her foot, hand raised again, ready for a second slap.

Caspian glowered. "I'd rather die."

Rose pulled her brother behind her as the school librarian came running through the crowd.

She stepped in front of the children. Her pinned curls unravelled.

"Juliet, that boy is disrespectful, defiant and spoiled!" Mrs. Clifford pointed to at Caspian. "He needs to apologize."

"Wouldn't you prefer a sincere apology?" Miss Welsh said, trying to catch her breath.

"After what their uncle did to your fiancé, I'm surprised–"

"What Roland does has nothing to do with these children. If I tell the board that you've been targeting them solely based on the allegations made against their uncle, I doubt you'll be able to teach here anymore."

Miss Pearson nodded slowly. "You weren't very nice to Roland when he was in school, either."

Mrs. Clifford glared at them. "Ask any of the other seasoned teachers at this school what that boy was like!"

"We know what he was like. We were friends," Miss Welsh said. "I've never once taken out my frustration on any of these children because of that."

Mrs. Clifford frowned, then pointed at Caspian. "I want this one removed from the premises. Disrespectful children have no place at this school."

∼

"Why are you in the same clothes as yesterday?" Rose said, scrutinizing him with her keen blue eyes.

Roland pressed his lips together, eyeing the ten-year-old. He opened his mouth, then shut it again.

She raised her brow. "If you're trying to be sneaky, you're doing a very bad job."

He took a step back, nodding.

"You smell funny," she said.

"Funny as in bad?"

She plugged her nose.

"Where's your grandmother?"

"She's with Lisa."

"And where, sweet flower, is Lisa?" Roland patted her on the head.

"She's feeding the babies."

He nodded. "Do me a favour and don't tell anyone that I just got in."

She stood akimbo. "But that's lying."

"Rose, I could do without the sass this morning. I have a headache," Roland mumbled.

She rolled her eyes, mouthing his words mockingly, then smiled, tracing an invisible cross over her heart. "Fine. Cross my heart, eat a fly, swear on Tabby's apple pie."

Dianna climbed up the sugar maple, cold bark scratching away at her fingertips. It had been years since she'd shimmed her way up and onto the thickest branch. She sat in her father's overalls, legs swinging as she listened to the sound of the school bell ringing off in the distance.

When she arrived the other night, her parents didn't ask questions. Her mother went to finish her knitting, and her father smoked his pipe while she slipped out of her dress and into her pyjamas. She sat at her father's feet, watching the wood crackle in the fireplace while they listened to the radio, rain knocking against the roof. When the tune to *Wicked Boys* began to play, her eyes burned with tears.

Mona, her mother, got up to put on the kettle. "That rain'll leave an awful mess."

Dianna glanced toward the window, heart skipping at the figure approaching the porch.

There was a knock at the door.

"Would you get that, Ken?" Mona said, popping her head out from the kitchen.

Dianna climbed to her feet, looking at her father. "Don't worry, I've got it."

He gave a low grunt, nodding.

She opened the door to find Roland pacing back and forth, soaked from head to toe. His face red and blotchy. She closed the door slightly, glancing back into the house. "What are you doing here?"

"Dianna." His trembling hand reached for hers.

She drew away from him, exhaling sharply.

Water droplets hung from his lashes. "D-do you know anything about vermin blood?"

Dianna shot her head back and came out onto the porch, shushing him. "Have you been drinking?" she asked, examining him carefully.

"Uh... Yeah. I think so? Just a bit."

He's definitely had more than a bit. Dianna folded her arms across her chest, tapping her foot. "I'll call my cousin to come get you."

"No. No, I need to talk to you. My mother she said...she said these things and I think... I don't know what I think. I just–" Roland ran his hands through his hair, sighing. "It's vermin blood. What does that mean?"

"We can talk once you've sobered up," Dianna muttered, turning toward the door.

He grabbed onto her hand, shivering. "Don't go. Please. I think I'm–"

"Dianna, who's at the door?"

Dianna ignored her mother, and stared at Roland, stomach twisting into knots as he held her tighter. She tried not to meet his gaze.

"Please listen. My mother, she–"

The door swung open, causing Dianna to jump.

Roland's eyes went wide. He opened his mouth to speak, but instead gave a little wave to Dianna's parents.

"Get off my property," her father said firmly, yanking her from Roland's grip.

Dianna jerked away from him, glaring. "I was about to call Peter to come get him."

"I need you to come with me," Roland said hoarsely.

"She's not going anywhere with you," Mona said, shooing him. "Make yourself scarce before I call the police."

Dianna stepped between Roland and her parents. "That's not necessary!" She noted the way he was trembling. "Roland, did something happen to your mother? Are you all right?"

"Dianna, get inside," her mother said sharply.

Roland blinked hard, stepping back off the porch. "I'm sorry. I wasn't trying to hurt you."

"I know that," Dianna said gently, wringing her hands together.

"Will you come home?"

Her father came marching toward him and swung, knocking Roland across the face and onto the frozen ground.

"Kenneth!"

Dianna charged off the porch, feet splashing against the slush, and pulled Roland up onto his feet.

Roland averted his gaze, shoulders shrinking.

"Dianna, get inside before someone sees," Mona said. "Mr. Crispin, if you're not gone in the next three minutes, I will notify the police."

Roland's lips curled into a wry smile. "As you wish."

Watching him fade off into the dark, Dianna's chest ached. She turned to her parents, shaking her head. "How could you?"

"I'm calling the police. That mans up to no good," Mona said, heading back inside.

Dianna turned to her father.

"If you go after him, you won't be welcome back into this house," he said, massaging his knuckles.

Dianna leaned against the trunk of the tree, replaying the night in her mind, listening to the front door slam behind her. She spotted her father smoking his pipe, coming out in his boots and winter coat.

Her father stood under the tree and crossed his arms. "You gonna hide up there all morning?"

Dianna looked away from him.

"Course you are," he muttered, blowing a puff of smoke up into the air. "We won't get a word from you for what? Another five years?"

"You didn't have to hit him," she said.

"Your mother realized you weren't at Peter's a long time ago. One of the neighbours spotted you in Roland's car. Do you know how that looks?"

Dianna rolled her eyes. "No. Please educate me."

"Did you lie to me? Have you been living with that man since you got back?"

She pressed her lips together. "I was."

Another puff of smoke.

"It was a mistake."

Her father gazed up at her. "After everything that family put us through."

"I'm going to Jakob's," Dianna said, jumping out of the tree. She dusted herself off.

"If you have any lingering feelings for that boy, I suggest you rid yourself of them, and quickly. People are beginning to talk."

"Let them," she said sullenly, shoving her hands into her pockets.

42

———————

A violent red ripped through the ether as the sun pulled away from the sky. Roland watched the window for what felt like years. He could feel their fingers in his hair, the low hums running through his ears, pulsing within his lethargic body. Nothing entered his mind. It was dark for hours. Nothing until the humming. Low, gentle, humming.

At first, when he opened his eyes, he thought it was Tabitha, but then he caught a whiff of bergamot. The scent overtook him as he fell back into the dark.

The flowers peeled away from the walls. Green moss oozing from them as Darius sat at his desk, eyes swelling with fear.

His mouth opened wide. "Don't."

Red polka dots splattered against the window and curtains.

Roland could taste metal. Tried to swallow it. Tried to grasp the hand running through his hair. Tried to breathe a word, but it slithered in his throat, scrapped the edges of his skull, pounded away at the cavity in his chest, and all he could see was Darius' eyes. Deep blue among green and red.

There was the darkness again.

Low humming, and bergamot, and gentle strokes in his hair.

He gripped the sheets, searching for a tether. Warmth washed over the room as Roland peered away from the window toward the strawberry red braid brushing against his neck. "D-Dianna?"

Her voice was dissonant, but it was hers. She was shushing him, urging him back to sleep, but Darius was watching them, and there was a gapping hole going through the centre of his forehead, oozing green sludge.

Roland stretched out his hand.

Dianna reached for it, lacing her fingers in his.

Roland's skin grew hot. They were face to face, his father's ghost at his back.

Dianna's green eyes swallowed the world, draining thoughts from his mind, until there was nothing but green, and her, and the freckles on her eyelids. She traced along his brow with her finger, smiling warmly.

Roland shut his eyes.

43

When she was eight, the dark was scary. In the dark, she saw her mother's face in the shadows that crept along the wall. This wasn't her room. The walls weren't her favourite shade of blue, and her dolls and books were missing. No one had tucked her in. Mama and Papa *always* tucked her in. Rose crept out of the nursery, careful not to wake her brothers, and went to the room next door. That was the room her parents stayed in whenever they visited Grandmother's house. The floors creaked as she tiptoed along, listening to the crickets chirping loudly up the hill. She pressed a hand against the wall, using it to guide her. The rooms were only a few feet apart, but in the dark, everything seemed so far away. Rose stopped in front of the door, ears catching an awful, heaving sound.

The door was open, just enough for her to peer inside. From that little sliver, she saw Grandmother squeezing her uncle's face between fingers, forcing a cup to his lips.

He was struggling to push away from her, gagging as the liquid spilled onto the bed.

Rose stood back, away from the door. Uncle Roland was looking at her, eyes glazed over. Something about the look told her she needed to leave, but her feet were glued in place. She crouched down beside the grandfather clock, staring as Grandmother rocked her uncle back and forth, shushing him.

"Mama, you're hurting me," he whispered.

"Why? Why did you kill your brother?" Grandmother said between sobs.

Rose covered her eyes, listening to the loud thud. When she peered between her fingers, Uncle Roland was on the floor, coughing up something foul. She yelped as Grandmother spotted her in the hall.

"Go back to bed Flower," Roland said hoarsely. "It's fine. Everything–" He gripped his stomach.

"I'll call the doctor," Grandmother said, going into the hall. She knelt down in front of Rose and kissed her forehead. "Your uncle's not feeling well, but it's nothing to worry about. Okay?"

Rose pulled away. "I-I want Papa."

Grandmother stood, nodded and headed toward the stairs. "Go back to bed, baby."

Rose looked back at her uncle, curled up on the floor. Once Grandmother was downstairs, she ran to him, throwing her arms around his neck. She squeezed. *Please don't die. Please don't die. Please. Please.* Her eyes fell on the light brown bulbs on the floor.

They were dirty, with roots jutting out beneath them.

She reached for one.

"Don't," her uncle whispered.

"Have you heard back from him yet?" Micah watched his mother carefully as she sat upside down in the armchair, tossing a ball of yarn up into the air.

"*Nei.*"

"What if he doesn't call back?"

Breena's pupils narrowed. "It's best you don't know."

Micah snatched the yarn from her, glowering. "You're not going to leave Nicholas there, are you?"

She swung her legs over onto the arm of the chair. "I can't. He's too important."

Micah noted the strained expression on her face. "Why? Because he's a full-blooded vermin?"

Breena chuckled. "It was strange, hearing that man's voice on the phone. He sounded like his father."

"*Musa...*"

"I think I'll take care of it. I expect you and your sister to start preparations for *Jare Guntin* before *Telehsei* arrives."

44

───────

Rose examined the dark circles under her eyes, pulling her hair up into a ponytail, and finishing it off with a light pink ribbon. She checked her curls in the vanity mirror before stepping out of her room. The skirt of her dress bounced around as she marched past Lisa down the stairs. After being forced to leave school for the day, she and her brothers decided it would be best to go on a little adventure.

After all these years, they were finally going to see their grandmother.

Rose had never been to an asylum before. She assumed it was like the hospital in East Tavern, where Julius was born, but it wasn't. There was a strong smell of bleach, and practically no colour at all. She couldn't believe how short the bus ride was, but none of the Crispin children had ever taken a bus before.

"Stop staring," Caspian said, walking toward the front desk.

"Sorry..." Rose's cheeks were hot. She'd witness her uncle talking to himself plenty of times, but not like that.

The man sitting down across from them seemed to be fully engaged in conversation with someone named Liesl. Or maybe he was Liesl? Either way, Caspian was right. She probably shouldn't stare. No one liked to be stared at.

"Hi, we're here to see Mrs. Crispin," Caspian said to the man at the front desk.

He seems so grown up. Her chest tightened as she wrapped the ribbon around her finger.

The man nodded, sliding a book toward them. "Sign in and be sure to sign out when you leave. Are you family?"

"Her grandchildren."

The man looked them over, nodded and passed a pen down to Caspian. "Usually, the son comes to visit."

"My uncle's busy today."

"Oh right. He's been arrested again for killing what's his name. That Keating fella."

"He didn't kill anyone," Rose said as Julius got up on his tiptoes to see what Caspian was writing.

The man shrugged, taking the book from Caspian as he finished signing it. "Nanette will show you where to go. Nanette!"

The siblings jumped as the man's voice boomed through the hall.

The nurse came racing toward them and smiled. "Hello, are you visiting or dropping off a new patient?"

"They're Mrs. Crispin's grandchildren," the man said gruffly. "Show them to her, would you?"

The nurse nodded quickly, then took off down the hall.

The Crispin's shot each other a look, then chased after her.

I've never seen anyone walk so fast. Rose hiked up her dress, practically sprinting after the woman. Julius and Caspian, lightly jogging behind.

"Hurry up slow poke." Caspian stuck his out tongue at their little brother.

Julius pouted, stomping his feet. "I am not a slowpoke!"

"Time and place." Rose shot them both a dirty look.

The nurse went into a room, and the children followed. "Mrs. Crispin, you have visitors."

Adeline lowered her brush. "Is the young man with the candy back?"

Rose planted her feet, swallowing the large lump in her throat, and curtsied.

Adeline stood. "Did Darius send you?"

"No. Um..." Rose pressed a hand to her chest, drawing in a deep breath.

"Hi," Julius started, easing into the room. "My, what a lovely painting."

Adeline circled Rose, then touched the top of her head, petting it gently. "Dear, you're shaking. Are you cold?"

Rose drew away.

"You look so much like my son," Adeline mumbled. "You could be his sister."

I'm his daughter. She wanted to say, but she held her tongue.

Caspian inched closer. "Did a man come see you yesterday?"

"Your face is bruised," Adeline said, examining him. "Who did you three say you were? Nanette, who did you say they were?"

"Your guests," Nanette said, hesitantly as she inched toward the door.

Adeline looked Rose over again. "Give me a moment. I'll remember your name, dear. It'll come to me."

Rose nodded.

"Have a seat. Would you like some chocolate or some cookies?"

"Yes please," Julius said, nodding.

The children sat on the bed while Adeline rummaged around in a drawer. "Darius always sends this nice young man with sweets. I've got so much I couldn't possibly eat it all. You kids should take some home with you."

Julius pointed at the painting again. "That looks just like my house."

"Really?" Adeline said, taking a tin from the drawer and placing it on the bed.

The children nodded.

Adeline opened the tin, eyes wide. "Roland."

Rose squirmed as her grandmother leaned in close.

"Young lady, you look so much like Roland. It's unsettling. Why are you three so quiet? Did he send you?"

"No." Rose was surprised at how small her voice had become. How small she felt.

"Is he dead?"

"No..."

Adeline handed Rose a shortbread cookie, then gave one to the boys. "He's dangerous. Stay away from him," she whispered. "He was here last night. Tell me, did he say something to you about that?"

Rose shook her head. "My... I um..."

Adeline took a step back and turned to Nanette. "I'm sure you have others to attend to."

Nanette nodded.

"We'll be fine, won't we, children?"

Rose wanted to shake her head but out of her mouth came, "Yes."

Julius took a bite of the cookie and smiled. "Tabby made these."

Adeline turned to him as Nanette hurried out of the room. "You know Tabitha?"

"Of course! She's the best cook in the whole wide world," Julius said sweetly.

Adeline pressed her lips together. "She was Roland's nanny. We let her go... well, Darius did. She had to go off and say all those stupid things. She's never lost a child. She doesn't know what it's like. I think highly of her, I do, but she kept overstepping. Darius had enough and–" She looked Rose over. "She didn't see what we saw. What that boy was becoming."

Rose met her grandmother's gaze. "What did you see?"

"You know, dear. If you didn't, you wouldn't have come."

Caspian bit his lip.

Adeline wrung her thin hands together. "He wasn't always a difficult child. Actually, it was quite the opposite. He was a good boy. Very sweet. When he was small, he'd brush my hair and chat with me, but he was sick all the time. Constantly. It was too much for us. We lost the twins before Lawrence was born, and then baby Darian.

We just wanted a big family. Lots of children running around, but it seemed like... like maybe we've been cursed? I thought it was my fault. Darius said it wasn't, but I thought it was..." She glanced toward the door. "Before we lost our son, we went on a trip to Dinara. We heard a rumour of this woman who saved several sick children there. Restored them to perfect health. I knew there was something about her. I just knew but Darius wouldn't listen. Our baby, Darian, only lived a year after we went to her. So, my husband, who seemed bewitched by this woman decided to trust her with our unborn child. After everything, he trusted her with Roland. He swore it would work this time. Oh, it worked all right! Now he and my son are both dead, and that monster killed them. I know he did. He's not right. I knew long before Darius made Tabitha leave that Roland wasn't right."

Rose nibbled on the cookie, glancing at Caspian as their grandmother scratched away at her skin.

"I need to get home. I need to keep him away from the children. H-have you... have you been to the house? He must've sent you. I swear, sometimes I see him, sitting in that chair there. He comes and watches me. Smiles. I don't know why he hasn't killed me yet. I think he enjoys it, watching me suffer in here."

"Did you give something to him to eat to make him sick so that you could protect your grandchildren?" Rose whispered. "Something from the garden?"

"Daffodil," she said, nodding. "I forced him to eat the daffodils from Wendy's garden. Not just the bulbs. The whole flower. My grandson, he was only five or six at the time, he got into them. I panicked. Roland he... he got so scary after that."

Rose shivered.

"But you knew that, didn't you Flower?"

She looked up at her grandmother.

Adeline wrapped her arms around her. "Please tell me he's dead. Please."

"He's not."

Adeline let her go, looking her over.

"Grandmother, how could you think he'd want to hurt us?" Rose asked, brows drawn together. "Uncle Roland's never–"

"He killed your parents. The gun was in the nursery."

Caspian shot a glance at his sister as Julius stared at the older woman.

"He killed Darius, and then he killed Lawrence. I don't think he meant to hurt Wendy. I really don't, but he... he did. He killed them, and Eloise and I we made the whole thing go away. We made it go away. Like idiots. I didn't want to lose another child. I couldn't. But then you three came to live with me, and when I saw how he looked at Julius. How he looked at all of you, I knew I had to do something. I wasn't trying to kill him. I just wanted to keep him away from you all. Just to... to keep him in bed. He was such a good boy when he was little. He was sick. He couldn't hurt a fly then, and with Tabitha back, he seemed himself again. It... please don't think I was trying to kill him. I just wanted to stop him." Adeline sank to the floor, sobbing into her hands.

"Rosie?" Julius shook her gently. "Is Uncle Roland bad?"

Caspian leaned back, staring straight ahead.

"All of this is nonsense. Our uncle didn't kill anyone," Rose said, helping Julius off the bed.

Adeline glanced up. "Did he marry her?"

"Who?"

"The Warren's daughter. Did he marry her?"

"He never married," Rose said softly. "He's been busy taking care of us."

Adeline rubbed her eyes. "H-he's been taking care of you?"

The ribbon was no longer in her hair. Rose weaved it between her fingers, stringing it along as she examined her grandmother's puzzled expression.

"Mrs. Crispin, are you all right?" the nurse, Nanette, said, coming back into the room. She turned to the youths, giving a faint smile. "She gets this way sometimes. Perhaps you can come back another time. Bring your uncle. He's very good with her."

Rose nodded, spying the carousel on the nightstand. "What's that?"

"He brought it last time," Adeline whispered. "That nice young man. The one who looks like Darius. He..." She met Rose's eyes. "Your uncle brought it. He asked what the song was called. Darius used to sing it to him when he was sick. That woman from Dinara taught it to him. She... your uncle can't know anything more about her. Please."

Rose laid the ribbon down next to the carousel, petting the mane of one of the white horses. "May we come again sometime for a visit?"

Adeline nodded. "With the letters, please."

Rose nodded, leading her brothers out of the room. "I think I have more questions than answers," she whispered.

Caspian shoved his hands into his pockets. "Do you think we should talk to Uncle Roland about it?"

Rose glanced back, giving Nanette a wave. "I don't know. Let's not talk about it here. For all we know, that woman could've overheard the entire thing."

45

—————

Dianna groaned, pressing her cheek against the counter. "Thanks for letting me come in so early."

"Like I said, I'm always here," Jakob said, scratching under his kitten's chin. "Did you hear? Your friend was arrested last night."

Dianna wrung her hands together. Heart beating rapidly. "I should check on him," she whispered. *It's bad enough that I left without a word. He seemed really upset about his mother. What if something awful happened to her, and it sent him spiralling?* Dianna sat there, unblinking. "Did he come in here last night for drinks?"

"He's banned."

"Well, he seemed drunk last night," she said, raising her head slightly.

"He didn't get it from here. Probably went to the Tavern Hotel or someplace on the east end."

The doors swung open, the chill from the wind blowing in.

Dianna gulped down air as Tabitha waltzed inside. She hid her face with her hand.

Tabitha's eyes pierced her like daggers. "What did you do to my boy?"

Dianna hung her head as Jakob cleared his throat. "I'm really not in the mood right now, Tabitha."

"Do I look like I care? According to all of Tavern, he was raving on like a madman outside your parent's house," she said firmly, nostrils flaring.

Dianna ran a hand through her hair, fingers catching in her matted braid.

"Were you together last night or not?"

Dianna stood, heading for the door.

Tabitha stepped in front of her. "Answer my question."

Dianna wrung her hands together, averting her gaze. "Whatever you've heard isn't true."

"The problem is that I've heard just about everything," Tabitha said, jabbing her in the shoulder. "And now the children are missing."

Dianna clasped her hands together. "Missing? What do you mean?"

Tabitha's hands dropped to her side. "The school had Evan come and collect them, and then when I went to check on them, they were gone."

Dianna pressed her lips together.

"What did you and Roland discuss last night? Did it have to do with Laurie?" Tabitha's hands were shaking. "Miss Warren!"

"He said something about his mother and vermin blood."

Tabitha's jaw dropped. "What?"

Jakob leaned in, his cat purring loudly. "Vermin blood?"

"My father struck him," Dianna said, throat tightening. *I should've went after him.*

"Struck him! Why? For what reason?"

"My parents wanted him to leave and–"

Tabitha started toward the exit; hands balled into tight fists. "Kenneth and Mona laid a hand on my boy?"

Dianna followed.

Tabitha stumbled onto the sidewalk, her short legs kicking up slush as she marched. "He's got the fever! The last thing he needs is to be worrying about you and the children!"

Dianna grabbed hold of her. "He what?"

"Probably got it from that girl, Charlotte... Look, just help me find the children. I don't want to waste another second while my boy's suffering back at home."

ROLAND SQUASHED Tabitha's cheeks with his hands, giggling as she scooped him up. "You look like a fish!"

"Quiet down, your brother's trying to study," she said, helping him into bed. Tabitha laid beside him and pulled the covers up under his chin. "Close your eyes, little love."

"But I'm not sleepy."

"I am," Lawrence mumbled from the table under the nursery window. The thirteen-year-old had been sulking over his history book all afternoon, scribbling notes while his chin sank into his palm.

Roland craned his neck, forcing himself up while Tabitha pressed gently against his tiny shoulders. His abs tightened as he scrunched up his face. "Why do you have to study?"

"Because, unlike you, I have school."

"I have school too."

"I have school outside of the house," Lawrence said, gesturing toward the window.

"You've had your bath. You've had your milk. It's time for bed," Tabitha said firmly, giving Roland her serious face.

He could tell by her voice that she wasn't really cross with him, but decided it was best to stop fighting and lay back down on the pillow. Roland rolled over to get a good look at her. "I don't want you to go home, Tabby. I want you to stay here with me."

"That wouldn't be fair to my boys, though, would it?" Tabitha said, kissing him on the forehead.

Roland pouted. "I'm your boy too."

"Roland."

Roland hid beneath the covers. He didn't like when Lawrence

used that tone. It sounded like Papa. Feeling around the bed, Roland pulled back the sheets, sitting up again. "Tabby, I can't find Pippi."

"She's right here," Tabitha said, picking the bear up off the floor.

He took Pippi from her, gently cradling the teddy bear. "Can I have something to eat?"

"You just ate," Lawrence said, furrowing his brow. "I watched you. You had cinnamon toast, and milk, *and* pudding."

"I didn't even eat that much pudding!"

Tabitha chuckled.

"Roland, if you don't go to sleep, Papa will get angry, and Tabitha will get in trouble. Do you want Nanny Tabby to get in trouble?" his older brother asked, getting up from the table.

Roland shook his head.

"Then say goodnight and go to sleep."

Roland frowned. "Goodnight, Tabby. I love you."

"I love you too, little one," Tabitha said, brushing back his hair. "Now promise me you'll be good and won't disturb your brother."

"I promise."

"Cross your heart, eat a fly, swear on Tabby's apple pie?" Lawrence said, looming over the bed. He crossed his eyes, wiggling his fingers at Roland as he inched closer.

Roland squealed, kicking at his older brother. "I promise Laurie!"

Lawrence grinned, folding his arms. "Good. Now I don't have to feed you to the monster in the creek."

"Goodness! Don't be putting thoughts like that into his head. You'll give the poor child nightmares," Tabitha said, getting to her feet. "He barely sleeps as it is with all the migraines."

Lawrence blushed.

"Go finish your schoolwork. And you, I want those eyes shut tight," Tabitha said firmly. "Understood?"

The boys nodded.

Tabitha left the room, closing the door halfway.

Roland snuggled up to Pippi, squeezing his eyes closed. He squeezed and squeezed until little wrinkles formed at the bridge of his nose.

"Roland?"

He tried not to laugh, feeling Lawrence's fingers pinching his big toe.

"Rolly! *Rolly*. Rolly?" Lawrence said, wiggling the four-year-old's toes. "Want to see something?"

Roland opened his eyes.

He wasn't in the nursery anymore.

"Laurie?" he said, looking around. He clutched his throat, listening to his voice crack. Pippi was gone too. Roland was outside at the lake, and up high. *What's happening?*

Miles pushed him toward the edge of the diving rock. "What's the matter? You scared?"

"Where's Laurie? Where am I?"

Miles shoved him hard, causing Roland to stumble backward toward the water.

He screamed, treading the best he could. He was sinking.

Vincent dragged him through the water, cursing.

Roland had known him for years, but he'd never seen Vincent so angry.

"He could've died!" Vincent took a swing at Miles as he ran toward over them.

"It was an accident," Miles said, stepping back.

As Roland sat up, he spotted Dianna charging toward them, pigtails flying behind her like flags in the wind.

"I outta give you a knuckle sandwich!" the twelve-year-old hollered as her older cousin Peter latched onto her.

"Keep your crazy cousin away from me," Miles said, crossing his arms.

Peter glared at him. "What did you just say?"

What's going on? Why am I at the lake? Roland turned to Vincent as Peter tackled Miles to the ground.

Peter whammed a fist into Miles' chest. "My cousin's not crazy! You're crazy!"

"Dog pile!" Nev and Cato said, cheering wildly as they jumped into the scrap.

"What's happening?" Roland said, eyeing Vincent. "Where's Laurie?"

Vincent shrugged, shaking his head. "At work probably."

"Work? No, that's not right, we were in our room and–"

Charlotte swung her leg over the stonewall, looking down at him. "What are you talking about?"

He blinked hard, glancing at the dirt on the skirt of her dress.

"Aren't you gonna help me down?"

Roland nodded, holding out his arms. "Hurry before someone sees."

She leapt down into his arms, knocking the two of them to the ground.

Roland chuckled as she dusted herself off. The tone of his voice seemed more familiar. He relaxed a little, sitting up.

She pulled him up onto his feet. "Are you okay?"

"Yeah. Can you believe Dianna, charging at Miles like that?" he said, shaking his head. "She was furious."

Charlotte's brown eyes looked him up and down. "How drunk are you?"

"Wait, weren't we at the lake?" He caught sight of himself in the window and jumped back. "Jeez! I look like my old man."

"You bump your head or something?" Charlotte said, circling around him.

"When did you get back from Augen? Where's my brother?"

"We haven't even gotten the money for the tickets yet," she said, hands on her hips. "Don't tell me you lost the ring."

"Dianna was... what ring? Your husband he–"

"Her ring. The one Dianna gave back. The one we're selling for tickets." Charlotte's brow drew together. Her eyes widened. "Wait, did you say husband?"

A hand slammed down on the back of his neck. "You stole your mother's ring?"

Roland jerked away, spinning toward his father. "Papa, what are you doing here?"

"Stop playing games!" Darius hollered, holding up an open palm. "What did you do with it? Who did you sell it to?"

Roland flinched. "I didn't sell it."

"Don't lie to me!"

"I swear. I didn't sell it. I–"

Darius struck him, then shuddered, taking a step back. "I'm sorry. I shouldn't have done that."

His eyes burned.

"Please just tell me what you did with it," Darius said, drawing in a deep breath.

Roland glared at him. "I hate you."

The room spun.

"I hate you, and I hate this city and I hate this stupid ring!" He threw it, and it bounced against his father's forehead, right through the centre of it, before hitting the wall with a loud bang.

Green liquid oozed from the hole in the middle Darius' skull.

Roland inched toward him, his skin burning. "P-Papa?" He whipped open the office door, muddy shoe prints covering the halls of Doren Shipping. His lungs hurt. Everything hurt. "Laurie..." Roland was gasping for air. "Laurie where are you? Laurie!"

Tabitha shushed him, placing a cloth on his forehead. "It's all right, dear. Everything's all right."

"Where's Laurie? Tabby, what's happening? Where–"

"Shh. It's okay, little one. You're okay. We've got to get your fever down."

Roland stared at Lisa, pouring medicine into a teaspoon. He struggled, trying to get up off the bed. Peter and Mr. Leon were holding him down. "What's happening? Where am I? Where's Laurie?"

"Roland, we need you to relax. You have the fever, and you need to take some medicine. Just a spoonful. Okay?" Peter said.

Roland's jaw was forced open by Mr. Leon as Lisa drove the spoon inside. He swallowed the medicine. It was bitter. Syrupy. It slithered partway down his throat before Roland coughed it back up.

"You stupid boy," Tabitha whispered, dabbing his forehead.

"Dr. Hagan is on the phone," Dianna said, entering the room.

Lisa nodded, placing the spoon and bottle on the table. "I'll speak with him."

Dr. Hagan? Roland tried to sit up. His stomach turned. *Why am I seeing Dr. Hagan? I haven't needed to see him since I was a kid.* He pushed Tabitha to the side, leaned over the bed, and threw up on the floor. Wiping the vomit onto his forearm, Roland gazed at her with glossy eyes. "What's going on?"

"Lay back down," she said softly.

"Where's Laurie?"

"Roland, your brother's not here."

He stared at her.

"Sweetheart, Laurie's..." Tabitha wrung her hands together. "Laurie's been gone for five years."

Roland trembled as Mr. Leon gripped onto his shoulder. "No. I just saw him. I was with him in our room."

"I'll fetch some towels," Dianna said, stepping out of the room with Lisa.

"Let me go!" Roland tried to rip free of Mr. Leon, sweat dripping down his neck. "Tabby, tell them to let me go."

"Roland, lay back down," Tabitha said gently, easing him back onto the pillow. "Everything's going to be fine. Peter, have Vincent and Dr. Gray found the children yet?"

"No. They're still looking," Peter said.

Roland's skull burned. "Tabby, I... I–"

"It's okay. Just relax. I'm not going anywhere, I promise."

46

"What do you think Grandmother meant by making the whole thing go away?" Caspian said looking at Rose. It was the third time he'd asked since the children boarded the bus.

Rose wrapped hair around her finger, shaking her head.

"I can't see Uncle Roland killing anyone," he said softly, as an older girl stared at them from across the seat.

The woman in front of them shot her head around, clutching her purse as the girl blew a bubble. When it popped, the woman nearly fell out of her seat.

Rose looked at the puddle of water beneath her black boots.

Julius leaned his weight onto her. "Can we go home now?"

"We're almost at the station. Once we get off the bus, I'll give you a piggyback home," Caspian said.

The bus came to a stop. The Crispin children crowded the window, along with the other passengers.

Julius turned to his older sister. "Isn't that Mr. Gray?"

Rose and Caspian ducked behind him.

There were two police cars blocking the road, just in front of the train station. Vincent entered the bus, peering into each seat until his heavy boots came to a halt.

"Hi, Mr. Gray!" Julius said, grinning sweetly.

Caspian and Rose waved sheepishly.

Vincent drew in a deep breath, gestured for the children to get up, and ushered them off the bus.

"How much trouble do you think we're in?" Caspian whispered.

"Enough," Vincent said gruffly.

Rose flinched, hiking up her skirt as she and her brothers scurried toward the other three officers. She looked up at Vincent, examining the cold expression on his face.

"What the heck were you three doing?" Vincent turned his attention to Caspian. "Everyone's out looking for you."

Rose gripped her stomach.

"Well?" He cleared his throat, took a quick breath, and gave them a weary grin. "Sorry, that came out wrong. We were all starting to worry, that's all. Are you three all right?"

She nodded, listening to the train pull into the station.

"Look Rosie, the trains here!" Julius said excitedly, tugging her hand.

"We had to send Dr. Hagan to the house earlier," Vincent said, opening the car door for them.

"Who?" She was watching the train. No passengers had gotten out. There wasn't a worker in sight. Her stomach fluttered as she twisted the ribbon around her finger.

"A friend of my father's from East Tavern Hospital. He treated your uncle a very long time ago."

Rose stared at him for a moment, then looked back at the train as Julius jumped around. Caspian and the other three officers were watching too, along with the people getting off the bus. The older officer went up to the train and peered around at one of the cars.

"Did you three run off to try and get medicine? Is that why Roland's been acting so strange?"

"Hey Vincent, there's no–"

Without warning, the officer was on the ground, shrieking.

The colour washed from Rose's face as she sank.

Julius knelt beside her. "Rosie?"

"Caspian, grab your brother," Vincent said, latching onto her. Holding her up by her armpits, he helped her into the car and closed the door, running around to the other side. Vincent's voice was muffled outside as Caspian put Julius between him and his sister and shut the door. The officers and other adults looked panicked.

Julius tugged on his sister's arm. "What's going on?"

A small figure came bolting off the train, skinny legs running, teeth bared.

"We need to go," Caspian said.

Rose threw the door open, launching herself out into the snow, her younger brothers chasing after her.

Vincent's eyes widened. "What the–"

Scrambling to her feet, she took off running. Boots kicking up slush as Vincent chased after them. Hiking up the pink skirt of her dress, she lifted her feet until she was sprinting on the balls of her feet.

Caspian pulled Julius along.

The vermin came flooding out of the train in droves, sending the humans into a scattered frenzy.

Vincent was closing in behind the Crispin's. "Stop, it's not safe!"

A loud bang sent Rose stumbling forward. Her heart stopped.

Vincent scooped her into his arms, shielding her body. "Caspian, Julius, get behind me!"

"They're trying to take the city!" a man shouted from behind them.

Rose's eyes widened as Vincent pulled the gun from the holster beneath his jacket and spun toward the crowd.

"Go!" He fired at the vermin bolting toward them.

"They're just kids," she said, voice catching in her throat.

Vincent glanced back at her. "Rose, it isn't safe. Take your brothers and go!"

A vermin in tattered grey clothes charged toward him, baring his teeth.

Rose pulled Vincent back as Caspian shielded their younger brother.

The vermin grabbed at them. Red streaks running down his face.

Vincent kicked the vermin in the chest, sending the young boy hurdling into the dirt, and aimed his gun.

"No!"

Without hesitation, Vincent fired three shots. "I'm taking the children to safety. Stay together and hold them off!" he shouted to the other two officers.

Rose shook, as he spun her around, grabbed her brother's hand, and lead them back to the car.

"Are any of you hurt?"

They shook their heads.

The other men surrounded the car, firing rapidly at the vermin as they got close.

"Get in and go!" one man hollered.

Rose climbed into the passenger's seat and shut the door, while Vincent piled her younger brothers into the back. She looked ahead at the vermin lying in the dirt, staring up at the ether as Vincent got into the car and hit the gas. Her stomach churned as the car zipped by. The vermin looked no older than she was. For a moment she thought its ear twitched. She buried her face in her hands.

"Are you okay? I'm sorry you had to see that. I..." Vincent held his breath a moment, running a shaky hand through his black hair. "You're okay right?"

Rose felt the tears swelling in her eyes. Through the spaces between her fingers, she could see the red spots on the skirt of her dress.

"Did you see them coming? Is that why you ran?" Vincent shook her gently as another round of shots echoed behind them. "Rose?"

Her chest tightened; lungs squeezed like lemons.

"Where did you three go earlier? Are you okay?"

She turned to Vincent, noting the quiver in his voice. "We went to ask Grandmother... we just wanted to ask her..." Rose was staring at the spots on her dress. The blood on her dress.

"I'll buy you a new one," Vincent said. "A better one."
Rose sank into the seat of the car.
"Caspian, what did you ask about? Was it about Roland?"
"Daffodils," Caspian said softly, cuddling Julius close.
Vincent winced. "I see."
Rose's gaze fixed on the blood again.

47

Suzanna squirmed as *Telehsei* ran the fine brush below her lash line. More than anything, she wanted this to be over. Zana didn't completely hate the blue beneath her eyes. It looked nice on Micah, but it wasn't something their pack would've done. It wasn't something Nyla would've done.

With *Jare Guntin* in a month, their mother asked *Telehsei* to come by and teach them proper *Mivos* customs. It didn't seem to matter to Breena Misk that Micah and Zana had their own customs, ones taught to them by their grandmother. Ones that were dear to them. It also didn't help that Breena had suddenly vanished again without a word.

Micah had said their mother would take care of the situation with Nicholas, but neither of them knew what that meant. They just wanted their brother back.

Telehsei finished the lines off by making two small dots above Zana's brow, then handed her a clean brush. "You should add your own colours."

Zana eyed her, ears twitching at a faint ringing sound. *Who calls at dinnertime?* She almost groaned. It had been the most *Hiloven* thought she'd had since coming to live with her father. Her pack never had any need for telephones. *Humans would probably be better off without them, too.* She took the brush, twirling it gently between her fingers. "Our pack didn't do things like this. We didn't even have a name for ourselves."

"I said, your colours, not your packs," *Telehsei* said, giving her a smile. "My daughter marked her skin with gold. Brushed it along her cheeks. We called her *Keltii* because she was warm like the sun."

Zana looked at the paints and powders, then turned to Micah, who laid on her bed, staring up at the ceiling. *Telehsei* wasn't the woman's name, but her position. She taught younger vermin in the pack, and over the years had become known only by her occupation. Zana found it strange that even her mother, who was around the same age as the woman, called her teacher. She would've preferred having Nyla or a member of her pack helping her prepare for *Jare Guntin.*

"In Tavern?"

Zana sprang from her seat, listening to her father's voice booming from downstairs.

Micah propped himself up onto his elbows and eyed her. "What?"

"Father is on the phone. It's about Tavern."

Micah got off the bed, racing his sister to the door. "Father?"

"How bad are your ears?" *Telehsei* muttered.

Zana turned to her.

"The *Valdinok* are in Tavern." *Telehsei* smirked, running a hand along the shaved side of her head. "You mother left to get the Slayden child."

"W-what?"

"Rumour has it that Tavern's been hoarding medicine in one of their warehouses. All those desperate vermin should give her enough time to retrieve our *Yunenik.*"

Micah glowered. "I stole medicine from one of the doctors there. He only had a handful of bottles. There's no way Tavern's hoarding it."

"Looks like there will be some casualties," Telehsei said, shrugging her shoulders. "While Tavern's busy dealing with weak packs like the *Riivo*, we'll have an easier time grabbing whatever they have locked up in their warehouse, and we'll get your brother also. I assumed your mother told you the plan."

"I thought she had a deal with Tavern," Zana said, turning to Micah.

"The deal was with the head of the Crispin family," Micah said softly. "And he's dead."

∽

THE TIPS OF NICHOLAS' ears tingled as he crouched down behind the bed in the nursery

"Vincent! What happened?" Tabitha's voice echoed from downstairs. "Are they all right?"

Nicholas shuddered, tucking his head into his shoulders, listening to the front door slam shut. Heavy feet pounded against the stairs.

"Vermin are trying to take the city!" Vincent shouted. "We need to board up the house. Make sure nothing can get inside."

Nicholas fell back onto his butt and stared at the nursery door, listening to the quickness of the feet approaching. *Rose.*

"Rose, everyone needs to stay together," Vincent said from the bottom of the stairs. "You've had a big shock. Why don't you change, and we can... we can talk through it while we get organized."

"I'm fine."

Nicholas could hear her hand gripping the knob of the door. He crawled into the bathroom and hid behind the wall as the door creaked open.

"Rose," Vincent said.

Nicholas spotted the brown lace-up boots following behind her. Those boots had kicked him once.

"I said I'm fine," Rose said sullenly.

From where he sat, Nicholas could see the mud on her stockings.

"You and your brothers were just attacked by vermin," Vincent said softly.

Nicholas furrowed his brow. *Attacked? Are they okay?*

"Please come downstairs." Vincent's voice seemed gentle, as it had when he'd initially asked Nicholas his name. When he'd asked him to return the gun.

"I'll be down in a moment. I just need to be alone for five seconds," Rose said, taking a seat on the bed with Roland's name etched into it.

Nicholas could see her clearly now, her hair wet, muddy and knotted. The skirt of her dress was dirty as well. *Is that blood? Is she hurt?* Nicholas held his breath, heart pounding.

Vincent placed a hand on her shoulder. "All right. I understand. I'll come find you in a few minutes."

Nicholas grimaced.

"Are you okay, Mr. Gray?" Rose said softly, turning to him as he headed toward the door.

Nicholas couldn't see his face, but the man's voice wavered.

"Yeah. Yes. I'm fine."

Once the door was closed, Rose scrambled toward the bathroom, and threw her arms around Nicholas, squeezing him tightly. She started to cry.

Nicholas held onto her; ears twitched at the sound of her sobbing. "Rose, what happened? Are you hurt?" he whispered.

"He killed a kid," she said through tears.

"Vincent Gray?" Nicholas shot his head in the direction of the door.

She nodded.

His stomach knotted.

"They were all on the train," she said, rubbing her eyes as she let go. She was taking sharp breaths, hiccupping between sobs.

Nicholas rubbed her back.

"Julius saw everything," Rose whispered. "What if something bad happened to him? What if I lost my brothers?"

Nicholas shushed her. "Your uncle's sick. He has the fever," he said softly. "I won't let anything bad happen. I'll protect you."

Rose went quiet.

"Look, the longer you're in here, the more dangerous it is for everyone," he said, listening to the commotion downstairs. "That man's not going to spare me a second time."

Rose drew in a shaky breath, gave a little nod and stepped out of the washroom. "My grandmother thinks Uncle Roland killed my parents."

"What do you think?"

"I... I don't know," she said softly, tugging at the loose button on her cardigan as she steadied her breathing. "Caspian doesn't know either, and that scares me."

Nicholas frowned. "Mr. Crispin's never given me any reason to think he'd do something like that."

"If I bring my brothers in here, will you look after them?"

"*Ha.*"

The nursery door whipped open. Nicholas darted behind the wall. "Who are you talking to?"

It was Vincent again.

Nicholas froze, clamping his hand down over his mouth as the button from Rose's cardigan popped off and rolled along the floor.

"You startled me," Rose said, softly.

"Who's in here?"

Nicholas held his breath. *Why didn't I hear him on the stairs? I should've been paying more attention.*

"No one," Rose said as Vincent paced around the room. "I was just talking to myself."

Books fell onto the floor.

"Stop, that one's my father's!"

He knows. Nicholas watched Vincent's boots come to a halt in front of the bathroom door. His mind raced. Every muscle in his body tensed. His ears perked up, nostrils flaring. There was no way he was letting that man hurt him again.

Rose grabbed Vincent by the waist. "I said I was fine," she said, trying to pull him away from the door.

"Rose, I know you're scared, but whatever's going on, you need to tell me," Vincent said, grunting as he tried to pry her off. "I'm trying to help."

Nicholas' eyes perked up at the sound Tabitha's heavy footsteps in the hall.

"What's going on in here?".

Nicholas' throat had gone dry. He spotted her short legs marching toward the pair.

"I heard her speaking to someone," Vincent said.

"Leon and I have dealt with vermin attacks before," Tabitha said. "You should regroup with the other officers. Find out what the plan is."

"I... I know but–"

"The children have had a shock, Vincent. So have you."

"I'm fine," Vincent whispered.

"Leave her to me. You go focus on getting those brutes out of our city," Tabitha said, pulling Rose off of him.

Vincent headed for the door. "I don't want anyone in here until after I've had a look around."

"That is completely understandable. Rose, why don't you let me help you get cleaned up?" Tabitha said, guiding Rose away from the bathroom door.

Nicholas was shaking. *I have to get out of here.*

"Rose, come," Tabitha said.

Nicholas could see Rose knelt over, grabbing books sprawled about the floor. Her fingers trembling.

"Rose, you're filthy and need to change," Tabitha said again, crouching down beside her. She pulled her close, kissing the top of her head. "I'll help you tidy them up after Mr. Gray's looked around."

"But–"

"How about I tuck your father's things into a safe place so they don't get knocked about again?" Tabitha said, looking directly at the bathroom.

Nicholas' pupils narrowed.

Rose nodded.

"Go with Mr. Gray. I'll be right behind you," Tabitha said, picking up the books.

Nicholas listened to Rose's footsteps on the stairs, heart racing. Tabitha walked past the bathroom door toward a short shelf at the back of the room that rested under a small, framed photograph of a boy holding a baby.

She kissed her teeth, glancing back at the bathroom. "You'd better get a move on," Tabitha said softly.

"*Deisso*." Nicholas stared at Tabitha as his ears twitched.

She met his gaze. "He's coming back, isn't he?"

Nicholas looked at her. There were a handful of places they could hide, but Vincent was getting closer. He slid into the closet and listened to the argument coming from downstairs as Tabitha hurried out of the nursery. He could hear Rose sobbing; it wrenched his heart.

Nicholas grabbed onto Harry, Julius' bear pressing it to his chest, the way Zana did when he was small. She would pull him close and combed her fingers through his hair until he drifted off to sleep. *If Zana didn't try to protect me from that man before, she never would've gotten hurt.* Nicholas' eyes swelled with tears. He fought them back and cuddled close to the teddy bear, listening to his uneven breaths. "It's okay. I'm here," he whispered over and over, the way his sister always did.

Nicholas' ears perked up at the sound of Vincent's boots in the hall. The nursery door swung open, creaking loudly.

Vincent went straight to the bathroom and began moving things about. "I'm telling you. They've all been acting strangely."

Nicholas' ears picked up on another set of footsteps coming into the room. They didn't step as roughly. Nicholas wrinkled his brow. *Dr. Gray?* He held his breath.

"Did you really kill a child?" Dr. Gray asked, keeping his voice low. "Vincent, what harm could a–"

"It was a vermin," Vincent said. "You, of all people, should know how stupid it would be to spare one."

"It was still a child, Vincent."

"The one that killed Mom wasn't any older," Vincent said.

Nicholas' ears tuned in on a banging noise coming from the room next door. His chest tightened. *That's Rose's room.*

"What is it you're expecting to find in here?"

"I know what I heard. A voice. It sounded like–"

"The girl's gone out front," a man hollered.

Girl? What girl? Rose? Miss Warren? Nicholas squeezed his eyes shut, listening to Vincent's boots slam against the wooden floors as he stomped toward the nursery door. There was another thud coming from one of the bedrooms. Nicholas angled himself, trying to shrink between the boxes, feather earring waving back and forth against his neck.

The button of his shirt scraped along the door.

Nicholas' pupils narrowed.

Vincent spun on his heels.

"Vincent," Dr. Gray said, moving toward his son.

Nicholas could smell Vincent's cologne. The closer he got, the stronger the smell of pine became. Before he had a chance to think, Vincent whipped the closet door open. Nicholas sprang forward and zipped by the doctor, eyes widening as Vincent reached for something beneath his long black coat.

"It's that boy," Vincent said, catching his footing. "The Wolfe's brother."

Blood rushed to his ears as Nicholas threw open the nursery door and bolted into the hall where Peter and Tabitha turned and stared at him, jaws dropped. Heart pounding, he slipped between them, glancing over his shoulder as Vincent came hurdling toward him, the doctor close behind.

Peter latched onto the collar of Vincent's jacket as the young man removed the pistol from under his coat. "What are you doing?"

"Move!" Vincent fired the gun.

Nicholas ducked into the guest room, body trembling. His eyes fell on Roland, sitting up in bed, drenched in sweat. The woman in the room looked startled. *He's gonna kill me.*

"Peter, that thing should be dead!"

Roland forced himself up, using the bed rail to steady himself.

"You can't go firing a gun in here. You could've killed someone!" Peter shouted angrily.

"One of those mutts nearly killed the children," Vincent said.

Nicholas took a sharp breath as Roland approached, weary eyed. The man held out his arms.

"Charlotte, it's okay," he said hoarsely.

"Is... is that a vermin?" she said, wide eyed.

Nicholas eyed Roland, then examined the expression of the stranger. *Is she the one who was staying in his room?*

"Charlotte, come with me," Roland whispered.

Nicholas watched Roland step out into the hall, legs buckling beneath him.

The woman standing on the other side of the bed raised her hands slowly, following behind him.

"I'm sorry," she said quietly.

Nicholas shot his head in Roland's direction, watching from the frame of the door as the man grabbed her hand.

"Charlotte?"

"Let me explain," Roland said.

"Explain what? The vermin or the murder suspect hiding in your house?" Vincent shouted.

"Vincent, she's sick and–"

Nicholas could hear Vincent's boots slam down along the wooden floor.

"Put that thing away before you do something stupid," Roland said firmly.

"Your niece was with that mutt in the nursery."

Roland massaged his forehead. "Vincent... the gun it–"

"That little girl kicked me and went running after Dianna," a man said gruffly, coming up the stairs.

"There's a vermin in the house," Vincent said, eyes falling on the entrance to the guest room.

The man gasped, stepping toward the far edge of the wall. He reached for his gun.

"You shot a bloody hole into my favourite clock," Roland grumbled.

"What are you on about?" Vincent marched toward him. "Cato, it's the mutt with the fever. The one whose brother stole from us."

"Hold on a minute, boys," Dr. Gray said hesitantly. "There are children present. I don't want anyone getting hurt."

"Besides, you can't shoot him," Peter said firmly. "He–"

A scream caused the men to flinch and turn toward the stairs.

Nicholas' ears perked up as he watched Roland's legs give way.

Vincent reached for him, then pulled away. "Was that Rose?"

Roland sank to the floor.

"Help!"

It is. Nicholas dashed from the room, tackling Vincent. They wrestled on the floor, the gun sliding toward Roland. *I have to get to her.*

"Cato, shoot!" Vincent drove his knee into Nicholas' gut.

Nicholas yelped, listening to Rose's terror filled screams coming from the front yard. *I can't lose her.* He dug into Vincent's neck, biting hard. He could feel the human squirming beneath him, panicked gasps fleeing his lips.

Click.

Nicholas' ears twitched. He glanced up, blood dripping down his chin.

Roland had the gun pressed to the back of his head. "Get off him."

Nicholas did as commanded and stood against the wall. "*Iya*... I was just... Rose."

Roland looked down at Vincent, trembling on the ground, nursing his wound, and then to Cato who stood at the other wall, gun aimed at Nicholas. He turned, pointing the gun in the young man's direction. "You will allow the vermin to leave."

Cato's hands shook. "H-he tried to kill Vincent!"

Roland lurched toward him, shoving the gun into the man's chest. "If he wanted Vincent dead, he'd be dead." Roland looked the man up and down, as Caspian and Julius peered into the hall from their bedroom. "Nicholas, whatever's out there... whoever it is, who's laid a finger on my niece, I want you to kill them."

Peter's eyes grew wide. "Roland."

"Go before I change my mind and put a bullet through your skull."

Nicholas nodded, dashing down the stairs. He opened the front door, the snow sticking to the bottom of his trousers as he leapt from the porch.

Rose stretched out her hand to him as a man pulled her toward the vehicle parked in the driveway. Rose started shrieking. "Miss Warren! They took her!"

Nicholas heard a low growl coming from his right as his fingers grazed hers.

The man shoved Rose into the snow. "What the–"

A blur of white came rushing from the edge of the property and slammed the man's face against the vehicle.

Rose crawled to Nicholas, shivering. "They took Miss Warren."

The man fell to the ground unconscious as the figure knelt and brushed the tawny blonde hair from their face.

"*Hallet Yunenik,*" she said, raising a brow at Rose.

"Zana?"

48

Nicholas held Rose close as the vermin drew near. Noting the way she trembled, spots of blood on her dress, he laced his fingers between hers. There was still blood on his face, running down his chin and neck. Human blood. The taste of it was foul in his mouth.

Nicholas had bitten the man with more force than he intended. He merely wanted to get to Rose as quickly as possible, to make sure she was okay. *She must be terrified of me.*

She squeezed his hand.

"You resemble Darius," the vermin said, peeling the white gloves from her fingers, eyes panning over Rose. "I have no intentions of killing you, girl. You can stop shaking."

"Rose!" Roland raced from within the house, the fear in his voice evident.

The pair looked back at the feverish young man stumbling outside with Peter and a shaken Vincent Gray on his heels.

The vermin's eyes grew wide. "Come Nicholas. Your brother and sister are waiting."

Rose held onto him tighter. "We have to help Miss Warren."

Nicholas listened to the men's feet crunch the snow, surveying the mass of human bodies scattered about the property. Had this one vermin taken them all down? Was that why Rose was screaming?

The vermin yanked him toward her, brows furrowed. "You're filthy. Did you kill one?"

Nicholas shook his head, Rose gripping his hand as tightly as she could.

"Why is she... Roland... what's going on?" Vincent said, hand pressed to his neck. He stumbled behind Roland, stopped, and began noting the surrounding them. "Detective Carson. Nev. Paisley. Roland, give me the gun!"

Roland, panting, pried his niece away from Nicholas, lifting her as she kicked wildly.

"They took Miss Warren!" Rose trembled, tears streaking her face. "They'll kill her!"

"What? Who?" Roland turned his head.

Peter took Rose from him as the man's legs began to buckle.

"Who has Dianna?" Roland said again, swaying slightly.

The vermin watched with narrow pupils. She smiled, revealing her fangs. "Where's your mother, *Yunenik*?" she asked, inching toward him.

"M-my mother?" Roland whispered.

The vermin ran a finger along his cheekbone, still smiling. She grabbed hold of his wrist, drawing him into her. "You're exactly as I pictured you."

Nicholas' stomach turned.

Vincent pulled something shiny from his pocket.

"You'll tell the humans we came to steal medicine," the vermin said softly. "I apologize for the mess."

"For what?" Roland turned to Nicholas. The mans face grew pale.

Vincent lunged forward.

~

Roland woke, ears ringing. It was cold. He propped himself up onto his elbows, then turned toward the parked police car in the driveway, where Detective Carson stirred, groaning loudly. *What happened?* The realization hit him. He sat up, head throbbing. "Rose?"

Through his daze, he spotted Vincent to his left. He dragged himself over, watching the man blink up at the night sky, blood-stained fingers pressed to his neck.

"My niece. Where is she?"

Vincent said nothing as he met Roland's gaze.

Roland sat him up, slowly. "Peter? Tabby?"

Tears rolled down Vincent's face. "They took her."

Roland eyed him.

"Why... why did you know its name?"

"Took who?" Roland's eyes darted about.

"You knew the mutt's name."

"Yes."

"Why?" Vincent said, staring at him.

Roland sighed. "I'll call for your father."

Vincent gripped onto him. "They took Rose."

Roland drew in a sharp breath, then another. Throat tightening.

Vincent struggled to his feet. "Why did you know its name?"

Roland gripped his chest, hugging himself.

"Answer me!"

Rose was gone. Dianna was gone. Nicholas was gone.

Roland trembled, something bubbling in his throat. He opened his mouth and screamed. He screamed and screamed and screamed, and Vincent stood there over him, watching. Roland's throat burned as the air left his lungs. He fell back into the snow and sobbed. *What have I done?*

ABOUT ARDIN PATTERSON

Ardin Patterson is a Canadian voice actress with Noble Caplan Abrams, and an author with a passion for storytelling. She is a Trent University Grad, who spent her years there geeking out over Shakespeare, hanging with her friends at the Trend, and going to bookstores every weekend. Her voice can be heard in animated series such as Polly Pocket, Hailey and the Hero Hearts and Matchbox Adventures. When she isn't telling stories or behind a mic, Ardin can be found playing games with her sister, drawing, hanging with her niece and nephew, or tackling her never-ending to-be-read pile.

Visit Ardin's website - https://ardinpatterson.com/

facebook.com/theverminseries

x.com/ArdinPatterson

instagram.com/ardinpatterson

tiktok.com/@theverminseries

www.ingramcontent.com/pod-product-compliance
Lightning Source LLC
Chambersburg PA
CBHW070408310726
48977CB00003B/604